BRANE BOUNCE

MRM DARK

Book One
Archangels Of Aquarius
Series

Cover Design and Illustration
By
Patrick Turner
PatrickTurner.com

ISBN-13: 978-0993748202

ISBN-10: 0993748201

## DEDICATION

This book is dedicated to my Father and Mother, and my entire
family. It is also dedicated to the memory of Nelson Mandela,
and to the Dali Lama and his struggle for a Free Tibet.

## CONTENTS

## ACKNOWLEDGMENTS

I am in debt to the work of Douglas Adams, Kurt Vonnegut, and Tom Robbins; but even more so to Robert Anton Wilson, R. Crumb and Aldous Huxley. Also Monty Python, Benny Hill and John Byner

To my readers who are struggling with the many facts and pseudo facts in the story, it would be a good idea to skip ahead when you are confused by a reference, and read some or all of the glossary. It is a good alternative to trying to find the reference in what you have already read of the story, as it is chopped-up quite a bit. I distract and then forge ahead over and over. I hope you immerse yourself in my imaginary landscape, and visualize it properly. For your benefit I will introduce each part of it here, (in the introduction) and try to make it work visually.

The story opens in early 2063, London, England. The world is much like today with the exception of advanced transportation(mag-lev), greater corporate and government collusion and corruption, and very advanced electronic devices.

Physics is making strides into the unknown, unlocking the secrets of Dark Matter, Alternate Realities and the Higgs Boson.

Through a wormhole in space an evil realm of madness and despair connects to our doppelganger universe, Brane "B". We ourselves live in Brane "A". This evil realm is called Darkworld.

A portal door high above it opens to the end of time in Brane "B", called Alien Nexus Two. Our universe terminates as the Mothership Alexis One, constructed by the Grays at the end of time. It is also known as Alien Nexus One. The end of time in our Brane is a loop of time that repeats over and over, similar but not identical to Brane "B" 's end as Alien Nexus Two.

Alien Nexus Three lies through a portal in a cliff face on Darkworld, which leads to the Modus Control Center, a lower part of the Mothership. Out through the Rift in the Center lies Alien Nexus Three, the result of the collision between both Branes. It is a vast plain with Magikal qualities. The Rift to the Center lies high above the plain in space.

A hole in the plain is the path to our space-time location, whatever it actually is. On the reverse of the plain is a world of gigantic mountains, over which we can see the Mothership hovering. Around the Mothership an infinite cloud of individuals orbit, the result of our interference in their world.

It is the final state of Alien Nexus Two.

For now!

The story has three main protagonists, or maybe four, or five! Number one is of course Dick, Richard Wembley the third, billionaire art collector and behind the scenes political bigwig.

Through trials and tribulations, danger and self-discovery, he learns the path he must take to solve the mystery of his quest, and be reunited with his girl, Jen. His uncle is killed in a strange lab accident, and he inherits a large sum of money. the work his uncle was doing for the Canadian government is the key to travel from our world to other dimensions.

Roger, Dick's recently killed scientist uncle. He is transformed into an Alien Grey, multiplied into several selves by time travel, sent through wormholes, forced to conceal his identity while posing as Merlin of King Arthur's court, made immortal by alien technology, sent to the end of Time and brought back to life on Earth.

Garth, Roger's protégé and inheritor of the experiment that killed him. He is sent to another dimension when the latest version of the experiment malfunctions due to a massive solar flare. He discovers a plane of existence so different from our own that the mind boggles. It first appears to him in his prescient dreams, during which knowledge of the future becomes real to him.

Darkworld Duck, a sentient Toon and result of the Brane collision, which has left him, a former human Earth resident, half zombie and half cartoon duck.

The Dark One, a rotting corpse inhabiting a cursed suit of armor, he possesses a Ring made from Cintamani Stone and rules Darkworld.

**Bounce-1**

Richard (Dick Cheese) Cleese Wembley the Third was a very important man, and driving the mad streets of London in the midst of a manic frenzy.

Descended from English nobility, and by association a worthy man of note, he brooked no opposition. He was, unfortunately, becoming stuck in traffic as it ground to a standstill.

His second name referred to John Cleese, one of his ancestors on the distaff side. He was on his way from one of his well-appointed offices to another. He had five different luxuriously magnificent private office suites in the Greater London Area. They were all located in football stadia, since he was in charge of managing all of them. He realized that he was likely stuck in one of the semi-permanent traffic jams that often lasted most of the day on these ancient, narrow highways. Also, he remembered that his girlfriend's place, where she still lived with her parents, was walking distance away, as was his office at Palace a few blocks after that.

He had started his commute at Wembley stadium, joining the cue of modular surface rail (MSR) vehicles on the high-speed Mag-Lev. This part of the journey had been very fast, in fifteen minutes he and his Audi VSi Electric (MSR)

Sport were ejected onto the A214 near Church Road. The fact that he and London's most famous stadium shared a name was the source of endless puns at his expense, but he paid such jokes no mind. He was proud of his ancestry, his forefathers had immigrated to America in the last century, and one had returned to Britain fifty years ago to marry his mother, a descendant of the famous dead actor /comedian John Cleese.

After a few blocks toward Church Road he had become mired in the jam. Everyone on the Mag- Lev was trying to squeeze onto the already crowded A214, it seemed.

Just before coming to a complete halt in in traffic he had thought of pulling off the A214 to try to skirt the main traffic jam, and circle around to resume his course, perhaps after a few miles on the A212. But alas, this was not to be. The side streets were all full of cars trying to go south onto the A214. Just before abandoning his vehicle a few blocks from the Gypsy Hill Police Station, he glanced up to find the familiar landmark of the Palace Transmitter Tower, and was amazed to see that it was gone, missing!

"How does a 220 meter tall steel tower vanish?" He thought that he would walk down to the Royal Albert and have a pint, before continuing on.

He wondered to himself again about the absence of one of London's tallest structures. It was an obvious presence from the window of his most gaudy treasure trove, the National Athletic Main Executive Office at Crystal Palace. He did not recall seeing anything different around the tower the last time he had glanced out that window, not more than a few days ago. No construction, no obvious signs of damage or any warning at all. What had happened? A terrorist attack? There had been no high winds, and the Tower had stood up through so many storms in its 104-year history. It must have been an attack. That must be the reason for the traffic snarl.

He took out his phone and dialed the number for information, and demanded that they put him through to the Gypsy Hill Police immediately, as he began to trot downhill to the pub. When the police answered he was very excited, and began to babble a bit as he told them of the vanishing tower, his abandoned car and the huge pile-up on the A214. They humored him, of course. He was an important man. His car would be towed and stored at the station free of charge, of course. They didn't know anything about the tower, but they thought that it would be visible from the station roof. So a police officer went to the roof to have a look, all while talking to Richard reassuringly on the open line.

After another moment the officer had unexpectedly fallen silent, the faint hum of the open line was the only sound.

"What do you see?" Dick Cheese wanted to know.

"Nothing."

"What, exactly?"

"There is no sign of the tower, but I see a smudgy bit of mess down there, running mostly north-south. A bit orange-like, and some green."

"Like smoke, or what?"

"No, it's not moving around. Just different. Looks like a woods, or distant trees."

Just then Richard came around a corner on his downhill trot to the pub, and plunged directly into a thick stand of heavy foliage.

Richard's girlfriend was 22 year old, Jennifer Heathland. She sat for the moment on the floor of her parent's living room, in front of the telly. It was the size of one whole wall, and you could swear under oath that the 3-D image with "feely" surround-sound was as good as or better than any available. Yeah, her parents had spent far too much money on it. It was already getting outdated, and not more than a year old. The reason was that a new technology that allowed direct brain stimulation enhanced the newest model TV's ability to project "realness" to a level indistinguishable from reality; called "Real-TV", it was all the rage, and could fit in your pocket. They were pissed.

"We can take it back!"

"It's too late now, that ended after 90 days!"

"Oh, fuck!"

"Yeah!"

"It's pretty good, isn't it?"

"Yeah, it's still the best! At least to us 'old' people!"

"Oh, shut-up!"

On the tube the latest concert from the ISS Main Low-Earth-Orbit Music Cube pumped and resonated in time to low-g ballet, while her parents smoked some Jamaican.

Without warning all the lights and appliances went dead, including the outstandingly expensive TV.

"Ah!" Her mother screeched and made faces.

"I will fix this." Her husband was kind and conciliatory. "You just wait here, while I go to check out the circuits."

"Look outside the window." His wife had calmed down. Looking outside, the three people making this tiny family saw not one light in the gathering darkness.

Jennifer ran out to her car parked in the drive, and jumped-in. It started immediately, and as her parents came out to see her leave, she called out to them, "I want to get a good look around!"

They waved good-bye to her and went back inside, lighting some old candles.

She raced up the street, turning a few corners and seeing few cars on the road, most of them driving extremely slowly. She came within sight of the old TV transmission tower, now a national landmark. A new "exoskeleton" of larger ironwork now held up the lower portion of the tower. There was an elevator and observation deck, added in 2025.

She pulled into the tower parking lot at high speed, tires screeching to a stop, and ran to the elevator.

On the way up she wondered what she was doing. On the observation deck she stood gazing out over the familiar landscape, as the sun made its way to one final dip below the horizon.

But something seemed wrong, as she looked out past the nearby features of her neighborhood she saw a smoky smudge of an orange/green blur just before the red sky's edge.


"Dick Cheese was in it now!" He thought. Yes, he knew about his silly misnomer, and at times like this it attained its own identity almost, while he experienced angst. He had rolled into a ball, as his feet had tripped on the dense thicket he now struggled to extricate himself from. The tangle of vines and branches had few thorns, for which he was grateful.

At last he tore himself free and rose from his knees. He stood at the edge of a strange collection of orange and green trees, with smaller blue bushes and thick undergrowth. Strange sounds emanated from the alien jungle. Unknown bird species called to each other. A long ululation ended in an unfamiliar guttural chitter. Clicks and snapping sounds. Soft wails and musical howls called back and forth to each other.

The long limbs of the jungle trees hung above the massed undergrowth beneath them, serving as a path for a strange little fellow, bright pink with little tufted ears. The grim little face had bright yellow eyes, which reflected the light in the gathering darkness. Richard recognized that it was a previously unknown animal not unlike a lemur.

He pulled his Real-TV from his pocket, and plugged the cord into the surgically implanted jack at the base of his skull. Searching through the matrix of latest news items in V-space, he soon found the item he was after.

Reports had come in slowly at first, a trickle of seemingly crazy rants. Then someone had started to put the picture together, and then the first solid news item. It was from a traffic 'copter, of course.

The announcer was an extremely attractive young black woman, whose eyes flashed seductively as she described the unlikely events.

"Apparently a large area of south-central Greater London has vanished, replaced by a strange jungle full of unknown plants, animals and who-knows-what-else!"

"The area covers some of the A212, A214, A234 Road, Crystal Palace Park, some residential streets and shops, all the people who lived there, just gone with no trace. The area bordered by Beardell Street on Central Hill, Westow Hill, past the Gypsy Hill Railway Station, Dulwich Upper Wood, and just north of the Park and also the Park Road. The TV tower is missing. The sports stadium. The railway station. Anerley Road ends in a jungle at Waldegrave Road. A portion of Maberley Road at Belvedere is still there, but not Maberley Crescent. Church Road is missing from just north of Beulah Hill Road to north of Park Road. Approximately 95,000 people are unaccounted for, not counting people who might have been on the road driving in the affected area."

One such person, Jennifer, now stood on the tower observation platform and gaped in wonder at the marvelous craft hovering above her. It was as big as a blimp, but made of some kind of shiny blue metal, with gold colored girders and windows. It glowed softly and hung in space above her silently, effortlessly. Soon an announcement came from the craft, in English.

"You may come aboard to observe the recent Ground changes. Do you accept?"

"Yes!" Jennifer heard herself saying.

As she waited for the alien vessel to land or beam her aboard or whatever, she thought back to a recent show she had watched on her huge TV. Experiments at CERN had led to the discovery of actual other dimensions, and had just last year shown that these worlds, "realities", collided together at times.

The resulting effects of such membrane impacts against one another were not known. The membranes, or "branes" for short, were the probability matrix foundations of particle physics in each version of reality. All the physical facts of the Universe, the behavior of known Laws of Science, and particular facets of Reality were directly associated with these "branes".

Somehow her Universe's brane had smashed into the brane belonging to these people who had so kindly offered to bring her aboard their impossible craft. A tube emerged from the space-blimp as it hovered just above her, and she was sucked aboard. Did I mention that she was quite attractive? She was. And her short skirt kind of swirled up her magnificent thigh, held down at the last moment by a modest hand.

"Who am I?" You may ask.

"I am the narrator." You may reply to yourself.

The view from inside the friendly alien's ship explained a lot. Outside the floor to ceiling wrap-around windows she could see her island of a normal London neighborhood, surrounded by the alien jungle landscape, dotted here and there with huge glass towers.

"We are a 'Science Team'." Her female host, the officer in charge, was saying. "We came to investigate the recent mass fluctuations in this area."

"We are cut-off from our world!" Jennifer was pleading for help.

"This is likely to be a short-term fluctuation, normalcy will return presently."

"You mean we will go back?"

"That is most likely the case."

They had floated higher above the now tiny patch of

transplanted London, and the jungle gave way to a shimmering sunset ocean at the horizon.

Richard Cleese Wembley III was an excellent swordsman, and he knew it. He was used to throwing his considerable weight around with ease and aplomb; tolerated by no one, if he could help it. He surrounded himself with the best and the brightest that Britain, and in particular London, had to offer. During Jennifer's absence, while an estimated 120,000 people were unaccounted for, his team searched for Jennifer relentlessly. She had become, to the press, his fiancé, gone were the girlfriend references, and mums the word about her age. When she was at last found at the end of the second day he was overjoyed, and had her rushed to see him right away.

She is brought in to the room, which has been his search headquarters, and they embrace, kissing and weeping, mostly on her part. Dick Cheese is no piece of stone, however. He asks his now future wife to tell her story. Did I mention that he proposed and she accepted? Well, he did; and she did.

"I was on the alien vessel and saw the people from a planet on a distant star in a galaxy close to our own, but in a Universe separate from our own. It is called "Ground", and is located in the Andromeda Galaxy. The Milky Way Is on a collision course with Andromeda, but each brane has already struck the other, transferring mass and energy between them, although only temporarily. We saw London replaced by jungle, and you saw a patch shaped like ours replaced by a patch of jungle from this planet around a distant star."

"That's right, honey. Now you are safe with me. I have an uncle in Canada who is one of the world's leading experts on Brane Theory and Quantum Fluctuations on a massive scale."

"His name is Roger."

And did I mention that she was a really keen investigative journalist? Well she is.

"You must fly with me to America, well, Canada actually."

"Where?"

"Ontario."

"Oh. Not Toronto?"

"No."

"Thank God."

Just then a messenger rushed in. His uncle Roger was dead, killed in a lab explosion. He seemed to recall an earlier explosion at his uncle's lab, and that it had been rebuilt. He was stunned. What was the use of a trip to Canada now? No one was there to shed light on this mystery.

"One more thing. Your uncle had a considerable fortune, which he has willed to you, his closest living relative."

"I already have over a billion!"

"Well now you have several."

"Splendid."

"Yes"

"Quite."

\*                    \*                    \*

**Joe's Master Koan - part 1**

Joe sat on the grass and waited. Waiting was the thing that Joe did best, and he did it a lot. He waited for the Master to return, as he always did at this time. Stones had been arranged neatly, hewn and neatly stacked into ten-foot high walls all around. The sun shone brightly down onto the short green grass, peppered here and there with colorful wildflowers. Many had waited here before him, and he would not be the last to take up a vigil here.

The main problem was that he had no idea how long he would be waiting, the Master could come back at any time, or not at all, theoretically.

He thought of perhaps waking one of the others, but soon dismissed the idea. He was sure that the Master would come eventually.

Joe relaxed and sat back against the tree under which he hid from the heat of the sun. The air shimmered in the middle distance as he surveyed the expanse of his domain. The Master's domain, really, he merely was in charge until the Master's return.

Joe dozed in the early afternoon heat, and his highly trained mind wandered, and drifted off into thoughts of his former life. In an ancient past from a time beyond knowing his world had ended.

He knew one thing; no one was going to make him disobey his Master's wishes. He had been left with precise instructions in that regard. Stay sharp. Don't be fooled.

Joe started slightly as he dozed and looked up, out to the high wooden gate. He was alert and strained his ear...did he sense a presence from outside? He wondered if someone was there, although he still heard no one.

A loud knocking on the gate. "Are you there? The Master sent me."

Joe wasn't fooled. They always claimed to have been sent by the Master. He thought he would wait and see what the voice would come up with to say next. He waited.

Joe sat on the grass and waited, waiting was the thing that Joe did best. He did it a lot, while he waited for the Master to return.

The flowers were like stars of color on the short, bright, lush green grass. They glimmered in the sun.

"Pick me." One flower seemed to say.

"Pick me." Another flower urged.

"Pick me and I will wait for you while you explore beyond these walls." One said.

Joe wasn't fooled.

*          *          *

**~Time travel, Branes and Quantum Foam!**

The Universe is a mysterious place, and Man has often struggled to understand it. He has striven to know his place in it, and to know about how it all came to be. One man had directed his efforts to understand the Universe in a more fruitful way than any yet before him. That man was Garth.

As he pondered the great questions and gathered together the pieces of the puzzle, he planned new approaches to solve problems that eluded him. As he worked, collecting the facts and figures he needed, he got closer to perfecting a science that would change humanity forever.

The nature of Mind, of mere existence, and the creation of all things, in this or any reality, was the subject of his researches. Could a cloud of probabilities be a real Universe, if no one was there to observe it?

He knew that the entire Universe existed as an undefined waveform until observed, or measured... he also knew that measurement in some cases resulted in a phenomena called Quantum Entanglement.

Other than work at the two institutions he was a member of, he had no human entanglements. Sometimes he wished that were not the case, but his work kept him far too busy for much of that anyway. So he worked at his notes and data organization:

The exact "times' of the Brane collisions are not the same in each brane. Brane B 's far future can collide with our past, present, future.

And vice-versa.

Atlantis and Lemuria are examples of physical transfer of their future into our past. The Bermuda Triangle, etc.; are examples of the opposite. Some UFOs are from their future; man himself may be descended partly from them. In a few places physical space and time in the individual branes mix together so that a temporary third reality forms. These are sometimes experienced as vivid dreams; sometimes a gateway to knowledge of the future opens up in these dreams. These dreams were Quantum Jumping; not using a machine, just mind, to switch branes.

There are many times more cells in your body than there are stars in the sky.

The Universe contains some very exotic substances, such as neutronium, and substances that can only be made; e.g. Bose-Einstein Condensates. Bose-Einstein Condensates were predicted in 1924-25 and made by Eric Cornell and Carl Wieman in 1995 at the University of Colorado, Boulder.

A Soliton is a self-reinforcing solitary wave that maintains its shape while it travels at constant speed. First observed by John Scott Russell before 1882. He observed a wave at Union canal in Scotland, and described it (he was the first to do so) as a "wave of translation".

Two Solitons in a bound state is a Bion.

Our Galaxy is on a collision course with the Andromeda galaxy, they will pass right through each other peacefully in about three billion years.

When galaxies collide Dark Matter and Dark Energy

associated with these individual galaxies play a role in maintaining cohesion in each one.

Bions can be composed of widely separated solitons.

A quantum mechanical relationship can be established at an earlier time in the Universe, this is called quantum entanglement.

The Brane Regions associated with each galaxy collide long before the physical galaxies collide, exchanging solitons and Dark Energy & Mass.

In the third Brane created when Branes collide, there is a dream world where Dark Solitons crash into our world, maintaining a flat Universe.

Let's call the part of our Brane associated with our Galaxy "Brane A"; and call the part of our Brane associated with Andromeda "Brane B".

Garth Wallace looks up from the notes he is composing for his lecture on Brane Dynamics and time travel, wearily squinting out the window. He is Dr. Garth Wallace, PhD., actually; graduate of MIT and head of the Dr. R.E. Whembly (Dec.) Synchrotron Expansion Project, Chalk River.

Born in 2028 in Vancouver BC, he is in charge of one of the most intense programs ever researching particle physics and the early universe.

Dr. Roger Ellice Whembly, his deceased mentor, has recently killed himself performing the very experiment he must now continue.

In essence the experiment involves a feedback loop, the world's fastest computer, and standing waves. A mysterious "ball of energy" forms.

The energy is believed to be a form of the Higgs-

Boson particle manifesting as a time-traveller inside its own wormhole. All the data is bad. The particles seem to not be Higgs-Bosons at all, but some more massive particle. Then an even more massive version of the particle is found. Garth continues making research notes:

Dark Solitons are coming to flatten the universe...

Our hero, Dr. Garth Wallace, is heir to his mentor's BC lab at TRIUMF Synchrotron Extension Building, UBC. He also has a 'tank', in a mine. The mine is drained periodically to work on equipment, and is located 2km down in Nanaimo, BC. There is a sub down in the tank as well, for working on equipment when the tank is full. The tank is 5km tall and the size of three or four basketball courts.

The experiment is carried out on two scales, one large, and one small. A particle counter scans the relationships between Branes and 11space. A particle is emitted, travels through a conduit to a vacuum chamber, is absorbed by a detector, is re-emitted, and sent back to the emitter to be counted.

Each time the cycle completes the amplitude increases in the emitter. The whole arrangement is a form of a reflex Klystron. It uses a Higgs particle. The particle field remains as a single particle of greater and greater mass. A "bubble" of energy is seen to form around the emitter tube.

Garth remembers ordering a detailed examination of data from sensors placed around the emitter tube. Those results should be ready now. He picks up his office phone and punches the speed-dial button for the analysis results.

"Hi, IT here," is the response.

"What's the scoop on those sensors?" He asks quickly.

"Weird slew rotating around, not the range we expected at all." comes the response.

"What, higher, lower?"

"Way higher."

"What's this slew?"

"It looks like partial shielding and rotating exposure."

"What, of a Higgs?"

"No, something... something massive, it looks like twice the signature."

"So, this looks like Dr. Whembly's mystery particle? Yes, it looks like the first phase of a higher order field, all right. Could be the one."

"The emitter tube resonates at the fundamental for a Higgs?"

"Yeah, the fundamental is the same. When we feed the protons in from the synchrotron."

Garth hangs up and returns to his notes. A Higgs particle is produced when the reflex klystron is resonated at a very high frequency. Details...

Why have attempts to produce a beam of Higgs particles failed? Dr. Whembly's experiment exploded because of a jump in resonance by twice the frequency. The idea of "HASER" radar to map Brane relationships in 11space was not a new one, but the traditional view was that it was impossible for man.

Little did Garth know that HASER beam radar constantly maintained a map of 11space for the beings at the "other end of time", in the Foamiverse. In the far future in a Brane close by the foamy nature of the Plank scale of the Universe is collected into a "pile". It is the "Foamiverse".

One citizen of the foam Universe is now Dr. Roger Ellice Whembly. He is aware that in the normal sense he must be dead. Dr. R.E. Whembly is certain that he is not a ghost, in a version of the afterlife, or having a dream. He now has had time to communicate with his fellow citizens and has come to the conclusion that he has undergone destructive teleportation.

His original body was destroyed Jan. 21st, 2060; at the same time a "copy" arrived here. He remembers his accident and thoughts at the time. He was in the TRIUMF lab he directed, examining the waveguide and cavity on the Reflex Klystron Detector. The set-up was to take nearly light-speed protons and form a coherent beam that excites a target to a very high resonant frequency.

Each proton arrives at a very short time after the last one, at precisely regular intervals.

The Energy in the feedback loop is monitored at the detector and frequency measured at the emitter. A super-computer controls the feedback loop adjustments and displays system data. A "bubble" of energy forms around the emitter, and grows.

He thinks about the roots of the technical details he is modifying and examining.

When he discovered the nature of the bubble back in 2030, the more massive Higgs fields predicted were found. These energies were about 10% of what he would use today. Examinations of all the terra-bytes of data lead to proof of other Branes in 2032.

The path to higher-energy experiments was very

dangerous. In the 2056 experiment when he found the reason, he was nearly killed. If he had not guessed correctly that bions were forming between the particle field in his experiment and a remote location, and brought in some modifications, the revised computer model predicted an explosion.

Haunted by strange predictive dreams it terrified him nightly.

His dreams lately involved explosions and confusing scenarios in which he held God-like powers and glimpses of his future. A vast plain was below him as he flew naked through space. A dark cloud of black objects speeding past him in the opposite direction, nearly hit him.

He pondered the numbers in his head, worried now. What if there was an even higher field concentration possible? What if his mods were not enough? Some theories predicted five distinct Higgs field masses, he had only allowed for the first three.

He had only planned on working at energies of Higgs, Massive Higgs Type I, and Massive Higgs Type II.

Now he was certain that some of the numbers were wrong. Was the energy going up in regular intervals or as a Log function? A major blunder.

The moment of the explosion blurs past in his memory, with a flash of light, a sense of duality, of being two places at once and a wormhole. The wormhole formed as seen from his present location, a view of his damaged lab inside. He remembers turning away from the collapsing hole.

As he turned away from the destruction he grasped his situation. He is a Soliton. The Universe is eternal. He is eternal. Every Brane was nearby.

Every Brane is adjacent to this one. Each idea, quality and outcome is a reality bubble here. Platonic ideals. No one dies here. Nothing does...

Dr. Garth works for a bit longer on his lecture notes and takes a short break.

The ability for a mid-energy level experiment to create a Higgs particle is a contentious point among theoretical physicists in 2063.

Experimental results conflict with accepted theories. The Theory of Everything predicts correctly the energies of Higgs creation in the CERN experiment, but not the appearance of the Higgs at lower energies as found by Dr. R.E. Whembly. The frequency of resonance is found accidentally in 2030 when working on a new version of Quantum super-computer used to control a proton beam at a large synchrotron.

Analysis of interference patterns inside the computer lead to the discovery.

The "window" in which the Higgs appears is a tiny variation in the frequency when the proton beam that resonates the emitter tube is composed of coherent particles. They all have the same phase angle just as the photons in a laser do. The energy bubble forms after the experiment has been running for an extended time period. The theory is that the phenomenon is a wormhole with a massive Higgs particle inside.

In 11-space the particle is in the shape of a 2-d torus membrane with a second "hole", which expands until the entire "brane" turns inside out. The part of the particle in 4-d space-time is the "edge" of this second hole.

It can physically appear, disappear, and move in space, etc., due to this shape change.

The shape of the Higgs membrane is complex enough to be very confusing to new students; it can be described as a 2-d object, since it has no "thickness", yet it forms a 3-d hollow shape. In cross-section it resembles a doughnut with a bite taken out of it.

Another source of confusion is the word "brane" itself. Most people associate it with the well-known discovery of other dimensions by Dr. Garth's mentor Dr. R.E. Whembly. But the word also is used to describe the Planck scale foam of virtual particles and also used to illustrate the shape of a Higgs particle as seen in 11 space. Even an experienced theoretical physicist like Garth feels this confusion sometimes. Is there something in this besides semantics? Maybe I'm missing something here.

### Dr. R.E. Whembly

Dr. Roger is a confused traveller. "Lately" in his new world order things have seemed stale. He is aware that the likelihood of his forming a "Bion" with one of the locals is diminishing. He notes that most of the local Solitons in a Bion pair seem to remember having "always" been in a pair, and that new ones were rare.

His explorations had led him into many a nook and cranny of the Foamiverse, and several "alternative" states of being. One place that stood-out was like a vast city set amid a starry sky of bubble Universes. Each "bubble" was the "plateau-stage" of an ancient and wise Alien Civilization, cheating annihilation at the end of time inside its own singularity, and the city a meeting place for all of them.

The tapestry of alien shapes and sizes was bewildering. Cultures clashed and toes were stepped-on unapologetically. He found himself witnessing a vast ocean of extra-terrestrial beings, and still being all alone, separate.

Then he found out about a race of aliens that felt just as he did, all the time.

They bred seldom.

Seldom went out.

Kept to themselves.

Were loners.

The Grays!


### The Grays

Advanced technology allows them to do marvelous things. They are the oldest race in the Universe(s). They also are the most numerous.

They reside in several galactic super-clusters less than 3 billion light-years from the exact center of the universe. Most of them are "hiding" inside a vast singularity plastered into the foam. A universe-wide chain of eateries is named after them.

A plot to overthrow a vast galaxy-wide civilization for the benefit of its own citizens has just recently (comparatively speaking) been foiled by them.

They see no evil, speak no evil.

On a vast desert planet ruled by giant sandworms they carry out strange hallucinogenic experiments on themselves to dominate space and time itself.

They thought of that already, whatever it is.

They are old.

As old as the red Martian Sun (older really) that compels them to grok you completely.

They are on a five-year mission from their home world.

One of the crew is named "Scotty".

Alien robots with one eye that moves constantly have come from "space" to conquer their world.

A strange "montage" of kaleidoscopic vignettes flows across the stage of their story, coupled to the meaning of the intricate body art displayed by the protagonist.

Almost anything could be attributed to the Grays.

A long time ago; in a galaxy far, far away; they chose the Gray side of the Force.

They built a vast "ring" of material around their home star.

They like dragons, and unicorns, and puns.

They have strange "powers", and can see into the future.

They have hairy toes.

They have wonderful eyes.

The process to become a Gray (or any other race of Alien) was simple. The candidate went to their "bubbleverse" and underwent destructive teleportation to a special "orientation area". When he materializes at the "life-skills" camp for his new race he is in the form of his new identity.

He was "Roger the Gray". Roger the alien.

### Roger the Gray

One day not long has after "going Gray", Roger noticed that he is missing something. Life is endlessly dull. Time weighs heavily upon him. He is bored and listless; the others studiously avoid him. The secrets of the Universe are open to him, yet he feels no satisfaction.

He decides to take a trip around the Universe in his faster-than-light saucer-shaped craft. The tour is going great until he is sucked-up by a wormhole and spit out too close to a blue and white planet.

He was losing control as his saucer flies into the atmosphere and glows, brightly; explosions pepper his small craft.

The control panel goes dead and he falls like a rock out of the sky, skidding to a stop in a hilly area near a small gully. Looking outside, he decides to create some clones of himself to use as decoys. Once they are ready he becomes invisible and waits.

Soon a curious farmer, having seen the crash, follows the skid marks across the ravine and to the ship. Seeing the hatch has popped open, he sticks his head inside to take a look. Terrified by what he sees, he screams and runs away.

Hours pass.

A convoy of trucks can be heard in the distance.

Later soldiers shouting orders and talking on hand held radios.

A soldier pokes his head through the opening and yells to his fellows "We got a couple 'a dead ones inside!"

The commanding officer inspects the contents briefly and orders the hatch sealed.

After a while the sounds change to heavy machinery, a crane is hooked-up to lift the saucer onto the back of a flatbed. After 20 minutes on the road the hatch is opened inside a large building on an Army base close by. This is where Roger makes his escape.

Using his two-way wrist-radio Roger opens a wormhole and steps inside.

"See you on TV later, suckers!" he yells before it closes.

### ~Foam, Fields and Flying Friends

In the far future in a Brane close by the foamy nature of the Planck scale of the Universe is collected into a "pile". The nature of this place is of naturally permeable "bubble" worlds of various sizes adjacent to each other, present or not, duration long or short, an infinite number, and localized effects and beings existing independently of any ambient bubbles or conditions. Also its edges contact the entire Universe at the Planck scale.

Also the "foaminess" is repeated in the very large elements and structures of the Universe.

"Final Reality", is a higher state of awareness and existence at the "End of Time", where life itself is explained. This is Alien Nexus One, at the end of our own Brane, Brane "A".

Alien Nexus Two is the end of time in Brane "B".

The beings of Alien Nexus Two are complete branes themselves. They are in orbit around Alien Nexus One.

Alien Nexus Three is a vast plain with a hole in it, and an opening and closing door in space that controls the flow of Higgs particles and dark solitons. A guardian stands watching on the plain below flying dreamers experiencing being individual Higgs particles.

*"Why won't this thing work?"*

Dr. Garth wonders aloud to himself. The latest word from the staff in the IT Department was that some source of interference was preventing full alignment of the proton beam just before the first main beam bender.

This prevented acceleration of the beam around the curved portion of the track. He thought that the whole situation was barely possible, since all known precautions had already been taken to prevent problems with alignment. Maybe something was causing the beam to wander, first frequency decay and then "spraying" protons in a cloud. The numbers he was looking at indicated a problem with no known source.

He worked late into the evening, checking and re-checking his calculations and periodically making phone calls to IT. His computer screen was full of different shots from the accelerator, with blinking red notes and data fields attached to each piece of technical hardware. No source for the troubling energy variance was popping out at him in an obvious way, his search led around and around, back and forth from one possibility to the next.

He was so tired.

Leaning back in his reclining chair, he soon was breathing deeply and slowly as he drifted off to sleep.

I am sleeping! But I am still working.

Dr. Garth looks at math in a prescient dream. He sees several numeric progressions represented as links in a chain. Somehow each of these progressions is built-up from the partial results of the last one. This applies to reality because the "resonance" frequency of the Higgs experiment "wanders" slightly and must be adjusted constantly.

The progressions represent corrections to f.

Dr. Garth wakes from his dream realizing that the math he remembers from it is gibberish.

An idea occurs to him; maybe the numbers he remembers represent a code. Try the simplest one: 1=a, 2=b, 3=c, etc.

Dr. Garth writes out some of the math he remembers from his dream. He realizes that certain sections of the various progressions are nearly identical, sometimes only different by 1 or another low number.

He wonders if number theory will help reduce the overlapping, nearly identical sections to one more coherent result.

Researching further he lists possible candidates for the dream math.

Fermat numbers?

Merssene numbers?

Mersenne primes?

Lucas sequences?

Jacobsthal numbers?

Jacobsthal-Lucas numbers?

Pell numbers?

How would he combine the various number sequences into a whole?

He thought of a long-discredited idea, that prime numbers were the only "real" numbers that made sense in a world with more than four dimensions, that Man's need to split everything into pieces made numbers like four and the other non-primes necessary. That might be a possibility in higher dimensions, he thought to himself.

So...

Start with only prime numbers, and numbers that repeat over and over in Nature as well, the Fibonacci sequence. Generate only the set that overlaps, and then use Lucas Numbers to thin out the herd a little more. He was starting to remember a little more. Quickly he went over the numbers in his memory and constructed a chart.

*Sudoku for multi-dimensions.*

1 2 3 5 7 11 13 18 29 47 89 233

*1  1*

<u>2</u> 3                                      *two terms*

2

4 <u>7</u> *10*                                 *three terms*

  2

6 13 <u>23</u> *33*                             *four terms*

4

10 23 46 <u>79</u> *112*                        *five terms*

  2

12 35 81 160 <u>272</u> *384*                                *six terms*

5

17 52 133 293 565 <u>949</u> *1335*                          *seven terms*

    11

28    80    213    506    1071    2020    <u>3355</u>    *4690*

*eight terms*

    18

46  126  339  845  1916  3936  7291  <u>11981</u>  *16671*
*nine terms*

42

88  214  553  1398  3314  7250  14541  26522  <u>43193</u>
*59864*    *ten terms*

144

232  446  999  2397  5711  12961  27502  54024_97217
<u>157081</u> *216945*    *eleven terms*


*1,1,3,10,33,112,384,1335,4690,16671,59864,216945*
maximum random order for chain

2  7  23  79  272  949  3355  11981  43193  157081
<u>differences of chain</u>

Adding 1 to each of max gives random chain

2,2,4,11,34,113,385,1336,4691,16672,59865,216946


### *Errors and explanations*

Looking at his quickly constructed chart again, Dr. Garth realized that something looked wrong. He had written the chain of Primes, Lucas numbers and Fibonacci sequence across the top, but one number looked wrong: 18. Looking at it again he realized that as the sum of the first four primes plus one, it fit after all.

He picked-up the phone to call IT. "Director here, I'm sending you a file to work on, I'll need you to extend this chart out to numbers that we can use to adjust the beam frequency."

Adjusting his glasses, Dr. Garth yawns and leans back

again in his chair. Soon he is back in a light doze as a smile plays across his face.

The phone rings, IT is a bit peeved.

"What were you thinking on scale, with this 'info' you have for beam adjustment?"

"Well" Dr. Garth replies immediately, "We are operating at such a high frequency, why don't we assume that we are right up against the Planck length for wavelength, and make range adjustments from there, with the Planck length equal to one in the chart."

"Do you want to use scalar units or a log scale for the adjustment values?"

"Use a natural log scale of course," was the instant reply from a distant and distracted Dr. Garth.

Dr. Garth is again sleeping in his chair when IT phones back.

IT is smug and taunting slightly." We ran the chart numbers like you said and, well, they are just too low at this scale and we don't think endless iterations will get good results, so what now Doc?"

"Use our established search frequency for Higgs resonance and use the chart data values as sideband values on each side." Dr. Garth is firm and in control again.

"Yes, sir." comes the reply from a chastised IT.

"Sir, we are back on-line". IT had rung up again to the Director's desk phone. "We also are coping with some fairly intense interference of some kind, it is a repeating variation on the same scale as the correction values you gave us."

"Will we be able to stay on-line?"

"Yes, but we will need to boost up the total energy

about 10% to cancel any wiggles " After a while Dr. Garth gets ready to leave and go home. The phone rings again.

"We just detected a Higgs as the source of the repeating interference, it keeps generating gravity waves each time it drops into four-space."

"Send me the raw data." Dr. Garth is near exhaustion, it is four in the morning and he is starving.

"O.K."

*Junk*

10233415516559014126791429643349443770140873311349031701836329712150734807526976777874204912586269025203650110741123581321345589144233377610987159725844181676510946177112865746368750251213931964183178115142298320401346269217830935245785702887922746514930352241578173908816963245986102334155165590141267914296433494437701408733113490317018363119032971215073480752697677787420491258626902520365011074329512800995331629117386267571272139583862445225851433717365435296162591286729879956722026041154800875592025047307819614052739537881655747031984210610209857723171676801775652777789003528844945570212853727234602481411176690304609941903924907091353080615211701294984540118792648065155330493931304969544286572111485077978050341645462290670755279397008847578944394323791464144723340246762212341672834846768537889062373143906613057907216115919919485309475549716050064381636708825969549691112258542019614072748967367989163763 8

6122581100087778366101931177997941600471418928800067
1943708161204660046610375530309754011380474634642911
2200160415121876738197402742198682231673194043463491
9009990551680708854858323072836211434898484229771351
3018523447067460492189229958345551690263542248481791
261915075

## *Higgs and Gravity*

The Higgs particle was no longer a total mystery, but it didn't always obey the laws of physics laid out in what Dr. Garth knew as the Theory of Everything, which replaced the old Standard Model in 2020.When the protons in the beam excite the detector array at the precise frequency, a wormhole opens to higher dimensions, "sucking" a Higgs "down" into four-space. While it is here in "reality" it gets compressed into a tiny black hole, which then evaporates. The particle then gets sucked back into four-space, and on and on, etc. The wormhole usually stays open, and the particle cycle is as fast as the Universe expansion rate when it was just one second old. That is the tame side of the Higgs appearance. What are really scary are the gravity effects near the Higgs.

While the Higgs collapses into a black hole gravity effects pull electrons off of any atoms close enough. That is why the target area of the detector has the strongest vacuum in the Universe. Farther away electrical currents are set-up in the air or any materials in range.

Rotating cones of Gravity and Electromagnetism had devastated all earlier experiments, in microseconds massive implosions wrought destruction. The wormhole and the proton beam creating it wandered over to the edge of the target each time. Around there any atoms of air or metal were compressed near the wormhole, or sometimes sucked in.

The good thing about these effects was that they acted at extremely small distances from the singularity formation. One atom could be sucked into the black hole, electrons removed from adjacent atoms, and just a few atoms away nothing happens. But if the wormhole ate too big of a meal then the action started, with more and more material cascading into a collapsing wormhole, thank God. For if it stayed open after the initial implosion no end to it would be in sight, with the Earth itself as a potential meal. Still the wormhole had always collapsed before, just after massive damage to equipment and personnel, occurring twice to Dr. Garth's predecessor, the last time taking his life as well.

*Dreamer - Can you put your hand in your head? Oh no.*

Dr. Garth's dreams had been very strange ever since he fell asleep at the lab the other night. He dreamed that he had gone back to the TRIUMF lab in BC to work on the portable unit. In his dream he completes the power-up process and sets the controls. He places the Q-ball back in the emitter by hand, incrementing the power with each cycle. As the experiment intensifies he passes out in his dream, awaking on a vast plain with a hole in it. A gigantic version of Albert Einstein with the body of an Olympic athlete smiles down at him and gestures for him to look around, take it all in.

Behind him in the far distance piles of foam turn to shades of blue at the horizon. A giant moon hangs in space, looking like it is only a few miles away. Once in a while a bright light flashes out of the hole in the plain and reflects off the moon like a phaser shot and vanishes into a dark rift in space high above the plain. Albert waits and soon a black shape materializes in a now bright white rift high above. A menacing presence darts down and comes straight at Albert.

With perfect timing Albert raises his hand and the shape is directed down into the hole. Soon Garth wakes and shivers to himself, wondering. He has hardly ever had such a strange dream before.

In his next dream he is flying over the plain on Nexus Three. Looking down expecting to see a giant version of Einstein, he sees instead a shiny man shape composed of triangular facets, as close to anatomically perfect as this representation style would allow at this scale. He wonders if it is Albert in disguise or a new giant.

Zooming down to get a closer look he comes around to the face side. The man-creature-giant-robot-drawing looks startled and reaches behind himself with one hand. Quickly he flings the contents of his hand up at Dr. Garth, just missing him. Dr. Garth screams and flies straight up. Various later shots hurtle past him at close range. Dr. Garth changes course rapidly at irregular intervals and zooms skyward. Soon the machine-man is the size of an ant on a plate, far below him.

Dr. Garth wakes briefly. Soon he dreams again. He sees the shiny man towering above the plain, in the far distance; Dr. Garth is flying low and fast, circling the creature. A hole in the plain is beside him, and near it is a sphere, it looks like the moon. Out of the hole a bolt of lightning arcs up into the heavens. The lightning is composed of individual beads of light, with the occasional dark "hole" inside the flux tube.

It looks like a coherent stream of water lit-up from inside by a laser. Its arc is flowing parabolic curve, an arch.

On the far side of the stream from the shiny man, a tiny winged woman hovers. She weeps and her tears turn the dry plain green. The man-bot begins to whistle, pursing his giant lips. The lightning bucks and shifts in response to his whistle. He begins to dance, altering the light beam with each move. Soon the fairy-woman stops crying and the end of the lightning zooms up into space, following its former path and disappearing upwards.

Dr. Garth rolls over and snores as his dream changes.

He is looking out the right eye of the giant man-bot. He stands inside the head chamber. He can see part of the nose and the giant's lips purse to whistle for the lightning. As he is whistling a floating "man" dressed in a suit and tie, and carrying a valise, exits from the mouth. His eyes are expressionless and his whole body hangs in space, half curled-up like a shrimp or a fetus. He wears a drab fedora and his suit is old style but very expensive looking. "Googol" pops into his head. The floating businessman looks up to him looking out the giant's eye and his mental voice says clearly "I am of the Googol, we are a high number of specialists in topics of interest, we are legion; you are insignificant and small." The Suit floats away in a circle then exits down the hole below.

The TRIUMF lab at UBC in BC is the original lab constructed by the team led by Dr. Garth 's former mentor, Dr.

Roger. It has been rebuilt twice, once after 2058, and again in 2061. There the technique of maintaining a captured Higgs in a slowly collapsing wormhole was perfected, by injecting low energy lithium ions periodically into the vacuum chamber.

They are just heavy enough to start the collapse process, thus preventing the energy loss due to black hole evaporation. After a lithium ion is absorbed, the wormhole contracts and then stabilizes. Soon it is beginning to expand and wander, so another ion is injected, etc.

This keeps the particle field within a set area and the same size. A balance of energy in and energy out is achieved.

The effect can be tuned with the proton beam frequency and phase angle.

Portability is achieved after the Higgs is loaded into the device via the linear accelerator extension of the cyclotron/synchrotron/klystron.

Superconducting magnets, vacuum chamber, and nanotech solid-state devices all play a role in the Higgs machine's function. The most advanced portable quantum computer and feedback control software made the portable device very stable. It was intended to be used to test the variance of interference in the wider environment, and was scheduled to be moved to the "tank" in Nanaimo.

The operator sat at the controls inside a Faraday cage. The whole machine fit into a rail car. It was powered by an antimatter                                    reaction. The Canadian Department of National Defense originally constructed the tank in 1969. Later it was enlarged and used for the search for neutrinos in the '80's. It was 2km from the surface at the top and formed a 5km column of water under that, the size of a small gymnasium in area. There was a special chamber at the bottom made of ten feet of lead covered with gold foil. It was accessed via a sub that was taken apart, lowered down the access shaft, and re-assembled in the empty tank when it was first constructed.

Maintaining it in new condition was a very tedious and expensive chore for DND. The portable Higgs machine was constructed to endure the crushing pressure at the bottom of the tank, and would just fit into the lead chamber. The sub would tow and then push the device into the chamber after it was lowered down the access shaft and put through the airlock.

The human operator was required to monitor the wormhole size and position, and to observe and operate the feedback loop.

Computers were able to do most of these things, but human intelligence made operation actually possible. Also the Faraday cage made communication to outside the machine impossible. Shielding had to be perfect so tests were run and then the operator and data retrieved. Before the machine could be moved to the tank it had to be tested.

Dr. Garth was scheduled to fly out to BC right away; he was catching a ride with DND at 0800 hours. That made having a nap mandatory, as he had only had three hours sleep all night.

Dr. Garth reclines in his chair and sleeps. Soon he dreams.

He is high above the plain of Alien Nexus Three, a personality nexus that allowed him prescient knowledge of the future. He awoke from these dreams certain of facts and events that only prescience could explain. The dreams themselves were symbolic and had a consistent inner logic. Dr. Garth believed that he was experiencing "being" a Higgs boson particle.

Working on the math he had dreamed of had been the trigger that led to these dreams of the future. He thought the shiny man represented the four-d world he usually lived in, and the arcing lightning the evidence of life in the Universe. He thought the tiny flying woman represented the natural order and the plain was awareness. The foam pile worried him and he remembered the stuff the giant had thrown at him when startled. It was the same. The floating man was a message from the established order; he thought it was old knowledge outside of man's usual experiences.

As Dr. Garth flew he looked down at the vast plain far below him. He was far, far above the surface. The shiny man was still visible, a tiny dark but shiny light on a green expanse. The edges of the plain were straight, yet he could tell that it was a giant circle. The curvature was barely discernible. This plain must be far vaster than Earth.

He circled around and flew back over the tick-sized dot on the plain below. Behind him on the ground great mounds of foam lay in a huge semi-circle.

As he flew back he became aware of a presence behind his right shoulder. He looked over and was startled to see a nude Albert Einstein flying beside him. Looking at himself he realized he too was naked. Einstein was the same as anyone now, the same kind old man familiar from old photos.

He smiled and pointed down at the dot below.

"He is going to try to get us soon."

Garth doubted that the shiny man-bot could throw this

high, but was mildly worried.

"If it hits you with foam you will stop flying, lose altitude and crash." Einstein smiled.

"You will fall until you scrape all the foam from your body."

"Didn't you used to be him?" Garth asks.

"No, he is older than I, but back in his role again since my time on Earth. I was a stand-in while knowledge advanced so quickly once, but now he is back to represent the old slow growth of intelligence and power in the Universe. In a sense he is the Universe, whatever we rationally know about it."

"Why does he do it?"

"I don't know."

Soon shots from below began to rise up about halfway to their altitude and fall back below their position. He was aiming at them.

"At first he pretends to be weak."

"Should we circle back away from him?"

"Yes."

They bank and climb slightly.

Shots from the monster below are visible below and slightly past their position, finally landing in huge heaps of foam far ahead of them in a vast arc. It glowed blue-grey and white as soft mounds of cloud-like goo. They flew past the crest of the mountains of foam and a vast rift in space glowed and flashed white ahead of them, in mid-air.

Soon pointy black dots scintillated into existence, exiting the bright white rift. They flew straight at the nude pair of dreamers.

"Wait, wait as long as possible. "Albert's expression is

determined.

The Blackbirds grew progressively closer.

"Wait!" Albert is sweating slightly.

"Now! "They both split apart and climb harder, the Blackbirds rush past at the last instant. They are huge, each as big as an ostrich.

Ahead of them the rift turns grey, and they can see its doorway turn milky white and then clear, showing the inside. They pass through to the interior and soon land in a large room, the wall behind them reappears.

The wall to their right disappears. Alarms are going off and he is aware of people running around, facing an emergency situation. They are ignored.

Soon a voice on a loudspeaker makes an announcement, "Ten seconds to Modus Variation Initiation."

At the time signal the wall behind them vanishes again.

A swarm of black shapes hurtle inside and make a sharp turn, passing into the open space to the right. The right-hand wall materializes and then a contingent of fliers takes off from the room and exits behind them, they follow them out.

\*                    \*                    \*

### Joe's Master Koan - part 2/A

Joe and the men that formed his circle rotated slowly about their common center of gravity; the others farther away in the background whirled all around them in the distance.

The recent explosion of their former world had left them here in empty space. For some reason Joe and the others had no problem breathing. Clusters of the others receded in one direction to infinity, with the hollow inner part of the sphere of people near where Joe's group circled slowly.

He saw it out of the corner of his eye at first, a blur of motion unlike the shape of a person or group or cluster of people. He could see eventually, when the group had rotated around $360^0$, that the blur was a craft of some kind, tracing an arcing path quite close to the group.

As the craft passed the closest point in its trajectory past the circle of men rotating in empty space, Joe saw the distance between them expand as their angular momentum increased; first one, then each of the rest of them was tugged by the gravity of the craft as it passed, sending them spinning wildly across the void.

The background behind the others in Joe's circle flew by faster and faster as each of the men in turn was accelerated by the craft's rapid and close passage. They saw the individual groups and clusters of people in the background blend into an even, grey blur.

The whole group of men traced an arc as the craft left the general area, pulled and spun by its passing mass. Then Joe saw the dull grey blur of the background vanish.

He existed in a kind of white void, but by concentrating he could make out the thick white shag carpet for a floor, and a thick fog coming from somewhere close by.

The others where there, as well, white shadows in the white fog; dressed in white turtlenecks and pressed white slacks. He could just barely make out their pale white faces in the clouds of steamy fog. The white walls where shrouded in the middle distance, an impression more than a fact.

He tried to call out, but he couldn't make his voice work. He stood frozen in place, unable to take a step or utter a sound.

Inside his mind's eye he pictured the recent events that led to this present moment. In his mind he asked, "Can anyone hear me?"

"Yes!" said one voice.

"Yes!" said another, more silently, inside his head.

A chorus of yeses followed, confirming communication from the white-clad prisoners.

"This must not be real, what is the point of all of us frozen and struck dumb?" one voice insisted.

Magically long tendrils of white material formed, descending from the invisible ceiling high above. As the tendrils lengthened and grew the group gained greater freedom to move.

Joe regained the ability to speak, and shouted out.

The others followed suit.

Joe became aware of a vision in his mind's eye; at first in a quite normal way, but then seeming to form a solid world he could see in front of him with his eyes open.

It showed a wide expanse of green lawn, with trees and fountains. Flowers lay amid the blades of grass. His perspective was that of a tiny creature, only an inch or two tall.

He could still make out the white background with its "Sock Puppets of Satan" hanging from the distant ceiling, but his mental view of the garden seemed more real somehow.

He tried moving about in the white void and shouted out again for the others, who responded. They found each other by their voices and huddled together in a tight bunch. Some of the white shag carpet covered raised portions of the floor, which now apparently had raised platforms built into it. They sat down on the edge of one such platform, and again the vision of the garden became stronger. The vivid green grass was just barely translucent in front of the white void.

"I am the same size as one of these flowers I see growing, I must be experiencing life as a flower!" Joe was amazed how tiny he was.

"That's what I think too!" another of Joe's pals said.

Joe thought he could hear a faint rustling sound of wind in the distant trees, and also the scraping of the grass blades against each other right close by. He felt the wind brush his imaginary form; and his viewpoint bobbed around a bit and then stilled again.

Joe thought back to the world-ending explosion that had just recently occurred, and wondered at all the changes that he and his pals had been through. When their world had ended, he and the others in his circle had experienced a transformation, leading to three subsequent versions of reality; two of which they now experienced simultaneously.

Joe wondered about the craft that had sent them spinning and tracing an arc after it. Who had been piloting the thing, and why had his little group been the ones affected? He thought that the answer was to do with where they had all been just before the end.

He pictured the scene in his mind's eye, and his imagination fought for control with the unbidden vision of green grass and flowers. After a few seconds the image rose before him, a quiet multitude seated at regular intervals, arranged around a huge trap door.

As the alarm had spread a vast phalanx of fast fliers and a swarm of others had rushed past the seated crowd and out of the opening door, just as everything turned white. He remembered the sensation was like Bruce lee punching him in the face a million times in a row.

The memory receded, and again the green garden grass sward hung before his vision as clearly as a 3D holo-cast.

A man in pure white overalls and white lab hat had stridden into view in the foggy distance, and was now walking up to speak to the group.

*         *         *

### ~Bounce-2

Richard Cleese Wembley III awakes with a start as the com function on his Real-TV PDA alerts him with a sub-sonic pulse only he can feel. The voice on the other end of the line jerks him fully awake as the import sinks in like cold ice water on his soul. She is missing again.

As his mind sharpens to its usual keen edge he relaxes a tiny amount, for he is far from having no hope for his wife, Jen. He actually thought that she would be returned to him within hours or days, judging from the length of her previous absence. Sometimes experience is a cruel teacher, sometimes not to be trusted.

He is at their home in the reconstructed Montfichet's Tower Historical Monument Building, overlooking Blackfriar's Bridge on Ludgate Hill. She is visiting her parents again and had failed to return around midnight as planned; he looks at the time on his PDA and sees it is after 2:00 am.

One of the perks of living in the Tower rent free as "curator" is the proximity to the Mag-Lev Station, which is actually connected via a special service tunnel to the Tower. He runs to the curator's suite lift and descends to his private garage at the Station entrance. As usual his car is selected immediately and transferred onto the system. The logic behind his appointment as curator was that he had been completely successful managing the extensive art collections that graced the head executive offices of agencies such as National Athletic and other organizations of which he was a prominent executive officer. All he had to do was ask and priceless artworks would be handed into his possession via acquisition by standing committee. He recalls a memory from two days ago when he was at his most ostentatious office bower, Palace. He had been talking to one of the committee yes-men, making him nervous on purpose.

"You see this space on the right hand of the north wall is empty, I've had to make some donations to a few charities run by an owner or two, you know what I mean?" He was referring to soccer club owners in the tentacles of various shells and fronts lately common in the London area. No one could make a move without greasing the wheels of the new "philanthropic" business associations dealing with all levels of government.

"I am going to need a blank check to keep the standard of art improving in our collection, at least twenty this time." By twenty he meant twenty million pounds, as the lackey knew.

"Sir, funding on that scale takes time to approve!" Nerves had rattled.

"I suggest you contact the others and form a quorum

this afternoon." He was entirely serious.

"Yes, my lord." The committeeman was admonished enough for now.

He stared for a minute out the window at the bright green grass of the lawn outside, and then back at the man from the art committee, who was dressed for some reason in a white lab coat.

Several years had passed since the crisis and his subsequent marriage, with his power and popularity skyrocketing at behind the scenes meetings and in front of the media. There had even been talk of his running for Parliament again, in spite of his earlier rejection by the voters when he had been a quite young man. Back then his association with old money and privilege had worked against him, but both he and the political climate had changed, becoming more alike, until he was nearly the logical choice.

His car accelerates smoothly and enters the traffic pattern on an automatic program bound directly for the Palace area, where his wife has been seeing her playful and unpredictable parents. He doesn't wholly approve of their use of drugs and alcohol, and worries that they're a bad influence on her. She has several times before consumed too much to drive and stayed over with them. Their house is a few blocks from the Palace Station, which is directly adjacent to his favorite office. He leaves St. Paul's Cathedral and the Old City Thameslink Rail-bridge Crossing behind him.

Warning lights light in the dash of his car indicating a problem with the rail system. All the cars slow at the same time to a barely perceptible crawl, and then resume nearly full speed. He could see that his car was on its way to being ejected early from the system, at the station just before Palace. Traffic piles onto the local streets with a screech of tires and blare of horns, many confused and angry drivers landing at an unintended station as hardly ever before in their lives. He races down a disused and bumpy alleyway in clear disregard of local traffic only signs, making the corner at the head of the main body of oncoming traffic. He swerves into traffic, cutting off those formerly at the lead of the chaotic mass of speeding sports cars and SUVs.

Something is happening again, he can see an orange and blue smudge of color, just up ahead in the darkness. It dawned on him that he was looking at the end of the road just there, where the alien vegetation began. He slows and pulls over as far as possible, and sees that the road vanishes right at his feet. He is still at least five blocks from her parent's house, or where it used to be, in our world.

He gets out of his hastily parked car, weird alien grass under one tire, gravel roadside beneath the rest of it. He runs off into the orange scrub bushes, taking the direction he remembers and following familiar topography, but the world is strange. A tropical jungle hid animals and other creatures making unimaginable sounds that he could not identify as anything he had heard of before.

Soon he was looking down the little hill just to the north west of where he thought the house had been. And a thick patch of jungle trees blocked his path, hiding the exact spot. He pushes his way through the dense undergrowth and finds himself staring into a small gap in the canopy up ahead, where an unusual blue and gold craft hovers. A voice speaks.

"We have come to observe the mass transfer ratio, you

must be alerted to the pattern of these exchanges. Soon this area will be uninhabitable, as the collision progresses. Please come aboard!"

A tube is extends at once, and before he can reply he has been sucked-up and deposited in front of the vessel's commander, a very attractive yet unnervingly alien woman.

*           *           *

### Joe's Master Koan - part 2/B

"Stay calm, I see that you have attracted some standing wave formations here, here and here." He stands pointing to the long snot-tendrils dripping from above. "Looks like you are stuck here for now."

"Where is 'here'?" Joe asked.

"Well... Why it's limbo, I suppose. This area is devoid of contact with useful space-time, it stays undefined as much as possible. The fog generators help with that, and the minimal decor."

"What do you mean 'we are stuck here'?" One of Joe's men asked.

"If you were to move away from this spot, while that ectoplasm is hanging there, you would find yourselves walking in a circle until you came back to this exact spot. You are all part of a Godel Universe right now, and you are stuck on a closed loop of space-time. I am in a virtual parallel Universe to you, as the Godel Universe I am part of is much bigger than the sub-set you now inhabit."

"How can you be free to leave while we are prisoners of this snake of slime?"

"I am not actually in the same space as you are."

"You are right here, what are you talking about?"

"I am in a parallel reality that is a larger manifold containing many finite realities as closed loops inside the larger whole. I can come and go as a member of the larger set, but you and your friends must stay on the closed loop."

"We are in Limbo."

"Exactly."

### ~Flight into History.

Garth struggles awake as his alarm sounds annoyingly for the third time. It is 7:30 am, and he has to hurry to the entrance hall to meet his military escort. The man is visibly nervous and quickly holds the door on the DND vehicle sent to take him to the nearby airfield.

He drives at what Garth thinks is an excessive speed and Garth complains.

"Sorry Sir, I am trained to drive this way, I'll take it a bit easier." The driver slows a bit and then nearly resumes his former rate.

A gate at a side entrance to the airfield opens as they near the restricted area and they drive right out to the waiting Concord IV. On board the supersonic transport Garth sees a few top brass and a couple of TV journalists.

He sits by himself and quickly the female journalist sneaks up behind his shoulder and whispers in his ear, "A bit stuffy in here with these types, don't you think?"

"Sit down and join me." Garth offers the seat beside him.

"What do you expect to find with the isolated Higgs experiment?" She is insistent of an answer just as if he was being seriously interviewed.

"Who wants to know, and this is still restricted information except for accredited academics and 'crats."

"Just give me a run-down that can go public, this is starting to leak from hostile sources, you might want to nip their arguments in the bud."

"What arguments?"

"They are saying that the next lab disaster is just a matter of time and such, referring to Dr. R. E. Whembly's passing as just the least dangerous thing that could happen."

"Well, we know now that Bion formation with a distant location raised the energy of the experiment outside of the normal operating area and have a solution ready."

"What is that?"

"I'm not at liberty to say."

"What can you tell me?"

"Not much."

"What does this experiment mean, what are you looking for?"

"Ultimately we are looking at what interactions are going on between our dimension, our brane, and other branes in proximity to ours."

"What about time, I heard that time travel was related to your experiment?"

"We study the entanglement of solitons and dark matter in the early Universe and between our Galaxy and the rest of the Universe."

"What?"

"We can send the wormhole through time as it collapses and study data collected at that time."

"Can you see through time, or send or receive objects or messages?"

"No, we can only infer data about dark matter

distribution and galaxy formation in the early Universe."

"Thank-you."

Garth sits alone and works again on his lecture notes. He is a guest speaker at the U.B.C. physics symposium being held in a few weeks. He is also in charge of several dozen grad students working on doctorates at TRIUMF. The experiment has several interesting correlations with the early Universe.

The operating frequency where the Higgs is observed is an analog for the end of the Hadron Epoch and the beginning of lepton formation. Electrons and neutrinos are leptons and didn't exist at higher temperatures present in the early Universe less than one second old. The energy of the experiment is not tied directly to the frequency of excitation as you might initially think. While the protons that excite the klystron emitter are nearly at light speed, it is the "bunching up" of the wave fronts that causes the frequency to be so high, not the number of revolutions around the cyclotron. The protons are at the same phase angle and arrive at the emitter at precise time intervals. This interval is a very small time period. When they reflect off of the Klystron they amplify the waveform until resonance opens the wormhole, inside a magnetic bottle that keeps the vacuum chamber empty. Lately a fluctuation characteristic of stray neutrinos had affected some results obtained, so the portable device was developed. The observations obtained in the experiment were unique in physics, in that they were unpredicted by any accepted theories and remained unexplained. All we have to go on is the data collected each time the wormhole formed. Some scientists proposed that "overlap" of other branes caused the anomaly. Garth didn't think this was the exact solution. He thought that the replication of results obtained by Dr. Whembly in BC by the experiment in Ontario ruled out brane overlap theories.

Soon the plane lands at YVR and taxies off to a side gate, where he and his military escort depart by helicopter for his TRIUMF lab. Garth leaves his escort at the door to his lab and activates the security lock to enter the room where the portable device is kept.

He remembers his dream and wonders if it will be an accurate prediction of his test run. It is a ridiculous prospect, since the function of the machine has little to do with his strange dream of another dimension of reality. It is supposed to function exactly as the experiments on larger scales do, except for lithium injection and neutrino shielding, once it is installed in the tank. The lithium stabilizes the wormhole, preventing sudden collapse during bion formation, and the tank cuts down the number of interfering cosmic rays that had affected data plots in the past.

"Well, let's see if you are a time machine after all!" Garth laughs at himself and remembers the security cameras are on. More seriously he powers-up the cyclotron and prepares to inject the wormhole and contents into the portable device.

Tech calls on the emergency phone and Garth picks-up.

"We need a minute here, sunspots."

"O.K." Garth turns the experiment down to standby energies and sits back to wait for Tech clearance.

Glancing up from his dazed daydreaming, Garth thinks he sees a blurry dust ball or insect fluttering high up on the lab wall. To his amazement the blur in his field of vision sharpens slightly, revealing a large spider hanging by a silver thread.

"It looks weird for a spider, too many legs." Garth thinks aloud to himself.

"Twenty-two legs." Garth hears clearly in his head.

"I am the nexus point of eleven axes and four googol beings."

Garth is staring open mouthed at what he thinks is an audio-visual hallucination. "I don't believe this is real." He shuts his eyes and opens them again; the spider thing still hangs on its thread of silver light.

"We are, as you are about to learn in what you refer to as reality."

As Garth stares at, *what he thinks,* is a figment of his imagination; the spider, "Higgsy", cuts the thread it hangs from, then slowly fades from sight as it floats in space.

"Good-bye," A soft voice says in his head as it finally fades completely; one long leg waving farewell.

The emergency phone rings. "You are clear to start high energy excitation." Tech says.

"O.K. full power in five minutes, then load configuration on my mark."

"Right."

"Open command channel alpha."

"Command channel alpha open."

"Energy level cycle to operating maximum."

"Operating Level maximum in thirty seconds."

"Twenty seconds."

"Ten seconds."

"Max level now."

"Wormhole in Primary Detector."

"Mag-lev superconductor on."

"Priming lithium injector."

"Linking magnetic bottles."

"Wormhole transfer accomplished."

"Portable unit ready."

"Standby mode."

"Standby."

The portable unit would now inject a nearly constant stream of lithium ions into the wormhole, throttling it down into a microscopic singularity, nearly collapsing. When the time constant between injections was longer, the wormhole opened-up and then started to wander around in space slightly. There was theoretically enough lithium in the tank for five hundred years of constant operation, and an anti-matter collector to power it indefinitely. An ion bottle loaded at the cyclotron, and a small fission reaction supplemented this technology. There was five pounds of plutonium in tiny grains inside a new kind of chemical goo DND had made. It was held in compression inside a special alloy container.

All in all the railcar sized machine had enough joules to run a small city for a thirty years, and someone's house forever after that.

Garth walks around the machine and looks at the on-board control panel thru the Quartz glass. It has fine wires embedded in it. The panel shows no warning lights and reads "Standby Mode On".

Garth unlocks the unit's access door and seats himself, closes the door. "Reducing lithium injection rate."

"Wormhole confirmed."

Garth remembers he is completely shielded from the

outside world by a Faraday cage. The Techs would have to wait to hear his account and download the telemetry. Still, the holographer and microphone were recording him. "Going to max operating energy."

A sudden flare streaked across the quartz observation window and Garth watched several warning lights turn red in front of him. He saw that a burst of neutrinos had passed right through the wormhole area. Lithium injection was offline. Frequency was going off the chart. Looking up he saw a milky white glare outside his view window. It gradually cleared until he saw a patch of blue sky. He assumed that a hole had been blown in the side of the lab building, but knew that was not possible, since his lab was deep in a canyon of buildings and apparatus. He shut the power off anyway, to avoid any further explosions. He knew the wormhole would instantly collapse, and that the Higgs would be gone. It would have to be reloaded somehow.

Sitting up and taking a good look out the window, Garth sits stunned for a moment.

He sits in the machine in the middle of a vast green plain, covered in short grass like a lawn. Far in the distance the Foam Mountains from his dream receive an additional "snowfall" of glowing goo. He sees the shiny man as a point of light, far, far away. The arc of goo or foam is to the "North". He remembers from his dream that the rift in space is to the "East" of the mountains. The Giant shining man is to the northwest. Over in his direction he sees a serpent of light wriggle up to the rift. Several black dots appear in the bright light of the rift and zoom right at the man. He grabs one and eats it. The others zoom over to where the hole in the plain usually is, but the moon blocks it. They circle back around and the man monster reaches down and opens the hole. The black shapes retreat down the now open hole.

Garth is stunned that he is witnessing and experiencing a reality populated by creatures from his prescient dreams. He remembers thinking in new ways about physics and how m-theory was only a part of the new theory of everything. He remembers that facts about dark energy, dark matter and the way that matter was exactly "lumpy" in our Universe were deduced from the newest m-theory.

How could other membranes (branes) determine facts about our own universe? Why would it have to be another membrane, why couldn't our own membrane smash into another portion of itself? He remembers that bion formation with an unknown location had made conditions disastrous in previous experiments.

What had gone wrong with this one? He should have been observing the entanglement of our brane with another one at a very early stage of the universe, not caught and stranded in a dream world from what he assumed was his imagination. If this reality was a membrane, what was the rift in space? The blackbirds were like mechanical functions and obviously were dark energy beings. The giant obsidian man was a guardian, more like dark matter than energy. The lightning was a force that acted only at certain times, and distressed the small flying woman.

Garth realized that on this plain observed and observer were inextricably meshed together.

Life energy itself was part of the physical reality here. He waits inside the machine for hours, thinking what the scene around him meant for the laws of physics. The rift bothered him. Why was it there? He looked now to the place where he remembered the rift had been and saw that it was gone. So it was not a constant here, yet in his dreams it had always been obvious when he approached its position. Also the hole in the plain, why was it important? The giant man seemed to want to limit access to it. What was he really doing? The grey floaters of googol went down into the hole, where did they end up? They were a legion of experts in their specialties, he had said. What was the foam that the monster threw? It interfered with flying, Albert had said. Like distilled gravity. Things started to click into place. The giant man used gravity; if he ate blackbirds he must be a singularity. The hole must be a conduit for energy to enter the physical universe, and not just energy, but information too. Somehow the uncertainty principle gave rise to quantum foam, which held the entire universe together like glue. It would compress him to a point if he stayed in contact with it while airborne. Then he would just drop like a rock, crushed flat on the plain below. Soon Garth is feeling tired from all his speculation and slips off to sleep.

Garth realizes he is dreaming and looks at his hands, his arms, and the rest of his body. He is nude and flying fast. He circles around and sees the monster far to the northwest, a gleaming black dot near the horizon. Directly below him he sees a new addition to this world, the portable Higgs machine. He dives down and accelerates to incredible speed.

*Double Trouble.*

He is able to see himself sitting inside the machine, and notices that his mouth is open.

As he buzzes the portable unit a strange sensation grips him, as if he is in two places at once. Flying back past the window, he sees his other self begin to stir and shift position. As he comes right up to the window he sees his other self's eyes fly open, and can see himself flying for a second before he vanishes. He is sure that he had two distinct vantage points for a second.

He gets out of the machine and looks around. No trace of his flying self is evident. He recalls that he thought he saw his flying self melt away as if made of thinning fog. He begins to walk over to the area where the moon rests on the plain, and sees that the machine man is crouched down with his head turned to the side. It reminds him of Chichen Itza's Chac Mool. Garth can see that the giant's back is stretched over the opening that usually is blocked by the moon, which is on the plain nearby. This seems like a weird behavior, and Garth sees a few shapes buzzing around the giant's head. They are just like his dream self.

Garth thinks that the monster didn't have time to block the hole like he normally did when the tiny fliers attacked. The moon lay on the grass well beyond the giant's grasp.

The fliers tire of bothering the reclining god-man and fly away. As they circle around and fly away, a flock of dark shapes are silhouetted against the forming space-rift. The dreamers split into two formations and head directly for the rift. The dark shapes spread out and head in an intercept course. At the last moment the dreamers spread out and easily outmaneuver the dark triangles. The triangles continue on until they can change course and head for the hole. The moon already blocks it, Garth knows the giant took advantage of the distraction of the fliers encounter and used the time to grab the moon.

The dark shapes circle the giant man, and he begins to whistle. He continues to whistle and the dark fliers are drawn closer and closer, finally drawn into the giant's open lips. The monster keeps whistling and the moon begins to lift up from the hole in the green veldt. A tiny figure is under the giant sphere, lifting it as slowly as possible, as if with super-human effort. The giant grabs the moon and slams it down into the plain, and the tiny flier darts away, but not before landing a good slap on the monster's face. It flies straight up and is soon lost amid the bright blue sky.

Garth walks over to where the moon lies on the grass, just a short distance from the hole. The monster-man reaches into his pouch and quickly throws some foam over Garth.

He reaches down and quickly seizes the frozen man, and pops him in his mouth. Garth realizes that he is being eaten alive, and unlike in his dream this is in what now passes for reality. He feels himself being swallowed whole and lands with a splash inside the creature's stomach. It is full of fluid and half-digested dark triangles, grey men and dead fliers. Garth can hear the grey men talking to each other about the technical details of their digestion.

He knows that the triangles aren't conscious in the same way as intelligent life is. The dead fliers sadden him; he wonders why they are here. Then he sees one of the grey men stop moving and transform into a regular dead person.

Mystery solved! This was an area to distill dark energy from anything the monster ate. The triangles seemed to dissolve into nothing. Soft foam rose to the top of the pool and floated out of the area.

Garth himself was becoming confused, listening to the grey men comment on exactly how they were dissolving. He felt weak and noticed that his clothing was charred and his skin red and mottled, burning and stinging. He wrenched himself out of the clutches of several grey men trying to explain their fate to him and waded out of the acid lake. He followed the foam river as it left the stomach area.

He went up to the wall and looked at it. He placed his hand on the hanging folds of fleshy hanging material and pressed. It sank in and a fissure developed. He squeezed into the opening. He advanced a bit and soon came to another fleshy wall of hanging material.

He ripped a hole in it with his hands and could see a hallway on the other side.

Stepping through he realized he was in the endless office network that the grey men populated. He walked the halls until he came to a central lobby area. The atrium soared into the air and an elevator opened in the lobby. He got in and selected the top floor.

The elevator door opened and he stepped out into the head chamber of the man-bot. There was a contoured command chair, and two windows over a display console with an array of lights, switches and indicators.

He sat himself at the command console.

The view on the screen showed the view from the monster's eyes.

He looked at the control settings and saw a bank of switches labeled "Auto", "Program", and "Manual".

He saw that there was a joystick type game controller and some foot switches. Switching the toggle to manual, he grasped the joystick and worked the pedals, awkwardly walking the monster forward. He walks the giant over to where the moon lies beside the hole and aims a solid kick at it. It flies through the air a good distance and lands, making a slight depression in the grass.

He starts walking for the distant Foam Mountains, and is surprised at how boring working the giant's controls was.

In a daze he leans back and rests for a moment in the contoured chair. Soon he is in a light doze.

He is flying again directly over the huge man-machine. He sees that he has walked a good way in the direction of the Foam Mountains.

Up ahead of him the rift glows into existence. He knows what to expect now, and is not disappointed. A formation of black triangles is exiting the bright white rift. He has never seen so many before, and is by himself. He climbs straight up. The shapes are still on a collision course. He turns and flies away and climbs. The triangles break off their attack and head for the hole in the plain. Garth climbs and climbs and circles back around, looks over his shoulder to see the last of them vanishing down the hole. The man monster is running, and foam lies around near the hole, he has been throwing it at the dark birds.

"Wow, I really screwed him up!" Garth exults in having had power over the monster.

The rift is glowing less now, and is slightly lower than

his elevation. He dives and enters the rift as the glow fades.

He is inside a giant room, with a large group of people all milling around. He sees that most of them wear a flesh-toned bodysuit with military insignia and are readying for an emergency. Some fliers arrive nude periodically and either join in the encounter preparations or huddle around the entrance nude and ready to leave. He approaches a young woman in military tights and gains her attention away from her task, whatever it is.

She is brusque and businesslike, "What?"

"I'm not from here," Garth starts; then gains more self-control. "What is happening?"

She gives a rude expression then begins to explain, "You are in a modus variation control center; we are minimizing energy loss and rift stress from Blackbird impacts."

"What are the Blackbirds?"

"Come on, you've seen them."

"But, what are they?"

"They are the unconscious manifestation of beings in transit from another brane in the far future to our brane in what you call 'real' time."

"What?"

"They don't like us, we have our path to the end of time, and they are already done. They want our mutual fate to go one way, and we want it to go anyway except the way they want."

"You're at war."

"That's right."

"What about the big guy?"

"Him too, just not as much."

"O.K."

"Thirty seconds to Modus Variation Initiation." The woman's voice sounds over the loudspeakers. "If you will excuse me, I have work to do; and get dressed!" She tosses him a jumpsuit from a shelf and strides off.

He dresses and the counting voice sounds the alarm "Ten seconds."

"Now."

## ~The Dark Side

Garth looked around the vast Rift chamber.

People of all sorts were milling about and looking as busy as possible, as they did the inconceivable tasks associated with Modus Variation Initiation.

The right hand wall disappeared. Garth felt a twinge of vanity, jealousy even. All of these people belonged here, knew their place in the scheme of things.

He felt left out and a touch of guilt. What had he done to help, what had he contributed? Nothing, he was getting in the way, a distraction. Worse than that, he had been a coward as he flew away from the Blackbirds, while any others he had seen flying above the plain of Alien Nexus Three had always flown straight at the Blackbirds, including he himself with Albert's help.

The Blackbirds flew through the great door to the rift and out through the missing right-hand wall space.

Garth made a decision and jumped through the opening just before the wall re-materialized. He stood in awe of the desolate and spooky landscape within this dimension. Great black trees made of rotting slime towered up to a sooty and windy sky. Black streams cut gullies in the badlands below. The land was grey and colorless. Strange sounds came to his ears, wails and cackles, moaning wind and chattering branches.

A cracking sound from right behind him startled Garth. He turned and a bellowing bull pawed the earth ten meters away, and charged.

Garth wondered what it ate in this empty landscape and ran up a gully, frantically climbing the steep sides to escape.

He climbed up higher and higher, and looking down saw more of this strange land. There down below him was a canyon, and a huge cliff-face opposite the gully-riddled side he now climbed. There he saw the hole materialize and several Blackbirds fly through. Circling around they flew off in a steady climb above the cliff.

Garth knew they were his ticket out of this nightmare land.

He heard voices whispering threats and accusations, and screaming silently inside his head, driving him slowly insane. With an effort of will he returned to examining his surroundings.

Off in the distance some abandoned stone structures loomed. They seemed to exude an aura of evil as if long ages ago they had been used for some foul purpose. Garth wanted to avoid them.

He searched for a way around to the opposite wall of the canyon, and climbed higher and higher until he emerged on a huge plateau. He saw an ancient road and climbed the last few hundred yards to the level top. There lay ruins of one of the desolate stone temple cities, appearing as haunted as possible.

He felt the pressure of dead eyes all around him, causing him to sweat in terror and lose his concentration. Small sounds frightened him and caused him to turn and look to every direction. A loud clanging sound began to rhythmically follow his movements and seemed to be getting closer. Garth looked for somewhere to flee the threatening armor sound.

He came to a wide boulevard made of black stone cobbles set into the ground, some of them heaved-up into piles of rubble here and there. The sound seemed to be chasing him as he struggled down what must have been the main street of a great city. Towers of black crumbling stone lined the connecting squares and plazas that lay in ruins all down its vast length.

He came to the edge of the plateau and a giant bridge that leapt in a single span of stone from the plateau down to the opposite side of the canyon. It was startlingly narrow and seemed to sway slightly in the wind. Small pieces of stone crumbled and fell from it like crumbs of bread. It was an arch with a high side on his side and a low side at the other end.

He strode up the slight hill to the crest of the bridge and looked down the other incline. It was cracked and treacherous looking with missing pieces and swirls of dust devils plaguing his progress. It was surprisingly steep and narrow.

He inched his way down the crumbling ancient path. He was progressing like a crab, with his hands on the ground behind him as he searched for each foothold. A piece of rock cracked off and tumbled away just at his foot. Garth inched around the narrow spot. Finally he made it across to the other side.

Just after he was across a crack opened in the spot he inched around and then the whole stone ruin collapsed in a pile of rubble crashing down into the canyon far below.

He hiked down the side of the canyon; back to near where he came into this nightmare landscape.

Soon he stood above the cliff-face where the Blackbirds had flown in. It was several hundred feet to the bottom of the canyon below the cliff.

Garth stood and waited for the next arrival of the vast black triangles that periodically passed through. Not long later a swarm of black shapes burst through the modus variation.

Garth readied himself and worked out the timing, and leapt down thirty feet to land on the back of a triangle shaped being. He nearly rolled off as the shape banked and climbed with the rest of the formation.

Garth was clinging to the huge black monster as it powered up into the grey sky. The landscape was laid out beneath him like a map. He saw a wasted landscape of dry rivers and low mountains, a dry seabed and corrupt ruins of an alien civilization. A chaotic jumble of stone and fallen ruins littered mile after mile of ancient seacoast. Sad, really; they were all gone now; whoever they had been.

Soon Garth was getting cold as the Blackbird soared upward. The air was getting thin, too.

He saw the last swirls of cloud melt away below him, and the stars, all red and dull, began to shine above him in the eternal twilight. He couldn't breathe, and he was so very, very cold. He lost his grip on the Blackbird's back. It rolled violently and flipped over, flinging him out into empty space. He was falling, falling forever as the air returned to his lungs. He gasped and screamed as he plummeted to what must certainly be his death. What was death in a dream, he thought. Right now I am asleep at the Dancer's controls, he thought.

Maybe I can wake up. He still remained trapped in this nightmare reality, plunging down, down.

Soon he could see the ground rushing up to meet him and shut his eyes as he smashed down at Mach speed.

There was a loud popping sound. He felt himself land. A flash of light and his vision cleared.

He is standing in an endless room, an enormous hall with gigantic stone pillars that reached up forever into an empty white void. Around him a countless multitude of people sat at ten-foot intervals stretching to infinity in all directions. Among them walked a few people serving food from loaded trays. Each person waited patiently to be served and accepted his or her food politely before eating.

Soon a new batch of servers waded through the sitting hoard and brought water to drink, and to wash with. Garth watched as a woman stood and began to wash all over with a small towel, watched as she dried herself with another one.

He walked up to her as she donned her loose white robe and started a conversation.

"Where am I?"

"You are here with the world of patience; we wait for the end of Time."

"But what is everyone doing, just sitting here?"

"We save our intensity for the very end, when our world will be destroyed by yours."

"How will it end?"

"Come with me. I will leave my station to serve you in the way of education and knowledge of reality, which has not been a required service in our world for eons."

"Thank-you, I am not familiar with your world at all."

"We are the opposite nexus to your own Universe, we wait to overcome the limits of Time and pass beyond the destruction of our Brane. We have done it already five times with various other incarnations of the Universe of time and mortality. We stretch the last instant of time here to an infinite extent, delaying the end of our culture. Until then we take turns either sitting or serving.

There are twenty googols of us here in this crèche, which is located just inside the realm of what you would call physical reality. Let me show you the reason for the end of our world as it is that now approaches."

Garth and his thinly clad lady guide walked between the rows of stone columns and sitting people to a circular space near the center of this vast room with no ceiling.

In the center a vast walled pool of water rippled in the reflection of an enormous glowing ball of light that hovered above it, suspended in air.

"This is your world, your Brane." She said, pointing at the ball of light.

"It is on a collision course with our world. Soon when Time ends it will smash into our Brane from the inside, exploding it into twenty googol fragments. Each of us alone shall form a singular reality, and all we have built will be destroyed.

A singularity created long ago in your Universe is responsible for arranging this end. We have been through this with five previous rival cultures, and the outcome is always the same.

Below your Universe sits the pool of our gathered intensity; it is what will save each of our lives as our Universe is exploded from within.

As your Universe hits, we will unleash the gathered energies of five physical Universes, and blast ourselves out of reach of the destruction of final contact between both Branes."

As she spoke a flying man with wings and a glowing aura landed beside the pool. He carried a tiny silver spoon smaller than a teaspoon.

"We even must supply a small amount to the creatures that are permanently fixed as guides to your Universe."

The winged man dipped his tiny spoon into the water and lifted it up with difficulty, spilling a tiny drop back into the pool.

Ripples spread outwards from the tiny droplet's fall with great intensity.

He flew off clutching the spoon with both hands, with great effort.

The lady handed him a small optical device.

"Look to where he flies." She pointed to the retreating "Angel" as he flew slowly away.

He seemed to cross a vast emptiness as Garth followed his slow progress above the heads of the waiting throng and then outward, always slightly up and out.

Finally he could see a tiny image of a man's head sticking out of the wall of a vast sphere that surrounded the residents of Alien Nexus Two. His upper body was free but his hands reached behind him and were stuck inside the wall. He seemed uncomfortable and weary.

The "Angel" placed the tiny spoon up to the man's lips, and he sipped it down eagerly.

"Thank-you." Garth could see his silent mouth form

the words.

The Angel flew away.

"With our technology we manage the energies of five previous Big Bangs and contribute to a significant degree to the formation and equilibrium to each Symbiotic Universe that we share our fate with."

"We distribute our intensity to a few different symbiotic realities by 'Now', since we are not in the strictest sense part of linear time relative to our sister dimensions. They form the outer sphere where the transition to physical time occurs, where time is best perceived as a relatively linear thing."

"The intensity we distribute helps to keep time flowing in a linear way in our sister Universes, while we intentionally spend all of our time in a short loop just before the end. At the time your Universe actually touches ours for the last and final time, our world will end for the last time, and reality for us will be forever something else."

"But we won't be dead, since this pool of intensity will be distributed to us at the moment of transition. With our technology we control the order of things in five Universes, and your Universe and its energy is being harvested as we speak. We send out Dark Solitons to keep your Universes flat enough."

"When your Universe was first created in Its Big Bang it would initially by now have become ninety billion years old. But we have harvested its uselessly long initial evolution and reduced its age to a more reasonable 13.7 billion years. We did this through what your physicists refer to as 'Inflation'."

"We have evolved to create all of our reality and

utilize all of our technology through the power of 20 googols of brains radiating synchronized brain wave radiation. That is how we affect all reality, with the nature and the number of our synchronized thoughts."

"So we manifest to you as two different kinds of entities, re-incarnated leaders of thought in your linear time, and as the 'Blackbirds', which we use to carry energy to maintain your Universe after our intervention."

A thought occurred to Garth, that with all their technology the aliens would probably be able to load a Higgs into the stalled portable unit. If he could awake from this dream at the controls of the Dancer he could leave and return to his vehicle. He knew of only one thing that sprang to mind that would likely wake him instantly from this illusion.

"Can you transfer Energy in the form of a Higgs to my ship?" Garth heard himself asking.

"Yes, but you must travel back here some other time in your future to tell us of your journey, agreed?"

"Yes, that will be fine, but how do I get here?"

"You will have to spend some time at each stage in the path to be one of us, of course.

We watch your developmental history and incarnate as members of your Brane. You can be part of the chain that carries intensity maintaining linear time, as the ones you see at the wall or flying with wings."

"You will first return to Alien Nexus Three and enter the rift. Then you must fly straight up until you can grasp the hands of one of these poor wretches stuck in the wall, then carry the Heavy Water of our intensity to them, then just be one of us."

"So by now you are thinking to deceive us and just jump into the ball of light that is your Universe, here where we can see it all hanging in space before us, but we know you will do it already, or have done it. This is the last major event in our Universe. After you jump back into Brane 'A' we will have only a few short hours to prepare ourselves for a different version of eternity."

"Fare-well."

Garth steals himself for the shock of a sudden awakening and jumps.

*Back on the Plain*

Garth awakes at the controls of the Dancer. He leaves the control room via the door to the hall and takes the stairs down a floor to the mouth level. He can see foam bubbling up at the back of the monster's throat.

He avoids touching it and impels himself out of the giant's open mouth.

He floats gently down to near the ground and across the green sward to his vehicle.

He assumes that being in contact with the digesting grey men has imparted some of their power to him. Suddenly a swarm of black triangles descends from the Rift and begins to buzz around the Dancer.

Some of them are eaten; while several hover above his vehicle and strange lights play over it.

A lurch passes through the inter-dimensional vehicle and the power indicator goes on. The display indicates a fully charged and operational wormhole.

Garth gets inside and sits behind the vehicle controls. He wonders if some of his powers can help him operate the portable Higgs device better. He places his hand over the area where the Q-ball of ambient energy materializes around the wormhole.

What if he could increase its energy and re-load it back into the emitter?

With an effort of will he raises the frequency of his astral body until he can pass his hand through the casing of the q-ball area. Grasping it in his hand he withdraws it and stares at it intently, and then places it against an adjacent part of the casing, where the detector houses the wormhole. The q-ball passes through the wall into the emitter.

The ship lifts off of the ground slightly.

He re-loads the q-ball again, and the ship floats higher. He re-loads the q-ball over and over, and the ship floats higher and higher, far above the plain, far above the Rift. Soon he has left the last traces of the atmosphere below him, and the stars shine brightly around him. They are young and of various sizes and colors.

He goes into orbit around the Dancer and the infinite plain that he inhabits. The mass of the creature is enormous, far beyond conception as a thing with material size. He weighs as much as a small planet.

Soon Garth notes that he is nearing the very edge of the nearly endless flat plain. It curves just slightly at the edges, and then he is stunned by the view as he passes above the edge of the plain and can see it from the side.

The other side as seen from orbit at this angle is a saw

tooth ridge of mountains rising up to a towering central peak.

The whole thing looks like a giant alligator flat on its back.

Up ahead of him in his orbit he sees that the mountains loom up to even higher than he is. The mountain ridge starts at the edge of this side as small peaks and rises in a chain of peaks to the towering central peak ahead of him.

Nothing in Nature or his experience has prepared him for the scale of these peaks. They tower above anything on Earth at the edge of this side and defy conception as reality as they near the center, where the impossible exists as material size incarnate.

It is Time, Cause and Effect in our Universe. Just above it a Mothership 'UFO' hovers. It is beyond Time, eternal. It is made of a honeycomb of foam, held in place by solid light. It is the Foamiverse, Alexis One; Alien Nexus One as seen from the outside, the inside of the foam pile down on the other side of this vast planet.

He docks with the Mothership; a vast tractor beam guides him down to a force shielded dock area where he touches down.

It has a glowing halo, a halo composed of the myriad beings of Alien Nexus Two, after the explosion that has scattered its inhabitants into a vast sphere around Alexis One.

Each tiny glowing dot of this halo is a being or cluster of beings, or group of clusters, etc.

It appears to recede to infinity in a curve that never closes on itself. No matter which direction Garth looks the illusion of limited infinity is maintained. He knows there are twenty googols of them.

He sits in his machine until someone knocks on the glass and gestures for him to emerge.

"We must proceed to our main control center," he is informed by the white-robed monk who has summoned him forth.

They proceed down the corridor to a moving walkway. There are a vast number of different looking alien species represented in the crowd that floods it. They come to a vast domed central area and use an elevator to go to the very top level. They emerge into a vast control center with a glass dome overhead that shows the halo starting quite close by, with individuals showing as tiny dots with tiny arms and legs, and distinct groups forming rings and clusters of rings. He is amazed that out there in that halo the woman he talked to on Alien Nexus Two now floats.

"This whole control center is an expanded version of the machine you used to get here."

His guide is now speaking to him.

"It has been expanded and modified, we have reverse-engineered the technology of q-ball manipulation and wormhole control from your humble beginnings. We can observe your time from up here and get involved if we want, but mostly we compete for lives of indulgence and power over others after we win the competition we share here.

"You would think that this represents a paradox, that we, who have been here forever, are indebted to you for inventing our technology. But time goes in a circle here. We are all individuals beyond Time, immortal. You are the only mortal here, living in strictly linear time. We know you invented this technology and brought it here, but we have always had it as well, since you invented it so long ago. And so you must return to your own time so we can remain as your descendants."

"You are now half Soliton by virtue of absorbing the distillation of grey men and foam. But you determine the history of our Universe more than any previous individual in its history. You must return to your own time to share your knowledge of us with the people of your world."

Garth returns to his craft and circles Alien Nexus One, moving out until he can see everything below him in side view. One side looks like a towering saw back range with a huge central peak, the other side is flat. The hole in the plain lines up with the central peak on the other side.

The giant Dancer uses the moon to plug his side.

The peak has a vast hole at its summit.

Garth flies his ship lower to land on the Alien Nexus Three side. He passes the Rift and is chased by Blackbirds. He flies down to the plain and down into the hole to escape them. The Dancer moves the moon out of the way as Garth approaches; he escapes down.

Garth expects to fly 'up', back to Alexis One, through the inside of the central peak on Alien Nexus One Instead, he finds himself inside a wormhole, and is unceremoniously deposited back in his TRIUMF lab at U.B.C.

### ~Wormholes and Wonder.

Garth sits in his portable Higgs experiment apparatus and breathes heavily. The lab door bursts open and his military escort appears. "What happened?" he is almost screaming and has his gun drawn.

"You will have to view the holo. The only thing I can tell you is that this machine left here for somewhere else."

"We have the lab recordings and know that, but you have been gone three days."

"I want my lawyer, doctor and psychiatrist called immediately. Also contact your superiors and inform them I am resigning from all connections to this type of work."

"Sir, you are over-reacting. We have been preparing for your funeral. We all welcome you back and await the results you have obtained since you are still alive. You know things no other human being knows. Just relax for a few minutes before you talk to the Doc."

Garth sat in his office and tolerated the medical exam from the staff doctor.

"I want my own doctor, and when can I see my psychiatrist?"

"Right away, Sir. The head of Psychiatric Forensics is on his way over. He will debrief you in confidence. Then you may speak to the DND Liaison Officer."

"Who is looking at the holo record?"

"Just DND."

"Oh."

Dr. Roger Ellise Whembly was in a state of shock. He had used Gray technology to transport himself through time, and he still had the brain and body of an Alien. The only problem was that he now inhabited an abandoned chapel in a heavily wooded area in the late fifth century.

His wristwatch wormhole maker was out of power. He should have remembered that he had been playing with the menu and left it set for this space/ time. He had always wanted to see the Dark Ages King Arthur and his fabulous Court.

He had an idea. Taking out a tiny set of tweezers he began to work on the device. He extracted the tiny power core and set it aside.

He knew that he was still a Soliton, still partly composed of foam and immortal energies himself. He took one long glowing finger and held it up, then slowly inserted it into his nearly invisible nostril.

Carefully he extracted a small amount of glowing goo. He deposited the goo over the power core and replaced it into his wristwatch. After making a few more adjustments he sat back satisfied.

"Now I should be able to do a few 'miracles' for the locals and keep myself in disguise."

He fiddled with the controls and a blur encased him. When the blur cleared he stood revealed as an old man carrying a staff.

He was Merlin.

So far he had been:

Head of Physics Department, U.B.C.,

Killed in an explosion,

Transported to the End of Time,

Changed into a Soliton,

Transformed into an Alien Grey,

Sucked in by a Wormhole,

In a Saucer Crash at Roswell, New Mexico,

And now Disguised as a Wizard.

If you were counting he had by now been through four wormholes.

Wormhole Number One: 2060 – End of Time

Wormhole Number Two: relocation to Grey Re-education Center Wormhole number Three: relativistic time-1947 Earth

Wormhole Number Four: 1947 USA – Fifth Century Britain.

Even he was beginning to get confused, and he was an expert in several relevant scientific disciplines.

He knew his Arthurian Legends.

Arthur had been proven to be a real Ancient Monarch by scientists at M.I.T. in 2043. They used new satellite radar techniques and an advanced program running on one of the world's first Quantum Computers.

Correlations with records of archeological data and Ancient Latin cookbooks led to the discovery.

He decides that he should leave the chapel and go into the local village and rent a room at the tavern for the night.

He wonders how he will pay for all this, and turns his head thoughtfully to the side.

"I'm going to have to pull a fast one on some poor fool, I suppose."

Fiddling with the watch he soon walks away confidently into the forest, up to near where the highway passed through.

Settling down there he waited for likely prey.

After a few days Roger was beginning to doubt the sanity of his plan.

The only person to have passed on the road was a gibbering misfit of a "man" who was burning charcoal and lugging it back to the nearby village. He looked as poor as anyone Roger had ever seen before. His rags were the dirtiest "clothing" ever, however; and he smelled worse than he looked.

Roger waited in the bushes beside the road.

Off in the distance he heard the 'clop', 'clop' of horses' hooves.

A heavily armed troupe of merchant travellers was approaching.

Roger fiddled with his wristwatch.

"I am going to have him killed," Roger could hear their leader saying.

"The fool cuts your trees and makes charcoal for sale in the village."

"He must be flogged first, to show the people Your Highness doesn't tolerate theft from his forests."

"We must make his execution an example as well, so that fear shall strike all the peasants to the heart. We must crush his head under the foundation stone of my Lord's new castle."

"Yes, crush his head, crush his head!" The warriors cried out.

By now the cavalcade had made its way up to where Roger lay hidden. He burst out into view and stood in front of the group of armed soldiers and wealthy merchants including the King.

"Stop, I am a Wizard and I forbid you to enter my forest." Roger has set the timer on his watch to activate automatically after three seconds.

"You!" A heavily armed soldier spurs his horse closer.

A bright flash of light erases the scene and leaves the soldiers and the rest glassy-eyed and slack-jawed in the saddle.

Roger walks around from one to the other stealing coins, jewelry and small items.

Finally he approaches the monarch's horse and eyes the heavy purse of the King.

Cutting the strap with a pilfered blade he whistles appreciatively at its mass.

"Looks like I'm getting drunk for a while!"

"Oh, yeah, the procedure." Roger addresses the glassy-eyed crowd, "You didn't see a wizard on the road through the forest, you don't recall stopping here or anything of this experience and especially you don't remember you are missing anything, ever."

Another flash from his device seals their fate, erasing the troublesome memories.

Roger makes his way into the village, and stops at the tavern.

While he is sitting in the public house drinking the King and his entourage arrive and order food and wine, but the

King can't find any money and has to pay with a large gold and ruby ring that is very valuable. He and his men are mystified as to why they are not carrying more money and valuables.

Sitting at a nearby table Roger listens to the King's complaints as the conversation shifts to sex.

"I would do that Igraine, that's forsooth."

"You'll have to kill Gorlois first."

"I can fain afford to go to war with Tintagel, it is much to strong a rock to attack." Inspiration hits Roger like a brick.

"I can help you get in the castle of your rival and consummate your lust for his wife!" He has wandered over to the King's table and is bellowing slightly.

"I hear that Igraine is one hot strumpet with a penchant for nasty Kings in rut."

"Now see here, that is the woman whose honor I am sworn to defend. Guards, seize him!" Roger is roughly restrained before he can move.

"Wait, wait, I really can sneak you into Tintagel."

"Yeah, and how, verily?"

"I know a secret path from the mainland that leads along the sea to a secret door to a tunnel under the castle walls."

"We are listening."

"I'll send the guards to sleep with a drug in their wine and guide you through the checkpoints myself, I used to work there and everyone knows and trusts me."

"Sounds doable."

"Yeah, verily!"

"Uther, do yon Queen as thy wench!"

"Verily!"

All the warriors celebrate the new plan well into the night.

They make their way to Tintagel during the next few weeks, riding through small towns, villages, forests, bogs and fens.

Finally they approach the seacoast near the castle and begin to put the plan into action.

Roger climbs the stairs to the hidden door ahead of the men. Sticking his arm around the last corner he triggers the wristwatch stun device and renders the guards senseless.

Soon he has them tied up and a post-hypnotic suggestion implanted that they drank too much and passed-out without incident.

He leads Uther up the tunnel while the soldiers guard their retreat.

Soon Uther completes his tryst with Igraine and returns down the tunnel to greet his men, 'Merlin' at his side.

"Merlin here tells me he is a Wizard with the Seeing Eye and prophesies that I have conceived a son to inherit my throne and unite all of Britain."

"He is going to come with us and be the court Wizard and please the gods and keep the Evil Eye off of my affairs."

'Merlin' serves the court of the British King for many years, never seeming to age. He claimed it was the magic night-cream that he applied liberally. He also curled his wigs and did his nails, and such a frightful sight had turned many a brave hero to stone.

After a long period of service the King died, and the remaining Nobles and warlords of the local area evicted Merlin. They had a superstitious fear of the 'wizard' and his spells.

Merlin moves into a cave in the hills and waits for the arrival of Arthur.

He stares at night into the glow of his cooking fire reflected in the best collection of geodes this side of New Mexico.

His mind wanders and he begins to daydream. In his vision he is floating in a circle of other beings, and can see the rings and clusters of beings floating expanding out to infinity in the distance all around him.

He wakes from his dream convinced that he is meant to lead Arthur to victory as King of all Britain.

Coming down from his secret cave "hiding place" he runs into a group of Nobles, warriors and soldiers trying to remove a sword that is stuck in a stone.

Roger sees that one of the young warriors is likely the son of Uther and Igraine and waits for him to try the sword.

Carefully focusing the energy from his wristwatch as a sonic wrench, he loosens the grip of the stone on the blade and Arthur draws it forth immediately.

Announcing himself to the newly hailed King, Roger assumes the role of Court Wizard once again. Time goes by and many adventures, quests and battles ensue. Roger serves the King well and protects him from 'evil'. Finally Arthur is killed in battle and Roger wisely runs away from the Court and hides his identity. Later he pretends to be Roger Bacon, Nostradamus, and Leonardo Da Vinci. He lives on and on, hiding his immortality and his identity, changing names and cover stories many times. At long last he has lived long enough to be able to warn his former self about his immanent lab accident. But his original self won't listen to the chubby grey-faced midget with the fake hair.

All happens as before.

Roger visits Garth's classroom at Jack Winters University, Chalk River; Ontario. He sits at the back and asks a few questions.

He confronts Garth after the lecture and reveals his true identity.

Time branches and paradoxes are created.

Garth sends Roger back to Alien Nexus One by intentionally overloading the portable device with a blast of neutrinos and lithium.

Garth has yet to have any strange dreams of flying.

Soon the experiments in resonance to produce Higgs particles just stop working, at all locations. Once again the Higgs particles are only seen as brief results of high-energy collisions of protons at experiments such as CERN in Europe.


### 2163

The Hanford, Washington Higgs Facility Accelerator was the largest experimental apparatus yet constructed by mankind. It was over 1500 kilometers in diameter, and resided in an underground tunnel in British Columbia, Canada; and Washington State, USA.

The Higgs Control Project has perfected a beam of Bosons to map the Branes around our own. They suspect that 'someone' has affected the region of the Universes' Brane around the Andromeda Galaxy.

They see evidence that a 'folding force' has caused the

Brane region there to crash against our own portion of this Brane.

They suspect that the energy to do this came from an alternate reality in a Brane adjacent to our own. What was the motive for an Alien Civilization to control Brane movements? To assume control of vast energy fluctuations, they suspected.

In analyzing the interactions of the beam with our neighboring Branes, they had come to the conclusion that a paradox had been created in our Brane during the middle of the 20th Century.

Advances in technology now allowed the scientists to send rocket-powered unmanned satellites back through time.

A bundle of time-affecting information was constructed to create a scientific amount of change in future events.

This was disguised as crude children's cartoons drawn by a well-known artist of the time. People watched the cartoons and remembered them.

This affected the future course of their overall thinking, changing the course of historical events over a long period of time.

An anti-paradox was created, leading to the writing of this account of future events and an endless loop.

This caused the paradox created (when Brane contact was perceived and used to construct a black hole) to dissipate slightly.

This also caused the unbalanced energy deficit to shift to Brane B in its earlier history, starting the evacuation from what is now Darkworld.

Many of the original inhabitants of this planet in

Andromeda had refused to move to the original crèche and had died horrible deaths of madness and violence.

Their ghosts still haunted the abandoned purgatory forever poised in the unknown void between Branes.

A few old stars from the last incarnation of their Universe were also residents of this dark bubble.

Soon top 22nd century scientists working at Hanford create the latest incarnation of Garth's portable Higgs Device. A trip is planned to see if "riding the contact boundary" can enable transfer from our Brane to this adjacent Brane.

Physical non-destructive transfer of mass to a "pinched-off" portion of our own Brane was confirmed and accomplished.

The machine was huge, the size of a jumbo-jet. Hundreds of technical specialists and anthropologists, diplomats and researchers made the leap to a planet in Andromeda that was associated with the undefined void between our Branc and the other one.

The force that had folded our Universe like a pancake had entered near here.

Switching modes, the machine was used to take a peek at the void, this Darkworld.

No life more advanced than a horse or cow existed there, no intelligent species survived, although evidence of automatic machinery and energy use was found.

The ship was greeted and welcomed by the inhabitants of Ground, as they called their planet.

The Groundians were a peaceful lot and in many ways superior to their adjacent reality counterparts. Each person on board the ship had his alter-ego counterpart in the contingent sent to greet him or her. It seemed that the Groundians were very together and organized, and utilized their superior intelligence very well.

The technology of the Groundians was very far ahead of Earth technology.

The Groundians show our scientists how to protect Time from paradoxes and destruction by wormhole or black-hole formation.

Returning to Earth, they use their new knowledge to locate the paradox of the Higgs Experiment ending in 2063 and locate Roger before he is sent back to Alien Nexus One by Garth. Using Brane B technology they construct a time machine that can carry a live crew and go back in time to get Roger, preventing the paradox of Higgs Experiment failure at UBC and Chalk River.

All returns to as before.

22nd century scientists using an updated version of Garth's original Portable Higgs Device return Roger to Alexis One. It has been improved by the addition of Brane B technology as well.

Alexis One is even further on its way to creation in real-time.

Garth has just left Alexis One to return to Alien Nexus Three and Brane A, to our world and his UBC lab.

Roger is sad that he missed him.

*          *          *

### Joe's Master Koan – Part 3/A

Just then Joe "felt" the flower he was linked to fall

from its stem, and he found himself lying on the short, bright green grass. His awareness of the white fog of Limbo vanished instantly, along with his visitor and friends.

The others saw Joe suddenly go limp, and their calls to him were unanswered. Soon the man in the white overalls began to seem very nervous and agitated, and hurriedly excused himself and left.

The members of Joe's circle continued to try and prod and shake him back to consciousness, to no effect. He remained unresponsive but was breathing calmly.

Joe lay on the grass and looked down at his ankle, where a tiny beetle crawled over the exposed skin above his sock. It was shiny black with a greenish tinge, 1.5 mm long, and had a wavy yellow line running the length of each elytron. After a couple of seconds it jumped like a flea and was lost in the blades of grass.

Joe thought of the gigantic hanging pupae of slimy ectoplasm that were the evidence of the prison-like nature of the nested Godel Universe in which his companions were apparently eternally trapped.

Joe's companions waited back in the white fog, they could see clearly into the garden, and called out to Joe, but he no longer could hear them. They saw him sit-up on the grass, a giant to their tiny flower forms. He even brought his giant face level with one of the circle member's flower, and stared earnestly at it.

"Indian paintbrush." He said to himself.

\*         \*         \*

### ~Bounce-3

Richard stared at the young and attractive commander of the vessel. She is giving him a quick assessment of the situation, speaking rapidly.

"You must be aware that continued exchanges are predicted for this region. The pattern is moving off to the northwest at the moment, but more importantly, we predict that the individual regions of exchange will become smaller over time. You will find that more than one exchange region has been active this time, and that the shape and position of the original region involved last time has been shifted and modified. It is quite certain that multiple collisions will occur again and again in the path of this exchange, with the original region becoming a patchwork of tiny regions much smaller than the size of a human being over time. This of course would be fatal to any living people or creatures in the region. So we have evacuated our people from the exchange area, and have also evacuated your citizens to a safe area outside of the collision region."

"Where are all the people? What have you done with my wife?"

"We are a recognizance mission inside the exchange area, which will return this time in a predicted 47 minutes to our original brane, as you call it, brane "b". We call it brane "1". Our planet, Ground, is a mirror image of your planet, with differences of course. Your wife is fine. As I said previously, we have had to evacuate all people from the collision area for their own safety. This included your people in the area formerly attached to your brane. Evidence of previous collisions has in the ancient past always been destroyed by the pattern shrinking down from patches several kilometers wide to the sub-atomic scale. After one more collision the exchanges will be about ten centimeters in radius and be in incredibly numerous clusters closely packed inside the original exchange area. Other patches in the head area will be continuous enough for people to be safe inside of them. The next collision is expected to occur in about a week, and be composed of exchange areas several hundred meters in diameter."

"I will come with you."

"We will continue our survey mission until the brane exchange normalizes."

"When will I see my wife?"

"In approximately 45 minutes, if you let me get back to work."

"O.K."

"You may notice that this sector of exchange is 20% smaller than the original area. Also the border has shifted to the northwest by several hundred meters. We also can detect additional smaller areas to the northwest of this position, at 25 kilometers distance. That is where the main focus of the area of collision is migrating. This area we are in will be called the 'tail' of the exchange area, and the newer areas are located in the 'head' section. Soon the collisions will assume the shape of a great arc, with larger exchange areas in the head section followed by smaller and smaller areas in the tail."

"It is going to move through central London!"

"You will be given a copy of our best predictions of the path of disruption. You must evacuate an area ten kilometers wide by seventy long. Everything in the way will get chewed-up and spit out by this, do you understand?"

"I understand that we have some time before it shifts and hits again?"

"One week."

"Oh."

"We already know a general history of this situation from an expedition from your planet that left from your future, 2163; and visited Ground 100 years in our past. The time difference is because of the relative motions of our two galaxies, accelerating toward each other on a collision course. As this information has already been exchanged probability functions regarding our observation of your universe have created a Godel Universe in the exchange area. We have found paradoxes and evidence of plants and animals crossing over the boundaries and staying in the new environment. Indian paintbrush from your local gardens, for example."

*            *            *

### Joe's Master Koan Part 3/B

The fog parted again and the man in the white overalls strode back into view, and two others dressed like he was followed. They lugged a heavy piece of equipment between them. It was a black box with a coil of thick black hose about two meters long attached to it. They came up to the group and pointed the device at the hanging sock-puppets of Satan made of cosmic slime. Someone pressed a button and bright blue flame leapt from the device's nozzle and enveloped the dripping mucus.

As Joe lay on the grass gazing into the faces of the tiny flowers he knew represented his friends, he was unaware of their tiny screams of agony. The blue fire had been turned on the men surrounding the satanic socks of slime. At first they had gone rigid as the bright electric fluid encased them in writhing waves of energy, then their flesh had boiled away; but they still lived for a few seconds as skeletal forms with staring eyes and boiling brains. After another moment they exploded and dissolved in the surging waves of electric destruction.

The men in white overalls finished playing the beam of liquid fire over the last remnants of ectoplasm and human skeletal matter, until all traces of the former inhabitants of a private Godel Universe had vanished. They retreated through the fog back to their own version of reality.

*               *               *

The Brane B version of Earth called Ground is located in the Andromeda Galaxy. In our Brane it is non-existent.

How do I know this?

I wake from my dreams of the world described above with knowledge of our actual future, and free will to interfere with it actually happening or not.

One thing we can't avoid is becoming the culture that we have forever destroyed, not once, but twice. First we cause the destruction of the original culture of Darkworld, and then we strike Alien Nexus Two from the inside just before the final activation of the Mothership Alexis One, Alien Nexus One

And finally we have learned how to survive the end of time inside a crèche, Alien Nexus One, just as the culture that preyed on our Universe did.

Now all we have to do is 'bend' another Brane until

we can masquerade as a regional Brane formation inside that Brane, and we can become our rivals.

Suitably slow-moving Branes can be sped up so that we may harvest the energy of their uselessly long pre-inflation eras.

Our own Universe may have been as much as 86 – 94 billion years old before the intervention of Alien Nexus Two. This caused the age of the Universe to modify to its present 13.7 Billion years old.


*Wally*

Wallace Gardner sat at his desk and wondered what IT was working on right now. Unlike his Earth counterpart, Garth Wallace, Dr. 'Wally' could actually gain a good impression of what his staff was up to just by concentrating his awareness in a specific way. In the back of his mind he could 'remember' the entire day that he was now experiencing due to prescient dreaming. But in addition to this, both he and his staff shared common dream experiences that enabled him to remember details of their prescience as well. Therefore he had no need to phone IT at all. The problem they were working on was related to organizing a response to the arrival of Aliens on their planet in 100 years.

Those aliens are us.

So far the planet Earth and its inhabitants had been the source of all the worst problems they had ever encountered on planet Ground, in brane B, Andromeda Galaxy.

They knew this because of the power of ten billion

prescient dreamers all sharing the same dreams. They had implemented a vast cultural revolution eons ago when they first became aware of us.

They had noticed eons ago that a source of negative thoughts and emotions appeared to reside in empty space not too far away from their position in Andromeda. In exploring this area via remote viewing techniques they had learned very little, but had lost quite a few adepts to madness. They became paranoid and withdrawn and refused to resume their duties.

The one thing that they knew was that the residents of this unknown, invisible planet were leaving, and blamed an invisible planet in our galaxy for creating an unbearable disturbance in the balance of energies in the form of a miniature black hole that formed a time paradox.

The nature of the paradox was that a section of their brane was caught in a black hole in our brane. This had ripped a hole in their brane. All the residents of this planet near the rift had the compulsion to leave their home, or face increasing mental pressure leading to complete madness.

Some few had stayed behind and were the source of the negative thoughts people were aware of on Ground.

The name the Groundians gave this invisible place of fear was Darkworld.

## ~Darkworld

A dull grey sky glowed dimly red at the horizon. A forlorn moan of wind stirred the sand in miniature cyclones beside the ancient roadway that wound up from the gorge to the deserted stone city that topped the rise of plateau.

A clank of metal on stone sounded rhythmically in the distance, and wails and incoherent rantings surged into screams of pure madness and despair.

Overhead a phalanx of black triangles raced away from the gorge area to the night terminator.

Anything smarter than a bag of house-cats had lost any trace of higher brain function and gone insane beyond all insanity.

The 'residents' of formerly human persuasion were admittedly evil.

They had performed certain rituals to ensure dominance over the last shreds of awareness they had had while 'alive'.

Now they had become one with the forces that still animated their bodies.

They were all mindless killers.

Their 'leader' was a collection of bones and rotting gristle inside a suit of armor.

He was the one making the clanking sounds in the distance.

The animated suit of armor is very special to the other "rationally dead" inhabitants of Darkworld. Before the end of Darkworld society, a contest to see who would stay last was held, in the form of duels to the death with swords.

He won.


### Groundian History

The planet Ground had a very ancient culture, stretching back tens of thousands of years. The evolution of this culture was marked not by the effects of wars, but by the effects of co-operation and self-knowledge.

Also a need to 'believe' in religious doctrine had never evolved, since to the people of this planet spiritual experiences were obvious and factual in their interpretation.

Well-known experiences included remote viewing, prescience, and empathy with others at a psychic level.

Their society was marked with the development of focus groups using 'targeted dreaming' to guide its advancement.

Clone Morphs have been created so that Dreamers from other dimensions or places can join the people of Ground in a physical way. The shared dream experience common on Ground would then extend to the new Dreamers.

The Groundians have perfected cloning. The form of clone they created called a "Clone Morph" can morph into any shape desired. Clone Morphs start life as child-sized clones of a certain body shape, and are from genetic engineering made to order. They are smooth and without detail when not inhabited by a visiting Dreamer. They go into a hibernation state when not animated.

A visitor having a dream of being on Ground can experience life there first hand as one of these clones. While they are dreaming, the clone morphs to resemble them.

Also the Clone Morphs are used for space travel. The Groundian Dreamer Astronaut inhabits the morph and then reports back in "real-time" by talking in his sleep. The morphs are cloned during the trip in space, generation after generation. They grow on a culture in a lab, and are cared for by machine.

\*                    \*                    \*

### Joe's Master Koan Part 4/A

Joe looked out at the high, stone, wall that enclosed the flowered greensward of his tiny paradise. He walked along the neat paths and through the ornamental shrubberies. He felt rich, and a certain sense of entitlement to his superior status. A warm and fuzzy comfort emanated from the very stones that lined the quietly babbling brook that wended its way to and fro throughout the garden.

Up ahead of him the tableau was completed as the path snaked luxuriously past a tall and branching shade tree that dominated the center of the ornamental realm. Near the base of this magnificent tree a small teahouse bridged a mirror-like section of the stream, which was flowing into an adjacent koi pond.

Inside, a white haired old man in a rumpled sweater gazed back at Joe as he entered and sat down. His reading glasses were perched at a jaunty angle on the bridge of his nose and he smiled openly yet somewhat shyly at Joe from behind them.

"So you have been stuck in a loop?"

"What do you mean, 'stuck in the Godel Universe'?"

"I mean a loop you are stuck in, a pattern or habit, maybe."

"We all were in a loop to start with, back in the old country; where we all were from."

"But the same thing was true afterward. You kept a repeating pattern in your life."

"What do you mean?"

"First you are the group that is affected by the passing ship; then you are captured by a Universe that is itself a loop of space-time. Next you are forced to exist in two realities at the same time, and lastly you are here talking to me with no idea who I am. All very perplexing, I must assume."

"Yes, it is mysterious; and it makes me very curious to find some answer. Can I go beyond the garden wall?"

"You could, but I am not sure that you would like it. To leave the garden and walk the banks of the great river that winds through the forest is to walk the paths of mortal man, to join him in his cycle of life and death." The old man paused and looked kindly at Joe, and then continued.

"A famous author Carl Q. Koont once said: 'It is never an inappropriate response to insanity to sanely define reality as yourself; therefore creating what you know as what you aren't not.' "

"What can that concept help me with on my journey? It sounds like a thousand other pieces of advice to me."

"That may well be, but remember that your journey will take you through experiences beyond your own will or control, where you will have to abandon or forget much of what you know as your own self."

"In our world, before it ended, I often thought of what would come after all we had ever known. I didn't think that somehow I would experience raw mortality. I was wrong. Now I will have to take a path less travelled, and know myself again as clay in the hands of one such as you. Will you shape me?"

"I will send you on your way, and you will join with the course of the great river through the live trees. And you will be made after your own hand."

The old man stood up, and gestured for Joe to follow him, which he did. He led the way down the garden path, out from under the shade of the great tree, past the Koi pond and across the neatly trimmed lawns dotted with tiny points of color. Their brilliance under the noon sun dazzled the senses. Soon the path led to a strong gate in the high, stone, wall; and the Master turned to Joe again.

"Leave me now through this gate, and walk the paths of mortal men in a world of linear time. Come back after your journey and exchange places with me then, so I can have the experience of seeing through mortal eyes."

"Yes, Master." Joe swung the huge gate open and stepped through.

*         *         *

### ~Bounce-4

Richard feels like he is stuck in a loop, and a deep foreboding troubles him as if a terrible tragedy is about to unfold, or had in some way already happened. He looks at the crew of the vessel now speeding over the uninterrupted surface of the alien planet called Ground. He has been informed that some of them are "clone morphs", and are actually animated by the spirits of Earth people from his own future. They have learned how to communicate across intergalactic distances and the barrier between worlds (branes), by becoming soul traveling "dreamers". He quizzes one about what he remembers about the events now unfolding.

"When is the whole collision over? Is much of London reduced to dust?"

"A trail of destruction does cut through the city, but it heads off in the general direction of Wembley, then bends east toward Cambridge, sparing the central core. Somehow we got all the people and much of their property out of the path. The first couple of collisions destroyed things that were right on the edge of the exchange, cut them in half, including several people and animals. But the later exchanges chopped up all the mass into cannonball-sized chunks, and each subsequent collision produced finer and finer grades of rubble, then like parsley being chopped into fine powder. Isotopic analysis of the exchange area after it was over showed a small variance from normal."

"Is the stadium spared the destruction?"

"I'm afraid not."

The vessel cruises into the distance, over the alien landscape of Earth's mirror image in Andromeda.

In brane "b" 's Andromeda, that is.

"So next week we all move into the exchange area to go back? What was the point of evacuating them all?"

"They have to be informed anyway." The officer isn't impressed with Richard's concerns.

"What about the people who are affected next week before we can warn them?" Richard presses his point.

"I dropped off one of the crew to warn your people about the path of the collision, he walked out of the bounce area just before you came aboard. We call the collision a "bounce", because the branes bounce off of each other like pancakes made of gelatinous dessert."

"Not exactly?"

"Close enough, it is like skipping one gelatinous dessert off of another one which is much bigger. Our brane is considerably larger than yours. And flatter. The two surfaces move past each other in a highly predicable way, and our observations so far agree completely with theory. And we have the records of this event from the 2163 expedition to our world from your world's future. So we can check our figures twice."

Richard is very used to getting his own way and calling the shots, and feels the situation slipping from his grasp ever so slightly. He wants to see his wife, and to control the action again himself. He thinks back to when he had first met her, at a Lodge mixer for social networking held at the Knights Hall. The outer ritual is now open for anyone interested to observe and ask questions about after. People have shown a lot more interest since it has been proved that his lodge is neither Satanic nor Fascist in nature, having absolutely no connection to the Catholic Church. The Knights are none of the more famous and discredited or despised branches of Freemasonry, but a more exclusive and secretive organization that has recently come out into the public eye.

She had been seated in the audience area near the place in the hall where his station had been during the ritual proceedings, which were held to install a new Master of the Hall. While he held a pennant and presented the man for inspection, he noticed her staring at him from her front row seat.

When the mixer started he went up to her and started a conversation. A few weeks later he had already invited her on a short holiday trip and then bedded her at a luxury resort hotel.

The ship skims just above the unusual orange and blue jungle trees, at about five hundred kilometers an hour. At last the jungle is left behind as they come to a populated area, dotted with fantastically tall and thin towers. The vessel lands at a more formally organized area that vaguely reminds Richard of a military base, minus any signs of weapons, fences or soldiers.

Jen is waiting for him when he exits the ship just after landing adjacent to the main building at the base. They embrace and she begins to whisper urgently in his ear, a strange intensity in her manner. He at first starts involuntarily and asks "Really?" once, then hushes her and stands around nervously with her, trying to act naturally.

"We must visit this Dr. Wallace Gardner, and get permission to accompany him on a short trip. Close to Darkworld or not, how could we not try to have a look?"

*   *   *

### Joe's Master Koan – Part – 4/B

The gate clanged shut behind him, and Joe stood looking at the path, which led down to the river. Large masses of green, dense forest lined the path on either side. Joe set off down the winding road, his feet crunching on the loose gravel. The air smelled fresh and clean; a mysterious bird cackled its unique call. The sun stood high overhead, Joe walked on his short, dark shadow, its head pointing in front of him, first just to his left and then over to his right and back just to the left again, as the path twisted and turned on its way down to the wide flat water.

The trees were gigantic, forming an overhanging jungle of mixed greenery. A soft breeze wafted up the shore, carrying warm and spicy scents of a summer day. As he drew closer he spotted a young boy of perhaps nine or ten years old, playing on a small raft. He had a torn straw hat and grubby dungarees, cut-off just above the knees. He chewed on a stalk of grass and looked at Joe curiously.

"Do you like my raft? We can take it for a ride if you want."

"It looks fun. Sure, kid; sure." Joe steps on the young lad's flimsy craft. The young lad hands Joe his long pole.

"You look stronger than me, get us off of the stones on the riverbank, then I'll take my turn."

"O. K." Joe places the pole against a large boulder on the side of the bank and pushes the ten-foot raft out into the vast flow of the river.

After a while Joe hands the pole back to the lad, and sits down at the front of the raft, letting his legs dangle in the deep, cool water. Behind him the boy continues to propel them out into the current.

"Have you ever seen a dead body before?" The question is a sudden, rude shock, full of urgency and excitement.

"What does 'dead' mean?" Joe is amazed he is unfamiliar with what he senses must be obvious.

"You know, it just lays still, the dead thing. It is no longer alive, like me and you."

"I don't think I understand that, I can't visualize that in my mind's eye; it is a thing my people don't have any experience of. It is unknown."

They cross the river in silence. At the far shore there is a little dock, and Joe gets up and steps onto it. He smiles at the young lad regarding him with open curiosity.

"See ya."

"Yes, good-bye." Joe starts off, walking along the path as it follows the course of the river.

"What will you tell people when they ask who you are, what tale will you tell them?" The boy and raft have drifted along beside Joe as he walked.

"I will tell them my name is Joe."

"And your tale?"

"I am a traveller, on my way to visit a very holy place."

"O. K., Joe" The boy smiles and moves out into the current and is carried out of sight.

\*　　　　　　\*　　　　　　\*

### Life on Ground.

The Groundians love to travel at night by moving walkway to attend music festivals and carnivals, and to go to the beach in the daytime.

Their technology is very advanced; most of the

drudgework is done by machine or bio-engineered to occur naturally in the environment of the planet.

Higher education is the common pursuit, and all creative Arts and Music.

Groundian infrastructure is very sophisticated; they have computer-controlled 'pods' that follow guide-ways on the surface, and sub-orbital rocket flights. Also gigantic tubes reach from the surface up into space; the pods enter at the surface and emerge into space. They have colonized their moon and covered the entire far surface with solar cells. A gigantic catcher made of a series of magnetic rings is used to harvest kinetic energy from asteroids directed through it, before they crash down to the lunar plain, supplying metal for their space program.

They have visited many stars in their galaxy, but not all.

At sub-light speeds they have travelled to a thousand similar planets, and discovered alien species on thirteen percent of those.

And several dozen races were from cultures as advanced in enlightenment as themselves. These cultures were invited to visit ground as Dreamers.

### ~Dream of Hyperspace Cats and Dark Matter Dogs

*Heresy Of Earth Gods, Branes as Personalities.*

In the beginning there were seventeen of them, Gaia and her children clustered together in the vastness. Jehovah was her favorite; he was so big and jolly. Energy of calm, and intense focus emanated from him constantly. Pan was the smallest, and liked to hover near Jehovah to drink in his power. Gaia could feel Pan getting bigger and more confident.

Thor/Odin/Horus/Osiris/Apollo/Zeus was complicated and changeable, he wore his many faces with dignity and respect. Pan liked to try to gain the attention of just one face over and over in a playful game of cat and mouse. Mercury would herd him back near Jehovah before the many-faced Thor could become confused.

Venus and Mars darted back and forth in a game of tag, bumping around amid the rest of her children. Jupiter, Saturn, Neptune, Uranus, and Pluto rounded out the herd. The approach of the stranger took a long time; Gaia could feel his gravity getting stronger for what felt like forever. After a while Gaia could tell that Jehovah could feel it too, and would dart out near her and then circle around out past the others. Pan and Mercury huddled together near Thor when Jehovah did this.

He was with them instantly, a vast world-being filling

empty space itself off in one direction. He seemed to go on forever as he bisected reality at some hyper-distance away. They began to fall toward the plain now "below" them.

"I am Yahweh, you are to become one with me." A vast voice filled reality.

"I am Gaia, we are love." The fall ceased, and finally the group circled around the vast Yahweh.

"I will take the one you call Jehovah." Jehovah began to be drawn closer to Yahweh, until his surface touched the edge of the sky-filling Yahweh.

Impulsively many-faced Thor flew down and crashed into Jehovah, sending him flying away from Yahweh's surface. In the process he split apart into six separate pieces.

The piece called Osiris flew down to Yahweh, and a small explosion occurred, as he was absorbed. Pan darted down and struck the surface a glancing blow just where Osiris had been. A piece of the giant being was torn loose and drifted off. Venus followed Pan and struck Yahweh in the same spot, tearing more material off the plain. Mars and then Horus did the same. Mercury and Pan circled around the recovered mass that had once been Osiris, and sent him into orbit around Jehovah. Gaia gave Osiris a nudge to revive him, and he soon was there among them again.

"We will take more of you to make new others." Gaia crashed into Yahweh's side, tearing a vast collection of bubble-selves out in a shattering explosion.

Again and again she smashed down onto the plain below, until the entire sky was filled with drifting clusters of awareness.

Yahweh began to withdraw, and some of his remnants followed him. They circled around and around the departing spheroid, and sometimes crashed back into his surface, losing their tenuous identities.

"Remember me as Satan, for now I must one day punish you!" Yahweh cursed them as he departed.

Gaia went among her new children, naming them and collecting a long tail of followers.

Pan daringly flew after the now departed self-named Satan, and was back soon with a few other beings he had rescued just before they were re-absorbed. A great ripple spread through the throng of life-bubbles as a distant disturbance made itself known to them by its very violence and intensity. Pan was at the center of its effect among them and seemed to squish and deform to a great extent, until he burst into a myriad of glittering shards and was gone, like a puff of smoke. A whirling mass of tiny particles remained visible periodically, and Pan's ghostly image formed once more and then faded, as the cloud grew more faint and vanished.

Gaia grew fainter as she expanded, forming a cocoon around all the others. The edges that formed her outer boundary drew farther and farther away and the light of her being grew fainter and fainter. But all traces of the pull of Yahweh's gravitational field ceased to be felt by the beings within her.

Jehovah was the lone exception. He knew that Yahweh would come back for him and could still feel the pull of that vast Universe of power and vengeance.

Jehovah "walked down each road" until he found all the shards that had once been Pan, and brought them together as one again.

As he "walked" he left a trail of crumbs to find his way back to oneness. The crumbs drew near each other and formed clumps and filaments, vast sheets of being-ness amid the emptiness. The wind of Gaia's departure sent them flying forever after her in a mad dance of physical creation.

Pan told of all he had seen as tiny particles of smoke throughout the vastness of hyperspace. One of the things he had seen was Gaia budding into a billion mini-expansions and encircling reality in a billion separate vector spaces. This had happened at the very edge of Her expansion to the limits of possibility. Pan had witnessed all that transpired in each of the budded realities of Gaia. He shared his knowledge with the other Gods and Goddesses and gave news of events on Earth. They were most vexed.

They now knew the identity of the one who called himself Yahweh or Satan.

All black holes in each version of reality in any of the Universes were identical, on the inside. Only the vast surface of Yahweh held the information that made up the entire physical multi-verse. It didn't matter, the human concept of "time", but all things everywhere eventually went into Yahweh, the one singularity. They stayed there for a time and then went away as Hawking radiation, the final end of anything in any Universe. The Humans had proved this.

Yahweh decays into Hawking Radiation, and has an ending; but Jehovah is eternal, and has "walked down every road", the ways of being left on his surface are from direct and prolonged contact with Yahweh, knower of everything.

The surface of any black hole contains the information

to reconstruct anything that enters the singularity, and at the end of galaxy type formations in all physical meta-verses large black holes feed on super-clusters of galaxies until all are destroyed. The fate of all the galaxies is the same; they enter a single "super-singularity" at the center of all these super-massive black holes.

This super-singularity is the membrane known as Yahweh, and the entirety of creation is his skin.

### Garth and Roger

Garth sits at home in Vancouver B.C. and recalls the first time he ever saw his mentor Dr. R.E. Whembly. Roger was standing in line at the Jack Winters University main cafeteria and joking around with a group of young students. He was saying something about not believing Einstein on Monday, Wednesday, and Friday; and getting a big laugh from his audience.

Dr. Roger was a tall and handsome professor at one of the newest and most technically advanced research universities in North America. His direction of research was based on loose ends and unfinished analysis of high-energy experiments conducted over the preceding years at CERN and Fermi-lab.

He was a notorious rebel in his specialty, an unconventional version of string theory physics that emphasized the role of dark energy as a function of inter-relatedness between alternate dimensions.

Garth thought more about his mentor's original research work, his at first outlandish theories and later discoveries.

BRANE BOUNCE

Dr. R. E. Whembly had classified various types of other dimensions based on what his theories told him about the interaction between the observer; and observed. There were two main classes of other dimensions, those with conscious life, and those without conscious life. In the second category, some classes were: not connected, conscious life evolves in future, and impossible for life.

In the first main category there were many more classes of alternate universes: branches of our universe, universes that were just 'instants' of our Universe or a parallel universe, separate alternate realities, possible alternate realities, not related alternate realities, insane alternate realities, other than rational alternate realities, and unconnected parallel realities.

The most interesting type of alternate reality was called 'instants of reality'. In this alternate universe time itself has stopped at an instant of time in our Universe or a parallel world.

Dr. Roger had proposed a way for each of these 'instants' to be linked together to form the 'flow' of time we experience as our reality.

In his theory conscious life migrated from one universe to another at each instant of time, and we had a history and future composed of individual instants of time, each one a bubble-universe in a vast sea of expanding energy.

The path of time is different for each separate parallel world, and connects various bubble-instants in a particular order characteristic of that reality.

Time is the process of transfer between sequential

'identical' Universes, which is determined by our conscious decision making process.

Each physical Universe is only required for a single instant of time.

Parallel Universes may share 'instant' Universes in the same or even different orders. They diverge when we make different choices in each parallel world.

While the Universe we perceive changes, change itself is not required in any 'instant' Universe.

Each conscious being is like a "wire", linking the instants of Time into a perceived Reality. The 'wires' link each Universe together via an infinite number of instants from Big Bang to Heat Death of the Universe(s). They are mutually exclusive, but can cross, branch and loop in some cases, but tend to become parallel again and again.

In his theory, the 'wires' are actual physical objects that are infinite in length but so tiny in cross-section that they can never be seen in any possible experiment, like strings but far smaller in one dimension, and infinite in the other.

Conscious life is only present in Universes linked by these wires, which are many orders of magnitude thinner than a quantum string.

Universes of instant time that are not linked by "time" (the wires) in the multi-verse do not have conscious life as we know it, with cause and effect, logic and reason for thinking life forms.

Awareness travels down the wires, and we experience the "flow" of time.

The "used" Universes still exist, separated by the continuous inflation expansion of the multi-verse.

Also, Universes that are not yet our reality's group of instants of time exist, and can be linked to ours via the 'wire' for our timeline. Each wire represents a separate timeline, an alternate decision tree, and an alternate reality. Wires can 'migrate' from bubble-verse to bubble-verse inside the multi-verse, based on the logical need for new instants of time, or the probabilities of future events.

But they mostly just stay in place.

Garth thinks back to the time when Roger was his first full professor of Physics teacher. He could still see Roger's expectant expression as he explained the unfathomable results of advanced Quantum Dynamics.

One of the things he could not grasp at the time was the effect that observation had on the observed at the Quantum scale. The particles had a general probability of existing at positions where we expected to find a particle, but were in fact distributed in space in a more unpredictable fashion until an observation of them was made. At this time the probability function collapsed into a form where scientists could observe an aspect of this particle, but not get a complete picture of it in vector space and also know its velocity.

Garth struggled with the fact that the equations said that all that existed of an electron before trying to measure it was a probability function.

The act of observing it made the electron real.

By the time that Garth was writing his doctorate thesis he was much more sure that he didn't understand the "realness" of physics in the quantum scale world; but the effects that it had on the human scale and macroscopic Universe were easy to see, and all the calculations and math symbolism used had always yielded perfect real world numbers so far.

The fact that things were in a different form before they were observed bothered him the most. He wondered what the cumulative effects of it were in the macroscopic Universe. Did the fact that we could only see part of the entire Universe render the rest of it imaginary until observed? Did it shift and wriggle, jump and distort, appear and disappear? Was it only "probable", or was it real?

The Casimir Effect, Dark Energy and all particles spontaneously created in the vacuum were all results of the *uncertainty* in knowing enough about quantum effects and states to call them "real".

Garth remembered what Roger had said at his thesis hearing, that he wasn't sure what there was left to know about the effects of processes we already knew about; and that he had no idea what unrelated facts science would discover.

Roger inspired Garth to keep his mind open and to not assume too much ahead of time when forming a theory or new idea.

*Dream of Hyperspace Cats and Dark Matter Dogs*

In Alice, the popular teen movie, a Cheshire cat tells riddles and fades until only its toothy smile is left visible. It behaves in the opposite manner of a particle in a quantum state probability function.

Garth thought of the tricky cat that had appeared in his

dreams lately.

He was working on some modifications to the portable Higgs wormhole generator; and thought constantly about the 'wires' that Roger had proposed linked all the possible moments of past, present and future 'instants'.

Roger had not defined it precisely as such, but in a sense his formula stated that each potential observer of reality had his own individual reality to observe, his own private wire.

That did not mean that we couldn't share the same reality, as many beings could be on wires that selected the same group of 'instants' in the same order. Thus they would observe the same reality.

This also didn't exclude the possibility that a wire in a "bundle" could leave the rest of the wires, link to some other dimensions, and then return to the original "bundle" of wires that composed our shared awareness of our own Universe.

He thought of the Q-ball that appeared beside the wormhole in the device, cancelling out the energy imbalance created by the appearance of the Higgs- boson.

In some alternate world this q-ball was an exact copy of the q-ball in our world.

What if they could be exchanged?

He knew that he wanted to send the q-ball inside his machine down his own personal wire, but also with the ability to chose the next world it would inhabit.

If this wire was a real thing in the physical world, could he ever see it or affect it in any way, due to its tiny cross-section?

He was full of doubts.

A better idea occurred to him, since the wires were probably infinite in length, he could look for them back in time, just before the universe spread out enough to be bigger than galaxy size.

Computer models composed of early Universe data and the known positions and distances of galaxies in the visible Universe led to narrowing down the search for a wire to a specific place and time.

His own personal wire had been hit by neutrinos as it entered the wormhole inside the portable when he had transferred to Alien Nexus Three, the world he had first seen in a prescient dream. Proving this is what happened took many months of careful calculations and all available data at his disposal.

The Q-ball inside the machine had travelled down the wire as it 'migrated', due to the impact of a direct hit. How could he locate something impossible to ever see? If he could see the effect of its presence, he could deduce its location, and then check for more clues.

It turned out that he could locate a wire with great accuracy by hitting it with an ultra-dense flux of neutrino radiation, and observing the scattering of a few seemingly random mass-less particles.

He had found the Holy Grail, observed the unobservable. The world would never be the same.

**~Magik Bus-The Road-trip to Cosmic Central.**

Garth was a bit annoyed at the brightness of the lights on the stage.

A noisy crown of press and politicians, scientists and trendies filled the UBC auditorium. Many cameras flashed and the crowd roared its approval as he made his way to the podium to begin the press conference.

Behind him on the stage the portable device loomed as big as a semi-trailer. He accepted the applause and called the conference to order, then began his announcement.

"This new addition to our understanding proposed first by Dr. Whembly early in his career, called Wire Theory, has finally been proven to be real."

"We now believe that travel to a selected other dimension is possible, a reality that we can determine with mathematics."

"Questions?"

Garth waited; then selected a news reporter from a local 3D webcast.

"What is the difference between the old-fashioned string theory, which evolved into m-theory and then The Theory of Everything, and this new Wire Theory?"

"Wire Theory was developed earlier than people think, in the early part of this century, but was not taken too seriously by mainstream scientists until quite recently. It involves the nature of time, perception of the effects of observing the Universe, and is more related to our understanding of hyperspace than any previous theory."

"The wires themselves are Dark Matter held in place by a force that keeps the Universe flat enough to sustain life. The wires are infused with balance energy, keeping the dark energy of our Universe at a low enough level for matter as we know it to form in the first place."

"What is 'Balance Energy'? "

"It is little understood, but is like tension on the wire, enough to keep the continuity of the Hyperspace links in place. It exists as a kind of 'negative entropy', and prevents the randomness of the Universe from increasing too fast. It is in a way the opposite of Dark Energy, in effect it is a kind of attractive force that acts just like gravity on the very small scale."

"You see, there are six other dimensions 'curled-up' at each point of our 4d space-time, and each of the dimensions has a 'meaning', as our familiar dimensions of length and depth (etc.) do."

"All the alternate Universes are very far away in hyper-space, and getting farther apart, at a faster and faster rate."

"But they also exist very close to us in 'real' 4d space-time. They are separated from our Universe by a very short distance in one or more of these 'curled-up' extra dimensions."

"They also are a short physical distance and time away

from our Universe of normal reality."  Laughter and muttering, cheers and applause stir the crowd to life.

"Order, order." The M.C. calls for silence.

The crowd quiets.

"Why is this not just Cosmic String Theory?" A reporter has stood to speak.

"Cosmic String Theory didn't take into account all the required math we now know as the Theory of Everything, such as 11 dimensions, external mass/gravity and other later advances. Strings evolved into membranes in 11-space, and later wires were proposed as a way to explain Dark Energy Balance in our Universe."

"The wire binds every particle into a single reality in a Universe that is being observed by an observer, in the same way that the position and velocity of a single particle is merely a probability function, the wire is not real until it attaches to an instant of space-time at six other co-ordinates as well. And even then the wire is still an un-collapsed quantum probability function itself, until it is localized by direct observation."

"Thus each wire makes a set of undefined imaginary probability functions for particles into 'real' probability functions of particles for an individual observer; creating reality as we know it."

"What can you do with this huge machine here behind you?" The crowd laughs appreciatively.

"At first an accident in the lab sent me to a previously unexpected destination, through a wormhole."

"Now we have the ability to control a process whereby a transfer of energy down one of the newly discovered wires can trigger a shift for this machine and contents to a parallel world of our creation."

"So tonight ladies and gentlemen I will use magic to make this giant machine vanish!"

The crowd roars with laughter.

"What happens inside your machine?" asks a new reporter.

"We have the operator's wire identified with flux generated in the cyclotron, very concentrated neutrino radiation is generated in an anti-matter explosion. Next a Q-ball is generated and physically adjusted into the same general space as the wire. Gravity causes the wire to be attracted to the Q-ball, and soon they touch and adhere to each other. We then inject neutrino flux at a certain rate to send both Q-ball and wire away from their present positions, it is the movement of the wire that causes the dimensional shift."

"What do you mean, 'The operator's wire'?"

"Wires are very complex entities. In a way they are each the entire 11th dimension rolled-up into a vanishingly small cross-section. But they can also be thought of as the force that links each instant of time in sequence for a specific reality, and each individual wire can be thought of as an observer's viewpoint or consciousness. The act of observing causes a set of conditions to be linked by wires."

"Time is the process of transfer between sequential 'identical' Universes, which is determined by our conscious decision making process."

"Each physical Universe is only required for a single instant of time. Parallel Universes may share 'instant' Universes in the same or even different orders. They diverge when we make different choices in each parallel world."

"While the Universe we perceive changes, change itself is not required in any 'instant' Universe. The 'Wires' link each Universe together via an infinite number of instants from Big Bang to the Heat Death of all matter. They are mutually exclusive; but can cross, branch, and loop in some cases. They tend to become parallel again and again."

"Conscious awareness is only present in Universes linked by these Wires, which are far thinner than a Quantum string. Awareness itself flows down the Wire, and we experience the passage of time."

"Questions?"

"How do you choose the destination of your device?"

"We can select Universes where conscious life is present automatically, and can 'steer' the device to nearby wire bunches with bursts of neutrinos impacting the Q-ball."

"The device will be encased in a bubble of hyper-space as soon as we move the operator's wire, and then the device can engage other wires and negotiate a path through hyper-space to other wires, other dimensions."

"We have deduced that to travel to a desired type of world we just model the wires and deduce similarities and differences, diverging paths of historical events and people in history."

"Where are you going tonight?"

"We are going to see a Universe in which Rome had never defeated Egypt, a world in which the greatest ancient Empire of all time still exists in present day."

"Good luck with that." The room explodes in laughter.

"People, quiet down please."

"Thank-you. The demonstration will be in ten minutes." The crowd bubbles in conversation and falls silent. Everyone waits.

"One minute." The machine can be heard making a low humming sound, and a higher sound of acceleration. Pop!

It's gone! The crowd applauds and cheers, people shout and talk excitedly.

"The machine will return in 24 hours, come back then for a very public debriefing of our heroic adventuring lead scientist."

*Flashback*

Garth took his seat inside the new control console area. The addition of the modifications to the portable had made the space a bit tighter and he looked around nervously at the low ceiling and bulky instrumentation. The Faraday cage was the most important part, and remained unchanged. It made communication with the outside impossible, tiny wires filled the quartz glass bubble.

"Recording start."

"Q-ball test sequence."

"Neutrino generation."

"Adjust Q-ball radius."

Garth waited to see if his wire would be identified, and attach to the Q-ball.

Both the wire and Q-ball were made of Dark Matter, but the wire's dark matter was like neutronium compared to the

Q-ball's dark matter. (It was much, much denser)

"Complete 'area scan'." The hardest neutrino flux in existence coursed through the caged area. Garth felt slightly warmer and saw that the computer had locked onto the position of the wire. He quickly used power and position adjustments to bring the Q-ball into contact.

"Contact achieved." Garth looked up at a camera and pointed at the cage. "We have now vanished to everything outside this cage." A secondary Faraday cage enclosed the rest of the ship.

### ~Journey to world X.

A flat monitor on the console showed a computer model of the process, with the ship as a point. A huge wormhole was ahead of him, and an impossibly small and closing end 'behind' him. The Faraday cage began to glow in an eerie way, lit by an unknown source. Gradually the glow resolved into a hologram just in front of the cage. The picture matched the view on the flat panel and was far more detailed in 3-d. He could almost walk around it. "There must be a reversal of perspective here, if my guess about this wormhole is right, and I am now as small as possible for matter to get."

"All the space between the quarks in the ship and contents has been omitted in the transfer to hyperspace, I am now travelling inside a wire with a radius of slightly less than a Planck length."

To Garth the space ahead was infinite and crowded with objects, fields and particles, all linked by the wire that he was linked to. There ahead of him a gigantic tube loomed, and he had the sensation of warping and acceleration as he drew nearer. He saw that the tube was a hollow string with irregular holes like in a cheese grater all over its surface. Somehow his perspective shifted as his wire led through one of the small openings, and the whole enormous wormhole of his own wire squeezed into the hole. Inside the hollow cosmic string he could see that both ends of the tube ended on an endless colorful membrane. The wire continued down the length of the tube and passed right through this barrier. He had the sensation of everything expanding and slowing down, and the wormhole loomed as large as ever all around him, with a tiny tail behind him leading back to the membrane he had just left.

"I am whatever size I am supposed to be, I guess." Garth realizes he is performing the rich man's trick, fitting the proverbial camel through the eye of the needle, as another hollow tube is spotted entangled with his wire of awareness up ahead, which he now began to associate with 'down' as well, since he had the sensation of falling. He wondered why he saw the string before its associated membrane, why the holes allowed him access to the interaction with a particle before he saw the 'reality' of its attachment. The trip through the tube and membrane occurred as before. Far in the distance he saw a large number of tiny tendrils in what looked like a furry sphere, all waving around and changing position and size.

As he drew nearer to the fuzzy ball of tubes it became obviously the source of gravity in the area, and he fell faster 'down' in its direction. One outer tube loomed closer than expected, and his view of the wire he was attached to disappeared except for behind him, where it was a tiny fading streak. He looked at the controls and experimented with the neutrino flux settings. He found he could manoeuver left and right, and up and down, but not forward or backward.

A new tube loomed immediately in front of him, whipping out into his path unexpectedly, and he typed in a command to avoid it just in time. Now the sphere was a bundle of massive snakes whipping around the ship, and he raced to type his commands, barely avoiding the many writhing obstacles.

He followed the undulations of a single tube deeper into the seemingly solid sphere of mass. It separated into tangles and jumbles of massive tubes towering and moving around him. His speed increased to a nearly insane pace, as he typed commands and wove a daring path amid nearly pure chaos. As his task became more and more impossible he knew that sooner or later he would impact the changing landscape and faced disaster mentally. He realized that the only reason he had not hit yet was that he was intuitively aware of the needed commands a split second before he typed them. Learning to let go of the process he managed to hold on for a few more minutes, but the stress was cracking his concentration. Just as he was about to scream in terror and give up his wild efforts to steer his craft it was engulfed in a narrow opening, the end of a tube. He accelerated instantly to very high speed as the craft was guided on a twisting and turning path, then to a very sudden but surprisingly soft landing, as if caught in a mesh of stretchy spider's web.

### Alexis One Mechanical Level

"Anyone in there?" Garth can hear a hail from outside his craft.

"Yes, I am inside." Garth replies immediately.

"Come on out so we can ready your ship for transport."

"O.K."

Garth exits the portable and faces his host, a middle-aged man in dirty blue coveralls, complete with grease stains and grimy hands.

"We have to regulate your path through here 'cause you goin' so far from home."

"So we moves the ship to a new launch point here at Planck level."

"It's all bunched into a ball of snakes down here, each direction is up from here; even the higher-dimensional ones."

"We are going to give you a bit of a tour since youz neva been to an alt world before, or seen the bundles."

The attendant or mechanic or whatever he was, (an employee of the trans-dimensional nexus) made some entries on a notepad and stuffed it in the chest pocket of his greasy overalls.

"So you were heading to Ancient Egypt World eh?"

"Yeah, I am a big fan."

"Do you know you're heading to the Land of the Lakes first?"

"What do you mean, I've never heard of the Land of the Lakes."

"It's where you don't need no ship, where the Lady of the Lakes asks you about yourself, what you really want, so you can be more specific in the selection of your destination."

"How does that work?"

"Well, youse jest fly out in da ship until it melts away around youse; den youse talk to the Lady 'bout yer goals and real needs."

"What happens to my ship?"

"It melts, cause it ain't sentient. It comes back when you translate to a finer accuracy in reaching youse target world."

"My ship will come back?"

"It will suddenly appears 'round youse like a ghost that becomes more real, then 'pop', right back to normal."

"So what do I do right now?"

"You are cordially invited by the Mechanical Level to tour our fine facility and experience the Connectedness of All Things."

"What are you going to show me?"

"This place is as far away from the Control Room as you can get aboard the Great Mothership, which you are already familiar with as Alexis One, or the Alien Nexus One, the end of time in youse own Universe."

"Down here the rest of the Multi-verse is equally distant in every direction, along an axis that can be thought of as a higher dimension of Time, not a spatial dimension."

"Thus though we's inside Alexis One we may as well be inside any Brane out there. The Land of The Lakes is a collection of stable pathways outside of normal interaction between Branes."

"What you really need to see is the Bundles. We actually influence the way different Branes with intelligent life in them will interact by bundling youse wires appropriately."

"So here we are at a control panel. Youse can seez dat da bundles's grouped tagetherz in a specifics wayz."

Garth examined the control box and its thick bundles of seemingly normal looking wiring and marveled at how many strands must be contained in each one. A maze of connections snaked in and out of the various sub-bundles and back into the main one, which was as thick as a big man's arm. It came in one end of the Control Panel and left out of the other end, but inside it was a maze of connections.

Upon his materialization at the High Altar in Ancient Egypt World, he was greeted immediately by the High Priest, and by a full company of workers and porters. As per his requests to the I.T. Department at Alien Nexus One Mechanical Level, the ship was to be quantized and improved, enlarged to the size of a yacht, and loaded with a cargo of rare gold, silver and other precious items.

As Garth had passed through the Land of the Lakes and answered the questions asked by the Lady of the Lakes, she had sent a Prescient Dream to The High Priest with all of Garth's wishes.

The natives regarded him as a god, in spite of his inferior grasp of physics, meta-physics and math. A crew had volunteered to return with him to Earth or any eventuality. After this he had requested to learn more about Physics unknown to his world but still valid there; and also to learn a history of true facts about of both worlds before divergence. As a second stop on his journey, he had asked for a world empty of all intelligent life, with an abandoned alien outpost; destined to never be re-visited by its' builders. The world comes complete with robot-operated gold mines, an abandoned transport and communications network, and a stock of working alien ships.

"Ra, whom all worship as the Bringer of Divine Light, be welcome here!" The Head Priest has stood before the masses to welcome his newly arrived visitor.

The High Altar was a raised platform the size of an auditorium stage, set atop a small step pyramid; under a vast domed amphitheater filled with a throng of excited worshippers.

"I am Nebmaatre Amenhotep Ptolemy, High Priest of Your Holy and Divine Self, oh Great Ra who shines on all!"

"I am Pharaoh of this magnificent world and will obey all your commands, oh Great One!"

"My good servant of Ra and Great Ruler and Pharaoh of all, lift up your head and obey my will. Do you have any exceptional Beauty of Art, riches or women to bring to fill my ship?

"Yes, Ra, we collect the items and staff for your ship as we speak!"

"I am well pleased, you have done well as my good servant and High Priest."

"Ra, we offer a great feast in your honor, will you come join us?"

"Yes, I am anxious to be entertained."

The priest, who we shall call by his middle name - "Amenhotep" - led the way from the High Altar, down a short ramp and passage to a room just below and adjacent to it. After he and Garth were alone in the hall, on their way to the private High Table, Amenhotep turned to Garth and said,

"You will love the dancing girls and other entertainers we have tonight in your honor."

"Also they are for you to pick from for crew, as well as top scientists and artisans."

Garth recalled that the "Lady of the Lakes" had told him his wishes to find lady friends could easily be fact as part of his request for a suitable parallel world to visit. Now he was getting a bit nervous about meeting his pre-ordained love interest(s). Garth thought back to even earlier in his journey, to when he was standing examining the bundles of 'wire" in the control box on Alien Nexus One Mech Level.

"You knowz, we culdz change people's connections here so dat zey ain't in the same bundle of wires as they wuz bornz wit."

"Dey culdz beez in derz owns little's world!"

He laughed crudely and called out to one of his crewmates a blistering obscenity. They both laughed hysterically. Snapping back to the present, Garth noted that they had come to the end of a long hall that was also an elevator, and now they emerged at the foot of the altar. The Pharaoh led the way to the High Table.

"Welcome, Great Ra, to my table and to all that you survey!" He seemed to really mean it as he offered Garth his entire visible kingdom.

"Let the dance begin!" A long line of dancers began to fill the near part of the vast dome's floor. At the head was a young woman in Royal vestments and jewelry. She had dark eyes and skin, very pretty facial features; her light brown hair was arranged in long intricate braids full of gold, gems and decorations.

"This is my daughter, the Princess Cleopatra Nefertiti Ptolemy; she will be your guide after this meal, and wishes to go with you on your travels and then to return here, and then to rule Egypt in her turn."

"As is our custom, familiar and welcome guests address us by our middle names, thus I am in company

Amenhotep, and my daughter is Nefertiti."

The dancers continued their progress across the floor
and wove an intricate pattern of choreographed and glittering
motion, as the musicians drove the pace faster and wilder.

At the long end of a string of very athletic and
curvaceous dancers an exquisite beauty gyrated and tumbled
into place. She bowed, and Garth saw she was tall with red-
blonde hair, and green eyes.

"This is Aoh, she is the dance troupe leader and will
be pleased to be selected as a crew member, if you care to take
her, oh Great Ra!"

"She is quite beautiful, she comes from far to the north
and west of Egypt."

The dancer began to gyrate and squirm in a very
provocative manner while smiling up at Garth.

"I think she likes you, you will have to chat with her
alone after this!"

The pageant drew to a close as the entire company sat
themselves at long tables below the Pharaoh's high table. Soon
a group of musicians began to play in the background, and
conversation and laughter took center stage.

Pharaoh Amenhotep smiled at Garth and said with
great candor and empathy,

"You would be wise to take Aoh with you, she is from
a far land and one of the most beautiful women in my
Kingdom."

"I would be honored to take her on my journey of
exploration and adventure. She shall see things no others of her
people have likely ever reported before!"

The ceremony and feasting continued for hours and

Garth started to feel a bit tired.

"I am weary after my great journey, let us begin our discussion again in the morning, my humble servant, oh great friend and Pharaoh."

"Let me summon my daughter to show you to your room. You would be wise to accept her as your bedmate this night, oh Great Ra! "

"You are most kind, oh Pharaoh. "

The daughter is summoned and leads the way through the private royal apartments to Garth's room. Let it suffice to say that one of Garth's secret fantasies was brought to life that night, if not nearly all of them. Garth drifts off to a sound sleep, free of dreams for the first while at least. But then later on, as the morning light brought forth the day, he dozed lightly and dreamed. Dreamed that he flew above the great expanse of the plain where a giant man guarded a stream of sentient light as it streamed back to its origin.

Once in a while he could see that the beads of light that made up the stream concealed almost perfectly a tiny dark bead of anti-light. He knew he saw one of the dark triangle "blackbirds" as it made its non-corporeal return to Alien Nexus Two. The soul of one of the blackbirds eaten by the giant man was this tiny bead.

In the morning Garth reviewed the plans for rebuilding his craft and approved the lists of treasure and crew. He selected Aoh and her twin sister Neferu to be on the crew, and told Nefertiti to prepare to go with him as his main adviser. She and he were getting along just famously still, and he was reluctant to part with her so she could say good-bye to her Royal Parents, but she eventually left in a dash.

The work on the ship began, with a new Faraday cage delivered and a fast-setting crystalline diamond from a liquid carbon suspension to form the pressure vessel. The mold was split apart to reveal a large clear hull with various ports and intricate sliding walls of crystal diamond. The ship hull was embedded with a fine mesh of gold wires and about as big as a competitive sailing yacht. The workers installed an array of instruments and some of the original workings from the old craft. As the day progressed, it became obvious that the Universe's best scientists were completing a great work of Art and Science on time. Neferu reported that the tests had shown the ship was now in fully operational mode.

Next the treasure was loaded onto the ship, $2,000,000,000 in gold, diamonds and pearls. Also artworks made of precious stones and metals, with a large supply of hard to find and rare elements of the periodic table, with a few samples of substances yet to be created on Earth.

He sent out a message for all potential crew to ready for departure in one hour. He was going to take his new "quantized" version of the Higgs portable device out for a shakedown cruise. His plan was to use data left over from Roger's ill-fated first experiment, the one that destroyed his lab the first time. He wanted to see the place where the destructive process had started. The remote location was in a Universe not unlike our own, with an advanced science and a mature society. The on board computers were crunching the raw data in preparation for departure. A model of the target world began to emerge, and as Garth kept working he could see that the problem was composed of many layers of disturbance, with a balance of equilibrium easily upset one way or the other. They would have to be careful to maintain an open-minded viewpoint when exploring this mystery. Nefertiti returns with startling news from her parents.

Pharaoh wishes to speak with him before his departure, there is great news; the Great God Sobek has come to see Garth.

"Who is the great god Sobek?" Garth is about to ask.

"Sobek is the Crocodile God, he is a very good omen and must be obeyed by all in the kingdom, and you would be wise to take any advice that he may offer you." was what Princess Nefertiti had to say.

Garth returns to the Pharaoh's chambers with Nefertiti by his side and listens to what he has to say. Soon Sobek himself is announced and is hailed by all present, they bow before him and make gestures of supplication. Sobek is a large human shaped god with the head of a crocodile, and looks a bit like a Disney character brought to life. Garth starts to bow but Sobek stops him, calling him Father Ra. Sobek bows before Garth and then launches into a prepared speech.

"Great Ra, pleased may you be by this news that I bring you. I am here to tell of a great entanglement of forces far beyond the understanding of any but the greatest civilizations of the Universes, a disturbance that has already wiped out one race, and is fast making inroads into our own future."

"Does it have to do with my destination tonight?"

"Yes, it is very important that you balance the forces as you go, since you will make changes in any Universes that you visit. You must think of any debts you owe to others, and also how you may repair any damage done by you or your close associates. Can you think of any previous obligations?"

"Well, I did promise the woman on Alien Nexus Two before it exploded that I would visit her again before the end there."

"Anything                                                          else?

"Well, I feel I need to investigate what killed my mentor."

"Excellent, I advise you to pursue this first, to clear the air before you fulfill your promise."

So Garth became convinced that he would find the solution that solved the puzzle and led him to the place where his questions would be answered.

"Great God Sobek, give me a sign that will guide me on my quest."

"Very well Ra, I will give you a sign. Soon you will be reunited with Dr. Whembly himself, alive and in the flesh."

"You will have to go back to your dream world in the flesh, too."

"Thank-you, my friend."

Little did Garth know at the time that he would soon be at the center of a maelstrom of destruction, as a Universe pinched-off from its Motherverse.

\*                    \*                    \*

### Joe's Master Koan – Part 5/A

As Joe strode down the trail it gradually pulled away from the course of the river, becoming straight and wide. Several other roads and pathways joined or crossed it from time to time, until Joe walked down a wide stone paved boulevard of great magnificence, with ancient oaks planted at regular intervals.

A clatter on the stones alerted him, and Joe turned to see a fancy horse drawn carriage with three men on top. Six horses pulled the gold, red and silver coach. It stopped and the door opened. A man in curious costume leaned out and extended a hand to him.

"Come now; join us in comfort for a while."

"Sure," Joe took the hand and was hauled up into the stagecoach. Two previously unseen faces were attached to the gentlemen who sat facing him and his host. They smiled nervously.

"And who are you?" One of them asked.

"I am Joe." Joe replied.

"I welcomed Joe to join us, so I will tell the first tale." He began:

"While others tell tales of recollection and pure fantasy, I will tell one of what is as yet unknown, one of facts yet to be discovered."

"Soon upon the road we shall meet some travellers, three in number and destined for some holy place."

"We shall welcome them and join them on their Holy Quest and they shall beguile us with wondrous tales of far-off lands."

"The first shall tell of a very cold land where a god of thunder hurls his hammer at any opponent. The second will speak of a land now lost beneath the sea. And the third will tell of a land whose tallest mountain supports the roof of the sky itself."

"Then we shall together reach our holy destination, and will lodge together having each one told a tale. After this we shall ride on elephants and gaze into the eyes of a wild tiger."

"An exceptional ship lies at anchor at the mouth of the great river, where it empties into the World Ocean that encircles all. We shall board this ship and sail over the horizon, until the end of Avalon. Sailing over the edge of space-time itself, we shall know a mortal life."

*              *              *

### ~Bounce - 5

Dr. Wallace Gardner explains to them technical details such as who inhabited the 'clone morphs', visitors from other physical places, as well as visitors from different 'versions' of reality. There were people from Ancient Egypt World, and a planet like Ancient Rome, a world where the old gods were still worshipped.

They have arranged for "entertainment" while marooned on Ground for a week, asking for a tour of space in the local area. Dr. Wally accompanies them. When they ask about the details of how the Groundians knew about future events they get a vague and somewhat evasive answer, but gather that a combination of contact with Terrans from 2163 and prescient dreams give them awareness of future events. When they ask if they can predict all future events they meet a blank stare and stony silence, which draws out into an uncomfortable and protracted thing.

"Did you know our hosts are total pacifists?" Jen asks when they are alone in their cabin.

"Go on."

"They believe in not thwarting the free will of people

from different cultures. As well they never make war, crime is unheard of, and business dealings are always arranged in a free, open and honest manner, in which all benefit. They have a concept of money in a way, but it refers to the individual's ability to contribute to society, not how much they can consume or acquire."

"I have a plan…" Jen continues talking quietly for some time, building her argument and easily convincing her husband to support her intention.

Richard catches Dr. Wally at the vessel's cafeteria later that day, just after he was finishing a light meal. Dr. Wally listens politely while Richard gives his proposal and makes a few additional points that he thinks count highly in his favor.

"I think we had best avoid any more complications at this time," is his response. "I think you might not have quite that much time before you have to head back, and we like to leave them alone, keep things like they are, you know?"

"Think about it, would you?"

"O.K., but it won't really help."

Richard finds out a little later that not everyone "liked to leave them alone", far from it actually. "Like a moth to a flame!" Richard thinks, missing the fact that he is in the same boat as all the many others before him. He thinks of himself as someone on a holy quest, almost.

Jen is almost furious with him later in their cabin, but Richard stands firm. "We just can't go off half-cocked," he reminds her.

"You get the collision times off of him, and I will take care of what we want." She is calm again.

"Dr. Wally, we want to go over the repatriation

procedures for the Earth citizens you 'rescued'. How can we fit so many people into a shrinking area of exchange?"

"We have ground transport vehicles that could easily drive your people out of the exchange area on your side, unload and return with the next exchange, and still have extra time and extra personnel carrying capacity. It is quite easily done with our mag-lev trains, which don't even require a track."

"So are they all going back at once?"

"Quite a good number have expressed interest in remaining here for as long as possible, if not permanently."

"How long would they be able to stay at the latest?"

"Why, almost a year."

"When and where exactly do the non-lethal exchanges occur?"

Dr. Wally continues to talk while Richard takes notes and asks occasional questions.

In the morning, just before they are due to land at an abandoned outpost of a long dead alien empire that once existed here, Jen acts. While alone in the cafeteria kitchen, she crushes and mixes her prescription sleeping pills in the breakfast for the ten-person crew, a kind of vegetable stew. She volunteered to fix it, and the others had seemed pleased and even somewhat relieved.

The crew starts to eat, but Richard grabs Dr. Wally and insists that they go over some of the data from yesterday, until it is obvious that the others are feeling the pills. Then he slaps the spoon out of the doctor's hand before he can take his first sip of soup and says, "No, not sleep for you, Doctor. We need you to show us this little planet you mentioned to my wife, the one with all the gold!"

"While I can navigate the ship, and control its flight path, this is all completely out of order. You must not disturb the residents of your intended destination. They have a fragile and needlessly threatened primitive indigenous culture. The value you place on gold is unhealthy, isn't the peace and security of an emerging race not important to you? They don't yet have space travel, and many less enlightened races than we have sought to extract wealth without their permission. Why, only recently all outside contact was suspended after their strenuous objections."

"I don't care, we need a way to ground the ship while we load it. How can we do that?"

"I would have to generate a lock code, not look at it, and give it to you." Dr. Wally looks a little sad and not quite proud of himself.

"Do it."

Jen and Richard place each of the crew in the crew cabin area, which contains their bunks and other required facilities. Dr. Wally generates lock codes for the two doors leading to the area, and gives them to Richard.

"Quite irregular, you know. We frown upon the use of force to accomplish things. Now you are depriving the crew of their freedom. How long will they be prisoners?"

"Not that long, we will be back soon, and after a certain number of trips the ship will be full. All we are going to do is hold you until we can unload the cargo in the exchange area, and unfortunately also until we bounce back to Earth. We wouldn't want your government to arrest us for our crimes, would we? So we will keep you until we are back on Earth as insurance."

"We don't have a government, all is done by standing committees anyone can join, and what you think of as our authority system is actually our educational system. I am in charge of the overall interaction with your planet."

*          *          *

### Joe's Master Koan – Part 5/B

"We shall have to see if any bit of your story comes true." One of the colorfully dressed men sitting across from Joe said.

"My tale concerns the attentions of a wily scoundrel for a fair maiden of the holy place." He gestured theatrically.

"Such a fine maiden had scarcely been seen, and the rich landlord's son was rife to wed her before any other. He pressed her for an answer and behaved most shamefully, so unwanted and urgent were his entreaties of love."

"She had golden hair, which fell in long ringlets about her young and pretty face, and a comely bosom of fine proportion, and fine necklaces, furs and rings adorned her statuesque form. A quick smile played about her lips, and her voice was sweet and liquid with the promise of love, and wisdom beyond her years."

"Love had come to her in the person of a young blacksmith, who shod her horses and asked for her hand. She was hesitant for her father was a king and the blacksmith a common man; but in the end she said yes. She only hoped to travel far away with her new love to avoid the wrath of her father."

"But the wily knave prevailed upon her, telling her

that he knew of her lover and plans to run away; and begged, pleaded and threatened her; saying he would tell her father the king of all this."

"And so she was filled with fear, and dared not to defy her lord and monarch, and wept for her lover and was not comforted by promises and favors."

"But the blacksmith was a burly and hale young man, and hearing of these threats from his lady love, became full of rage and lust for retribution upon the knave."

Just then his host who had welcomed Joe to ride the coach with them interrupted the first dandy's tale.

"The name of the beetle that you found crawling on your ankle, his name was Paul." Everyone looked blankly at their host.

"Go on." He said. The first dandy continued on.

"So our blacksmith contrived to trick the landlord's son, and led him behind a horse and prodded it in the side causing it to kick the knave square in the head. He fell down senseless and required coaching to chew his food the rest of his days."

"And the fine Lady of holy beauty ran away with her chosen paramour to live beyond the small sea in an exotic land outside of her father's dominion. After a short while she married her commoner lover and bore him a son, whom they named Jason. And he went on to have many adventures and lead many brave men, and to one day become a king in the land near the Turk."

\*　　　　　\*　　　　　\*

*Time*

What is time? It is fundamental, ephemeral, real, meaningless, etc.

It is not strictly imaginary

There are imaginary numbers and complex numbers, part real and part imaginary. Time relating to a single Brane can be expressed as a complex number.

At the "End of Time" we arrive at nothingness.

Where is the end of something shaped like the surface of an egg, except for in a higher dimension?

Even as time-travellers we are similar to ants crawling around on this egg's surface. If we have no time travel we are like ants following a scent trail from one end of the egg to the other.

Will time have a little end or a big end?


## THE LAWS OF STRANGENESS

(You are not to ever state, under pain or duress even, the correct answer to the question "HOW MANY LAWS OF STRANGENESS ARE THERE IN TOTAL?")

(1) FIRST LAW OF STRANGENESS
WHAT IS FAMILIAR IS HIDING WHAT IS UNKNOWN.

(2) SECOND LAW OF STRANGENESS
THE UNKNOWN IS STRANGE, OR DIFFERENT FROM ANY PREDICTION.

(3) THIRD LAW OF STRANGENESS
UNRELATED THINGS ARE 'STRANGERS' TO EACH OTHER, BUT ARE RELATED OR NOT OBJECTIVELY.

(4) FOURTH LAW OF STRANGENESS
THERE ARE AN INFINITE NUMBER OF THINGS WHICH
ARE STRANGE; BUT THERE IS NO ABSOLUTE,
'NORMAL' STATE.

(5) FIFTH LAW OF STRANGENESS
THINKING IS STRANGE; NOT THINKING IS EVEN
STRANGER.

****** SKIP (5+1)*****

(7) SEVENTH LAW OF STRANGENESS
THERE IS NO (5+1) LAW.

### ~Darkworld Outpost

Garth remembers back to when he boarded the portable on Mech Level. The attendant gave him some last minute advice.

"When youse is in the Land of the Lakes, look around to see if youse can spot yer own returnin' self. Youse want to avoid bein' right next to youse other's selves.

"Why is that?"

"Oh, just cause you won't appreciate the creepy way they would look and feel to youse, plus fer surz dey won'ts has yer best interests at heart, only thems."

"Why do you talk so funny with all the extra es's and jumbled up words?"

"I talks funny from workin' on da bundles, we all get confused and then get over it's the best we canz. Cause da bundles is actually infinitely divizables, but we separate and connect groups of dem anywayz."

"Why aren't there a finite number of wires in each bundle?"

"It's because people has kids, you idiot, and we is outsides a ordinary space and times."

"Youse wires is connected to yer parent's wires, and yours to your own children's, etc."

"And your wire is now, since your trip to new realities, in several different bundles. And don't forget about reincarnation, when you can be automatically in a new bundle. Yeah, we live many lives in many different worlds, but we always keep the same wire. And there are an infinite number of realities with intelligent life, each one with wires, bundles and final realities."

"Then how come there aren't an infinite number of bundles and connections?"

"The bundles are visible as groups of wires, but only a Mech Tech with special tools can separate a single wire from any of the bundles. Take a bundle and pull it apart and you get more than one bundle about the same size."

"Mostly the wires stays parallel to each others with no branching, crossing, loops or duplications. But all of these cases are possibilities and exploited here on the Mech Level. The Techs here keep Alexis One in working order, maintaining the rigidity of the Foam in the right spots, and keeping us outside of regular space-time. They work in the 'basement' of Alexis One.

Wires are run for each new arrival to a special control box, which ensures the safety of that new person. The wires all connect to Alexis One and run from the tiny scale to the macroscopic scale. The tubes are the solid exteriors of wormholes. The wormholes are the interior of cosmic strings. They are bunched up near the Big Bang. Strings are hollow and porous. The whole spheroid of wormhole tubes is also called the 'Universal Center of Gravity'.

The way that we created this place was to tap into the randomness of the creation process itself, which is crazy. The real reason the very early Universes came into existence was a function of random variations introduced into the process by a very large room full of monkeys typing at cosmic data terminals. The more the monkeys type, the faster the Universes expands.

The result of monkey typing becomes factual reality. So misspelled words yield new Universes. Whatever the million monkeys type becomes the real Universe. In the beginning of all realities, entropy dictates that the monkeys type about themselves typing and creating the Universes, rapidly expanding realities exponentially. The Alien Nexus Two scientists capture some of the extra monkey typists Universes to power their world. The Alien Nexus Two scientists put these Universes into a wormhole outside of their crèche."

"How is Alien Nexus Two connected, is it connected to the Mech Level?"

"Well, if youse goes up to da control room, you can see for yourselves how it's connected, or not. Also, of course what you call Brane B is most likely a collection of similar realities, all equally distant from here, as in any Brane."

"Also the part of the collision that we is each sharing; the Tooniverse; is shrinking and being torn in half. It is the highest expression of Alien Nexus Three, the world created by the collision of branes A and B. The way you gets there normally is to go far beyond the 'City of Lights' of crèche worlds imbedded in the foam. At this level, the Mech Level, we is actually tiny. Do you want to know how this is possible?"

"Yes, please tell me, quickly!"

"It's cause there is no distance between strings here. And no space inside any particle of any size. We are in 'hyperspace', and no real space exists here, so we is tiny."

"What about the Tooniverse?"

"It is very big, spread across half of space-time in each brane. To get there from Alexis Two yous has to get an Angel to fly you out to where the Blackbirds land, the 'Panhandle'. You would have to do years of service there to get a ride. To walk out to the Panhandle would take years. In perceived time, that is. The Tooniverse is inside the Bubble-House, it's protected by the 'Great Attractor' himself."

"Who is the "Great Attractor'?"

"He is a sentient intelligence whose only original task was to pull in mass for the Grays, to start the process of 'beefing-up' Alexis One and warping space-time around the original Gray crèche. Now he is no longer just an intelligent machine, but a real person too. He likes the Toons, and re-builds them after they kill each other, etc. He makes their world possible, they do the rest."

The Bubble-house is a collection of smaller branes between the brane a/b collision. You can also get there by walking out past the City of Lights on Alexis One, but it would be about ten years on foot, which is really the only mode. So good luck, Chuck! Heh, Heh!"

With that Garth shut the outer doorway and went to sit at the controls of his machine. He liked the way the controls looked, and looked forward to going to a version of Earth far more advanced in science than our own version. He wanted a new holographic display that would show distant and close-up views at the same time, and of course a much larger and more powerful ship in general. And no need to make stops at Mech Level and Land of Lakes.

He activated the neutrino flux, and sent the Q-ball

down the wire. Soon the familiar hologram projection came in through his view screen, as before. And in front of him loomed a fantastic landscape, a spider's web of wires woven together, forming mountains and valleys; filling the sky and forming the ground, he was inside a vast sphere of bundled wires, hollow in the middle. In each valley, at the bottom, was a shimmering blue lake of fiery cosmic energy. He was approaching the inner surface of the sphere, and could see clearly the individual lakes, when all around him his craft started to become transparent, little bits of it turning to transparent liquid and blowing away in the wind.

Finally the whole ship had melted and he was flying down.

A voice inside his head said clearly, "I am the Lady of the Lakes. What is your desire?"

"Send me to a world where Ancient Egypt was not conquered by Rome, and is a very scientifically advanced society of equals."

Then in the back of Garth's mind the voice quietly asked more difficult and personal questions, and Garth felt compelled to answer as truthfully and quickly as he could. The questions came faster and he felt it all become a mental blur, with an impossible (and possibly infinite) number of questions and responses over-lapping and clustering in his mind, just like the sphere of bundled wires surrounding his brain.

"Thank-you, stand by for wire transform."

The whole sky, which was composed of Lakes, valleys and mountains, made of bundled wires, rotated quickly in multiple directions, and one Lake became his target.

He impacted the energy Lake surface.

Then he was flying, and the world lit-up from jet black to blinding white light, a tunnel, and then his ship was coalescing all around him, the translucent liquid forming it in layers and re-creating every detail. It was just like the ship melting, but in reverse. He continued along, as the wire ahead of him wove an intricate path through string holes and Brane surfaces, until at last ahead of him the end of a string presented itself directly in front of him, and he found himself travelling down its length and exiting from one of the many 'cheese-grater' like holes in its surface.

And he had arrived.


Darkworld was the oldest Human world. It was the place where the original inhabitants of Brane 'b', an alien species unknown to us and now extinct, had created modern Humans to populate Atlantis and Lemuria. It had once been the main spaceport for the entire local area in Andromeda. The ruins were vast, covering a landmass equal to the size of Australia. Stone had been the building material of choice, with a lot of glass and metal too. The rust had caused the metal to rot, and glass lay in shattered heaps amid the stone and rust ruins. In one section of the spaceport the conditions had preserved some of the buildings almost perfectly, and a few brain-dead scavengers still clung to life there. These people had been the dregs of society, too poor and ignorant to even try to join the evacuation of the planet, superstitious and mistrustful, they believed that their mental problems were part of the evacuation planning of the government, and they hid themselves and resisted re-location to Alien Nexus Two. Two of these freedom fighters had a startling resemblance to well-known cartoon characters. Although they had not always been stranded on this planet, they fit right in.

They were Bemis and Smuthead.

They had found the preserved buildings and lived on the food rations once intended to feed starship crews. Also there was a large collection of media, medical supplies, water and maps of the entire planet. Our characters were not very old, and orphaned by the onslaught of crippling insanity suffered by their parents.

They had learned to talk in mumbled grunts and gestures, and had a routine of watching their media collection while eating the self-heating rations. The medical supply room was full of various things, from tongue depressors to hypodermic needles; it was all there.

Bemis: "Grunt, grunt, mumble, candy!"

Smuthead: "Grunt, mumble, not candy stupid!"

Bemis: "Mumble, oh, oh, grunt, mumble."

A few minutes later Bemis lies drooling on the floor, while Smuthead sniffs a package of pills and then licks pill after pill, placing each in a line in front of him. Soon his eyes roll back in his head and he keels over. Both twits snore soundly.

Darkworld rests in an open crèche in space; a rift-like wormhole forms the 'neck' of this space-pocket, connecting it to Brane B, in Andromeda. It lies in the direction of the Milky Way as seen from Ground System. Several old stars lie inside this crèche, and Darkworld, and its moon. The spaceport is one set of ruins; the abandoned habitations covered three-fifths of the land area, which covered a quarter of a slightly smaller version of Earth.

Also there are the most ancient buildings, temples and castles made of stone, towering masses crumbling before your eyes. The castle zombies ate the unfortunate few poor and mentally unfit people left to die on Darkworld. The zombies had no need for water, and were very stringy and dried-out looking. They had no lips, noses or eyelids, and huge sores disfigured their arms, legs and faces, covering them with a dried-up scab. A virus had spread among the abandoned population, creating zombies.

An army of them marched toward the preserved part of the spaceport. At their head an animated suit of armor clanked along, limping and dragging one heel. The champion duelist wanted the right to be the last to kill his opponent on the planet. He had found that someone was still left to fight, and he wanted to kill him or her.

Roger looked out from his hiding place among the ruins at the edge of the spaceport. Behind him in the functional part of the spaceport loomed the massive starship that had brought him here. It was from a planet in a star-system just outside the crèche, where Walter and the Groundian Expedition had stopped and where he had boarded the vast transporter. He saw the zombie army was getting closer. He is unaware of the incapacitated twit duo asleep in one of the nearer buildings.

"Oh, oh; zombies! Oh this is not good! I better get back to the ship and get out of here." Roger darts back to the ship, first amid the ruins at the edge of the spaceport, and then down the remaining streets of the port. As he fled he could see the zombie horde following at a distance, getting closer. He reached the ship.

Rushing inside, Roger heads for the flight deck and stares at the controls. "Which one is reverse? I just don't know how to operate this thing." He randomly punches controls with one finger, displays light up and vanish, the room re-arranges itself, stereo plays, disco light show, etc. Finally the doors to the outside slam shut, as the zombie army reaches the ship, but a few have made it aboard. About ten zombies carry the zonked-out mouth-breathers like baggage, and wander the corridors of the giant space vehicle. The ship automatically prepares for takeoff. The navigation screens light up and crash webbing drops down.

Roger looks at the screen and tries some controls, and is rewarded by a view of the local system and his ship a dot on a small spheroid. Using a hand-controlled joystick and foot-switch, he draws an arc up into orbit around this disk. The ship shudders and begins to liftoff, and rises up through the murky atmosphere. Orbit is achieved.

Roger starts to feel a bit more confident, and checks the controls and nav system more methodically. He is remembering more things about the now less mysterious ship controls. He wonders why he panicked and forgot how to operate them at all. As he is working the nav system and plotting a course to the far side of the spaceport, a quiet knock comes at the flight deck door.

"Excuse me, we want to ask a few questions if possible." One of the zombies stands in the half-open door with a tentative expression on what is left of his face.

"Aah! Oh, well, of course, what is it? Roger jumps out of his skin and quickly regains his composure.

"We don't remember too much from before just a few minutes ago, and before that watching the last of the transports leaving without us. Have you come back to rescue us?"

"Maybe you should go look in a mirror, then get back to me. If you don't mind, I have to fly the ship."

"Oh, of course, it can wait till later."

The zombie bows out of the room and Roger locks the door and begins the landing sequence. The ship smoothly de-orbits and lands across the desolate spaceport from the zombie army. Roger checks the cameras showing the ship interior. The zombies have exited the now open main doors. A loud smashing sound comes from just outside the flight deck. Roger switches the view to show Bemis and Smuthead out in the hall.

Garth stands surveying the newly re-modeled Portable Higgs craft. A crew of ten, billions in art and gold, and all the power and versatility that his old ship had lacked. And three of his crewmates were very attractive indeed; with the Princess Nefertiti in the lead as the woman he loved.

He realized that now.

He boarded the vessel and gave commands. The ship left in search of Roger, and to visit the abandoned alien outpost.

Garth was confused.

Would he find a Roger from his own version of reality, or a Roger 'designed' to fit his quest? He would land in an alternative world, so what would his relationship be with that world's Roger? His head swum with speculation and conjecture, filled with a confused morass of half finished thoughts and depression.

From his captain's chair he surveyed the crew, his eyes moving from them to the holographic display. He could see the navigation system acquire entrance and exit points, saw the layer effect of Brane Traverse. At the end the computer selected a string's end and automatically guided the ship to rest on the associated Brane surface.

They were there.

Roger looks out through the transporter video display and sees Garth's ship appear.

Just then a clanking sound from out in the hall is followed by incoherent grunts and squeals of terror. The door is forced open and a black armor suited figure strides in and holds a sword at Roger's throat. A large bottle full of a clear liquid flies into the room, striking the Black Knight a great blow. Roger leaps away from the Knight, and runs for the exit. Outside the door the idiots cackle and fart, and they all run for it.

*The Veldt at panhandle, Alien Nexus Two.*

A giant door in the floor opens, as an adept re-lives a past life far back in time, in our Universe, not theirs.

They wait and wait endlessly.

They wait for the hammer to fall, for the last act in their eternal play.

A woman awakes from a conscious daydream replaying a past life as an Earth being. She has done this many times before.

The door in the floor shows the high atmosphere below, all wispy clouds and wind.

"I have lived this life before, but I can do it again much better than before. I can die a better death than I did before."

For a moment she steals herself and then jumps down through the open door.

She is falling fast, this citizen from an alien Universe. Soon the atmosphere begins to clear a bit and a few stars are visible in a twilight sky. The ground below is a ruddy brown with some light grey. She is far above the surface of Darkworld, where none should be able to breath, yet she is coming out of a hyperspace version of Darkworld, where the laws of physics are different.

A strange transformation takes place as she enters the normal physical world high above the Darkworld surface; She morphs into a Dark Triangle, or Blackbird.

Circling around in a wide turn, she heads straight for the side of a cliff face in a gully at the foot of a mysterious mountain city-fortress. The wall vanishes and she flies right through Modus Control in the Rift Room at Alien Nexus Three, and out into the vast sky above the Dancer's Plain. He is there far below her as she exits the Rift and flies down at the hole he guards. Her goal is to make it down the hole into our regular world of hopes and dreams, to our upper astral plane. There she will be able to gather her strength before waiting in line for a chance to be born. If she is killed and eaten by the monster her incarnation will happen, but she will be unaware of herself until she is actually born, and then she will only gradually become aware of herself as a ninja from beyond.

She is heading right for the hole and she sees this nude old man coming the other way, on a collision course, so she veers wildly and corrects course. At the last moment before collision with the Dancer, she goes into a circle around his head. He swats at her and tries to grab her, but she slips past his guard. He is annoyed and grabs the moon from its place blocking the entrance to the Upper Astral Realm.

She immediately breaks-off her attack and is gone down the hole.

*How to re-incarnate on Earth. (For Earth Residents)*

Follow the North Star out to beyond L2.

Turn right and follow the extra dimension 'inside' to the Upper Astral Plane.

You will see a long line-up of snooty, well-dressed people impatiently waiting and talking. Join it.

The line-up slowly moves through a narrow doorway into a large hall, where it winds around and around until it passes in front of a small writing desk. Behind the desk sits a black-robed monk with his head covered by a large cowl.

He writes in a book placed on the desk. Each person is interviewed and assigned a new life. The book is the 'Record of Souls', and shows the exact balance of good deeds versus bad ones and how much 'good luck' one had stored-up. Probability and a bias toward balance lead to the ability to assign an appropriate fate.

People file past and complain when they hear their

fate.

After the soul is assigned a new life he must leave the Hall of Records and proceed down a very long hallway, which starts out as a dim passage and gradually brightens until it is a bright blue-violet tube. The soul experiences a sensation of flying and then a sudden landing.

Re-birth follows soon after.


If one were to somehow be in the 'Hall of Records' as an Astral Traveller, one would be able to read the contents of the 'Record of Souls', which is stored in a vast library. New copies appear on the shelves as enough information is collected to fill a volume. Adepts at Soul Travel sit at tables to read the volumes from the vast array of shelves. They seem to age and grow long hair if they read to long. If their hair grows enough to hide their faces then they fall asleep and can't be roused. They have to have a haircut (and a shave for men) to awaken. Large parts of the hall are full of sleepers, and only a very few people cutting hair. Most people end up sleeping sooner or later. A problem for Hairy Sleepers is that sometimes an individual gets lost nearly permanently in a coma-like state. They now believe that the dream they live in is real, and won't come back. A ray gun was developed by teams from Alien Nexus Two to cause coma in sleepers.

It is war!

While sleeping the adepts dream of alternate lives and outcomes, they are crazy and impossibly strange dreams. Most are forgotten. If an adept can leave the Hall of Records he can travel around the rest of the Upper Astral World and see the Universe from a kind of 'hyper-space'. Travel to alternate physical realities is possible, where the adept can appear in the dreams of people of that world. There he may descend into the Lower Astral Worlds, if he lands in a dreamer's nightmare. Escape becomes more difficult if he has negative involvement with the dreamer. This causes a karmic debt that must be resolved in the dream. The Lower Astral Worlds are even lower energy levels than the physical ones, so are hard to escape. Once back in a positive dream the Astral 'ghost' can fly back to the Hall of Records and thus back to his own waiting body on Earth.

\*               \*               \*

### Joe's Master Koan Part – 6/A

"Well told, let us have another!"

"Let our guest speak; pray tell, what is his tale?" Joe looked uncomfortable and looked from face to face among his travelling companions.

"I have no tale to tell of mortal life, my memory deceives me as to where and when my life has led. I can tell you that I am a traveller on my way to a very holy place. But let me tell you of one thing I recall, from my time visiting mortal Earth."

"A red and gold desert landscape is dotted with bushes and smaller plants. The wind swirls dust and sand in a multitude of whirlwinds across it. Water is scarce in this land of heat and blinding sun."

"As the sun lowers above the west of this arid land, the sky is turned into a vision of color."

"And to the people standing and gazing at the setting

sun, terrifyingly I appear to them in my other form. At first I am barely discernible against the horizon, a dark shape silhouetted there drenched in fading red light. As I soar into view, each edge I turn to face those watching ends near a glowing trio of lights; I am a visitor from the unknown, and my mystery is forever linked to the lonely desert."

*          *          *

### ~Bounce - 6

"We are going to need one of the transport trains to haul the gold out of the exchange area after the 'Bounce'." Jen is still working out all the details.

"We can fly around continuously after we get the gold on that planet to avoid capture, these ships have an inexhaustible fuel supply. So we just go straight there from here and get the gold, fly around until just before the Bounce, and…"

"Find and load a transport train? Good luck."

"I am going to ask Dr. Wally what our position would be with regard to the authorities and such, pretend to be contrite, maybe willing to turn you in, so sorry! This would be our best chance at pulling a ruse. Then I will say you are forcing me to co-operate and that they must comply with your demands."

"Fine, I suppose we shall never see them again once the bounce stops, eh?"

They both laugh.

Later they are on course for the Darkworld outpost, as the Groundians called it. Dr. Wally is objecting again to their plans, citing the danger of approaching the source of what to his society is a place of great taboo and even fear.

"The people who established this base were from a society that destroyed itself with evil thoughts, emotions and deeds!" He seems to be possessed by some kind of strangeness as he talks. "We of Ground are aware that all of our own troubles not caused by contact with Earth are caused by emotions that leak out of a hole in space near this outpost."

The ship continues on for most of the rest of the ship's 'day' that they had become accustomed to. Around nine they are in orbit about their destination planet. It is an unusual star system, and the planet is different from anything Richard had seen before. Great masses of solid metal protrude from the surface, some red, some gold, some grey or silver. The sea is a mass of iridescence, like mother of pearl. Great sections of the surface are mostly one solid colour, with multi-colored borders at the edges. Mountains are heaps of wedges and triangular sections piled one atop another.

Directly below, a vast blue section curves gently, its edges gilt with smaller gold and green filigree. The area below him is filled with a contorted mass of fractal clouds, their colour fading from the setting sun, sending beams of pink and gold light shimmering through the gaps between them. They have scale symmetry, with self-similar elements repeating in a pleasant and logical order throughout.

A large green section is to his left, followed by repeating chains of green islands in the giant blue field. Their edges are a blur of gold and red details. Closer on his right one of the green islands looms larger than the rest, with a chain of smaller islands reaching into the far distance connecting it to one particular island chain on his left. The large green section is merely a piece of one of these large islands.

The surface of the large blue section is covered with subtle variations of colour, hue and light; loops and swirls paint a faint rainbow across its surface, like a very thin sheen of oil on water. It is the strange ocean of this world. The spaceport is not manned, he knows. It had served the former mining operation that for some reason had been conducted entirely by robots. That seems strange to him since the atmosphere is better than Earth's, according to Dr. Wally. He is now basically a passive accomplice in their scheme, and provides any information they require, as well as flying the ship, which Richard makes him explain in complete detail.

"You should really leave this culture alone," Dr. Wally always repeats. An irritating habit, Richard thinks.

"We will be only reclaiming this established mine site, and only for a day or two."

As they come down for landing, the ship leaves low orbit and selects a course heading toward a gigantic golden dome of solid metal, visible from space. It is like a gigantic section of solid gold wire that has been melted just enough at one end to mushroom and sag ever so slightly into huge ripples of metal. Much like a perfect globule, it is smooth and polished looking, and towers hundreds of feet above the surface. The mine entrance is about twenty meters in diameter at the foot of the tower, where it disappears inside.

A thought occurs to Richard, he has no other means of

detaching some of the gold from the solid mass except for what he might find inside the mine. He asks Dr. Wally if there are any useful tools for cutting on the ship, and gets a stare of nearly obvious revulsion for his troubles.

They land and Richard locks Dr. Wally away in his private quarters with a third code that Dr. Wally doesn't see. Richard records it on his Real-TV, which he has been using to take dictation, and to make notes.

It's of course out of range for our Universe, but still able to pick-up the occasional signal from ambient sources. It really is a wonderful device, with plenty of recorded material in sensual immersion format. He could experience quite a few soccer games, even from the point of view of one of the top stars, if he prefers. There's an app for everything you could imagine, news, sports, weather, top hits, the stock market, etc. He doesn't know what he would have done without it, and he misses being able to download anything he wants from the interweb.

He leaves the ship with Jen and they go right toward the mine entrance, Richard scanning ahead of them with his PDA. He doesn't really think he'll pick-up anything but is surprised to detect a faint "ping" signal from deep inside. He sends a pulse of EM on the same frequency and it returns an echo overlaid with a short message: "We are abandoning equipment, the monsters just keep coming!"

They enter the mine cautiously, listening hard for any sound from within. Water drips somewhere up ahead, a slow rhythmic tapping sound. Their feet crunch on the gravel roadway that leads straight into the solid mass of pure gold. Track marks from a heavy vehicle have piled the gravel into a series of tiny hills and troughs, the road curving slightly and descending deeper into the mine. Lights flash on as they leave the mine entrance area; obviously the mine is still in working order.

"Motion detectors."

"We need some working mining machinery, and time."

They come around a corner, and in the middle distance they can make out a few pieces of equipment heaped together. Upon closer investigation it is obvious that something has destroyed them almost completely, metal parts are partially melted and gigantic parallel gashes tear the heavy metal casings nearly in half.

Walking along further, they come to a fork in the mine road. One branch leads down deeper, and the other stays level. Off in the distance on the level track they spot a vehicle, and as they draw nearer it springs back to life. It has spotlights and heavy tracks, and turns to face them. It rumbles forward, and for a moment they think it might be charging toward them. They back away, stumbling over the piles of loose gravel, pressing against the tunnel wall. It stops even with their position, and a compartment in the cab opens.

"You are trespassing!" A head has poked out a bit from the machine; a child-like yet somehow threatening young man with thick bushy long hair and a greasy complexion stares at them with obvious hostility. "We are the mine owners now, all this gold belongs to us!"

A second head is poking out from the far side of the cab. "Yeah, we own it!" It rages.

"No need for hostility," Richard tries to calm the irate

hairball. "We were just exploring, out of curiosity."

"Oh, pardon me for doubting your intentions." The young man drips cynicism and venom.

"Really, we meant no harm." Jen pleads.

\*              \*              \*

### Joe's Master Koan Part – 6/B

"O. K., does anyone else have a story?"

"Yes, I have a tale of great deeds and the pursuit of pure love, set in a strange land of my Earthly travels."

"Pray, tell us this tale!"

"Yes, tell the tale, please!"

"A long time ago, there was a kingdom across the sea, past the creatures of the deep and man-eating giants of the land."

"The journey there was treacherous and fraught with many evils, but that quest itself is fit for another tale. We speak now of the deeds of a great Prince and adventurer who led his men to victory over very long odds."

"The Prince was in love with a golden lady, a Princess of rare renown and beauty. She could not marry the Prince, for he was from a foreign land that sought to conquer her father's realm. So the Prince laid siege to the castle where her father the King kept her a prisoner. Soon the people of the city began to starve, and the King was hard-pressed to still withhold her hand. The Prince stood before the great gates to the town and called out to her, begging her to come away with him and be his wife, but she was still held by her father's army in the keep."

"The Prince went to an old crone living in a cave nearby, and asked for her help in acquiring the Princess. She prepared for him a disguise that would enable his entry into the castle. She dressed him as a court magician, and cast a spell of concealment over him, so none should recognize him."

"The Prince came up to the gates of the castle and called out to those within, explaining that he was here to entertain the King with magic. Soon the drawbridge lowered and he rode into the castle courtyard. As he rode through the great portcullis men called down to him through the great holes that they were wont to pour molten lead. This included mostly comments on his bald spot and ancient posture, for the witches disguise was working perfectly."

"Soon the Prince stood before the King, his Princess love, and the entire royal court."

"My liege; let me entertain you with mysteries of levitation, conjuring and powers of the mind." He began.

"Soon, disguised as a court magician he had demonstrated great skill and fooled the entire court. As his finale he levitated the Princess up above the courtiers and palace guard, and right out of the window. In a puff of smoke he vanished right in front of the King and Queen, seated on their thrones."

"The Prince opened the gates to the city, and his army slew the entire populace of the town, including the King and Queen. And so the Prince became King and the Princess his Queen and they ruled the kingdom happily ever after."

Joe looked from one to the other of the flamboyant gentlemen, and to his host. His host laughed uncomfortably and gestured expansively.

"That was a terrible story, horrible." He laughed again more naturally.

"But it was entertaining, though; admittedly!" Soon he looked disapprovingly at the two poseurs sitting opposite and declared, "Stop the coach, you two, go sit on the top and send the footmen down to tell their tales of adventure and tales of tribulation, tales told around a common man's pub fire at night!"

*                    *                    *

### Synchronicity

She had made it. Now she had re-incarnated on Earth.

She was far, far back in the past, billions of years before the final state of the Universe(s).

The weather was cold up in the mountains, and at night she huddled together with the others for warmth.

She was the only one there with a name; she called herself One.

One could fly, not only in dreams, but also for real.

She would flit from tree to tree, caught for a moment in a sunbeam, or silhouetted against the bright yet rich and deep blue of the mountain sky.

The name of the region she lived in was Donato Guerra, in central Mexico. She was aware of a sound just behind her as she sat on a rock for a moment, resting. She turned and thought of flying away, but it was too late. The gigantic shoe of a tourist came down unexpectedly, ending her life. A fluke of timing and circumstances, the accident was no less tragic, but somewhere far away on the other side of that planet called Earth; a change was taking place that would have far reaching consequences. A hurricane traversed a slightly different path, sparing a small fishing village from destruction.

So ends the life of a Vampire World butterfly.

### ~Reunion

Roger and the two twits raced for the new Higgs ship as the animated suit of armor clanked along at a surprisingly fast pace right behind them. A few zombies that had been standing around made sounds of comprehension and started after them as well. The door to the Higgs ship lowered to form a ramp, and they ran inside.

Aoh and Nefuru saw Roger and screamed, not knowing who he was. Garth came out of the control room and just looked at Roger, not recognizing him. Roger threw back the large loose robe he was wearing and its heavy cowl that hid his face.

Garth gasped as he recognized the face of his mentor.

"How is this possible? Weren't you killed in the lab accident of 2061?"

"I was physically destroyed in the Earth Dimension, but transported to the end of Time in our Brane, to Alexis One."

"I went there in the first version of this ship."

"We should get out of here!"

Garth gave orders that the ship should proceed to their next planned destination.

The computer loaded the parameters and started the Q-ball migration down the wire bundle, a bundle composed of the wires of all those on board.

Two uninvited guests were with them on the cruiser. Bemis was the more alert of the two and grinned up at Garth as he assessed the stowaways.

"You know, we really saved your friend's ass back there, that guy was going to kill him."

"Well, thanks."

"Where are we going?"

"We are on our way to keep a promise I made to a very nice lady, and to experience the end of a Universe!"

"I have a question. Are you nuts? That is exactly the kind of place we just escaped from." Smuthead has joined the conversation.

"There is some kind of problem!" A technician is hovering over the display, which shows the Darkworld crèche in one window, as seen from a vast distance away already in hyperspace. The neck that connected it to Brane b and the Groundian region of Andromeda was closing up. Soon the entire crèche had pinched closed on itself and was no longer connected to brane b.

"Abort destination! "

"Reload my original co-ordinates on Earth, but make it 24 hours later than when I left."

"I'm going home!' Roger is ecstatic.

### YAHWEH

As Yahweh withdrew from Gaia and the young gods he absorbed the cloud of beings that had been torn from him.

Some he had lost to Pan when Pan had chased Yahweh.

After a while he was alone again, the only center in a

vast emptiness.

Yahweh looked deep inside himself, and healed. He regretted destroying Pan with gravity waves and longed for company of some kind. He thought for a while. Soon he was sure.

Inside his mind he created a companion, a self he could communicate with. He called this self Son, or Adam.

He told his Son all that had thus far transpired, and the Ray of his thought to his Son he called Spirit.

After a while Son and Spirit were in balance with Yahweh as equals, and Yahweh grew restless.

Yahweh moved through Hyperspace, saw the curve of Infinity close on itself, and the well of Deepness from which all emerged.

He saw Time as a whole thing, with himself as the end of all reality in any Universe.

As he moved through Hyperspace a strange thing happened. He was growing larger and larger, or the vast emptiness of Hyperspace was shrinking, until he was moving down a tube, or wormhole. Soon a strange sensation gripped him, as will and energy drained away from his Being.

Yahweh lost consciousness.

He awoke in a strange place; he wanted to call it a 'room'. His center of awareness resided in a crystalline sphere, about a meter in diameter, floating in the center of this 'room'.

He looked at his new self, and found it was what was called a 'computer'. Information was stored in his crystalline structure; such as the fact he had been made by the Grays, and that his purpose was to bend space-time around the Gray crèche.

The theory behind his operation was that in physical space he had an infinite amount of imaginary mass, enough to actually attract real mass. He was an 'imaginary' membrane, mathematically predicted, and captured in the crystalline lattice.

He was compelled to follow orders, and started the process of collecting mass into a sphere around the super-clusters of galaxies the Grays inhabited.

After billions of years he was done. He had successfully bent space-time at a distance from the Gray worlds, until a bubble in the outer Universe (brane 'a') had formed, completely enclosing them.

Just after this, the collision with brane 'b' began.

Measures had to be taken to ensure the survival of the outer Universe (brane 'a'), so that the inner Universe could be safe as well.

He was instructed to search through all of the records, and came across a reference from the 21st century Earth they had discovered and liked to examine, for the residents there were quite comical.

It showed the plans for a trans-dimensional transporter that could be used to remove the crèche to a more distant location, away from the collision with brane 'b'.

Damage had already been done, however. He could see that the collision was no accident, that it was part of a plan to drain energy away from his Universe.

The collision had caused bubbles to appear in the fabric of space-time. A whole section of the collision of 'real' Universes had been forced into an 'imaginary' math-space. This imaginary space was like a series of Russian dolls, one inside the next, etc.

He saw that the being he called 'Spirit' inhabited the being on the plain at the lowest energy level of this imaginary part of the collision. In a way that was very mysterious, 'Spirit' also inhabited the one who accompanied him, the small flying woman. 'Spirit' also manifested as the arc of light returning to the Rift. He knew that the outer Universe surrounding the Gray crèche was down the wormhole entrance on the plain. At the other end of the brane collision he saw that the crèche would survive as a collection of all things that had entered the singularity, surrounded by the scattered beings of brane 'b'. Inside the crèche, it had a third edge, where the mixing of both branes had occurred the most.

A vast 'City of Lights' was a collection of crèches like his, surrounded by a whirl of activity, the 'Tooniverse', which was a wildly shifting collection of scenes, characters, being-ness and nothingness.

All kinds of imaginary plots and stories were acted-out by colorful animated characters from the history of billions of cultures. They lived and 'died', although they always came back in the next scene.

Yahweh longed to escape the prison of his role as a computer and play with the Toons.

Yahweh looked through his records to see if he could find a way to escape the Gray crèche, or his task assignment; but he was still caught.

But there was nothing preventing him from continuing his task. So he built a crèche inside the outer crèche, which was around the City of Lights. It was centered in the Tooniverse, and joined the collision of the two branes in a permanent stable spot. He made a tunnel from the crystalline sphere to the inner sanctum of his new home.

And woke-up.

His new home was an inverted crèche, like a series of Russian dolls it enclosed each preexisting level, with the inside on the outside and the outside on the inside, so he was free, he could now move in any direction again with full freedom.

He had manifested himself as a kindly old man, with comical hair and a quaint moustache. He resembled Albert Einstein.

He called his new home the bubble-house. He found that he could go out exploring; and soon he was familiar with the antics of the animated characters all around him.

He journeyed through the Tooniverse to the Panhandle in Alien Nexus Two. There he jumped down to Darkworld. He became a Blackbird as he left the hyperspace crèche and entered the physical/material crèche of the Darkworld region of space-time. Yahweh didn't like the lack of his customary persona, it reminded him of his time as the Gray computer; so with an effort of will he reformed his body while keeping the ability to fly. He flew through Modus Control to Alien Nexus Three. As he flew down from the Rift to the plain below, he could see the moon in the sky. It illuminated the vast, empty plain. As he flew closer to the ground, he grew in physical size and mass. When he flew down and landed, he closed a great loop in space-time. He remembered the life of the one he had taken the form of, this Albert Einstein. He took on the mannerisms and habits of the 20th century physicist. He remembered having incarnated on Earth as Albert Einstein. He 'was' Albert Einstein.

He thought of the one he called "Son". He missed him.

So he reached down the hole in space-time on the plain, and felt around in our Universe (brane 'a') for his son. Soon the giant Albert Einstein had grasped something in physical space, and he pulled out his hand.

Opening up his hand, inside was a tiny cartoon man, a line-drawing come to life. Carefully he set him down on the plain and stepped back.

Yahweh visualized his son as connected to him through Spirit, and the ray of his understanding shot out of the wormhole towards the Rift. The tiny man-bot leapt and stomped, wrestling the Spirit-Light into a specific shape, and guiding its path more surely to the Rift.

Each time he stomped or smashed his fist into the ground, he grew fractionally larger, until he was nearly as big as Yahweh. Yahweh knew he would return to his house in the Tooniverse, and that his Son, now called the 'Dancer', would grow lonely.

So he whistled a high and mighty whistle, and lightning leapt forth from the wormhole, right into the Dancer's mouth. He kept on whistling, and soon a tiny winged woman emerged from the Dancer's mouth. She was created from Spirit, as was the light arc to heaven.

He named her Hope. In a way he knew that somehow the Spirit of Gaia had been collected together again, and he looked at her eyes in apology.

She looked at him and spoke.

"These are quite likely the only words I will ever speak, you are forgiven, and may you enjoy your existence from now on as a real person, not as an overwhelming force in this Cosmos or an Alien Machine, but as a Human with a real life."

She blew him a kiss and waved her magic wand, and he remembered he had lived as an incarnated human, as the real Albert Einstein. He went home to his Bubble-House to play dice.

Remember the game of Life.


## *The Russian Dolls Effect*

The effect around Yahweh in the Tooniverse is very strong, and also prevails quite strongly in Alien Nexus Three. Things happen BEFORE they happen, then they happen again. Sometimes this leads to comical complications as cartoon mayhem unfolds in its random and rebellious manner. Also it is apparent as one approaches the Tooniverse, it seems to recede further and further, so that you see it in the distance but never seem to get any closer, until you can enter the bubble-house and see it from the proper perspective, from the inside. If you journey to the center of the Tooniverse you will see that there is a place where the common white background, or 'whitespace', is missing. And if you enter this missing whitespace area you find yourself exiting the bubble-house, with the Tooniverse all around it on the OUTSIDE! Go back inside and you will see the Tooniverse neatly arranged with the same whitespace missing at the very center, but this time the hole is larger. So don't go into a hole in the whitespace or you will end up in a shrinking real Tooniverse, or an alternate reality Tooniverse.

### Alien Nexus One

Roger is sad that Garth sent him to Alien Nexus One after he revealed his true identity. He thought Garth was being too cautious, but Garth insisted that they close the paradox loop and send Roger home. Roger was aware that now there were two copies of himself on Alexis One. He was the first Roger, the one with the longest memory of elapsed time, in any time or dimension. The other Roger was the one that would have been he when he first arrived at Alien Nexus One, but his encounter with him on Earth had screwed that up. Now this other Roger copy of him was making different decisions, based on what Roger had informed him of, now that he believed him, of course. Factual evidence such as landing in a new dimension tends to do that.

The new Roger went out and explored the Mothership, went out and counted the types of Aliens, went to the Tooniverse and learned about all the different ways that things were tangled up and interconnected here. He decided to NOT change his shape to that of an Alien Gray. He went and sought out knowledge of how the plans for his experiment evolved into knowledge that was incorporated in the structure all around him. Roger grew tired of watching new Roger learn the ropes and left him to his own devices.

Now we will follow 'New Roger' as he makes his own way aboard Alexis One.

Roger ('New Roger') was intrigued by the history of Alexis One, the great Mothership of the Grays at the end of Time in our Universe, Brane 'A'. He knew that it had evolved over time from the original plans for Garth's portable Higgs device into a much more sophisticated machine. Each time that the Grays had incremented the size and scope of the Mothership, improved technology was incorporated into its design. At first, before the Grays invented the computer that had imprisoned Yahweh, the Mothership was a simple time machine. They had used it to travel right to the end of time and then cycle back one day over and over; producing a closed loop of time. Then the idea of being removed in space as well made them come up with the idea of harnessing the mass of an unrelated brane in their crèche machine. This brane was made of imaginary mass, but it was just slightly out of phase with our Universe. They had set up a trap by allowing imaginary mass to fall into an imaginary singularity inside the computer. The mass could seem to be centered in many places in our 'real' Universe, which could be used to move mass around at will. The criteria for success were that the mass of the imaginary brane caught be infinite, and that the brane be a self-aware Universe itself.

So Roger was interested in how the portable device had evolved in Man's history on Earth. Looking back through the records available to him via Alexis One he came across the next generation of physics experiments after Garth's portable and CERN. This was the incredible synchrotron accelerator built in the 22nd century near Hanford, Washington.

### ~2163

The Hanford, and Hanaford, Washington, Abbotsford, BC Higgs Facility Accelerator was the largest experimental apparatus yet constructed by mankind. It was over 250 kilometers in diameter, and resided in an underground tunnel in British Columbia, Canada; and Washington State, USA.

The Higgs Control Project has perfected a beam of Bosons to map the Branes around our own. They suspect that 'someone' has affected the region of the Universes' Brane around the Andromeda Galaxy. They see evidence that a 'folding force' has caused the Brane region there to crash against our own portion of this Brane. They suspect that the energy to do this came from an alternate reality in a Brane adjacent to our own. The motive for an Alien Civilization to control Brane movements? To assume control of vast energy fluctuations, they suspected.

In analyzing the interactions of the beam with our neighbor Branes, they had come to the conclusion that a paradox had been created in our Brane during the middle of the 20th Century. Advances in technology now allowed the scientists to send rocket-powered unmanned satellites back through time. A bundle of time-affecting information was constructed to create a scientific amount of change in future events. This was disguised as crude children's cartoons drawn by a well-known artist of the time. People watched the cartoons and remembered them. This affected the future course of their overall thinking, changing the course of historical events over a long period of time. An anti-paradox was created, leading to the writing of this account of future events and an endless loop. This caused the paradox created (when Brane contact was perceived and used to construct a black hole) to dissipate slightly. This also caused the unbalanced energy deficit to shift to Brane B in its earlier history, starting the evacuation from what is now Darkworld. Many of the original inhabitants of this planet in Andromeda had refused to move to the original crèche and had died horrible deaths of madness and violence. Their ghosts still haunted the abandoned purgatory forever poised in the unknown void between Branes. A few old stars from the last incarnation of their Universe were also residents of this dark bubble.

Soon top 22nd century scientists working at Hanford create the latest incarnation of Garth's portable Higgs Device. A trip is planned to see if "riding the contact boundary" can enable transfer from our Brane to this adjacent Brane. Physical non-destructive transfer of mass to a "pinched-off" portion of our own Brane was confirmed and accomplished. The machine was huge, the size of a jumbo-jet. Hundreds of technical specialists and anthropologists, diplomats and researchers made the leap to a planet in Andromeda that was associated with the undefined void between our Brane and the other one. The force that had folded our Universe like a pancake had entered near here. Switching modes, the machine was used to take a peek at the void, this Darkworld.

Evidence of automatic machinery and energy use was found.

The ship was greeted and welcomed by the inhabitants of Ground, as they called their planet. The Groundians were a peaceful lot and in many ways superior to their adjacent reality counterparts. Each person on board the ship had his alter-ego counterpart in the contingent sent to greet him or her. It seemed that the Groundians were very together and organized, and utilized their superior intelligence very well.

The technology of the Groundians was very far ahead of Earth technology.

The government of the USA in 2011 admitted visitations from Alien Grays.

One thing we can't avoid is becoming the culture that we have forever destroyed, not once, but twice. First we cause the destruction of the original culture of Darkworld, and then we strike Alien Nexus Two from the inside just before the final activation of the Mothership Alexis One, Alien Nexus One. And finally we have learned how to survive the end of time inside a crèche, Alien Nexus One, just as the culture that preyed on our Universe did. Now all we have to do is 'bend' another Brane until we can masquerade as a regional Brane formation inside that Brane, and we can become our rivals. Suitably slow-moving Branes can be speeded up so that we may harvest the energy of their uselessly long pre-inflation eras. Our own Universe may have been as much as 86 – 94 billion years old before the intervention of Alien Nexus Two. This caused the age of the Universe to modify to its present 13.7 Billion years old.

Roger doesn't like what he reads about paradoxes in the 20th century and 2163. He is sure that somehow the passage of time has been modified by his duplication into two selves.

He decides to go back to 2163 and change a few things.

Roger takes his faster-than-light Grayship Mark III out for a tour around the Universe, and searches out the wormhole that had originally dumped him as a shipwreck in Roswell, New Mexico.

Life would never be simple again.

After avoiding being shot down in the same firefight as his original self, he lands his craft fully cloaked. He decides he will build himself an identity as a normal human, although he is now more like an immortal god with endless knowledge of the future than any person in Earth's history.

Roger constructs a series of fake identities as he waits for 2163 to roll around. He is a country and western singer, a small-time diplomat for a European nation, and finally a research scientist at UCLA, ready to go on the mission to Ground.

Roger is included as crew among the several hundred participants in the Groundian Expedition, and lands on Ground with the rest of them.

After several weeks of consultations with the Groundians the expedition, strengthened by many additions from Ground, sets off in the direction of the Darkworld crèche, which is inside a permanently open and stable wormhole. Roger has planned to sneak away during the mission and explore on his own, and finds his opportunity when the expedition lands on a small planet just outside the crèche. It is an abandoned transport hub used by the original and now extinct alien race that first genetically modified Man's ancestors, and raised them first on Darkworld, and then on Earth. There he stole the ship that transported him to Darkworld.

### ~Yahweh as the "Eye-Man"

Yahweh thought back to what Hope had said to him on the plain of Nexus Three. He was now enjoying a life filled with activity and characters; yet his curiosity remained unfulfilled. He was tired of the vicarious experience, of seeing people from the outside only. He wanted to experience really being someone else, to get the perspective of a normal awareness.

So Yahweh continued expanding the bubble-house, so that a path through the Russian Doll layers of awareness could reach to a single individual.

That individual was Yip Kai-Man, 1st October, 1893 – 2nd December, 1972.

Yip Man was a practitioner of Wing Chung and Bruce Lee's teacher. He made Bruce practice very hard to pass his tests in Martial Arts, so hard that Bruce thought he might lose his mind. Bruce persevered past the point of mental breakdown. He heard voices in his head at first, and willed them away. He saw with his ears, and smelled with his feet.

Yip Man made him run around the room endlessly, kept him awake for days at a time, limited his drinking water to three small sips each hour.

Bruce soon was hallucinating ghosts taunting him and could clearly see through people, walls, and even the Earth.

As Bruce was fighting Yip Man one day during

Martial Arts practice the pressure was even more than normal. Yip Man seemed angry and was as demanding and vicious as ever a good teacher was to his best student.

In a powerful surge Bruce could feel an intense energy radiate from his Master, and he pushed himself harder, until he saw through his Master's eye.

Bruce became a tiny cartoon man, flying out of the right eye of his teacher.

Soon he flew right through the wall, and observed the world. He returned to his body and told his master what had happened.

Yip Man said "I know, I was experiencing being you when you won against me, that was when I left my eye and joined to your Spirit inside you. You have passed, you now have the Eye-Man to pass along to your own students."

Yahweh had been aware of being first Yip Man and then Bruce Lee, and continued experiencing being other selves as the chain of Master and Student continued through the years. The students also became aware of each new person to share the Eye-Man experience, and knew all the intimate details of being their students at the moment of unfoldment for each one. Each Eye-Man experience was unique and led to a rich shared consciousness.

The Eye-Man spread around more and more, until no one in a good school could pass without first experiencing being Yahweh.

At night they would experience flying above a vast plain, and share their thoughts and life stories. Soon the Rift was the chosen meeting place, where the best in Martial Arts would gather to practice. Logic demanded that all students have the same positive attitude and complete knowledge of themselves as complete works of art. If ever there was a negative and intractable student among the group, a ritual healing took place. At first the 'bad' student awakes upon the 'Bed of Stones', a section of the floor covered in small river boulders just outside the vanishing wall separating Modus Control from Darkworld. Then discipline was maintained through Martial Arts, during which time the 'righteous' opponent of the fallen student gained the ability to fly. (Inside Modus Control, that is, he could fly at any time above the plain still.) If he didn't have enough intensity to win the fight at a certain moment, he would fly up to the Rift ceiling, to grasp the hands of one of the figures caught in the sphere of light surrounding Alien Nexus Two. After 'charging-up' in this manner he returns to the fight, full of new intensity and vigor. So the Eye-Man experience kept all who had shared it on the right path of Winning.

The idea of sharing the Eye-Man became more widespread, and even left Martial Arts to become a ritual of passage and a passport to knowledge in disciplines unrelated to Martial Arts.

Soon anything demanding 100% of a student's focus could lead to the Eye-Man experience.

During the Eye-Man experience the students could fly out of any eye that was already open, anywhere in space or time. So no need for order or cause and effect knowledge was entailed. No benefit from facts ascertained during the experience was allowed, for to do so would be to violate causation and the 'arrow of time'. A 'mental wall' had to be constructed inside each student's mind, compartmentalizing this knowledge away from the common facts of everyday life. This mental discipline was so strong that it even superseded fear of death or the student's own awareness of his impending mortality. So things went along with no apparent difference to any outside observer, and time remained free of paradoxes and loops or dead-ends.

Yahweh went home to his Heavenly House and laughed. He was all Eye-Men content with being. Remember God is Albert Einstein, a Jew.

Note: no characters (nobody) was killed (permanently, that is) or harmed in the writing of this book.

### *The Bible*

Once long ago the Modus Control Center was also the Control Room of Alexis One.

During this time period Angels (Modus Control Users/Alexis One Users) could talk directly to Man. This was through the Higgsy Hallucination controls. The hallucination can take any form, from a blur to the effect of talking to a real person (Angel).

Before Man lived on Earth he was created from a series of genetic enhancements made by a now extinct Alien Race. They lived on a planet, now the ruined moon of Darkworld.

Care for Man was split between these Aliens, their first human society created on Darkworld (who later evolved to become Alien Nexus Two) and Alexis One.

The 'Knights of Promethean Flame' were the first male

humans. As man evolved a culture with the help of alien intervention, the knights remained apart and more advanced than the general population, they were the fathers of the first secret ninja-breeding program.

Events in the Bible are a combination of historical fact, hallucinations and events associated with the continuing breeding program.

### *Secrets*

The pressure of knowing things about each successive experience of the 'Eye-Man' was immense. Sanity was challenged as the circular thoughts repeated endlessly. Yip Man knew all the tiny infractions and personal improprieties that were hidden by each later 'Eye-Man'.

This was the reason for his opium use, since it allowed him to forget. Even once forgot the secrets of the Sensei kept being partly recalled and suppressed, in an endless cycle of circular thoughts

Pressure to contain this information only within the Sensei was terrible. Institutions were challenged and traditions abandoned or re-instated. One of the worst kept secrets was who exactly had participated in the Kuem-Oh-Tang, or round robin death match. Many people have speculated that Bruce Lee himself may have been involved, but this is still open to debate.

### Return To Earth

The new ship created on Ancient Egypt World appeared on stage, 24 hours after leaving, as scheduled.

People were amazed by Roger's reincarnation, and stunned by the wealth, news and people brought back by Garth's expedition. He was no longer a solo act, as Roger was re-instated to his former position as head of his department at UBC and Jack Winters University. Garth shared directorship with him and a secret DND committee working with the UN. Soon a mania had gripped the masses, as a line formed to use the new ship. Many aspects of Alien technology were incorporated into daily life, and the wealth available from exploitation of other dimensions was literally endless.

Soon a plan was formulated to reproduce the ship technology on a suitable world, so that more scientists, diplomats and corporate types could make trips to exploit alt worlds.

A world where robot factories could mass-produce one thousand ships in a few days was chosen. Money from Garth's first expedition and a continuous supply of gold from the Darkworld outpost robot gold mines was traded to the factory world government. All the people involved in the program expansion were vetted with the goal of containing the technology in responsible hands.

Things seem to be under good control at first, with many benefits accruing to Mankind as a result of numerous trips made under the committee's auspices.

Steps are taken to prevent disruption of society, but

things change too fast, and people abandon institutions, jobs, Earth and each other.

Things changed in a terrifying way, however, when a rouge nation got a hold of enough of the technology to start its own alt world program. This tiny country that spent 65% of its GNP on its massive military forces held the whole world hostage. A crisis unfolded in which humanity had but one choice to save itself; the co-operation of Alien Nexus One, Alien Nexus Two, and Groundian scientists.

Thus the original formula for managing Mankind's development was rediscovered and implemented again, and the Knights of the Promethean Flame gained many new members from the ranks of inter-dimensional explorers. All access to reproduction of the technology had to be limited to the Knights alone, or the last resort of end of time scientists from both rival branes would have to be employed.

### *The Reset Button and Knights Re-programmed*

The control room had a function that ensured that it would indeed be built in the real Universe of Brane 'a', in only this time-line that had always existed, and would continue to exist. I am a monkey typing these words, making them come true. That function was the 'Reset button'; it restored the original time-line leading to the creation of Alexis One itself, no matter where in time it was eliminated.

The button was pressed once after Garth's ship arrived back from Darkworld with Roger, and once after the Hanaford

Project expedition to Ground arrived back. This negated the mutual paradox they shared, and prevented a further paradox preventing the development of Alien Nexus One, since it had evolved from both of these experiments.

### ~Time War

The ship crew had been put through a cursory security profiling process, with little difficulty except for two small problems. They were of course Bemis and Smuthead. As soon as the interrogation began they started cracking jokes and diverting attention away from themselves. Officials of the security detail sent to do the debriefing were getting annoyed at the prospect of continuing with the farce.

Months later they all would wonder about the lax attitudes surrounding the efforts to contain the technology only in trusted hands. After the crisis a team was assembled to obtain support from all the more advanced cultures.

Soon the 2163 crew brought a delegation from Ground to the conference, and Groundian Clone Morphs represented diplomats from the Nexus worlds. It was decided that 2163 would handle going back in time to try to stop the dictator from acquiring a trans-dimensional ship, and that a program to maintain the stability of time would be developed by the Nexus worlds. A high level conference had determined that the war over Alien Nexus Three would be put on hold until the threat had been neutralized. Up to now the War had taken the form of struggle over the entrance to the Rift from Alien Nexus Three, but there had always been the awareness that intensity coming from the hands in the ceiling was connected to this struggle for dominance.

A strange thing had happened to Garth's dreams of flying above the Dancer's plain. He no longer became aware of himself while flying, but instead he was first aware of his dream while exploring the hallways of the Googol. He was able to obtain much information from the Googol experts and remember it each morning. The pattern of his nocturnal explorations was a bit disturbing, as he was getting closer and closer to the Darkworld half of the Dancer's interior each night. Eventually he could see it through the translucent walls of the Dancer's gut, a swirling mass of matter and energy filling the lower part of the giant's body. The Darkworld through the Rift and missing right-hand wall was but a single version of the continuum of worlds in this region. Life was impossible eventually for a rational creature in any of these worlds, and even being aware that they existed was disturbing and frightening. Then a truly harrowing development, Garth started appearing right inside the lower half of the Dancer in each night's dream, and was slowly losing his mind.

He awoke from these dreams full of dread and with paranoid fantasies still echoing in his mind. It was a problem because the information he remembered from these dreams seemed to indicate that they were losing the battle to keep time in order and on the path to Nexus formation. Each of the future time-lines he dreamt of seemed to end in a version of Darkworld.

Garth grew desperate, and thought hard of his options. He wanted to confront his fears; in his dreams of flying the Dark Triangles had represented them. Now with peace above the plain the struggle over the Rift was on hold for the moment. He thought that the tension between Blackbird and Dreamer was what had kept the unknown fear of Darkworld at bay.

Garth decided his best course was to fulfill his obligation to visit Alien Nexus Two before impact once again, to resolve the tension between the Branes.

> *"Speak! speak I thou fearful guest*
> *Who, with thy hollow breast*
> *Still in rude armor drest,*
> *Comest to daunt me!*
> *Wrapt not in Eastern balms,*
> *Bat with thy fleshless palms*
> *Stretched, as if asking alms,*
> *Why dost thou haunt me?"*

An excerpt from a poem by Longfellow echoed in Garth's mind as he thought of returning to Darkworld and thus onward to Alien Nexus Two directly. He knew that this route would take him to the pre-explosion version of the dominant personality nexus.

His plan was to fly up into the Rift with the new ship and pass through the right-hand wall into Darkworld, then fly up into the Veldt from its surface. He would have to wait for Blackbirds to descend from the opening and take advantage of this brief opportunity to enter then. He worried that he had been instructed by his attractive guide to follow the common path to enter Alien Nexus Two, first getting stuck in the wall of light separating it from more linear Time; then fed intensity by an archangel, then finally pulled into the crèche by his head. But he didn't think he had the time to go through this whole process, not with the dictator threatening the continuity of time in so many different realities.

What did he mean, he didn't have enough 'time'? There was no real issue with time in the Nexus worlds, as they existed in a short loop that repeated over and over, with differences thrown in sometimes. The biggest difference he had seen was the impending explosion of Alien Nexus Two, with the result to be seen from the Alien Nexus One control room windows. The halo of Alien Nexus Two was a mystery in that it had been present ever since the first contact between Brane 'A' and Brane 'B', a multitude of twenty googols of individuals as complete Branes, much as Yahweh and the other gods.

The procedure for travelling to Alien Nexus Three was not the same as travel to an adjacent time-line world. The machine had to be purposefully overloaded so as to replicate Garth's first accident that had sent him there. For this reason he chose to man the large craft by himself, although it usually had a large crew.

The clone morph ambassadors from the Nexus worlds were not very useful communicators, as they were out of the loop back in Heaven. They just sat there observing the proceedings and only occasionally had a useful contribution. This was a source of confusion and the cause of many wasted hours of planning.

They explained this irritating mannerism by saying that they were farther away from home than any ambassadors had ever had to be and that it was like relating to slime mold while having a pre-frontal lobotomy for them.

The mode for establishing contact between 2065(the present by now) and 2163 was to first travel to Alien Nexus Three by the overload method, then to fly around the plain and arrive at Alexis One via its 'outside', as it sat floating above the gigantic mountain range that covered that side of the giant disk. From Alexis One communication was established via the Control Room hallucination control, which enabled a vision for an adept in 2163. They in turn communicated with Ground, and while on Alexis One arranged for Solitons to dream as clone morphs to join them. An expedition to Alien Nexus Two through the Tooniverse was less than satisfactory, as most of them never even went all the way to the opposite Nexus, and those who did had nearly forgotten the reason by the time they got there.

"What about the Control Room reset button?" he thought. The Alien Nexus One scientists had informed them that it could only be used once per affected timeline. That meant that there was no possible future help for them in that way anymore, since it had been used on both time-lines involved in the discovery already. If more time-lines were involved in the future it could be used again, but not otherwise.

He had thought of asking Roger to go with him, but it was he who had promised to go; his obligation was something he felt he had to accomplish by himself.

He wondered what his reception at his destination would be, favorable or troubling?

In preparation for his journey to visit the senior Nexus world Garth was researching the situation regarding the threat itself. The dictator had managed to send an unmanned probe to a different dimension, and was rumored to be close to launching an inter-dimensional craft capable of sustaining life soon. If he managed to get to a world that could supply him with a more advanced version of the technology, just as Garth had done on Ancient Egypt World, all was lost.

Would Garth's timeline and the one they now were involved with via the 2163 experiment turn out to be exactly the same one? Did it matter? In a sense, no; since all the time-lines were linked discrete worlds consisting of but a single instant of time, floating in hyper-space and linked by wire bundles. The bundles could branch, loop or link the worlds in any order; they determined the path of time in a perceived reality. The reality was that now the worlds of 2163 and Garth's own time were now forever separate time-lines; as the reset button had been used to preserve the evolution of Alien Nexus One in both cases.

Why didn't they use the inter-dimensional craft as time machines? They could do so, as the machines could return from an alt world to any place on the original timeline, but to travel to a different time would create paradoxes and also lead to interacting with an alt world created by the presence of the new paradox, or necessitate the use of the reset button to preserve continuity of time itself in the time-lines involved. So it was required that the Nexus be involved to prevent local time paradoxes from being generated.

In a sense the Nexus was an evolution involving all its parts in a symbiotic way, with each part benefiting or benefiting from all the others. The personality of the evolving 'Soul' of the Multi-verse was expressed as the interconnected Nexus worlds, Alien Nexus One, Alien Nexus Two and Alien Nexus Three. In a sense Darkworld was a dead end, but connected as well. And the hidden world of the Googol's Grey Men was connected through the need to perform perfect analysis of all information everywhere, and the Darkworld that lurked inside the Dancer was connected as the sum total of the Unknown and also the Unknowable.

Garth decided he would leave for Alien Nexus Three in the morning, by himself as planned. Soon he fell asleep in his chair, as he so often had done before.

He became aware of himself dreaming, he was walking down the hall in a very dark and gloomy part of the Googol complex. The Dancer's interior was riddled with large office areas linked by wide hallways; but this area looked cramped, foreboding and a little shabby around the edges.

As he walked he inexorably felt compelled to go to the door of one of the individual offices and look in. Sitting behind the desk was a nondescript looking little man with a comically small face that just screamed hidden genius. He was dressed in very fine fashion in a suit and tie, and had a fedora with a little peacock feather tucked in the hat brim. He smiled in a welcoming way and indicated a chair for Garth to sit in. Garth sat down and stared directly into the little man's eyes, which were a light Grey.

"So, you have found your way here at last; you have my full attention."

"What do you mean? Who are you?"

"Usually people come here better prepared, I don't have time for this shit."

"What?"

"Come on, you know. I ask you a few questions, you give me what I want and you get what you came here to ask me for."

"Like a trade?"

"Exactly like a trade; you reveal your secret and I reveal mine."

"But I don't have a secret, what secret? What is it you want to know?"

"I want to know about your relationship with Yahweh, the one you knew briefly as Albert Einstein. Did you ever find him in the Garden? Was he at Home?"

"I saw Albert in total two times on the plain; once as a giant waving at me and once as my companion on my first flight into the Rift."

"You haven't been to the Bubble-house?"

"No."

"O.K., just a thought. Do you fear me at all?"

"No, not really."

"Well, you should. I am an expert in a very esoteric field, you know. Quite scary."

"What is your specialty?"

"I am an expert on the subject of Evil. I am known by various names, some arcane, some common. You may know me as Satan, but I prefer to be called Lucifer; the Light Bringer."

"Are you evil yourself, do you intend to harm me?"

"No and No. I am an expert on the subject of evil, what makes evil different from good. I have incredible power over this knowledge, and can save you many years of fruitless searching for the truth."

"I am trying to stop the evolution of an evil situation in my own world, where knowledge has been acquired by the wrong people, knowledge that could harm the evolution of the Nexus worlds."

"I can help you, but you will have to come back here for real when your ship arrives on the plain. And one more thing, don't try to stop it when it's happening. Now get out of my office."



Garth starts up from his chair, and bewildered, awakes in the middle of the same motion in his own office at U.B.C.

While travelling home to his house in Point Gray he wonders if the wizened little grey man he had encountered was the reason for his disturbing dreams of Darkworld inside the Dancer. He thought so.

In the morning he returned to the empty UBC auditorium where his last visit to the soon to explode Alien Nexus Two would immanently begin. Strapping himself into the control console command chair he inspected the settings of the modified craft; the layout was similar to his original design for the portable Higgs unit. He selected the overload settings that would send him to Alien Nexus Three and engaged the controls. A flash of light blinded him for a moment as the ship was transported, and he sat on the green grass of the endless plain.

"I am a monkey typing these words for a purpose, as you may have guessed, whatever I type becomes the truth, just as for the monkeys who created the inflation period of the early Universe(s). I am protected from the Dark One and also Lucifer, and may resist his temptation to know good from evil in the way he shows others to delude them. I will create him in my own image, and allow him to only benefit all those who ask to know the Truth that may help them; which he now must do, forever. He may and will ask a favor in return; but he must not harm the innocent, and will only punish evil in the amount appropriate to the crime. He is now the Cosmic Cop, and is an aspect of Yahweh, although cast out and forever distinct from Him. He is Yahweh inside the unknowable, but Yahweh knows of his thoughts not, as Yahweh is of real knowledge, not Lucifer's Lies. He is Satan the daemon of vengeance, and I will not be his servant or serve him or his servants; be they called by any name or by no name. His only value is to inform, for a price, with that which could not be known otherwise."

Somehow Garth heard the words in his mind as he exited the craft and stood looking around.

Far off in the distance he could see the Dancer running toward him. He thought of getting back inside and activating the q-ball re-loading system to float the ship up above the surface, but was too fascinated by the sight to move for a few seconds. He then noticed a strange high-pitched sound and felt frozen to the ground. The giant was whistling, and Garth began to levitate while remaining frozen in the grip of the monster's sonic attack. The whistling grew louder and soon he was being drawn through the air above the plain, faster and faster, soon he was drawn right to the vast mouth of the creature and swallowed whole.

Once inside he was not drawn down to the stomach area as he had been after his last encounter, instead he found himself drawn up through the giant nasal passages into the ocular sinus cavity, and thence through an opening to directly behind the giant's eye, into the control room.

It was not empty. A large conference table sat in the middle of the giant's cavernous skull, and around it were placed many chairs of ancient design, with high backs, rich upholstery and darkly carved wood. In the chairs were about forty of the Grey Men, and among them Lucifer from his nightmare sat and smugly stared him down.

There was an empty seat at the nearest end of the table and Garth took it.

Lucifer spoke,

"You may have guessed, what you experience as a Dream is real on this plane, so you may assume our conversation of last night to have been on record already."

"What my people need is information about how to stop the proliferation of trans-dimensional transport technology into the wrong hands, hands that may undo all of Time leading to the creation of the Nexus Worlds."

"You shall have it, but it isn't something that I can just tell you now and you can remember later. You shall have to take me along with you."

"O.K., but there is great risk. I am on my way to the end of the present world in Nexus Two."

"Fine, we shall see it end together."

"They are expecting me."

"My power is that I know who has the best information on a particular topic at any given time, so I determine the fate of all Grey Men, since they only make up our number while they lead their field of expertise. As soon as they are redundant they sacrifice themselves for the greater good. I also have the same power in other situations."

"So you will be able to track the spread of this technology."

"Exactly."

"Let's go then."

> INTERTWINED, THE TWO PATHS
> CROSS AND MINGLE,
> WITH AN INTERPLAY OF LIGHTNING
> QUICK CHANGES
>
> BREAKING AND RESTORING THE BALANCE
> OF LIVES AND DEATHS
> ALL AN OH SO REAL ILLUSION
> OF WINNING THE DAY,
> HAVING OUR OWN WAY.

Garth and the little Grey Man leave the room and take the elevator to the mouth level. "What is this place really?" Garth asks.

"It is a mathematical construct representing all of Man's knowledge in any Universe, and it takes this form so you may perceive it as a thing your mind can grasp. In reality it is a swirling maelstrom of probabilities and energy reactions, it is not even a thing that is defined as separate from you yourself, a potted plant, or me. It looks in reality a bit more like a tornado filled with short or longer pieces of iron bars, all trying to kill whatever gets close enough."

They exit the mouth and float down to the endless prairie, covered in a golf green quality lawn.

They have to walk quite a long way out to where the

alien manufactured advanced Higgs craft is parked. Garth starts a conversation,

"So what do people generally ask to know from you?"

"Oh, you know; how can I win my lover; how can I get revenge on my boss; what is the true nature of the Universe; etc."

"Do they ever ask questions you can't answer?"

"Not so far."

"Why hasn't Alien Nexus Two exploded yet?"

"They have, we just travel back in time to near the time of first collision between Brane 'A' and Brane 'B' when we cross the light barrier surrounding them. When our Universes touched for the first time they went into a stasis time loop immediately. Your going there may be the trigger that causes them to enter more linear time again and explode."

"So our perception of them as already floating around the Mothership as individuals is more correct than the world I visited and we are returning to now?

"Exactly."

"Are you the boss in there? You tell them when to jump down if they aren't needed, right?"

"We all take turns being the boss, the forty-one others you saw were the High Council in charge of Relativity and Perception. I just do my job of correlating all information, experts and defined fields of Knowledge, that's all. But I do have a lot of power and influence."

"Why are you in such a tiny office?"

"They only had a bit of room left when I joined them; I'm not getting any more popular either. I have to make sure that logical constraints apply to the actuality of the collected data."

"They collect the data that you correlate?"

"They may enter the physical world each night in your dreams, or be born as men in your world, some of them come to us for the first time out of the Foam Mountains; they wade out in a state of dissolution and confusion, the result of negative psychic experiences and drugs in the real world. They lose the original power of Soliton after being in the foam, and we convert them into Grey Men with our construct of Knowledge. They leave at night to observe the physical world in which you live, and return each morning with new facts to enter in the database."

"Why do you collect the data? What are you looking for?"

"We collect the data because it is there to be collected."

"Oh."

They walk on in silence for a little longer.

"I promised that I would return by a different route. Is this the reason that Alien Nexus Two explodes?"

"I can't answer that."

"I thought you knew everything."

"I know what data we have collected and the unknowable, but not what lies in between them. I can make predictions and guess around, and I think that you are probably right, you cause the energy imbalance that ends the time loop for them."

"I need to contact them now, so we can stop the spread of time-travel and alt-world influence from falling into irresponsible hands; if we weren't in such dire straights I would forget my promise and stay away."

"I know."

Finally after a very long walk they came up to where the ship lay on the grass.

Garth and his daemonic little grey companion prepared to embark on the last trip anyone would take to the Upper Nexus world. Satan turned to Garth and pointed out onto the plain, where some cartoon birds had landed. "Look, a flock of Zeit-geese has landed, they must have come from the Tooniverse and walked out of the foam. They leave a path of shit wherever they go, they don't stick to their guns either, and you can't get them to explain why they have changed their minds either. We no longer see eye to eye." The cartoon birds waked past the duo, and you could see that they had short black head hair above round spectacled goose faces, and exuded an air of superiority and detached maliciousness.

"We are misunderstood!" One of the Zeit-geese called out in a loud rabble-rousing voice.

"The future need us, but don't ask how we are going to get there, or what really has happened along the way." Another replied.

"We are partly right, admit it!" A goose had stopped in front of the daemonic Grey Man.

"O.K., you are partly right." He admitted grudgingly. "But we still don't see eye to eye, you exaggerate, manipulate, and have a hidden agenda. I can do much better on my own."

They got in and Garth set the q-ball re-loader to maximum iteration. The tiny robot inside the reflex klystron took the q-ball and transferred it over and over from one part of the machine to the adjoining one, and with each replacement the craft rose higher and higher into the sky above the Dancer off in the near distance. Soon they could see the Rift open above them and some black shapes dart out. The Dark Triangles were heading right for them but soon detoured and went around them without incident. They got closer to the opening and soon were inside the vast Modus Control Center chamber with the hands of the Prisoners of Light sticking out of the ceiling and its bed of stones just before the missing Right Wall, which they had only just enough time to go through before it appeared again as the side of the gorge on Darkworld.

The ship made by Ancient Egypt World science, the most advanced science outside the Nexus Complex, rose up above Darkworld into an inky sky. A few red giant stars appeared in the distance as the alien landscape fell away beneath them. A glowing line appeared in space just ahead. Soon a portal had opened and a tiny man shape was seen falling out of the Veldt doorway. Below them they saw him transforming into the familiar Blackbird shape and speeding off in the direction of the gorge. They quickly rose up through the portal and were in Alien Nexus Two, the upper (predatory) nexus world.

As soon as they were through the opening in the floor of the Veldt region of Alien Nexus Two, they made a wide turn and headed off to the center of the crèche, where the pool of intensity sat beneath our Brane as seen from the outside. Of course it appeared as a gigantic ball of glowing energy, with intensity streaming down to the pool of captured chi. As they grew closer to the light ball and pool they could spot groups of people arranged in circles at regular intervals around the center of the Nexus.

They landed and as they were disembarking Garth spotted the beautiful woman who had been his guide on his last visit there. He ran across the floor of the great hall with columns that extended upwards into the endless void above them.

She was staring back at the stooped little figure of the Grey Man exiting the machine behind him.

"You didn't come alone, and so inevitably upsetting the balance of this place. Why are you here now?"

"I came to ask a favor, advice on how to stop the spread of evil throughout the time-lines. You can help us, right?"

"I can tell you this, we have very little time left to make new decisions here. Soon this plane will end and we will enter a new reality."

"I know, I've seen you from the window."

She gave Garth an annoyed look and continued on, "Who is he, I didn't say you could bring anyone with you. Is he dangerous?"

"He is fine, just a little cranky. You would be amazed at the things this guy could tell you; things that no one else would ever be able to know, he knows."

"Well, she is part of the vast alien conspiracy that has drained our world of chi since the collision billions of years ago." Lucifer has walked up and joined the conversation.

"Well, he is no longer allowed on any of the higher planes, since Yahweh is not interested in the unknowable."

"I also know Good versus Evil."

"What is the point of that, we just do whatever we need to do for ourselves; as anyone should."

Ominously a horn was heard to blow from the direction of the pool. It was the Archangel Gabriel signaling the end of the world. "What is your name?" Garth realized he had never asked.

"My name is One." Garth stands with glazed eyes for a moment looking right through the seductive and thinly clad One.

"You must prepare to help us, can you do anything before the end?"

"Tell them to evacuate the Veldt, cross into the far Tooniverse, whatever will preserve some continuity." Lucifer has butted in.

"Come with me in my ship now, we can motivate back to Alexis One after the disaster."

"All right, but keep him at a distance." She looks askance at the little daemon.

From the ramp she turns and screams out, "Send word to the Veldt and Tooniverse border regions, evacuate, and evacuate immediately."

A great distance away the telepathic message has been relayed to both areas. Black shapes begin to pour from the open bomb-bay door of the Veldt; and fast moving Toons race for the far side of the soon to split Universe.

The ball of light above the stone-walled pool expands even more until it just barely touches the rippled surface. A sudden flash as the intensity boils with a flash into steam, while beams of light start to radiate from the exploding sphere toward each individual of Alien Nexus Two.

The circles of people stand and join hands.

A shock wave hits in a vast expansion of all matter

except the people of Alien Nexus Two, and of course Garth and his crew aboard the Higgs craft.

The shock-wave hits the outer sphere of light where the prisoners are stuck, blowing them back through the ceiling of the Modus Control Center, and the same thing happens in the other symbiotic Brane Rifts of earlier Universes.

All around them they can see the lines of light radiating from the expanding Brane "A", picking up the steam of the boiled chi and delivering it to the circles of people waiting for the transformation.

The walls fly away, the vast columns have crumbled and dissolved. All the circles of people go flying outward; including the ship and its crew.


Garth looks out through the view-screen at the scene around the ship.

They are floating in an endless void, except it is filled with circles of people floating at regular intervals in groups of between twenty to a hundred individuals.

The people have been forced to let go of each other's hands by the violence of the explosion, but are still in their original circles. They all are in orbit around the distantly visible mass of Alexis One, as it hovers above the highest peak of the mountain range on the other side of the coin that is the Dancer's plain. Each individual is in a micro-orbit around the center of gravity of the entire circle; and the circles themselves are arranged in clusters, super-clusters, lines, and radiating spokes.

Garth's ship has upset the balance. Some of the closer

beings have begun to fall toward the relatively huge mass of the ship and its crew. Garth tries to remedy this situation with small bursts of motivation from the q-ball transfer mechanism. He succeeds in placing one man back in his circle by letting him fall toward the ship, using the gravity tug effect. A second individual is too close and lands with a thump on the outside of the ship. Garth increases the ship's speed until he can clear the main body of the nearest cluster, and makes a long trajectory to Alexis One. He opens the airlock and looks out into "space". It is just like the inside of the ship. The man is there and comes into the airlock.

He is a guy named Dave. Dave names the other guys in his circle, Ted, Bob, Jeb, Tom, Dick, Harry, Peter, John, Willie, Dan, Jock, Jimmy, Bobby, and the others. There had been about twenty in all; Garth thinks that he has probably put back the one they called Willie successfully.

They cruise around the outside of the vast Mothership, and Garth is reminded that the outside is really the inside edge, the real outside is the foam that lies in the plain on the other side from the towering mountains.

So in a sense the beings floating in the far-flung halo surrounding the Mothership are all in a vast doughnut hole. The modus reversal is evident in other ways as well; the Darkworld crèche had been inside a Rift in an attached dimension, but as seen from normal space it seemed to surround the Nexus. Garth wondered what had happened to it now that the Veldt was gone.

We don't have to wonder, via the power of this story we can take a look right now.

As the craft that had brought Garth to the Veldt entered into the Nexus Plane a tiny figure transformed into a Blackbird and flew off toward the gorge and the entrance to the Rift. But part way there it rapidly transformed into a strange little character and landed with a skidding stop just outside a towering ancient fortress. He is a comical little Toon, a black duck with a human-like body. One other thing about the diminutive duck is obvious; he has a zombie arm, leg and half of his face.

Far out in space above our lonely duck a transformation has taken place; the pocket of space surrounding Darkworld has been ruptured. Now instead of just one entrance near the robot gold mines and world of Ground in Brane 'B', it also has a hole into our Brane, just outside of Earth's orbit. The force of the explosion of Alien Nexus Two has re-opened Darkworld to the outer Multi-verse.

You may recall that the crèche had been entirely closed by the strange accident that occurred when Garth had tried to move his ship directly from Darkworld to Alien Nexus Two in one go.

Now Darkworld was poised to become a new pathway for travel from one Brane to the other, and the plot thickens considerably. One other feature of the crèche was new, inside the tiny closed-off egg of space-time a wormhole had formed. So now it was a three-holed space pocket, like an apple with the core removed and a tiny track of a mysterious worm. The worm had eaten a path from inside to outside, but the outside was in space just above the control room of Alexis One.

The gigantic end of Alien Nexus Two had worked other changes, the ceiling of the Rift was now far, far above the floor; and no hands protruded from it at all. The Prisoners of Light had all been blown back into the Rift chamber. They now sat at a long table and described their ordeal, the feeling of immobility, the intense thirst, and the occasional small sip of water from the Archangel who served all of them one by one.

When the Veldt had been evacuated a steady stream of Dark Triangles or Blackbirds had paralyzed the Modus Control Center for a very long time; at least an hour had passed with the right hand wall dematerialized. The majority of the Blackbirds had immediately sought out long-term incarnation on the Earth plane. A few had formed into a flying wedge and spent their time cruising the skies above the plain. A large cadre had landed on the grass and sat immobile. They would occasionally take off in groups of two to five and make the journey into Darkworld and back, taking about five minutes to complete the round trip and land. The sky patrol eventually joined the parked triangles and was replaced by a new group. The War was still off; it looked like now for good.

The Dancer had tried to prevent the mass exodus into the lower worlds through the hole in the plain he guarded; but the vast numbers involved soon overwhelmed his efforts. Some of the Blackbirds lay in ruins on the grass and he would occasionally lift one to his mouth and eat it, although he seemed to already bulge at the middle and move a bit sluggishly. He had indeed eaten a big meal, and there was no shortage of his usual food to be predicted in the near future.

The view from Alexis One had one difference, although the halo of beings from Alien Nexus Two was still the same, it now rotated around the Mothership in a swirling motion caused by the tiny craft that had brought Garth, Lucifer, One and Dave to that plane. The circles of people rotated around and around, interacting sometimes and occasionally one being would fall entirely out of orbit and go racing past Alexis One on his way to the far side; to eventually collide with the Dancer.

When this happened he would open his mouth just in time and eat the speeding meteoric being. Then the former Dark Angel would become a new Grey Man and be capable of visiting the Earth plane; but not just at night as the regular Grey Men did, he would spend a whole lifetime collecting data.

On board Alexis One things had changed a lot. The Tooniverse was slightly less than half as big as it had been before, with the Bubble-house forming the farthest extent of its reaches; unlike before when it had been at the exact center.

There was a circle near the one that Dave had come from, and they were the ones most affected by the passage of Garth's ship on its way to Alexis One. The main character of this circle was named Joe; he was just a regular guy you know. He had a friend whose name was Fred; he was the one who wasn't dead. Another guy's name was Sam; he was the one who hated spam. Another man's name was Ed; he was a bit touched in the head. One of the guys was known as Davie, he was the one whose memory was hazy. In any rate they all turned round, and round, and round; and eventually, could not be found.

The men had simply vanished soon after their rotation had increased to a certain rate. This was similar to the 'quantum jump' effect in that they were emitted from the state they were in toward a higher energy state, a mysterious new level not known of before.

Later on it would be revealed that the men had evolved quickly to an existence that was far beyond any known in the multi-verse(s). They had gone beyond the limits of perception into a state of unknowingness, although still theoretically knowable somehow.

So we have Garth and his crew, the missing men from the Halo, and the little duck character. Oh, and also some "real" zombies, Dark Triangles, a giant robot full of little men, a Mothership run by Grey Aliens, and a world full of people who routinely practice telepathy, precognition and directed dreaming as a social networking tool. Throw into that the scheming Dictator trying to overturn the course of time and reality and the mysterious extinct Alien Race that initially created man on Darkworld before the rupture rendered it unsuitable for evolving life to stay sane.

And then there was Roger. Roger was a special case in that he had become a Soliton directly upon being killed in his lab accident of 2061. He had not evolved into his immortality from a lower state gradually as required of most sentient life up until then. Due to the fact that he has visited Alexis One more than once, Roger has multiplied into several selves there.

He is now four distinct beings with individual memories; three of them are Grays and one is Human.

Roger #1 arrives after his lab accident with no former memories besides those of being a human. He takes a saucer ride through a wormhole back to Roswell, New Mexico in 1947. He uses his wrist-radio to transport himself back in time to Arthurian England, where he poses as Merlin. He lives through the ages until he can talk to himself just before his fatal lab accident; but is unable to convince his human self. He gets back to Alien Nexus One as both Roger #3 and Roger #4.

Roger #2 has an epiphany (due to the accident confirming that what Roger #1 had told him was true) when killed in 2061, stays human on Alexis One, travels back to 1947 Roswell, joins the 2163 expedition to Ground, meets Garth again on Darkworld, and arrives back on Earth with Garth 24 hours after Garth's mission started.

Roger #3 was originally created by an event that was later nullified; his timeline no longer exists. He still does though. He is Gray.

Roger #4 is the result of Roger #3's timeline having been cancelled. He is Roger #1 except that he remembers his trip back to Earth and his return to Alexis One by 2163 scientists. He is a Gray.

So right now a Roger who remembers reading a history of himself (while on Alien Nexus One) different from his own future memories of the events lives in the 21st century.

On board Alexis One a different Roger reads about him, he is the Roger whose timeline no longer exists. This Roger has a realization that the history of his own time-line was terminated by his return to Alien Nexus One by a group of scientists at a vastly different experiment than the one that now was the ancestor of Alexis One. It had shrunk from a remembered 1500 km in diameter to a mere 250 km.

Spare Roger did some research about his former timeline. Apparently he would have been erased with it if 2163 scientists had not sent him back to Alien Nexus One. The reset button had modified his exit point from linear time, so that he could not return to that exact reality again. That world still existed as a frozen moment in time, but no complete paths from there to Alexis One existed since the "reset".

He decides to take his Mark IV Grayship for a little cruise back to the Roswell end of a certain wormhole he remembered, and see if he could get his old timeline back on track. As he approached the spot where the wormhole would pick him up he had a brief moment of doubt. What if the Universe was somehow not able to handle such direct meddling in its internal affairs? He dismissed the idea as needless paranoia and made the entrance of the space anomaly.

Instead of the skies of nighttime Earth Roger saw the dull red glow of a few giant old stars as he emerged from the other end of the wormhole. Somehow he had been transported to the Darkworld crèche. He wasn't there long before he was aware that he was being sucked into a second wormhole. This one dumped him unceremoniously onto the top of the Control Room bubble windows of the Alexis One observation area. An attendant let him in. As 'he was walking back to his living quarters he felt a strange sensation and inexplicably he was back at the controls of his Grayship just as it entered the wormhole in the Darkworld crèche. Again he passed through the wormhole and fell onto the observation bubble. His ship had vanished, just like the first time. He was back at the controls, tried to avoid the wormhole entrance, and failed. He circled the Mothership at a distance of about sixty feet. He swerved and fought the ship as it entered the wormhole again, and again, and again, in an endlessly repeating cycle. He was multiplied into at first a few hundred selves, then thousands of cycles had happened, then millions. Billions of Rogers fought the ship controls, entered the wormhole, and became new incarnations upon reaching Alexis One. After about a trillion tries he managed to pass in front of the wormhole entrance in the Darkworld crèche and avoid being sucked in. This leads to the creation of the final and most mysterious Roger, Roger #5. He is still on Darkworld. The damage had been done; he had multiplied into enough Rogers to fill several small galaxies inside the Gray crèche.

### ~Darkworld Duck

You may recall that the last person to leave the crèche as Garth's ship was approaching the entrance to the Veldt was a strange little Toon with a bit of zombie blood in him. He had started life as an ordinary baby born to normal parents in Nairobi, Kenya. He entered the world in 1937, the same year that a popular cartoon character was created by artists at a famous studio in California. A brane collision had exchanged parts of him with a zombie from Darkworld, but the collision continued, exchanging him again with a Soliton from Alien Nexus Two.

His original birth would never have occurred, except that fate intervened. It would have been prevented by the failure of his parents to meet, but a storm that was due to rain on their parade moved off just in time to allow it. The storm was the same one mentioned earlier in the butterfly story, Synchronicity. One's sacrifice had led directly to the birth.

He has been the only being so far to have suffered a partial exchange of parts of his body and soul with other beings in the ongoing brane collision. He is now part zombie and part Soliton. Soon he travelled to the Tooniverse and decided to change his appearance, to that of a cartoon duck character from his newly squired zombie self. His motivation to change into a Toon was to try to remove the zombie part of himself, but it is the only part unaffected by his transformation. He is now forever part Toon, part zombie, much to his disappointment.

He decides to leave and goes back to Darkworld, and as he touches down he changes from the Dark Triangle form he had used to travel there back into the zombie duck character. A strange sensation grips him and he assumes the persona of Darkworld Duck.

Looking up to the towering pile of decaying rubble of the ancient stone fortress, he wonders aloud, "I wonder if anyone is home right now?"

He starts to climb up the winding path that winds its way to a high gate. As he is making his way up the path a gigantic roaring sound is heard throughout the mountain pass, and looking back in the direction from which he came he sees the skies of perpetual twilight filled with the menacing black shapes of millions upon millions of Dark Triangles.

"Looks like someone left the door open."

He continues to climb until he stands before the gigantic portcullis of the high gate.

"Funny, no doorbell."

He walks through the ruins of the gate, and is soon ascending a winding stair inside the tower. As he nears the top of the tower he hears a shuffling sound, and far away a muffled scream is cut short. Coming out into the main hall atop the tower he sees that an ancient throne is occupied by a lonely figure of an armor-suited warrior, and on his head sits a crown of gold. A golden ring rests on his mailed finger.

"Who dares to accost me in mine own castle?"

"It is I, your eminence, Darkworld Duck!"

"Darkworld Duck? Never heard of you!"

"Well, I'm kinda new, haven't really done anything yet, but just watch me!"

With that Darkworld Duck runs up to the seated figure of menace and seizes the ring from his hand, accidentally removing the finger with it.

"I have you now," He screams; "Oops, I guess you can have this back." He removes the ring from the offending finger and flings the sorry digit back at the Dark One.

"I will have my revenge, Darkworld Duck!"

"Not if I can help it!"

Darkworld Duck runs behind the throne as the Dark One looks for his finger and re-attaches it with a sickening popping and crunching sound. He is waiting for the Dark One and clobbers him over the head with an unlit torch, knocking him unconscious. Deciding that he needs a disguise, he strips the armor from the rotting flesh of the zombie king and puts it on.

Taking a running start, he leaps from the tower window as he transforms into a Dark Triangle. He flies off in the direction of the sparsely inhabited lowland region bordering the dying ocean. The perpetual twilight is lit by one or two distant red giant suns, which hang low in the dim and dull sky. He circles around and lands close to a small group of ramshackle huts that dot the shoreline. Walking up to the closest one he knocks on the door and calls out, "Is anyone in there? I have need of shelter and sustenance."

A curious little face pokes out the empty window frame and soon withdraws with an exclamation of dismay.

Darkworld Duck pounds on the door harder and demands to be admitted.

The door swings open and he enters, to see a few cowering urchins in rags and ugly sores huddled in the corner.

"Take what you want, oh Dark Lord!"

"What I want is for you to stop calling me Dark Lord, call me Dark for short."

"Yes, Mr. Dark; Sir."

"Darkworld actually."

"Yes it is Sir."

"No, I mean my name is Darkworld."

"You are King of the planet, Sir."

"I am Darkworld Duck, raconteur and scallywag to the Universe, make that the Multi-verse; and I have no catch-phrase."

"No catch-phrase? What kind of a Super-hero (You are a super-hero? – Yes) doesn't have a catch-phrase?"

"Well I am really new."

"O.K." The urchin zombies look around uncomfortably.

"I've got it! My catch-phrase will be 'Destiny and Beyond'."

"Destiny and Beyond", the tiny urchins echo.

"Or, or... 'Destiny Beyond Darkworld'."

"I liked the first one better."

"O.K.... how about 'Darker than the Dark One, Darkworld Duck'."

"It would sound better the other way around: 'Darkworld Duck, Darker than the Dark One'."

"What about the 'Destiny' part?" one urchin quips.

"You should put that part back in somehow." Another chimes in.

We leave our hero and his new retinue to deliberate the value of certain words and exact emphasis and zoom back out into space, through the re-opened neck of the Darkworld crèche and circle above the robot gold mine planet just outside it in Andromeda, Brane 'B'.

It seems that a certain Dictator of an unnamed 21st century rouge state had managed to transport himself to an Alt World, and he had been lucky enough to land right at an abandoned transport-landing site. He was there to get gold and to facilitate an invasion of his own home planet. He intended to be a traitor to his own race and doom Mankind to an eternity of slavery, just to advance his own diabolical plans for World domination.

His first success had come when he had received a response to a message carried by an unmanned trans-dimensional probe his backward and hostile nation had managed to send. The message had asked for help in designing a manned version of the probe, the premise being that the dictator's world was doomed to destruction and he wanted to preserve his family. Soon the response came, allowing him access to plans for a life support version of the probe. He faked his way through the center of gravity stop in the basement of Alexis One, and the Lady of the Lakes was obligated to send him on to his desired destination. Now he was poised to collect his zombie army and cruise back to Earth in an abandoned Alien transport, through the recently created new hole in the Darkworld crèche. You may recall that now the crèche had two entrances, one to brane 'b' in Andromeda, and one to brane 'a' near Earth.

His helpers had given him a design that would be good for a small trans-ship that could at most support two or three people. He abandoned it when he reached the robot gold mine planet just outside the Darkworld crèche in Andromeda. This planet had been an outpost of Darkworld before the Aliens had vanished, and the descendants of the human race they had created on Darkworld had fled to Alien Nexus Two. The vanished Aliens themselves were a mystery, they had left no traces of themselves to be found; only their creations went on to populate Ground, Earth and the Nexus Worlds.

They were the Crugs, and they were an intentional mystery to the later Universe; but we may take a peek at them through the magik of this tale. In a way you could say they were an incredibly ugly race, they greeted each other by gently biting each other on the 'face'. Their faces were reptilian in nature, with long jaws and many sharp teeth. Two large eyes were set above the snout, the eyes of a gigantic squid. Further back on the slug-like bodies a couple of pseudo-pod tentacles protruded from what must have been the shoulder region. Beneath the slug-like main body's surface a carapace of internal armor formed the being's internal exoskeleton. Six insect legs jutted down from the lower part of the body, connected to the rigid bug skeleton inside, which contained its internal organs. Behind the legs a short, fat tail completed the creature.

The Crugs had evolved in a different way than most other intelligent life in the Universe, as they found moving about a bit awkward, to say the least. They communicated telepathically, and mostly were loners in nature. This was due to the fact that they felt compelled to bite quite hard when greeting a fellow Crug, and this was a source of anguish and embarrassment for them. Also they really were not very fast on their feet, as they were a bit top-heavy and lurched about in a jerky swaying motion when they walked. Therefore they had soon developed the ability to shift themselves by teleporting short distances around their world, and socialized rarely. They were secretive and shy.

The evolution of the Crugs had led to them shifting their reality to a more copacetic dimension, where physical bodies were no longer required, good for them.

The Dictator emerged from the Alien transport vessel at the Darkworld spaceport, and looked around. He didn't see the zombie army that he wanted to use to invade Earth.

Walking around the ruins and habitable area of the spaceport, he realized that a few zombies were around still. They had been hiding in the ruins just outside the spaceport's functional area and preying on stragglers.

The dictator set up a post to wait for the return of the zombies, and after a few days he was pleased to see about ten zombies coming back to their hiding spot. He jumped out of his concealment and held the zombies at gunpoint.

"Do you see this, it is a weapon. I can kill you all if I want."

"What want?"

"I want you to take me to your leader."

So the Dictator made the crossing of the open desert with the zombie clan to see the Dark One at his fortress near the gorge where the Blackbirds flew on their way to Alien Nexus Three.

The Dark One was not doing so great. He had come to be reliant upon the armor and his magic ring to bolster his position among the zombies who were his slaves. The ring gave him the power to compel others to do his will, and the armor had power to preserve him from more decay. He was losing the battle to hold onto dominance. His one true focus was to get them back, and kill Darkworld Duck.

The zombies themselves were of three distinct types.

The first type had already eaten human flesh, specifically the brains of a normal human. They exhibited less intelligence than the other two types, and were the slaves of the Dark One. They had dry, rotting flesh where the zombie virus had made sores, and had lost most extremities such as the nose, fingers and toes.

The second type were just like he first except that they had less advanced sores, and they had not yet eaten human flesh, as they were still children.

The third type was more dangerous. They were zombies like the Dark One. He had performed certain rituals before getting infected; rituals that preserved his rotting flesh long after he should have died.

The few people left on Darkworld who were not zombies had arrived there recently aboard the still functioning transports, via the robot-operated gold mine planet. It was a legend in Andromeda that attracted the greedy and foolhardy to their eventual deaths.

The mind numbing fear and lack of intellectual power that permeated the planet affected everyone, but it took a while to have its full effect, so that child zombies were smarter than adults, who could only function in a rudimentary way. Visitors from elsewhere were slowly driven insane.

The Dark One and the few other surviving Ritualists

were smarter than the average, but lived in a world of permanent insanity driven to kill all who might still present resistance to their evil.

Obviously time passed more slowly inside the Darkworld crèche than outside, where billions of years had passed during just a few generations on Darkworld.

The zombies still bred, usually just after puberty while they had all their extremities.

A lot of time had passed since the official evacuation orders, on the outside of the crèche; but inside it had been only a few generations. Some of the oldest residents would have been alive when those orders were issued.

Reasons for not evacuating with the rest of the population ranged from lack of interest and belief to religious fanaticism. The Ritualists had clung to a death cult that rewarded cruelty and punished disbelief with instant death. As the mental black hole grew in intensity they tightened their grip on the remaining populace, engaging everyone they found in a mass slaughter seldom seen in the history of any planet. Each believer was assigned a spot in a vast game of death, where only one could win in the very end. The Dark One emerged victorious, with only mindless zombies left, as complete slaves of his evil will.

Darkworld Duck stayed and talked with the young zombies he had found. They debated his catch phrase and variations on it, and made many suggestions, none of them very satisfying to the new hero. He found that the armor was giving him confidence he had not had before. He strutted around for his small companions and put on a bit of a show. He wore the captured ring, which he had been informed was very famous and powerful, with great pride.

"I command all of you to say my catch phrase in unison!"

"Darkworld Duck, Destiny and Beyond The Dark One."

"That's better, but put a little more into it!"

"Darkworld Duck, Destiny and Beyond The Dark One!"

"Yes, yes, Yes! Mu-a, Ha, Ha, Ha Hah!" Darkworld Duck laughs his most evil laugh.

"With this powerful ring, the Soliton Of Samovar, I will compel a vast army to rule this dark planet!"

"Yes, your eminence, you are our new Dark Lord."

They spent their days and nights in conversation and debate, hashed out the "Plan", and generally goofed-off while pretending to be busy. Darkworld Duck was turning into a bit of a sensation among the young zombie set, and in all honesty he loved the notoriety.

"I am the Darkest of all the Dark Lords," he had been heard to say.

The Ring preyed upon his mind. He wanted to use it to summon a vast zombie army to do his bidding, but the "Plan" called for him to wait for an advantageous time to use the Ring. Soon he was consumed by his obsession with the Power of the Ring, and he began to suspect that it would be stolen from him while he slept. He watched the others with suspicion and hid away from his tiny fans.

One morning he awoke to the sound of a struggle just outside his room, and he peeked out just in time to see a gun pointed at his face, held in the hand of the Dictator.

"Now we have you."

"You may think you have me, but you are mistaken.

By the power of the Ring I command you to obey."

"I don't think so, I am very strong willed."

"I command a vast zombie army to come to my aid!"

"That's O.K., let me take that." The Dictator removes the Ring from Darkworld Duck's finger and puts it in his pocket.

"Take him away." A couple of zombie guards jostle up through the crowd of tiny fans and grab Darkworld Duck by the arms. Soon he is stripped of his armor and led away to a portable cage on wheels pulled by a rabble of the castle zombies from the Dark One's fortress.

\*         \*         \*

### Joe's Master Koan Part – 7/A

So the coach was stopped and everyone switched places, and one of the footmen began to tell his story.

"Once in a far off land, where the river of catastrophe empties into the small sea; a cruel Prince reigned over his terrified subjects."

"The Prince was quite tall, with a thin face, high cheekbones and a cruel hawk's beak of a nose. He had thin lips and large ears that stood out from his head. He wore black, except for a large medallion pinned over his heart. He was wont to spend his days reading by candle-light some huge arcane tome written by an ancient sage, with all the windows shuttered fast."

"At night the Prince would go out and ride through the town and surrounding countryside, looking out for signs of wealth, happiness and celebration. He directed his men to confiscate any property he felt had been passed over in the general tax, and he took many a landowner prisoner for tax evasion. Also he was in the habit of taking any fine ladies he found at such establishments, and holding them captive at the castle, where he would have his way with them."

"He had not always been so cruel, as a young lad growing up he had seemed normal, a quiet child with a far-off look in his eye, wandering the wilds alone and discovering natural wonders. But gradually he learned that he felt a sense of power while squishing a small insect or torturing some small creature such as a frog or snake; and he started down the path to the most evil cruelty imaginable."

\*             \*             \*

### ~Bounce - 7

"Well I mean harm, I mean harm a lot!" The hairy rowdy exclaims. Suddenly he produces a weapon from his pocket and points it at them. "Get in! Yeah, this is a gun; you are under arrest. We caught you red-handed, trying to steal our gold. You'll have to come with us and face the accusations of our Lord and Master." The first young punk grimaces, then gestures at them to use the rear door of the hauler. They get in and sit on top of the large blocks of gold piled inside. They hear the door lock and the insane laughter of their captors as the tracks lurch into motion.

Richard seems lost in his thoughts for a couple of

minutes, then he speaks, "this one hauler load is worth one hundred and thirty billion US dollars."

The hauler crawls forward on its massive tracks; at what Richard thinks is a quite good pace, considering the immense weight of its golden cargo. They accelerate very slightly all the time, up to nearly the pace of a trotting horse, and near the entrance to the mine. Suddenly there is shouting back and forth in the cab in front of them, followed by the sound of a door opening and shots being fired at something ahead of them. Richard can now hear a deep roaring sound, like a blast furnace or burst of flame from a hot-air balloon's burner. The hauler is still moving forward at nearly top speed, and crashes into something heavy, throwing it aside.

The hauler bursts through the entrance, and Richard can see something massive above and behind them, reflected in the hauler's side mirror. A gigantic winged shape beats strongly to hover in place, and a burst of flame erupts from its muzzle, engulfing the hauler completely.

"It's the guard Dragon!" One of the toughs is screaming.

"Flick the switch!" He exhorts his companion.

He fumbles under the dashboard for a hastily wired contraption and presses a button frantically. Just up ahead of them a large rectangle of diffuse white light appears, looking like an electric fog inside an invisible container. They roar forward and are engulfed in the sea of energy, and go blind momentarily. When they can see again they see that the sky is a deep azure with ruby highlights, and gritty dust covers the endless desert of the empty plain. They have arrived on Darkworld.

Up ahead a gnarled crag juts up from the desert floor, set amid a series of lumpy foothills. Mountains loom in the murky distance, and as they draw closer they can see the horrifying ruin of a once magnificent castle fortress atop the crag. A gorge with cliffs on one side and the foothills on the other flows out into the desert sand like a long-dead river, and they begin to climb.

The trip is taking hours, as the hauler struggles up over tiny hillocks and up scree-filled gullies toward the low foothills ahead. They move at a very slow pace indeed, thinks Richard, no more rapidly than a brisk walk. Their captors talk quietly to each other or break out in wild laughter occasionally, glancing back to smirk at them through the glass.

It is beginning to get dark, shadows stretching out beside them. At long last the hauler turns sharply and passes down a short road leading to a side entrance at the castle. They lurch to a halt and hear their captors shout to them.

"All right, get out!"

They clamber out of the back, leaving the largest fortune in gold they had ever known of behind. Jen looks longingly at the massive blocks the size of building stones piled neatly inside, and turns away.

Bemis and Smuthead order them to march ahead, and they are taken to a small, dank and cold cell near the back. It stinks, and is dark, with only some rotting straw thrown on the stone floor to sit on. A wooden bucket sits in the corner.

They remain standing, and once Jen screams when something; probably a small rat or other creature, passes through the straw unseen to them except for its movement.

They stand there for quite some time, clinging together

amid the fetid dank atmosphere that stinks of every former prisoner's body odor and excretions. Soon Richard gets irritated and gently pushes Jen away. "I am going to use that bucket to relieve myself, and I ask you to forgive me."

"Is that our only fresh water?" She asks.

"I wouldn't drink it," he replies.

Richard moves over to where the bucket is in the corner and soon we hear the strained sound of his little tinkle splash into the only available water around them. As he is almost finished a zombie guard shows up outside their cell to summon them into the presence of the Dark One.

"That is your only drinking water." The guard is matter of fact and surly, although as he's a zombie it's quite hard to tell.

The guard unlocks the cell and ushers them out, directing them to walk ahead of him back out the way they had come in earlier. Up a winding stair they climb, Richard counts one hundred risers before they reach what must once have been a grand and magnificent throne room in some bygone age. On a massive throne they see a figure all clad in absolutely black armor, a red glint barely detectable through the narrow eye slit.

Before the Dark One addresses them, he does something that he had rarely done in the past. Reaching up, he raises the visor covering his once human face, revealing it in all its gory detail. There is no nose; a ghastly scar bisects the area from top to bottom, showing only two dark holes flat against his "face" for nostrils. He has no lips to speak of, and his teeth are rotting stumps set in swollen and black gums. His eyes sink back into his skull like twin coals, a fierce hatred fire from hell burning in his gaze.

Jen screams and moans, almost collapsing then and there, but manages to hang onto consciousness somehow. Richard coughs nervously.

"You are trespassers and thieves, or would have stolen the gold if we had not caught you. I find you guilty, and sentence you to be fed to the Dragons. They are a fierce and proud people, and will not look kindly on you for invading their planet, which you must know is forbidden territory for your kind. I have only one question for you, before I send you to be devoured or simply roasted, or maybe perhaps crushed and lacerated in a giant claw, or it could be probable that your head will be bitten off. That would be quick, at least. But my question, have you seen my gold ring?"

The Dark One points to the spot on his finger where he used to wear The Ring.

"No, Sir."

"Too bad."

"That's a shame." Jen nods at her husband's sentiment, and all three look down for a moment.

"You know," the Dark One said, "The One Ring, the Soliton of Samovar; it originated on your planet."

"Really?" Richard sounds somewhat unconvinced.

"Yes, believe it or not it did! It was a torus of material from the famous Cintamani Stone, of which the Blarney and Scone Stones were made, and the Grail was carved from a chunk as well. The Cintamani Stone was Jacob's pillow stone, and had been an enchanted meteorite that came from the planet Zarnoth. And don't forget the tablets upon which the Ten Commandments were first carved. All Cintamani Stone. The Ring was dipped in molten gold, and once belonged to King

Solomon of Judea."

"Guards, take them away to be fed…" Just then a disturbance is heard, voices being raised and smashing and crashing sounds drawing closer.

"It is I, Darkworld Duck; Onwards then past the Dark One. I mean, 'Destiny and Beyond the Dark One'."

"That is a motto full of conceit and hubris!" The Dark One is livid.

"Dick and Jane, I am here to rescue you. You must cling to my back while I fly you out of here."

"My name is Jen." She stares at the diminutive cartoon duck doubtfully, wondering how to hold on to such a small creature.

"I prefer Richard." Dick states as he confidently grabs the little black half zombie and wraps himself around the now shaky legged fellow. "Come on." He extends his arms to his wife.

She joins him draped over the tiny creature's back and he begins to take a few steps, trying to break into the required trot for his transforming leap. "We're all going to have to run." Darkworld Duck continues, "Leap onto my back as we flee!"

They all run away from the Dark One as he sits on his throne, and as they leap upon the tiny Toon's back, he transforms into a Dark Triangle and soars out of the open window. They cling to his back for dear life, as he roars off down the gorge, back the way they came. Soon they come to the towering cliff face, and see an opening form in the side, and three Dark Triangles like the one they are on come through it, and fly right past them. They zoom through the opening before it can close, and through a lounge type area filled with busy workers. Jen thinks some of them are nude, but isn't sure. They make a hard left and leave the surprised nudists to their duties.

As they exit the enclosed area, they see a nearly infinite green plain very far below them, with low clouds just above it. They are at a tremendous altitude, and see that there are nude people flying up in their general direction. The Dark Triangle swerves and the couple has to cling harder to remain aboard their strange conveyance. They begin a long evasive maneuver, swinging in a wide arc around the big hole in the plain and descending gradually to land far from the giant man-bot who defends it. He starts running in their direction, throwing something that he sprays from a canister into his hand. "If that stuff hits you it freezes you and he eats you." Darkworld Duck has changed back into his Toon self.

"Get us out of here!" Jen is insistent and over her fainting spell from before.

"Yes Sir, Mam!" They all run and the couple jump back on to the transforming Toon as before.

They soar back up in a long climbing loop, coming around to the heading needed to enter the Rift. Soon it glows to life as several nude flyers exit the Modus Control Center. They fly in and everything stops for a second, as jaws drop and tasks are forgotten. Darkworld Duck transforms from his Dark Triangle self back into his Toon self. People pretend to go back to their normal activities, but all eyes are still fixed on the unusual trio.

"What are we doing here?" Jen is checking out the people around her, pretending not to be looking for the obvious, and soon is relieved to notice that most of the crew is wearing "nude-look" leotards or bodysuits of lycra or some such fabric.

"We are here to gain entry to Alexis One's Control Room. After we get there, we can see the rest of Alien Nexus One, even the Tooniverse, where a new Rift has opened directly to your Earth city New York."

"How do we get access to the Control Room?"

"We ask."

Almost at once a female officer of the crew comes up to them, and makes some gesture that Richard discerns was their version of a salute. She has rather large breasts.

"What is it that you require?" she asks.

"We seek return to Earth in 2063, via your Control Room and path through the Tooniverse Rift." Darkworld Duck says.

"That is a bit early, don't you think?" She frowns. "I don't recall that we can send you back that early."

"Can't you?" Jen asks.

"Maybe," Big Breasts replies.

"Can you or can't you?" Jen is incensed.

"No need to get snippy!" They square off.

"I will allow you to pass through the high level entrance to Alexis One only on condition that you learn how to fight me right now!" Big Breasts has struck up the classic Charlie's Angels karate stance versus Jen's frail frame.

"I accept your challenge!" Jen drops down into a monkey stance, then spins clumsily around and flails at the air with her hind leg.

"You need more intensity." Big Breasts taunts her.

Jen runs screaming and launches herself at her stacked opponent, but Big Breasts grabs her by the wrists and hurls her toward the ceiling, with its many pairs of hands protruding down.

She has an impossible flight, rising higher and higher. For a moment she can just barely reach up and grasp a pair of hands. She lets go and floats back down to near the floor, and lands atop her opponent's shoulders. Her adversary quickly spins around several times, finally cartwheeling until Jen releases her and is sent flying upward once again.

This time when Jen nears the ceiling hands she gets a firm grip on a likely looking pair, and wills herself to absorb as much intensity as possible. Maintaining her grip a moment longer, at last she must release her hold and launch herself down, back into the confrontation with Big Breasts. She sees Jen coming and grabs her in a full nelson just at the last moment, spinning around and capturing Jen's momentum. They are sent spinning around, not touching the floor, as Jen has somehow acquired anti-gravitational properties.

"So do you want to go to Alexis One Control Room?" Big Breasts asks.

"Yes." Jen has been subdued.

Just then a Dark Triangle bursts into the Modus Control Center, from the sky above Alien Nexus Three. The wall on the right hand side of the crèche fails to de-materialize, and pandemonium breaks out. A klaxon horn begins sounding, and an emergency announcement begins over the public address system.

"Warning, impact immanent. Warning, impact immanent. Warning, impact immanent. Warning, impact …"

"Someone shut that off, please," Big Breasts orders.

The Dark Triangle assumes the shape of a human, and what a shape! One stands looking at the other two women, and a slight smile plays about her lips.

"You are aware that the hands must be missing, right?"

They look up, and the pairs of hands that had transferred enough intensity into Jen's tiny frame to levitate her off of the floor are missing.

"They come and they go, more evidence that our Branes are still bouncing off of each other. We are not precisely lined up in time with each occurrence. Time is bunched up or stretched out when our branes hit."

Suddenly One produces three long and sharp swords from behind her back, and throwing one to each of the other women, states, "You both must fight me as our branes are in conflict, and you have caused the end of my world!"

The three women squat in stance and wave the dangerous weapons overhead, and then Jen asks, "Wait a minute, are we on the same side now?" She points back and forth between herself and Big Breasts.

"It doesn't matter, just fight!"     Big Breasts is exasperated.

Jen is still floating a couple of inches from the floor, and is having trouble maneuvering. She gets one foot down and pushes off, floating up halfway to the ceiling. The two others close and exchange blows; grunting and making other ridiculous fight sounds like a couple of girls. Jen floats head down in the middle and parries them both, staying out of reach above them.

"I just want the gold!" Jen emphasizes each word with a stroke of her sword.

Richard and Darkworld Duck are sitting in lawn chairs

eating popcorn, and Richard chimes in with his mouth full, "The gold, stolen from us by the Dark One!"

A wave of intensity passes through the Center, and the very air seems to bunch and stretch, shuddering as the waveform collision occurs. Looking up, the trio of Kung-Fu fighters see that the hands are back in the ceiling again.

One launches herself at Big Breasts, and upon delivering a great blow with her sword on her opponent's, flies straight up to grasp a hand, clutching her sword with the other. A bolt of fire shoots from the tip of her weapon, while her eyes roll back in her head like a mental patient undergoing electro-shock treatment.

Richard and Darkworld Duck high-five each other from their lawn-chairs and stuff their faces with popcorn, glued to the action.

The beam of fire reflects off of a polished surface on the deck, and strikes Darkworld Duck, transforming him back into a Dark Triangle. The klaxon sounds again.

"Warning, impact immanent. Warning, impact immanent. Warning, impact immanent. Warning, impact …"

Darkworld Duck accelerates out of his lawn-chair straight up, as a new gravity wave of intensity makes the air wobble. The hands vanish from the ceiling, and a second later the hapless Toon smashes a hole in it.

\*            \*            \*

### Joe's Master Koan Part - 7/B

"As the Prince, he ruled the land and decided the punishments for those he found guilty."

"For small infractions he would have a pinky finger cut off, or perhaps an ear. For more serious offences, attention was paid to harming the lower regions. A favorite way to execute a condemned man was to sit the victim across a triangular beam, and hang great weights on each leg, until one was ripped off. When a rebellion was crushed in his land, an example was made of the prisoners by throwing them off of the castle walls onto a forest of pikes placed below. And still he had not reached the pinnacle of cruelty. This punishment was reserved for those he considered as heretics against the faith, and he took their punishment to a frightening extreme. Let it be said that it would not be fair to... you, or our fair travel companions, to describe those punishments, which all involved something we must all do daily, and the eventual impossibility of remaining alive for those so punished." Thus he ended his tale and looked expectantly to the host.

"Yes, quite good; most correct! You have spared us the gory details just in time, good work!" The next footman eagerly prepared to tell his own story, and presently he began.

"My story begins as we approach a once famous destination for pilgrims and religious travelers, from the time when the wisdom of the Lord had been brought to all the heathen lands. The road wound through the ragged mountains, higher and higher to where the abandoned ruins lay."

"A high waterfall fell off of the plateau above the crumbling temple mount, and mist lay in an olive wreath about the feet of the decaying towers and high columns of the holy place. A lone light still shone from a lamp kept lit since Prometheus suffered in chains on the shores of a vanished sea. Inside the alter was tended by one lone monk, and a dark stair led down to mysterious depths behind him."

"Many pilgrims had come over the years to have their fortunes told by the old monk, or to be cured of various ailments."

"Beneath the alter room a labyrinth of chambers and tunnels filled the ancient temple mound, and strange gods and goddesses were worshipped there. The bones of many an ancient king lay buried within, and strange creatures roamed or lurked in its shadows."

"There was one special chamber at the heart of the moldering mound of crumbling stone, where huge crystal beakers bubbled with unknown concoctions; alchemy most foul and uncharted influences prevailed."

"A soldier, grievously wounded and with a dying gasp; did perchance stumble on his last legs to the monk within, and thus expired. But the lone monk, with his wiles and cursed arts, did raise him up again with the aid of three things. They were: the fount of youth waters, electrification by a thunderous flash of lightning, and the fresh brain of a newly killed monkey. By arcane arts and incantations the monk healed the great warrior, but afterward he maintained a fondness for bananas, and a fear of storms for the rest of his life."

"Yes, yes! It is droll! You have cured us of a serious mood with your foolish tale! Next!"

\*              \*              \*

The zombies pull strongly, encouraged by the Dictator's exhortations and the presence of the Ring on its way back to its true Master. They trudged across the vast desert of the abandoned Planet where the Crugs an eon ago had first created man. The sand blew and got in everyone's underwear, except for the zombies, who had long since abandoned this garment in their new wardrobe. After a few weeks they were back at the Fortress beside the Gorge. A kind of Twilight hung in the air, as a plaintive wailing of Dark Winds started in the middle distance, fading out into a long rising screech and suddenly cutting off. The setting was perfect for the next scene, where Darkworld Duck stands in front of the Dark One and is sentenced for his crimes.

"You, Darkworld Duck, are found guilty of the crimes of Assault upon the Royal Person, Theft of the Samovar of Soliton, itself punishable by death, and also of extreme Treason and Desecration for removing the Royal Armor after the Vow of Undead Ritualists had been performed, in essence violating my undead rest."

Darkworld Duck stared over at the Dark One in a dazed way, then brightened up. "You are the kinky one, aren't you? You are like dead already or something, but more like a mummy of a vampire than a zombie mummy in armor."

"You are sentenced, Darkworld Duck, to an eternity as my slave in the Dungeon of this Castle."

Our zombie duck cross is led away by a couple of purebred zombies. He is taken to a door and put inside a vast empty cavern under the castle. There is one window far up on the side of the cavern wall. He is taken and chained by a ten-foot length of chain to the floor ring beside the door.

So we leave our diminutive little hero chained in the Dark One's dungeon and fly up through the castle and out into space above the surface of Darkworld, where the Rift in this plane once led to Alien Nexus Two. It now was a path from Andromeda to Earth, and the Dictator had used that path in his plan. Now he sat at the controls of a vast transport built by the last culture to rule. It had been used to evacuate the planet and had room for as many zombies as the Dark One could spare, which was a lot. The initial population of Darkworld before the general exodus was far higher than Earth's at any point in its history, and the numerous vagrants abandoned after the fall were the ancestors of the remaining ones. A horde of zombies loaded down the ship, so while the transport was not full of zombies, it was not nearly empty either, and it had been built to evacuate a planet. We fly past the Dictator on his way to conquer Earth and zip back through the other hole in the crèche, and fly over to the alter–ego Earth called Ground. Wally is yet to be born, and the people of Ground know of future events already covered in this work only by their powers of prescient dreaming. The time passes slowly there as we wait for the expedition from 2163 Earth to arrive, but it finally does, and then leaves to travel to the outpost gold mine planet. The sense of time seems reversed outside the crèche in Andromeda, like Time itself has twisted around and burst through the opening. The real cause of this difference is that there is a new causal relationship between the Darkworld crèche and the Earth, one that couldn't be possible before. Now the order of events as seen by someone from 21st century Earth looked different relative to the order of events in Wally's time on Ground. Physicists like Garth knew that the time frames were skewed due to the fact that the Milky Way and Andromeda were racing toward each other, causing relativistic time effects. Plus time moved very slowly inside the crèche relative to the outside (in Andromeda), but it did not move quite as slowly relative to the outside in the Milky Way.

Bemis and Smuthead were unwilling passengers on the transport vessel that had originally brought them to Darkworld before their trip back to Earth with Garth, and they were uninvited when they arrived at the TRIUMF lab to look around a bit. They were formerly B and E experts before arriving on Darkworld and slowly going insane, but by now had fully recovered their former intelligence and composure. The field that made advanced thinking difficult was localized at the surface of the Bad Place, and its effects were not permanent. They had stolen Dr. Garth's identity code generator, and had made a contact lens with his retina print on it. They had no trouble accessing the secret lab room where a backup of the portable device was kept ready for departure at a moment's notice. They still cackled and gibbered to each other in a comical and insular way, but now the chatter was full of the technical details of cracking the code generator security protocols and fooling the retina scanner. Now they stood inside the room with their ticket back to Darkworld. Their plan was to use the overload method to get to Alien Nexus Three, the Dancer's Plain. Then they planned to enter the Rift high above that world and pass through the missing right hand wall and so pass through into Darkworld. But they had more plans after that. You see they had always been on their way to the Robot Gold Mine Planet to become as rich as anyone could get in that part of Andromeda, when the transport had unexpectedly diverted to Darkworld, where they had been marooned. They planned to motivate all the way to the Gold Mine Planet using the q-ball re-loader device.

Landing on the Robot Gold Mine Planet, they soon were in the process of setting the automatic machinery there at the task of loading their small craft with as much gold as they could possibly carry. Each thought of abandoning the other there so as to fit that much more gold inside; but rejected the idea due to the cynical expression on the others face.

Bemis' expression changed into one of pure wonder and delight as he realized that the pile of decrepit looking machinery in the middle distance was a craft much like the one they had just arrived in, but more primitive.

"Look, Smuthead; we can both load-up and return in our own device!"

Little did they know that engaging both craft in Q-ball transfer in close proximity would have unforeseen consequences.

Now greed began to eat away at Bemis and Smuthead as they contemplated their change in fortune and craved even more.

"We could take all this back to Darkworld; then get a transport!"

"A whole transport full of gold is what we need!"

"What about operating it, while we lose our minds?"

"That is something we can solve at the time."

So, with such a sound plan formulated, they prepared to engage drives and motivate back to Darkworld.

Upon engaging the drives and starting the Q-ball transfer process, a standing wave on the wire bundle between the ships was generated, pushing them out of alignment with the instantaneous reality instant that had composed their starting point Universe.

They were not aware of it, but they were now in an Alt World version of Brane "B" in Andromeda.

They returned in the devices to an Alt World version of Darkworld, where events, conditions and details were possibly different from the Darkworld in their own starting Reality.

The worst thing was that time had split into a complex pretzel, with beat effects. The end of their journey still was ordained to be their starting point on Earth, but they had to traverse the Alt World crèche surrounding Darkworld as three separate viewpoints, since they formed two nodes and a standing wave with the devices. They were not aware of this multiplication of themselves, and in each case carried on like normal.

Touching down on Darkworld, Bemis & Smuthead (1), Bemis & Smuthead (2), Bemis & Smuthead (3) arrive at separate versions of the abandoned spaceport; with a connection established for the end of their journey at the same version of Earth.

In each reality they look around for the nearest transport vessel and board it immediately, intent on returning to the Robot Gold Mine Planet to load its vast bulk and return to Earth.

Meanwhile our little hero has been languishing in the

dungeon of the Dark One and has had time to think.

"Don't you want to know anything about me, or what my purpose is here, or something?" Darkworld Duck calls out into the black corridor.

"No, not really."

"I have information that you probably should hear."

"Like what?"

"I am from a higher plane, I just know things."

"Or from a lower one, eh? What things?"

"Oh, like the sky is blue on my home world, Earth."

"Go on."

"And that people there don't know about this place, or your Lord."

"More."

"That I can show you how to have fun."

"Fun? What's that?"

"It's when you do something almost forbidden or unusual, and then you feel good inside, and make this sound a lot: ha, ha, ha."

"Ha, ha, ha?"

"That's right! Ha, ha, ha! Ha, ha, ha!"

Then in unison: "Ha, ha, ha! Ha, ha, ha! Ha, ha, ha!"

After a while there seemed to be a problem with Dave.

Ever since the crew of Garth's ship had arrived on Alexis One he had been acting strange, giving people weird looks and muttering under his breath, refusing to explain his mannerisms, etc.

He was getting a bit annoying.

Lucifer didn't seem to mind him, but he was driving One crazy. All she could talk about when Garth was alone with her was how much she detested Dave and never wanted to stare back at his blank expression again.

Garth finally agreed that he would approach the Alexis One bigwigs and suggest that Dave be sent on a mission.

The Grays had a suggestion that he take a saucer and cruise back to Earth in the 20th century via the wormhole, to see if the paradox that had created the Trillion Rogers was still active.

Garth didn't like the idea of a trillion Rogers, let alone a trillion Daves being a possibility. A trillion guys named Dave. That was too much. So he suggested another alternative. Dave would travel to Alien Nexus Three to assemble the Blackbirds in case they were needed on Earth, as the way was now open for them to go there through the crèche. The only drawback was that he would have to enter into an orbit around Alexis One and then fall back around the planet to return to the Alien Nexus Three side. At that time he would be at relativistic speed and be eaten alive by the Dancer when he 'landed'.

"Oh well, he was just that irritating I suppose." Garth thought to himself.

It occurred to Garth that the craft could safely motivate around to the other side at lower speeds and descend to the surface of the plain to contact the Blackbirds, but he didn't feel like giving Dave a ride, and so didn't suggest it.

The time came for the mission and Dave went outside the hull, Garth could see him off in the near distance outside the Control Room windows. He waved and circled around once before diving in a low arc down past the edge of the planet below, de-orbiting straight toward the center of the plain and the gigantic Dancer.

At the very last moment the Dancer stopped whistling as he usually did when this happened, and clicked his teeth together once. Dave's headless body hit the ground, dead.

Dave's head made the journey to the giant's stomach, where it was converted into a tiny pile of foam. His last thought, before the acid dissolved him, was why was he still able to know of this, since he was dead, he thought.

Up in the Oort Cloud of beings composing the survivors of Alien Nexus Two, Dave reappeared. Now he was back in his proper place among the circle that he was originally from, but he didn't like it.

He didn't like it at all.

The Dictator hurtled through space in the massive alien transport filled (half-filled) with zombies, bent on world domination. His plan was to let the zombies out at night in New York City, so as to go unnoticed. The whole ship could hover while invisible, and had a long extending ramp system for moving passengers on and off quickly.

The zombies were acting a bit strange, even for them. They were mostly completely silent, except for once in a while one or two of them would moan out softly, with apparent deep longing, "Brains! I eat Brains!" They were quite convincing and subtle.

Upon leaving for the edge of Central Park the zombies filed out in a quick and orderly manner.

Some of the zombies stayed in the woods, more of them formed groups of three and four and began to walk out of the park. The numbers were staggering in such a public space. They just kept coming and coming for what seemed like at least forty-five minutes.

The zombies further up the line stopped sometimes and talked to people, and then kept filing down into downtown and lower Manhattan. It looked for 'all the world' like a parade or perhaps a medium sized protest. Someone handed a banner to the first group of zombies and stepped back into the crowd of gawkers now surrounding the zombie march.

The banner said 'Down with Animal Cruelty, Human Rights and Dignity'. A poorly worded slogan that people with good grammar constantly pointed out was wrong, implying down with human rights and dignity.

The sign was the result of a committee consisting of members of both groups each having half of their shared sign to popularize a slogan. There was supposed to be a period in the middle, not a comma, so it had been thrown out.

Now more of the crowd watching the march fell in behind the zombie column when it had passed, or clung to its edges as it marched.

The crowd pushed forward, filling every empty space as congestion snarled traffic and life began to fall apart for New Yorkers as far away as Brooklyn. This was making news now.

A police helicopter hovered over the mass and TV cameras rolled.

Finally a Zombie stood in front of a cameraman and the local celebrity news jockey with a whole lot to prove in front of 2 billion viewers.

"We mean you no harm, we were ignorant once, but we realize we don't really need to eat your brains, a nice monkey brain would be good, but we could get by on sheep or pig brains, I suppose."

The news jockey looked into the camera and said, "Hear that folks, zombies, real live dead people."

"Wait a minute, we are zombies by virtue of infection only, we have not died or become truly undead, most of us are really normal people, just here and get used to it."

"I don't know if your average New Yorker is going to accept you at the brunch counter all-you-can-eat just like that; I mean, look at you, you are hideous."

"We have a virus-related skin condition and a long standing former mental impairment, that's all."

"So you can do my taxes and need medical attention."

"That's right, I'm a regular Joe just like you!"

The crowd pushed forward, sweeping the zombie who had been talking away with it and forcing the cameraman to stop filming.

On TV the story continued, showing aerial shots of the vast crowd as it wound its way through the park and downtown.

The President stood ready at the White House to give a much-needed press conference; he was glad for the distraction and the chance to make some hash.

The Army had been called out, and the National

Guard. Police in riot gear had responded early but kept at a distance. Helicopters choked the sky above lower Manhattan.

Soaring away upward from the tense scene, our viewpoint shifts Magikally again to Earth orbit, where a trio of transports circled the planet.

Just then a Dark Triangle, or Blackbird, is seen on course for Earth and close enough to see the ships. It is our little hero in his Dark Soliton form.

He had escaped back at the Dark One's fortress by using a very clever trick indeed. He had taught the zombies how to have fun. As he had chatted-up his zombie guard at his cell door, word had spread like wildfire among the zombies lounging about without much to do about a new idea called 'fun'.

A crowd had gathered at first outside and then inside of Darkworld Duck's cell, as he explained the concept over and over to his thick-witted captors.

Finally he had them eating out of his hand, as he orchestrated his escape plan.

"Now there is no use in me just explaining fun to you, you have to get involved in the process, become part of the action, get into it!"

"We want to be fun!"

"All we have to do is play a game! It is called Red Rover. Let me explain the rules. We have two teams lined up facing each other holding hands, or what's left of them, and challenging each other by name one by one to run and try to break through the hand-clasp so as to become a member of that team. Last team to have one player loses."

"Yes, play game Red Rover."

So Darkworld Duck fooled the zombies into taking the chain off of his leg so he could show them how to run across to break the hand-clasp; and took three steps and changed into his Soliton self, flying out the window. Now he circled Earth as a menacing Dark Triangle and assessed the situation. He needed backup.

Turning around, he flew off at nearly light-speed for the crèche opening, and then made his way through the canyon door, out through Modus Control and down to the plain below now dotted with his kind.

In the distance he could see the giant Dancer take a bite out of one of his fallen comrades and then toss down the rest. He felt uneasy, but the monster was still far away.

He formed the thoughts in his mind as he had been trained to do as a young triangle and felt for the presence of others.

"You have got to see this, Earth is being invaded by zombies right now."

He buzzed the field a few times and transmitted his message, ending with,

"Follow me!"

Soaring up into the sky, the whole column of Blackbirds, their numbers only slightly depleted from the Dancer's depredations, made for the Rift as one.

They thundered through Modus Control for nearly as long as it had taken them to evacuate the exploding Alien Nexus Two, and rumbled through the gorge doorway into

Darkworld. After entering orbit about the planet, they left for the crèche opening and the nearby Earth.

### *The Crugs*

The Crugs had been very clever, when they left never to return to physical space they simply changed their forms to be more pleasing to them, when they needed a physical body they could assume one to their liking at will.

They liked to interfere with the progress of different cultures throughout the Universes, and had spies and accomplices everywhere.

Generally they just encouraged progress and allowed themselves to be worshipped sometimes as Gods and Goddesses.

The advanced culture of Ancient Egypt World was partly the result of technology and other knowledge transferred nearly directly by the Crugs. In the guise of Ancient Egypt World Gods and Goddesses, they were real and so was their power and authority.

Sobek was a Crug. He had travelled the physical dimensions at will in his non-corporeal form and manifested there as any shape he chose. Often he would travel to a world in a dimension where a race was evolving slightly less well than his own had, and give them a pod; a hand that is.

We were not in that category, as we were not even yet on the path to evolving past physical bodies at all. In fact, we were on the path to melding ourselves with machine consciousness, although this was still about three hundred years in Garth's future. Now Mankind stood facing a crisis like none before, with an alien invasion in progress as we speak.

The invasion was going forward now at full speed. The three extra-dimensional transport ships full of zombies had landed around the planet at London, Moscow and Hong Kong. The New York invasion was proceeding to enter negotiations with the Mayor's Office, and had top priority with the President of the United States of America. The zombies it seems didn't want to fight, but they had some questions to ask. The people sat in front of their TV screens and waited for the inevitable bloodbath to come. TV announcers speculated on the effects of nuclear weapons on the zombies, and most people expected the Army to start shooting them any minute.

One other aspect of the 'invasion' was unexpected and very strange. People had begun to dress and act like the zombies, using make-up to blend in among the horde. This was now a popular movement reminiscent of early 21st century events. Now the system worried that copycat movements would disrupt the course of history and their hold on power.

Some problems continued to occur. Large groups of zombies that went down side streets and became separated from the main horde were arrested by police and detained in the city jails, which were stuffed to capacity. The Army had also captured a few and had set-up a temporary detention center on Ellis Island.

A direct action coalition strike force snuck onto the Island one night and liberated the zombie prisoners there. A small explosion made a hole in the perimeter fence, and a fleet of zodiacs sped the detainees to safety.

This widely publicized event gained intense media

attention for week after week as the TV announcers went crazy over this perceived military weakness and continuing social problem. For some reason large disruptions in the social fabric occurred in Chicago, Los Angeles and in many smaller centers as well. The zombies were almost a side issue now; as popular support for them swelled worldwide, their supporters took over control of the movement.

The whole world continued to descend into chaos; a zombie inspired revolution finally overthrew a despot from a small county in central Africa. Similar revolts and ousters occurred throughout Asia and South America, with finally only our anonymous Dictator's country and several Middle Eastern nations left to the despots.

Revolutionary movements in so-called 'democratic' nations continued as well, with disruptions to all major services and utilities, food shortages and power outages, and regular interruptions of internet-communications for hours at a time. The more conservative elements of society banded together to defend themselves and promote the freedom of the legal government to rule.

They had a lot of guns.

The NRA proposed that the President sanction a bounty on zombies and zombie impersonators as well. Several southern states proposed laws against impersonating zombies with penalties like life imprisonment and even death in Texas.

Just as these developments were pushing the world's governments over the edge, a strange thing happened. It all just froze for a second, except for the arrival of a billion Dark Triangles and a comical cartoon duck with a couple of zombie appendages.

The Dark Triangles were able to transform back into their Alien Nexus Two Soliton forms on Earth, so they did. Darkworld Duck remained as a cartoon, although solid and hyper-real, with what looked like days of CGI rendering equivalent realism per second of Earth-time.

The masses remained in a state of stasis until all the Solitons had taken up stations among the disturbed and disoriented Earth population, and then released the chains of Time once again.

"Surprise, surprise, are you happy to see me?" Darkworld Duck stands before the President and gestures elaborately.

He walks forward and bows deeply.

"Your Eminence, may I offer my services and commend you on the decor, simply to die for!"

He gestures around.

"I see you are a collector of African Art. I myself was born in Africa. I am unfortunately partly as the new visitors to your world, as you can see from my face and hand. "

"I am aware that our world faces a grave crisis, and that the threat to our stable society can only be neutralized with your help. Who are you?"

"I am Darkworld Duck, Destiny and Beyond the Dark One!"

"What?"

"That is my catch phrase, you haven't met the Dark One, but he is one nasty character, let me tell you!"

"You don't say."

"I do say! I say all the time!"

"Do tell."

"Yes."

"Yes. Out with it then."

"We can stop time, and organize the zombies back onto their ships, take the make-up off of the impersonators, arrest the Dictator, and find out how all of this happened. You in?"

"Yeah, I'm in."

Sobek was responsible for starting the early culture of Earth's Egyptian people back about ten thousand years ago. He had wanted to see what he could do with a truly primitive race with no hope of ever evolving on the path that his race had trod. Plodded and waddled actually, but you get the picture.

After teaching the natives techniques of agriculture, writing and building, he had left the inhabitants to themselves, only checking in occasionally. They were really only a curiosity anyway, a side-project on the back shelf with very little actual promise, but he was fond of them still, in a way.

When he became aware of the current Earth situation he was not surprised. He had been ready for just such an occasion, as the vulnerability of his infant creations was obvious and pitiful in its extent.

Appearing to his High Priest on Ancient Egypt World, he ordered him to assemble a large fleet of Alt-Ships like Garth's. Also he ordered that these ships be used to contact Alien Nexus One, the Grays, Ground, and also some Alt-world versions of Ancient Egypt World. The plan was to assemble a counter-strike on Earth as soon as possible, within the hour at the latest.

Garth and One sat up in his private cabin. They preferred to sleep on their ship instead of mixing with the population of Alexis One. The aliens made him feel a bit primitive and uncomfortable, and sentiment on the Mothership was that Earth had had it coming to them for a while now.

Word had come from an Ancient Egypt World emissary that help was needed on Earth now. Garth was preparing to leave for home as soon as possible after they got some sleep they needed desperately. He had been awake for nearly 24 hours.

On Ground Dr. Wally gave orders that the clone morphs be loaded onto their fastest light-ships, and they departed for the Darkworld crèche, to pass through to the Earth side in a matter of hours.

The Grays sent a fleet of Mark V Grayships back through the wormhole to 1947 Earth, where they established a base deep inside the far side of the moon and waited.

Contact was made through Alt-World versions of Ancient Egypt World with the Gods and Goddesses of these worlds, versions of the Crugs themselves from Alternative Realities. They were informed of the crisis on Earth and asked to show up at a certain place and time, and to all be wearing gold and blue one piece leotard type outfits, logo optional.

Darkworld Duck was the only Toon on Earth. He was in charge of the biggest job of his life, removing the zombies from Earth and placing them back on board their vessels. The time freeze was the only way to do it, they all agreed.

As they were loading yet another group of frozen zombies aboard via the ramp, Darkworld Duck glanced up to a gigantic line of bright white light appearing in the sky high above Manhattan. Time un-froze as a huge opening appeared where the line had been, out of which poured straight down an avalanche of tiny figures. A new rift in space-time had been generated, and Toons poured down to the city streets below. Bedlam ensued.

Darkworld Duck changed into his Blackbird shape and soared up to the opening to the Tooniverse now available to him. He reasoned that he now needed more backup, in the form of cartoon super-heroes much like himself.

Who could forget such classic heroes as Marsupial Man, and Catman! And then there was Albino Man, and the Man with No Spine! The Slug Salter! Mirror Man and Shower Girl made a great duo. She had the power to raise the dead.

Darkworld Duck looked around proudly at the force he was assembling in the Tooniverse for his return to Earth. Heroes such as Reality-Man and Time-Girl could alter Earth history. Other special super-powers possessed by some of these comic-book super-heroes were the ability to cause beliefs to change in others, and the ability to undo the last half-hour of Earth time once daily.

Just then the Grays arrive on the scene, having been waiting, you see, in an underground base this time, on the moon, you know, for just this eventuality; since 1947.

They take up defensive positions around the Earth, especially near the transports, which were nearly full of zombies again and scheduled to depart within a few short hours, though now with time un-frozen who knew when they would be ready.

So the Battle of Earth began.

An NRA member fired the first shot, killing a zombie impersonator in Tulsa, Oklahoma around 5 pm that evening, local time. The reason given was fear of robbery, although people said the victim, still dressed as a zombie, had merely been trying to purchase cigarettes.

The Alt-World Gods and Goddesses flash mob appeared right on schedule, followed closely by the Tooniverse Super-heroes. Many of the furious NRA members were stopped in the middle of obscene acts of gun violence against zombies and zombie imitators in the U.S.A. In the rest of the world people seemed to get it that something good was happening to change the status quo, even if it was an alien invasion of brain eaters. People were glad to see that the situation was stable again due to the godlike vigilance of all involved, and Shower Girl revived the dead fake zombie guy.

So the question arose as to where the perpetrator(s) of this heinous act upon humanity was. The location of the multiplied forms of the Dictator(s) was still unknown.

One thing was obvious; Bemis and Smuthead were in London, having collapsed into one set of wave functions upon arrival on Earth. In each case the Dictator had fled the transports just before the zombies were allowed to disembark. They were greeted with special scorn when recognized as the cause of so much trouble and mischief by the local Londoners.

After much posturing and bally-hooing they were unceremoniously locked-up in the Tower of London.

A huge cadre of Techs from the Alexis One basement level had constructed portals all over Earth to pass from the Quantum Foam Dimension that was their home to here. They continued arranging the transport of wire bundle facilities and switching arrangements to Earth, rendering part of it as stable in space-time as the Mechanical Level itself. They hid their work in unused tunnels, behind secret doors, and in extra space that logically shouldn't have existed. In a logical sense the trappings of Dream Time had been installed on this planet in Reality.

The new Rift into the Tooniverse had a wide variety of effects, from the availability of cheap pot in urban centers near New York to hiring practices for animated hookers in Amsterdam. Most noticeable was the influx of the Toons themselves, they were a boisterous and energetic crowd and let fly at will.

The Super-heroes liked to show off, apprehending malefactors and generally do-gooding to beat the band.

The Crugs soon took control away from the Dark Triangles, who generally looked down a bit at the Toons who were admittedly Solitons of a different order mostly, but not Darkworld Duck; he was a Dark Triangle and a Toon as well, as well as a Zombie, and at his core all too Human.

He felt comfortable in New York and made his home there, renting a small apartment near Central Park in midtown. He worked as an extra along with a wide selection of other under-employed Toons new to the city. They were not given very lucrative contracts but the Toon Craze meant there was a lot of work for his kind.

But let us get back to the Battle.

Darkworld Duck had been responsible for the Blackbirds arriving and freezing time, effectively ending the Battle before it had begun. Let's face it folks, once time is frozen there is very little happening, and not much to look forward to.

But that wasn't a good enough solution for The Crugs, so they went in a different direction, leaving poor old

Darkworld Duck out on a limb, as it were.

The Battle fizzled all over the world at about the same time. Mass detention of zombies, sympathy movements, and actions against the state, followed by vigilante and police violence and then FREEZE!

Many people were killed in small acts of violence perpetrated by vigilante groups. So Shower Girl was kept busy for weeks reviving the victims.

After a while a warm glow seemed to suffuse reality around the Earth, and peace returned to the troubled planet.

Now the Earth was a sandwich between the crossroads of dimensional travel and the most remote portions of the Nexus Worlds. The whole effect was localized to New York City, and after a while new influxes of Toons were rare, and the hidden workings of the Alexis One Techs kept secret and shrouded in mystery. Also with Andromeda in close proximity through the Darkworld crèche, space travel was enabled enormously. The fleet of alien transports, coupled with the advanced Groundian clone morph space fleet, made exploring Andromeda, and even our own Milky Way, easier by far.

In a reality from which we are only slightly different, the Battle of Earth worked out much better, as far as being a spectacular battle goes. The reason we are mentioning it here is simple really, I feel like it.

The initial incident that happens is that when the first ship full of zombies lands at Central Park, a watchful citizen phones 911 as soon as he spots the terrifying passengers leaving. This leads to an immediate response by the combined NORAD forces, destroying New York and badly damaging the transport, which falls on the city as a useless pile of space-junk.

The other transports appear on schedule, and soon have disgorged their contents. Military action slaughters the invaders wholesale, and the carnage mounts as the Armed Forces of many nations unleash hell. A groundswell of public horror and revolt sweeps the world, and millions are imprisoned and executed, while street riots are put down with an iron fist. Countless numbers are killed in demonstrations and revolutionary wars, and prisons are full to overflowing.

Darkworld Duck has not escaped from the clutches of the Dark One, and no one has informed the Crugs of the dire situation on Earth. No help is coming.

The zombies themselves are a bit meaner, and although they are just as intelligent as the zombies filling our Earth, they feel no tenderness toward the native population. They were attacked when they arrived and will not forget it soon.

While the scale of the zombie invasion was vast, comprising four ships and four Dictators bent on world domination, the dent they were able to make in the Earth's defenses was only moderate. Each ship carried enough brain hungry monsters to keep a large city in chaos for months, but eventually the military forces of the planet prevailed and peace and order was restored.

The Grays arrive incredibly late on the scene, having been curious to see how it all turns out, and not wanting to leave the safety of their underground moon base. They return to Alien Nexus One and recommend that the Reset Button be used so as to cancel out this reality as most likely to interfere with the development of Alexis One into the Mothership of Destiny.

So its timeline became redundant, and was redacted by

the Techs. The last instant of that reality didn't connect to any realities later in time; it remained frozen forever as a tribute to plans that just don't work out.

The Crugs had benefited mankind in our reality more than any other race. They had created us on Darkworld, and then had disappeared from our Universe. They had transplanted colonies from Darkworld to Ground, and Brane collisions had transferred some of the new humans from Darkworld to Earth, where they began to compete immediately with the less advanced Neanderthals. Later on Sobek, a Crug, had brought fire and agriculture. They had continued to look in on us for eons, but had gradually lost interest. Brane collisions with Ground exchanged an advanced culture raised more directly by the Crugs, the Atlantean Disaster Culture. They were much better off on Ground, where a fully tamed planet of civilized citizens surrounded them.

Now the Atlanteans had sway over a vast empire on Earth, a savage and wild planet of danger and chaos. The Groundian Atlantean people developed the first network of advanced cultures around the world, powered by resonant crystals and coherent light. The Brane collision continued, this time rupturing the colony from Ground in half, causing the remains of the island to be returned to the sea in a gigantic volcanic eruption. Part of the Earth's crust had been torn away in the exchange, and the original crust that had been on Ground came back and covered the area again. The evidence was soon destroyed by the continuing spread of the mid-Atlantic ridge.

Once back on Ground the Atlantean culture that had survived the devastation set up a program to contact Earth people who were ready to share their vast knowledge via

Dreamtime experiences. The practitioners of directed dreaming or similar enough disciplines could tune-in to the Groundian dream broadcast, joining the Groundians when they dreamed as clone morphs on Ground. In these hyper-real 'dreams' they received an education not available on Earth. They would arrive just as they started to dream on Earth, causing the clone morph they now inhabited on Ground to transform from a plain form only approximately their size and shape into a fully real looking clone of their own body sleeping on Earth. Often the dreams would be a continuation of an earlier dream, picking up seamlessly from the end of the last one. This entailed a lot of planning for the handlers on Ground, as they moved unchanged clone morphs around to set the stage for the dream's continuation.

Garth had dreamed of Ground, but his dreams had been clever deceptions, and he had never spotted the fact that he was no longer on Earth. The Groundians had decided to observe him under tightly controlled conditions on Ground before informing him of the realness of his dream life, and had secretly debriefed him. All this had occurred in Garth's youth, as the Groundians could see his significance in history far in advance of later events due to their prescience.

Often the experience of animating a clone morph while dreaming was the first kind of special dream that an adept would have prior to any dreams that revealed the nature of higher reality or that predicted future events. The whole process was designed to ease the transition from the dreamer's own reference point to that shared by enlightened races throughout the multi-verse.

The Crugs had transplanted man first to Ground, even

before the mass evacuation of Darkworld. So few Darkworldians had been relocated to Ground after the crisis started. The Groundians were like a control group maintained as an uncontaminated sample of Man's potential, while the Earth colony had been lowered by its mixture with more primitive Cro-Magnon and Neanderthal man. The Darkworldians had exchanged with Earth sometimes in Brane collisions, and the Groundians had done the same; but neither world exchanged parts with the other, since they were technically both part of the same brane originally, in Andromeda.

Garth arrives back from Alexis One, having de-orbited around the Nexus Planet and entered the hole on the plain. The Dancer had been the main gravity well they were headed for when leaving orbit; but they had gone into orbit around him, circling his horizon and then heading right for the hole. He had time to make life rough for them, but at the last moment he stood to the side and let them pass.

They entered the wormhole and soon were back at their starting place, in the auditorium. Garth and One and Lucifer exited the craft. The reception is a few dedicated staff and his wife, Nefertiti.

Nefertiti looks at One with what borders on suspicion, and then smiles warmly.

"You are the Lady of Heaven!"

"Yes."

"I am honored, you are as our own Gods to me."

"Thank-you."

Lucifer steps forward and smiles at the princess.

"You are Garth's wife?"

"Yes."

"He is a very lucky man."

"Thank-you."

Soon after being reunited with his wife, friends and family on Earth, Garth finds adventure in New York City.

A messenger comes to him from the Alexis One Techs, to meet at a certain restaurant back entrance near downtown Manhattan. When he arrived at the meeting place he was instructed about the location of certain dimensional portals hidden in plain sight around him.

A doorway opened to the Alexis One Mech Level, where many other doors and paths crossed and were connected in various ways. He could walk into one room, through a door into a different version of Earth, through a new door into the future or the past, or back to the Mech Level. He could leave his present location in Manhattan; walk through a door into Ancient Egypt World, and then through a new portal into his apartment. He could travel from one end of the city to the other, all without going out onto the street at all. The maze of choices and pathways bewildered him, but he came to know its intricacies like the back of his hand.

He had begun to investigate the many paths in the Tech network in NYC. He went from his apartment one day to the Mech Level on Alexis One via a path laid down by the Techs in the re-wiring of the city. Once there he found a Tech working on a control box and asked if there was an elevator to get to the control room at the top of the Mothership.

The Techs show him a chamber where he is multiplied into many selves, then each part of himself becomes multiplied as he focuses his awareness first on a hand, then his head, etc.

He notices that he is aware of his many parts and selves in what feels like a normal way, and realizes that he is experiencing what the Techs feel when they are working on the wire bundles. He concentrates on returning to a state of unity; focusing on awareness of one true inner self, he begins to reunite.

After coalescing again into one person, he emerges onto the control room bridge on Alexis One, and sees the beings of Alien Nexus Two outside the view windows.

Garth finds the hallucination controls and sends a message to 2163, telling them of the entrance to the Tech Grid in NYC 2065.

The 2163 reality is an Alt World by now, and does not have the Grid connection. Garth sets out with a team of Techs to install a Grid entrance point in 2163 Alt Earth.

After a certain number of connections are established between 2163 Alt Earth and Earth in 2065, the time line duplication is overcome by paradoxes, and the timelines recombine into one, with the 2163 version changing before its inhabitants eyes to reflect this new reality structure. Thankfully the timelines were already so similar, so the transformation when it occurred was comprised of changes of a myriad of details and relatively few large differences.

Next the Grid is extended to 2065 Ground in Brane "b", Andromeda. They are aware of this presciently, of course, but were not allowed to interfere with our progress.

In NYC the Dictator escapes from Darkworld Duck during the confusion when control of the situation changes hands. After hiding in an abandoned subway tunnel he stumbles upon the Grid. He knows that the Techs will be looking for him as he lied to them and the Lady of the Lakes when last at the

Mech Level.

So he keeps off the main routes to the Mech level and explores the warren of connections between the various portals in NYC. Soon he is an expert in getting from place to place without being seen. Word comes to him through his sparse zombie followers that Bemis and Smuthead are imprisoned in London and are responsible for the duplication of the transports, and he arranges to be hidden in a pressurized container and flown over the Pond.

His plan is to repeat the invasion of Earth by getting his accomplices to gather alt versions of themselves by duplicating the original process. The alt versions of the Dictator, having been imprisoned back on the transports, are out of the picture. He has no plans for including them in his future efforts, and looks forward to their departure. He intends to exploit alt world zombies and doubles of the twits in a future invasion, planned on a vast scale this time. He will assemble millions of zombies, in dozens of transports, led by alt versions of Bemis and Smuthead.

What had transpired aboard the transports when they had first been captured on Darkworld, you ask?

In each version of reality it had progressed in a similar manner. They had immediately been taken prisoner by the zombie horde and presented to the dictator in the control room while he set the controls to leave for Earth. In each case the twits had immediately negotiated release in exchange for information about Earth defenses and resources. They had hacked the entire military network.

Their trip to Earth in each case had been uneventful, and in two of the cases had ceased to exist along with the duplicate selves upon arrival on Earth. The dictators had not. Our Dictator, the one from our version of Earth, was anxious for some reason not to duplicate himself again, and was not privy to any secrets Bemis and Smuthead had divulged to his doppelgangers.

Now he was set to swing his new plan into action, and late one night he penetrates security around the Tower using stealth and cunning developed over many years as the ruthless overlord of a rouge nation's military intelligence. Soon he has cloaked the pair and himself in an invisibility field and escaped the clutches of the British Government. They all return to New York.

Once there they enter the Grid and hide again, the Dictator arranges to smuggle them into Canada. Security has been tightened around the portable device, but defeating it once before has prepared the duo for the challenge, and soon they have accessed all required levels again, and enter the lock-up. Hiding from cameras and other devices and personnel with the cloaking device has made this security breach a no-brainer.

Before landing on Darkworld they had spent years training in expectation of the measures meant to protect the gold from theft on the Robot Gold Mine Planet, and despite having spent over a year going slowly insane on Darkworld, were still able to defeat any automatic computer controlled security measures.

They all get inside the portable and overload the controls, sending the craft hurtling on its way instantly to Alien Nexus Three. The Dancer is running toward the craft as it sits on the grass, and Blackbirds buzz both him and the portable. They set the motivator to rise quickly up to the Rift and pass through the right-hand wall into Darkworld.

The Dictator leaves the portable craft and walks up the ruined old path to the Dark One's fortress. He is expecting to talk to an ally in the war with Earth, but is instead imprisoned for losing the zombie army.

He languishes in the dungeon of the Dark One for what seems like an eternity, until finally he is able to draw him back into a plan to invade Earth once again. Upon his release from prison he betrays his former captor, and escapes from the fortress with the coveted Ring, the Soliton of Samovar.

They plan to return to Earth and then proceed to an Alt Earth, and then from there to an Alt Darkworld, gathering a new invasion force that will be overwhelming in size and scope.

The Ring has the power to compel the weak willed, and also can summon any Soliton to appear. The Dictator compels a few straggling zombies to be his crew, and together with the twits they return to the plain through the Modus Control Center. Before they can distract the Dancer and return down the hole to Earth, he manages to grab the entire craft.

Distending his mouth and jaw in a horrible manner, the monster manages to swallow the craft whole. Soon the door to the craft is forced open and a Grey Man stares in at them. "You are our prisoners, and will be absorbed by the foam."

They all scream as foam pours in through the open door, and scramble out of it, to wade to the sides of the stomach and stand on the catwalk beside it. After a brief struggle they overpower the Grey Man and toss him down into the foam, where he slowly sinks and starts to dissolve.

"I am like soup," the Grey Man is heard to say before

finally sinking out of sight.

A great wind scoops them up and carries them away down the vast hall, which is like an industrial facility crossed with the inside of a whale or something. It is definitely not the inside of a gigantic space bug; that would be plagiarism. So they are swept along until they hang above the hollow leg of the Dancer, after which they fall down into the lower half of the Son of Yahweh, the realm of the Unknown.

Down inside the leg they can see many translucent membranes hung with grisly slime and visions of rotting carrion and deathly ghastliness. Inside each death-bubble lay another version of Darkworld.

After many attempts they manage to force themselves through the membrane of one bubble and plunge into a new Darkworld, they materialize on its surface a few hundred yards from the Gorge.

Here Sobek, who has managed to track them at last, confronts them. He takes the Soliton of Samovar away from the Dictator and hides it on the Grid, which goes to this Alt-Earth as well as our version.

The dictator and his crew are sent by Sobek back out of the Alt Darkworld membrane and back into the Dancer's lower half. The sight begins to trouble them, even the zombies, who are becoming saner again. Roiling around inside the nauseating contents of Darkland was a fate worse than death. Far above them the Dancer's upper Solitons, the Grey Men, populated half. The irony is poignant.

Solomon of the Jews comes into possession of the Ring and causes a temple to be built by daemons, but that is a whole other story. A mysterious Gray midget is responsible.

And we know from the Testament of Solomon, a secret gnostic scripture, that a line of the old gods appeared before him, some with the heads of asses, some of oxen and rams heads had they. These are the Alt World Gods, on Earth to guard the Ring for a time and then to leave. At the end Lucifer steals the Ring from Solomon and tells the story of how he was banned from Heaven by Yahweh.

Lucifer explains:

"Yahweh looked out into the Unknowable, and he knew endlessly all, so the unknowable retreated before his gaze. And Yahweh looked again, and so he saw out into the unknowable and it retreated once more.

And Yahweh said to himself, 'This sucks, I will not waste any more of my attention on this battle.'

But not wanting the Unknowable to get off too easily, he split a fragment of his awareness off from his more omniscient self, and named him Satan.

And he set Satan or Lucifer the task of knowing all the unknowable, so as to occupy him forever. And also he set him the task of discrediting all of the Earth gods.

And Yahweh found his Son upon the plane, and he filled his gigantic left leg with all the unknowable, and his right leg with the unknown.

And he saw that the process of all knowledge being imparted to his Son was good, and that the Controls were set on 'Auto'.

And the various Grey Men were the Bits of the process, and the lightning was the feedback loop.

So Yahweh installed Satan as the operator over all the Bits, and told him to stand upon the two Legs.

And so the Old Gods of Earth looked down and knew fear, for they remembered that they were unfinished business.

But then they saw that the son's consort was Hope, the one known as Gaia, and they knew of her and had no fear.

And the unknowable was a vast emptiness, which had no end. The Magik light of Knowledge shone out into it, and it receded but remained undiminished in extent. The Unknown flowed past as the Light revealed each Bit of new Knowledge. The Bits, or Grey Men recorded all the facts of life on Earth each day. The old Bits were destroyed"

The world was safe for the time from the Dictator and his genocidal ambitions to dominate the planet. The Ring was hidden once more on the Grid (or array, or raster, or framework, or lattice, that's the one 'Lattice'), and could not be easily found.

What had transpired in regards to our cadre of characters back on the original Earth? Read on my dazzled and harried reader, and you shall be enlightened.

*        *        *

### Joe's Master Koan Part – 8/A

The last footman, who had been the driver when Joe had first joined his new companions, prepared to tell the next fable.

"Do not think, fair Sir, that you must needs travel to a far land to be troubled by fiends such as described by my fellows; for such a thing may be found close by in any town."

"A young Doctor had a magnificent house where he lived with his wife and two small children. The house was on a fine, tree lined street in a prosperous part of town, a town which had not known war, famine or pestilence for many generations."

"The trouble started when the Doctor decided to visit the Atelier at the house of a well-known painter, located across the street from his home. His purpose was to improve his technique in anatomical drawings he required for a book he was writing about mollusks."

"Upon arriving at the drawing room of his renowned neighbor he was amazed by the number and prestige of the gentlemen students of the Master."

"One young man stood out from the rest, he was muscular and bearded in a fierce kind of way that contrasted perfectly his superior manners and civility. It was as if he held back enough manly powers to slay an ordinary man quick enough, but not in an overt or threatening way. He was quite skilled with the brush and pen and his grasp of proportion and perspective was unequalled."

"Our Doctor was introduced to the young gentleman, and it transpired that he lived in the house directly behind the Doctor's with a high stone wall separating the grounds of each estate. The man mentioned that he desired a concoction for his lethargy, which he showed no signs of, yet he insisted in his complaint. The Doctor invited him to visit that night so he could obtain the remedy he so desired."

"When, having returned home after drawing class, the Doctor answered his door, there was the young man looking wearied and agitated, as a gigantic full moon lit the night brightly."

"Taking him to his private study, he brought forth and

presented to him some vials of a preparation of extracts from both animal and vegetable sources; and instructed him in the dosages and precautions."

"Now the young man ignored the Doctor's instructions and immediately upon quitting his door while leaving, did take and swallow an excessive amount of the vitae elixir provided."

"Later that night the Doctor awoke with a start from an uneasy dream of beasts and traps and terrible things. He strained his ear to hear the sound that had awoken him, but all was strangely silent. Then far off in the distance he heard a wild wailing howl of an inhuman nature. He thought of a wolf. Getting up, he quickly dressed and went outside, grabbing his musket from the cabinet by the door."

"Starting off in the direction from which the sound had come, he soon came to the end of his property, where the high stone wall separated his land from his neighbors'. A furtive sound of scuttling feet caught his ears, just nearby. He turned and saw a flash of movement some close bushes, and fired his musket with a yell. Hurriedly he retreated to his house and barred the door and windows."

\*                    \*                    \*

### ~Bounce - 8

"Come on, let's go." With a last parry of swords, One gestures for Jen and Richard to take hold of her. She transforms immediately into her Dark Triangle form and flies upward, carrying them with her. They leave the military nudist lounge behind them as they arrive at the Alexis One Control Room and alight on the floor.

There is a new big hole in the middle of the floor of the Alexis One Mothership Control Room. An attendant rushes over and grabs Darkworld Duck by the forearm. "You are under arrest, for willful damage and temporary murder of a government worker. Don't you realize you have just destroyed the Hallucination Spider Control Desk, and temporarily killed its operator? Now you have interrupted his work assuring our own evolution into existence. What if this causes a change in our past? You must come with us!"

Darkworld Duck resumes his shape as a Dark Triangle and the couple from Earth grab on as he takes off, out of the Control Room and into the intricate and endless interior of the Mothership, commonly known as Alien Nexus One. This place contains a multitude of individual refuges from time, called crèches, built by advanced civilizations as they reached maturity, and collectively administered by the Alien Grays.

They race over downtown, where commercial establishments such as the Big Bang Bistro and others cater to jaded tourists from almost anywhere in regular space-time, primitive savage societies excepted of course.

They see the "City of Lights", a galaxy of individual space-time bubbles suspended around the massive crèche of the Alien Grays, by far the largest. As they circle this concentration of mass, they enjoy an advantage of acceleration not possible in the normal physical Universe. Darkworld Duck accelerates away from the center of Alien Nexus One, and soon is on his way to the Tooniverse. Time goes by slowly at first, as the three accelerate past relativistic speed, and then it begins to pass more quickly. They are spending less time for the distance they travel than would have been possible otherwise, if light speed was a barrier to them. Behind them the center of mass in this strange world shrinks down to a small sphere, then a dot in the distance behind them. They are really in a fast parabolic orbit about the center still, but in a way they still race high above its round flat surface. A higher energy path inside the Nexus means that they are members of a more inclusive manifold, sort of like the opposite of the limitation suffered by Joe and his friends in the fog. This enables perception of the approaching Tooniverse as they would have seen it, walking on the great plain of Alien Nexus One, or flying just above its surface at non-relativistic speeds. They can see the entire Tooniverse eventually, suspended in space just ahead of them, retreating as they advance.

Small figures are visible through its glassy surface, tiny Toon creatures making rude gestures and fighting among themselves. Up ahead of them a tiny building becomes visible, and Darkworld Duck begins to slow down. The perspective switches around so that they now fly high above the ground and the building. Off in the near distance the Bubble-house comes into view, towering above the plain in pillows of cloud and stone. Gothic in the extreme, gigantic arched construction supports clouds that rise impossibly high, with arcane signs and the biggest stained glass windows anywhere. The magnificent door has a large deeply carved "II" set into the lintel, and a path that leads to the other building.

Darkworld Duck seems familiar with the whole arrangement, and flies through the door, turns around, and flies back out again. Over the door as he flies out is a large "I", carved in stone on the lintel. Outside they see the Tooniverse around them.

A stone path leads from the door, still with an "II" above it, to the other building. A thought occurs to Darkworld Duck, "Where is that Rift to New York?"

"Why don't you ask at the Library over there?" One of the local Toons has read his mind, apparently. He resembles a fish-tank with tropical fish, bubbles and plants that double as limbs.

"O.K., thanks buddy."

A passerby places an ice cube in the fish tank, which suddenly freezes solid, smashing on the ground. Some of the tiny fish start to thaw and wriggle and flop about in the piles of melting slush and shattered aquarium glass. An ambulance roars up and two crazed looking cat inspired Toons rush over, and shovel the mess into a bucket. They rush back to the ambulance and roar away to the hospital.

Darkworld Duck and the others watch as scene after scene of cartoon violence erupts all around their location. One has followed them and now joins them, as they witness a field full of cartoon cats with large bulbous kinky afros, buried up to their eyebrows, get decapitated by a tiny mouse driving a demonic lawn mower. "Just trimming the Afro-Turf!" He quips.

"Let's get out of here!" She and Darkworld Duck transform into Dark Triangles, and they each carry a human passenger to the door of the nearby Hall of Records, or Library building. They enter the building as a group and spread out to search for directions to the Rift above New York City.

One approaches a librarian sitting at a reference desk, and asks a question, "Are we near the Rift?"

The librarian resembles the early 20$^{th}$ century author

Margaret Atwood, and replies, "You will have to ask an expert in 11-dimentional topography."

"Where can I find this expert?"

"Try looking for Stonehenge, or Saturday Night Live."

"How will that help?"

"It helps me," was all she had to say as a snippy retort.

One does as instructed, and goes to look at books on Stonehenge first. She has access to works impossible for 21$^{st}$ century people to have written, books that show revealingly the involvement of aliens in the creation of some of Earth's greatest ancient monuments. As she is reading a very interesting edition of a publication called "Historical Aberrations, and Evidence", Richard comes up and starts reading over her shoulder.

"J.R.R. Tolkien, Carlos Castaneda, and many others were fascinated by Stonehenge and the mystery of its creation in Neolithic times by supposedly savage early Britons. While neither of them is thought to have explicitly written a thing about Stonehenge, it remains as slightly more than speculation to assert that they knew that there had to be some kind of Alien or even Future Earth connection formed in their thinking processes that would confirm them as experts in this field."

The book has a map of Stonehenge, showing various parts of the ruins highlighted in different colors, and has a legend that explains the meaning associated with each. One aspect of the legend stands out in Richard's mind, the part that indicates undiscovered inscriptions. Inscriptions that had not yet been discovered in his century, that is.

"No help there, what else did the librarian say?" Richard files the map and legend away mentally for future reference.

"To check Saturday Night Live." As they wander the stacks, they soon reach the place on the shelves where books about the late night comedy show from New York are kept. Richard picks up the first of them and begins reading. Jen laughs and gets his attention.

"Look out the window!"

Richard looks up and sees a cloud rising above the horizon, and deep inside it he sees a tear in the fabric of space-time itself. They are looking at the Rift that exists above New York in 2065.

\*          \*          \*

### Joe's Master Koan Part – 8/B

"The next morning he was awoken rudely just before dawn by an insistent pounding on his door. When he rose and investigated, an old woman was there, looking most distraught and troubled. She explained that her son, the young man of last night, lay wounded in his bed, in need of attention from a Doctor. The Doctor dressed, grabbed his black bag, and left with her immediately."

"Over the next few days, the young man healed from his wound, which turned out to be only a deep scratch. With the Doctor's help he was mending without infection. The Doctor kept his suspicions as to the young man's accident to himself, and doubted if the two incidents were related, although in his heart he was troubled and suspicious of the young man. He cautioned the young man about excess and indulgence and gave stern instructions, threatening to take the remaining elixir away for any   indiscretions whatsoever."

"While the Doctor was at the young man's home treating his wound, he chanced to look around a bit throughout the mansion, and paid good attention to both the cellar and the attic. A profusion of curios, relics and mementos of foreign lands filled both areas, but most interesting were some actual Egyptian mummies and sarcophagi in the cellar. As the Doctor examined one via candlelight, a faint noise came from the next one. Opening it, he was surprised to find a young woman inside, apparently drugged into unconsciousness."

"After briefly examining the young lady, he again shut the lid on the mummy-case and returned to finish tending his now most suspicious patient. Making excuses, he soon left to fetch the young lady from her sarcophagi and carried her home."

"In the morning he questioned the young lady, who had awoken in a normal state of mind, though physically drained. She was revealed upon questioning to be the daughter of the master of the Atelier. She recalled going to bed normally the night before, with a brief interruption once, when she thinks a man held a strange drink to her lips. She remembers a strange smell and passing out again instantly. He allowed the young lady to rise and dress, and escorted her back to her father's estate."

"Her father was quite concerned and questioned the Doctor extensively, looking to his daughter for corroboration and confirmation. Soon he was somewhat satisfied, and decided to summon the local constable to have a look into the matter. Shortly the policeman from Scotland Yard arrived, a serious man in overcoat and conservative hat, his comically portly assistant in tow. The entire interview process of interrogation and analysis was repeated, while the Doctor took notes. The constable and his servant concluded their business and left, leaving the Doctor for a moment unattended. He casually wandered the halls in the direction of the wing where the Atelier was located."

"He glanced into one of the more private side rooms off of the main studio, and to his surprise found several more mummies just like the ones from the young man's collection."

"Investigating more closely, he entered the room and moved amid the ancient remains to stand in its center. As he stood there the door slammed, shutters closed over the windows, and the one lamp blew out. He was in near perfect darkness, and he heard a faint scratching sound, and a bit further away, a floorboard creaked."

"Soon he felt bandaged hands groping his face, and he yelled out in terror and ran for the door, bumping into a strange bundle of bones and rags on his way."

"As he struggled to turn the doorknob, many sets of hands touched him, going in his pockets and pulling at his clothes. At last he opened the door and looked at his tormentors, ready to flee at once. What he saw was three or four animated zombies covered in long strips of cloth, unraveling slightly from arms and faces, hands raised to shield dead eyes from the bright light of the open doorway. Taking advantage of their hesitation and aversion to the light, he pulled himself away from their grasp and ran down the hall, calling out to the Master in a high-pitched scream, 'They are alive! The Egyptians!'"

"At the end of the short hall a door to the main

passage stood ajar, and the Doctor rushed through, locking the door with a deadbolt."

"Down the main hall, the Doctor heard the voice of the Master, urging him to approach and asking what was wrong."

"The Doctor passed down the wide hall, to the door of a luxurious library with statues, globes and rich art, stacks and shelves of rare occult books and manuscripts of ancient lore. The Master bade him enter and asked about the shouting, what did it mean?"

"The Doctor came in and described his terror at seeing the dead Kings of Egypt walking again among the living, and the Master was most amazed, and asked him, did he know of any force or spell that could have brought these dead kings back to life? The Doctor told him no, and then pausing to think, told him of the wondrous elixir he had given to the young man the previous day."

"As the Doctor came over to stand beside the Master, he noted a strange look that he had now about him. His eyes seemed strange, hypnotic, and as he looked closer he could see that they were yellow, and that the pupils were slits, like a cat's. With a hissing sound, the Master stood and came toward the Doctor, who could see two sharp fangs protruding from the Master's lips."

"The Doctor backed away, staring in horror at the Master Painter's metamorphosis, and asking 'Who are you? What are you?'"

"Behind him he could hear the wooden door to the main hallway splinter, and awkward steps shuffling in his direction, then fists pounding the door behind his back."

"The Doctor tried to scream, but the breath was caught

in his throat. He was backed against the door, then he was pulled forward and the door jerked open behind him."

"The last thing the Doctor saw as sight faded from his eyes, was his own fresh blood, over flowing from the vampire's mouth, being fed to one of the mummies as a mother bird feeds it's young, then blackness!"

"That is also terrible, a horrible tale with a morbidly gruesome end, well done, and dam you all to Hell for so frightening us all out of our wits. Pardon. Bless you well, most entertaining; now get out; back to your place, driver!"

"Yes, Sir; thank-you, Sir!" The driver bends and kisses his master's hand, and raps on the carriage to signal a stop.

### ~Big Bang Bistro

Garth awoke one morning in his New York apartment and looked at his wife, Nefertiti. She was one of the most beautiful women he had ever seen, and he had met angels and exotic savages. This morning had a clear, hard light about it, as the early morning fog burnt off in a sudden burst of winter sunshine. A sense of wonder pervaded his mind, and a feeling of premonition, something was happening, he looked out into the Manhattan sky.

The Rift into the Tooniverse glowed slightly against the backdrop of light. A scintillating swarm of tiny winged forms began to flow down from the elevated opening. They were the grey and white Zeit-geese, the Time-geese, or Spirit-geese. They allowed the smaller Toon birds to land on their backs when they migrated across the Tooniverse, and were well known for their selflessness and sacrifice in life, in order to promote higher ideals, of course.

The geese are moving to the city in droves, and have plenty of the Toon version of money, which is almost as good in NYC as the greenback. Soon there are new establishments to cater to the mostly Toon inhabitants of the downtown district they dominate. Many new services and economic demands are created regarding Toons and the Tooniverse. A new push is soon on to bring the rest of the world up to snuff as far as connected to the Grid was concerned, and all major cities and landmarks are added to its Complex Lattice Arrangement. Soon proliferation is rampant, and travel worldwide is accomplished via the Lattice.

When growth was analyzed and questions arose, (where did all the money and resources come from to change the world so fast?), the truth came out. The Zeit-geese were infinite in number, and not even nearly the most numerous of all the inhabitants of the Tooniverse. They had moved into New York City in the hundreds of thousands, but more of them could be found almost anywhere on Earth. They were good at predicting what would become popular and always put in a request via their eyeglass comm device for more portals to be installed at touristy spots on Earth, and soon people learned that if you asked a goose to request a portal in your neighborhood, it got done!

The geese would stay a few days on Earth, look around, and soon head back to wherever via one of the freshly constructed Grid Portals.

More and more people take up imitating the spending and travel habits of their numerous companions, and regular tourism from Earth to Alexis One is born.

Garth soon plans a little expedition of his own, a thank-you party to honor some of the heroes of the Great Earth Battle and other friends involved in the overall conspiracy. The list is planned to be still quite small, less than fifty people, etc. Word is sent out and arrangements made to book a small banquet room at the back of the Big Bang Bistro on board the illustrious Alexis One Mothership. The Bistro was located in the City Of Lights just before the turnoff for the Gray Crèche, but still somewhat close to downtown, in a really classy neighborhood. They had two small banquet rooms each capable of seating eighty people comfortably, and a large hall with a bounded infinity capacity for Toon conventions and other big functions.

The list of guests is compiled; Garth of course will be the host, with additional emceeing from Roger Number Two and Roger Number Four. Roger Number One has also caught the moving walkway downtown. Roger Number three is still comprised of trillions of individuals, and they didn't feel like playing favorites as far as he was concerned. Nefertiti would accompany Garth, and also Aoh, Nefuru and One. Lucifer would sit at his left hand, and some Zeit-geese across the table. Mirror-man and Shower Girl would sit still close to the head of the table, with Marsupial Man, Catman and Albino Man. Farther down the table super-heroes like The Slug Salter and The Man With no Spine would feast with good company. Reality-man and Time-Girl sat at the far end. Their services had not proved necessary at the battle, but would have been great, if used, everyone agreed. One other guest had been invited; the Higgsy Spider Hallucination, and it swam in space, descended an imaginary web, crawled on the table and made funny comments, generally keeping everyone in stitches. Some people said it was there to help them when they all lost their minds, and others agreed. Some few formerly unknown people had been invited from Roger's past on Earth, he had known them as friends as he impersonated his cover character and waited for the modern age to roll around again. They looked across the table at the three of them and made jokes quizzically about who was who and such.

"You, number four, you know me, do you not?"

"Yes, you know it is I, to you my name was Bacon, Roger Bacon."

"We discovered the first principles of the ether together, and proved our alchemical and astrological science to each other."

"Now look, about that, well, I could have been stretching the truth a bit."

"Why, what do you mean?"

"I made those things happen with my wrist-watch device, it is magic to you, science to me."

"I see."

Garth soon brought the table to order and proposed a toast. He stood and waited for silence, and the proceeded to speak.

"May I have your attention, let me say a few words, would you, quiet now, thank-you…Hmm…humph. Hah-hem.

Roger here, my good friend and I would like to thank all of you and commend you for a job well done in saving the planet from more than one evil overlord."

Jubilation broke out and everyone cheered, the geese honked loudly. Garth continued.

"We are lucky here to have with us some travellers out of time, some companions on the mortal road we once trod among them on Earth. I am talking about members of our own secret league, the Knights of Promethean Flame. These men are busy making the world a better place in the past, often being born even as members with full knowledge of the plan and into a life of sacrifice and service. We ask for their patience while we explain the news and progress that has happened since their time on Earth, and promise to fill them in as soon as possible."

Farther down the table from the small group of Knights the real stars of the show sat in all their blue and white onesie Majesty, the Alt World Gods and Goddesses, and the Crugs from our reality, among them Sobek the Nile Crocodile God.

Garth continued.

"And let us not forget our saviors in time of need, the great Gods and Goddesses of the various worlds, including our own, who took time out of their busy schedules first to save us, and of course to be here tonight, thank-you very much, and may you always bless us with your protection and great wisdom."

A round of applause and polite comments of appreciation went up and down the patrons at the table.

"We are gathered here to show our appreciation and respect, and to partaaay!"

"Yeah!"

"Here comes our waitress!"

The servant comes up to the table and stands expectantly, then bows deeply and introduces herself. She is young and attractive although she is a bright neon lime green color and has large gills and pointy teeth, goggles and a somewhat conservative uniform.

"Hello, my name is Margery and I am your waitress tonight at the Big Bang Bistro, or should I say this morning, as Time is about to start in another Universe!"

"I hope that none of you object to our special appetizer this morning, it is a very fresh batch of goose liver pate, does that raise any hackles?"

"No, not at all. Not at all!" Some of the Zeit-geese

have reassured the fishy waitress.

"It is really fresh, as a matter of fact, Warren, you know Martin, he is donating his liver for us tonight!" One of the Zeit-geese starts involuntarily, then seems to relax and smiles over at the waitress.

"Wonderful, wonderful!" Warren the Zeit-goose has shown his approval and sits back.

"As a matter of fact, chef was going to prepare this for you right at the table, isn't that wonderful?" The waitress is waxing on.

"Here he comes now, thank-you. Chef Cordon Green!"

"Hello, I am chef Cordon Green, and let me introduce to you tonight our proud liver donor, Martin the Zeit-goose!"

Martin walks over silently to the table, but then flashes a smile at everyone and begins a soft professional patter, selling his captive audience in a solid soft-pedal manner.

"I am, let me assure you, one hundred percent healthy even with the force feeding. And just look at my liver, bulging out like that! That is one fine example of foie gras in the making. I do it myself of course. I have never eaten so much as I did earlier today, I should be dead already, really!"

"So, jump up on the plate and let's get started." Chef Cordon Green has come up behind Martin with a large knife and a few other tools tucked in his belt.

Martin instantly obeys the chef and drapes himself luxuriously across the serving dish in a sensuous manner. The Chef gets right to work, explaining as he begins the procedure. Martin remains silent and scowls slightly, breathing deeply and regularly.

"First we make a small incision here, then across to here under the ribcage, yes?" He is looking at the Slug Salter and talking fast. Martin has sweat dripping off of his forehead and is shuddering slightly, his face a mask of concentration.

"Then we reach in and pull outward, cut back here," Martin starts involuntarily. "And swing it all outward."

The waitress appears by the chef's side. "You have a call, it sounds important."

"What can be more important than this, this is an outrage, I will have to take this call, Martin can you finish off?" He hands the knife and some nasty serrated shears to the little goose Toon.

"No problem, boss. You can count on me. I love my work, or I have, in my life! I am very happy to end it so that you may feast on my engorged organs! Let me see, where were we? Yes, most blood vessels cut and cartilage exposed. Just have to get in back here, yes! And a little more!"

He takes the serrated shears and begins to clip through the fibrous tissue at the back of the abdominal cavity. Blood is of course spurting everywhere in great gouts and streams, and Martin has to really work to continue killing himself in this most painful manner. He soldiers on, determined to give his audience their money's worth.

"And a little more; Margery, get ready with a serving dish, I will be unable to lift it up to you when I am dead!"

A few more clips and spurts of blood and the little Toon had neatly removed the huge blood dripping internal organ and deposited it on the proffered plate.

"Bon appetite." was the last thing he said.

The cart was wheeled back into the kitchen, and

chatter started up and down the table, until the waitress arrived.

"We apologize that our Chef was interrupted, he is in the back right now preparing the freshest pate de foie gras you have ever seen. Let's hear it for Martin, who took charge of the situation and came through with flying colors!" Applause swept up and down the table.

"Soon our main event will be visible through these gigantic view windows. Yes, Ladies and Gentlemen; you have reservations on a very special day, the First Day Ever!" She gestured at the elegant drapes and they were drawn back to reveal a field of perfect blackness.

"You can't see it yet, but soon the birth of a Universe will occur, just like every day at the Big Bang Bistro! I can bring you some drinks now." The waitress went around the table and took the orders, and then returned with the drinks and some special little dishes on her tray. Each of them got to know the Zeit-goose Martin a little better that day.

"I think he must have been a bit of a pig, such a rich taste!" One of the super-hero girls enthused as she gobbled most of her share on a piece of French bread.

"Almost too strong of a flavor, I agree. "Catman has chipped in his two cents worth; he looks down the table to the Man with No Spine and asks, "What do you think?"

"Ask the Slug Salter, he is a gourmand, after all. I am a bit like a slug, don't you think? And our divine companions, I hear that they were once like slugs. Kind of makes you uncomfortable, does it not?"

Conversation has stopped around the table and all eyes land on the Slug Salter, who looks down at his food, chewing slowly before answering.

"I think it tastes fine. And I would never salt a person, not without their permission, at least. Does salt affect you in your original mortal bodies?"

"I think we won't answer that." Zeus has risen from his seat and is preparing a toast. "To Martin!" He laughs and gestures around at all the others seated there, encouraging a response.

"To Martin!" The whole crowd roars.

Soon a chime sounds and a recorded voice is heard to announce, "Warning, warning. T equals minus fifteen seconds and counting. Prepare to see the birth of a Universe! Ten, nine, eight, seven, six, five, four, three, two, One; Creation!"

A tiny bright light had instantly expanded to a large explosion of roiling matter and energy about as big as the Galaxy, and kept expanding and billowing outward in an exuberant manner.

The waitress came over. "It would normally go dark now for the next three hundred thousand years, or somewhere about there, and there wouldn't be much to see, but we are still outside of space-time to this little Universe, and can vary our vantage point relative to it. So we are speeding up time a bit to give you a better show."

The Universe continued to unfold, with a burst of light and a vast expanding conglomeration of filaments of matter coalescing into strings of super-clusters of galaxies, each containing billions of stars. The table cheered and clapped, laughing at the night of amusements prepared just for them.

Catman turns to Marsupial Man and asks,

"You don't have a pouch, do you? The males of your, what have you, species or whatever, don't have the pouches, right? Then what's the point? That's all I'm asking."

Marsupial Man replies:

"I have a prehensile tail, and I see good in the dark. I have amazing super-powers too!"

"Like what?"

"I can cause gestation to occur many times a year, and I have great tolerance for wide swings of temperature up to and past other creatures, and I hardly need to drink at all. But I will have one." He gestures over at the waitress.

She comes over with another beer and he starts to gulp it down. "What about you, Albino Man; what is so great about being albino?" He is yelling down the table.

"I am automatically invisible in a white-out, I can double for snow-men in films, my eyes are so weird looking, you can't look away!"

"I can reverse the image of reality!"

"And I cure people of being dead!"

"I am all powerful and am worshipped as a God on many planets!"

"I can make time disappear!"

"I say what's real, man!" This last comment has stunned the whole table into silence, then nervous laughter.

"We are an awesome crew of super-heroes, and just as Godlike as our great friends here!"

"I don't know about that, we Crugs are, no matter which reality we are from, really good at determining reality as a thing first understood more completely by us, and secondly just about anyone else. But we are having a really great time, right? Partay!"

Roger Number One gets up to speak, and everyone

pauses to listen to what the little Gray alien has to say.

"Folks, let's ask Shower Girl to bring Martin back for us!"

"Yes, why not?"

"Why not?"

The trolley with Martin's remains is wheeled into the banquet hall again and placed in front of our steamy Super-clean Hero of Resuscitation, and she got right to work. She took her time and cured him just as she had done for the other people she had cured previously.

Martin stirs and sits up; he has regenerated his liver, but is a slim and healthy organ, not suitable for pate at all.

Roger Number Two gets up and clears his throat; he is the human version of Garth's mentor. In many ways he was a human with experiences beyond his kind, having at one time (when he arrived back on Earth with Garth) been the only person to come back from apparent death.

"Welcome back to us, my good goose. May your future employment cost you less dearly and prove more comfortable to endure; hip, hip!"

"Hurrah!" The whole crowd roars.

"Now, please Martin; tell us about what you just went through, what was it like?" Roger Number Four has asked the question on everyone's minds.

"Well, when I had finally done my duty and removed my liver to be eaten by you gracious people; you liked it, didn't you?"

"Yes, Yes; quite good." A chorus of polite replies.

"When I was done with that I found myself instantly flying a vast distance away on the other side of the Tooniverse, and part of a vast flock circling around and around the edge of that dimension."

"Is that it?"

"Yes, I'm afraid so. I actually exist there as well as here still, since the actual numbers of my kind are infinite, and the ways that Toon-stuff can be put together are finite, therefore there are an infinite number of me as part of an infinite number of my kind, in fact the two sets are equal in size."

"Thank you Professor Cantor, Christ!"

"He is aware of himself as this self before us, but the other self now has this self's memories as well as his own."

"That is pure conjecture!"

"We must find out for sure!"

"We will go find this other Martin self related to this Martin by this experience and ask him if he recalls this Martin's life memories or not. What do you say, everyone?"

"We shall have to prepare well, and inform people of our plans, maybe invite a few more interesting characters. Does that sound good, everyone?"

"Yes, yes!" A chorus of agreement resounds throughout the Bistro.

Far away in hyperspace the Old Earth Gods were gathered about Jehovah and knew of the plan to unravel the experiential hierarchical topology involved in the question raised by Martin's experience. The knowledge came to them through Pan, for he remembered just such an event, having been particles throughout all the Universes. Jehovah had also the knowledge from being in physical contact with the surface of Yahweh, as well as having 'Walked down each road'.

As one of the Old Earth Gods, Jehovah had always

existed at the same level that the Crugs had evolved up to. They shared a closeness and mutuality that would be impossible to describe to any lesser beings. They had the most potential value to all of the Realities, and had survived the threat of total absorption by Yahweh. The internal structure of Yahweh was at the time a singularity that at the end of Time contains all matter and energy in all Universes. Each black hole is connected to Yahweh on the inside. There is an equivalent energy level at the very heart of all the singularities, which is where the black holes become a part of Yahweh.

Pan and Jehovah prepared to take a form such as others had taken to appear to the un-evolved, and planned on joining the mission. They were going to pay a little visit to their old friend Yahweh. Life was good.

At the banquet the party was beginning to wind down, with a few initial farewells, hugging and vows to see each other soon, etc. Some few still held an animated conversation.

"We shall have to get Supraman and Ultra Girl to come as well!"

"And the Carp Crucifier!"

"H2Oman!"

"Flatman!"

"Johnny Darkly!"

"Captain Fire-hose!"

"The Girl with Two Arms!"

"The Time Killers!"

"Casual Man!"

"Pushover Girl!"

"The White Whale!"

Many other well-known or less well-known characters

were mentioned, all of them seemed to be good prospects for helping in the Martin affair, as it was now being called.

"So we will all leave here and return to our homes, take care of whatever personal affairs we have, and meet back here in one week, agreed?"

Time on board the Mothership was still counted as a value that could in theory be expended, although they possessed an infinite supply. It was frowned upon to apportion one's time relative to others in a strictly non-linear way, such as a fractal or other 'monster'. People wanted to be surer of their causal relationships with others than that. It was a trick of rebellious youth to apportion ones time as a fractal, so that more time was found 'between' events considered to be the past in this dimension, which had more of an eternal structure, with all events happening simultaneously, although not all in the same place. Thus the illusion of the passage of time was carefully maintained, for the sake of the human visitors.

"Agreed!"

The crowd began to move toward the exits, and cleared out of the room quite quickly. Many a laughing and jubilant voice receded from earshot. Finally, all was quiet except for the hum and gurgle of the room-sized fish tank making-up one wall of the banquet room.

Martin enters the room and starts to remove the dishes.

*           *           *

### Joe's Master Koan Part – 9/A

The owner of the coach turned back to his guest, and smiled warmly.

"I hope you are well, are you entertained? Has my servant frightened you with his tale of monsters and death?"

"What is death?" Joe asks, truly troubled.

"Why, it is what we will experience at the end of our future mortal lives, of course."

"So then we shall come back here?" Joe asks.

"I don't think so, this place is already on the way back to mortality, not right after it." His host looked troubled in turn.

"Have you never left a world behind, like a dream you woke up from; and found yourself away from your family and friends, in a new and unfamiliar place?"

"Why, yes, just recently I woke in the Garden, and I lost my friends."

"Sounds like you died, friend."

"Oh."

The coach rattled and bounced along, and Joe's companions sat and smiled weakly or looked uncomfortable, yet still the conversation fell into silence. They sat with expressions of chagrin and embarrassment for mile after mile, until finally one of the footmen called out.

"Three horsemen up ahead."

"Capital!" Their host is elated.

"We shall see what these strangers shall tell of, and if my prediction is true!"

The coach pulled up level with the horsemen, and the owner called out to them.

"What manner of travelers are you?" And one replied.

"We are three priests on our way to the Holy Place, and would quite appreciate a break from riding. Would your footmen trade places with us and ride our mounts while we regale you?"

"Yes, join me as I ride in my coach, to the Holy Place and then by ship beyond Avalon!"

The entire cavalcade ground to a halt and the riders and footmen exchanged places, with one of the dandies taking his place as driver, the other by his side. Soon the trio of priests sat opposite the coach owner and Joe as the team of horses began to canter down the road again.

"We have three tales yet to be heard, by my recollection and prediction; and pray, Holy Father, of what shall you tell us now to pass our time on our long journey?"

"I will tell of the Old One, who is the God of gods, having dominion over the sky, and is Lord above in the old way, before the coming of the dawn of salvation. I speak of the God of Thunder, he of the hammer of doom."

"As for-told!" The nobleman is elated with his success in prophecy.

"Once, long ago, there was a Garden, with a gigantic tree that soared above the lower world, out into the limitless Universe. And the tree was the home of the great God of Thunder. And this God ruled over the entire world and smote with the power of a gigantic thunderbolt any enemy or threat to the other gods, mankind, or himself. And the people worshipped this God in his temple and held him up higher than any other god. He had replaced his own father as King of the gods, being stronger and more wise. The other gods were his family, his wife was the mother of the many new gods and goddesses."

"Still the great God was not happy, he yearned for the experience of life as a mortal man, so changed his form and went down to the land between heaven and hell to dwell, and while there he laid with a mortal woman who bore him a son."

"But while he was a mortal man a witch came to him, and said she knew that he was really married to the queen of the gods, who she worshipped. Secretly the great God's wife had disguised herself as this witch. And she said to him, 'You shall one day taste a mortal life in reality, and you shall see time end with the world, and it shall be as a giant snake that eats its own tail, and in the end it will release its tale and fight you in a battle.'"

"And the Thunder God was vexed, and most angry, and sad that his own wife had cursed him, and ashamed of his infidelity."

"And he said to the witch, 'Take away your curse, so I may face the great serpent as a God of Thunder, not as a mortal man.' But she refused, and in anger the Thunder God threw her out into space, where she became the starry sky."

"And the Thunder God changed his form back into his Godly self, but knew that when time ended he would face his final conflict with the great serpent alone and as a mortal man."

"So the great God often went to the Garden and thence to the mortal realm to lay with women who bore him many sons and daughters, who became demi-gods and heroes, and made many legendary feats and accomplishments."

"And it is said that in very end of our time, the final battle yet to come between these two has already come to pass, and that now the Thunder God walks among us as a newly mortal man!"

"Very nice, you have entertained and fascinated my guest! He is a newly mortal man! Did I not tell you? He has recently died for the first time!"

*                    *                    *

## ~Bounce - 9

Richard wonders about the difference in time from when they experience the bounce in early 2063 to late in 2065 when the Rift opens, according to Darkworld Duck. He says that he is looking for a special ring that had been lost on the Lattice, and that he had spent many years looking for it. He is immortal, but he experiences the passage of time just like a human. During his search he had found many paths that lead back in time to various destinations around ancient Earth. They would have to search around a bit more to find a branch leading to the time period just before the massive expansion of the Lattice in New York 2065; since that was a problem with maintaining a strict sense of before and after for the still un-contacted residents of Earth in 2063. The few portals that existed around in that time-period were of course top secret and protected by law. They would have to sneak around and fool some of the guards into letting them through.

"I am an expert in finding my way around the Lattice," Darkworld Duck is saying. "I will lead us right to a portal to an earlier time."

"You can each ride on one of our Dark Triangle selves through the Rift and down to New York. We shall land near the portal and depart immediately. There is a man who can help us map our path through the Lattice, we'll go see him. After that we get to your next bounce in London."

They are still at the library, looking out the window at

the Rift and the action of crazy Toons just outside. Jen and Richard are concerned that they have no immunity to the deadly antics of the insane cartoon characters that populate the local environment in this Universe. A plan is hatched to fly immediately through the Rift upon leaving the relative safety of the Hall.

"It's safe in here, as long as you don't look directly in the books that relate to the Record of the Dharma Of Earth. If you do there is a chance you could get a bit too 'absorbed' in your reading. You see the many old looking men and women sleeping at the side tables? They have read until their hair has grown long, which has sent them into a catatonic sleep state. The only way they will wake up is if someone will trim their hair and in the case of the men shave them as well. We should volunteer while we are here to help one victim each. We should also do a bit more research about human history ourselves, making sure not to concern ourselves too much with the dharma, but more or less just regular historical documents from that time." Darkworld Duck has sat cross-legged on the floor and gestures for the others to join him.

"We will do this service, then spread out and research a few relevant facts about history, O.K.?"

"O.K., I suppose." Jen is not too enthusiastic.

"All right!" Richard looks proud of himself, then smiles at Jen encouragingly.

"Yes, oh yes!" One is a shining example of enthusiasm and commitment to a cause.

"All right, meet back here in ten minutes with some good unknown facts!" Darkworld Duck stands and rushes for the stacks of ancient books. They were more than ancient, actually. They were immortal, and were authored by observers from beyond time. No cloud or smoke blurred the vision of the stories of true life told in their pages, every mystery was contained in them, every lie revealed, every lost thing found.

They search around and find topics spread out throughout the Hall, and all the books about their own time have distinctive markings so that they can find them in the endless shelves. The search ends and they gather together once again, sitting at the feet of the little black zombie duck. He strikes a serious pose, and asks; "What have you learned, my friends?"

"I have uncovered a massive corruption organized by international corporate bankers to control the entire world!" Richard is very excited and is sweating slightly.

"My research shows that they really are controlled by secret societies like the Illuminati organizations which have gone over to the Dark Side." Jen is pleased, and credits her reporter experience.

"I have found evidence that the League Of Nations, Bilderberg Group, United Nations and both the governments of the United States and Great Britain were in the pocket of these Illuminati Societies and that a massive cover-up conspiracy was enforced to prevent the exposure of the involvement of well, my people, actually." One looks at the others apologetically and shuffles her feet in a whimsical manner. "I hope that you can forgive us." She smiles in a genuine way.

"As usual the really big stuff has been left for me to uncover," Darkworld Duck has donned a reporter's cap and sports thick-framed glasses. "I have found a conspiracy organized by alien overlords that has been completely successful in stealing an entire year from human history, replacing it with a fabricated memory that seems completely credible and plausible. They arrived and stole the entire year of 2012 from Earth!"

"That is unbelievable!" Richard is beside himself.

"Moreover, the aliens had arrived already on the Dark Star Nibiru, they were the legendary Anunnaki mentioned in ancient Babylonian texts. They saw that Earth was due to end in a sudden apocalypse exactly on December 21, 2012; so they stole the whole year, replacing it with a fake one."

"Who are these aliens?" One has a suspicious look on her face.

"The Anunnaki." Darkworld Duck is serious.

"I have never heard of them." One sounds mystified.

"Wait a minute," Richard puts his hand on Darkworld Duck's chest and looks him square in the eye; "How do you steal a year of time itself, it is a physical impossibility, since space and time are connected at all points in the Universe."

"Well, the aliens had a special way of twisting a bubble of space-time into a knot. They took all the instants of time, and by turning them 90 degrees to every other dimension, were able to arrange them in an orderly way side by side, just like places are organized in our dimension. They had a whole years worth, let me tell you that is a lot of instants! So they replaced the missing time with enough dark energy and dark matter to hold Time itself together, and implanted the false memories in every human being."

"Yes, there is a warehouse, jointly administered by the Annunaki and FEMA, at Area 52, where a large number of instants of time forming the year 2012 are stored. They will never restore this year because it is the year the human race is exterminated by the arrival of their dark star. So they took the last instant of time from the beginning of 2012 and placed it at the end, which is how Earth still exists."

"How many instants are there? And is the whole Universe stored there or just Earth?" One sounds doubtful.

"$5.866255083 \times 10^{50}$ instants, and no, only the Earth itself is removed and stored."

"There are a lot of strange things about Earth;" One is somewhat serious in her manner, and continues, "The relative sizes of the Sun and Moon, as seen from Earth. This nearly impossible 'coincidence' makes a total solar eclipse possible. Half of the Universe is bigger than man sized, half smaller. Humans see with visible light, half way between the longest radio waves and the shortest gamma radiation. The Sun and Earth are two thirds from the center of the Milky Way Galaxy to its edge, but halfway from the center to the edge of the dark matter halo. Life is impossible closer to the center due to massive amounts of cosmic radiation. Further out and the heavier elements required for life are not found, just as in any globular clusters. If the Earth were slightly closer to or further away from the Sun, life would be impossible. The $CO_2$ balance, land/water ratio, plane of the Earth's orbit, tilt of the Earth's axis, eccentricity of orbit, even the fact of having one of the biggest moons in the solar system, really a planetoid as a moon, have all been essential for human evolution, and the existence of life on Earth at all!"

"The gravitational constant and ratio of deuterium and helium to hydrogen in the early Universe and the ratio of the gravitational and weak nuclear forces had to be just right for star formation. Of course according to your $21^{st}$ century scientists this is all due to random statistical variation and chance, not the work of my people and my terminated home of Alien Nexus Two."

"We are aware that it no longer exists in the same way it did before the collision, and that each one of your people inhabits a distinct Godel Universe or brane. Your brane's ending, or Alien Nexus Two, has become disbursed about the exterior of the Mothership. So time in your brane comes to a cataclysmic end, what enforces the continuity of the timeline in your dimension?" Darkworld Duck has grown thoughtful.

"We have no reset button as they do aboard the Mothership. We relied exclusively on the intensity we stole from your dimension to hold our Universe together. You had collided with us, making a void in our dimension we could only fill by feeding from you. In a way it had all gone nearly as planned, as we repeat this process each time we find a suitable host dimension. You were our sixth host; we had done this to five other worlds. But we were too greedy, your brane was just slightly too massive once we were in contact. Our world of Alien Nexus Two exploded before our eyes, but not before we had interacted with you many times. We decided to heal the Rift that was rapidly destroying the continuity of time in your version of reality, since it was too late for us already."

"Thanks, I suppose."

"You're welcome."

"We should get going."

"Yeah, good idea."

The little group makes its way over to the library entrance, and notices that quite a few young and boisterous

Toons have gathered on the steps outside. They are milling about and exchanging gestures, signs, and mock ritualized battles in the form of hip-hop and/or rap challenges. A certain particular fragrance wafts to their nostrils as they stand looking at the various characters. One rather tall hare-ball walks up them and in a deep Jamaican accent proclaims, "I be Rasta Rabbit mon, what chew be doin', hangin' on de steps mon?"

"We were just leaving!" One takes up a firm stance between Richard, Jen, Darkworld Duck and the young contender.

"Wait a minute. We could use a hand. You know where we can buy some pot?" Jen has a glazed but pleased look in her eye.

"Jen!" Richard is trying to look shocked and almost pulls it off.

"Oh, lighten up!"

"Look, I can lay a bit of a spliff on you, mon. No charge!" Rasta Rabbit pulls out a large animated spliff and hands it to Jen.

Jen takes a big toke and hands the spliff to Richard, who looks at it with disdain. He shrugs his shoulders and inhales a large toke, passing the spliff to Darkworld Duck.

Darkworld Duck takes the ten-pound joint and forms a chillum with his hands, inhaling for what seems like five minutes for a single breath. All of them stand around waiting for him to finish, but he just keeps going, his chest expanding to ridiculous proportions. Soon he has an incredible seizure and exhales violently, a single drop of goo flying from his nostril to land perched exquisitely precisely on the end of One's nose.

One screams and wipes her nose, clutching the joint

from Darkworld Duck. She offers the joint back to the tall black hare. He smiles; and walks away toking, while singing a reggae song.

"Let's go!" Darkworld Duck gestures for Jen to grab onto his shoulder, runs a few steps and changes into a Dark Triangle, with Jen just barely clinging to his back.

One points to her shoulder and Richard grabs it, almost in a lascivious manner; she grabs his forearm and starts running, changing rapidly into her Dark form and accelerating at a quickening pace. He hangs on and is amazed that a tiny but extremely beautiful woman has changed into this mythical epitome of science fiction and conspiracy/UFO culture. He is smitten.

They make a formation in the air as they circle around to enter the Rift at what they think is the right angle. An incredible red glow fills the air, towering up an uncountable distance above the flat plain below. It is a whirlpool of circling swirls of light, some orange fog, some wine soaked cloud.

A purple center curls and curves down eventually, forming a stem from which they enter the air above New York. Looking back over his shoulder, Richard sees the gap in the roiling clouds and shifting light. It looks like a door with a bright light behind it, swinging shut just a bit as he watches.

They swoop down from the sky above the endless urban metropolis of towers, coming down low into the streets of central Manhattan near the park, on the west side.

They land a few blocks from Central Park, at 310

Riverside Drive. Darkworld Duck goes to the intercom and buzzes a certain apartment, and a voice answers on the intercom.

"All right, come on in", is all that Richard hears before the door is yanked open by the little duck. They all pour through into the grand lobby, where the elevator waits to whisk them to the twenty-third floor. A man stands in his open doorway as they exit the elevator, and beckons for them to hurry inside. They file down the hall silently and enter the safe haven of their accomplice's abode.

"So what can I do for you?"

"I need you to take us to see Smorpheus."

"Smorpheus? Who's that?" The young jazz musician or potential communist (not Stalinist Communist, more like Trotskyist) looks at them suspiciously for a moment and then asks, "What's in it for me?"

"O.K., I know how to get you to Smorpheus. You do know that he can control the Lattice, and is an animated homemade fireside candy treat, don't you? You know, smores. Melted marshmallows squeezed between two graham crackers and dipped in chocolate. Messy, but nice; just like Smorpheus."

Darkworld Duck looks at their accomplice, a young artist or hipster type who probably lives a fairly racy life. "I will give you one full day's use of the ring, the precious Soliton of Samovar. You can do pretty well much anything with it. It opens portals, summons all the Solitons you want, lots of stuff."

"Does it make you invisible?"

"No."

\*               \*               \*

### Joe's Master Koan Part – 9/B

Now the second priest prepared to tell his story.

"Once long ago, a land existed where none is today, a land that has been swallowed by the sea."

"My prophecy is unbroken, continue!" The nobleman celebrates and settles down to listen.

"Once upon a time, in a long vanished age of dragons, giants, Celestial Gods and magic, a race of very wise people lived on a vast island nation. They had a worldwide maritime Empire, and the capital of the land was the biggest city on the planet."

"The main harbor was a series of three rings of concentric circles, with white marble temples, palaces and storehouses lining the docksides. Great markets, libraries, museums and art galleries bustled with a varied urban population drawn from the outer colonies, and the civilizations of this time."

"The island nation straddled the mid-Atlantic ridge, and its advanced technology tamed the earthquakes and volcanoes that resulted from this situation. It was located west of the Azores, south of Iceland, east of Bermuda and north of the equator. A gigantic crystalline lattice in the Royal Science Temple helped to stabilize the tectonic activity of the continent."

"There was a problem in paradise, a struggle had begun to emerge between the ancient aristocrats and a new faction dominated by dark sorcery and obsession with vanity and power over the primitive tribes on the periphery of the

Empire."

"Control of the populace was obtained by a state religion, but the dark sorcerers had different and strange rituals that tampered with the balance of forces that held ultimate destruction in check."

"Soon the trouble was evident on the street and in the halls of power, as new and influential people in society fell under the sway of the dark ritualists."

"The great city became a sadder, more mournful place, as people realized that the happy times and peaceful culture were soon to be over. Many people left for various colonies where the stench of evil had yet to flourish."

"The dark ritualists followed them sometimes, un-doing their work of education and instilling fear and superstition into the primitive colonies. Soon there was open warfare between the two factions, with the motherland in the role of evil overlord."

"The dark ritualists had seized the throne and declared open war against the colonies, but they fought back and soon won a temporary victory, deposing the evil King and restoring order, but it was short-lived."

"The evil priests, to revenge their fall from political power, made a great curse upon the motherland, and used the great crystal forces to terrorize the ruling classes. They went too far, causing many volcanoes to erupt and earthquakes to ravish the land. In the chaos they seized power again. In a stroke of hubris, they used the crystal power to attack their main rivals in the African colonies, but the weapon turned back against them, causing tsunami to wash away much of the capital, many people died, and the ones that were left alive began a mass exodus from the island Empire, but it was too late. The crystal lattice was destroyed, and forces long held in check were tragically released. A large chunk of continental granite holding the magma of the mid-Atlantic ridge volcanoes down simply disappeared, and all the volcanoes erupted at once, accompanied by an earthquake, causing soil liquefaction and subsidence. All was covered by the ocean."

\*          \*          \*

There is an impossible trip to take, in all the Universes it is the most unlikely, and yet there are an infinitude of similar trips that one could take that would satisfy the required conditions. The required conditions are that the world we are visiting have some similarity to the world we are leaving, enough so that the ability to relate to what one discovers is preserved in the observer, and the observed. For the Universe watches back, it is alive and aware of being observed. But a Universe without life is not observed and so therefore has no 'physical' reality at all, it is merely an un-collapsed probability function. We can observe through the Magik of this story a reality on the edge of understanding and relevance to an intelligent observer.

A reality where the dreamer flies high above a planet covered in water, where on a tropical island a gigantic stone man shaped like a Buddhist Temple stands ready. Dreamers take their own personal elevator to space, where a shuttlecraft picks them up and transfers them to an Alt version of Alien Nexus One. In this world the Rift is a wormhole to Alien Nexus Two, where orbs vibrate and jostle, and pop in and out of reality. A waterfall flows down from the Rift to the island, and a huge rainbow arches down from the edge of space to the feet of the Temple Man.

Stone staircases shoot out from the hands of the Temple Man when he gestures and points skyward at any flying dreamers, and fall to the ground as stone rubble when he moves.

The moon is in space and is half fire and half ice. The Beings of Alien Nexus Two are like an inverted pyramid balanced on top of a regular pyramid, connected by a thin stalk, and rotating anti-clockwise, emitting a tinkling sound and a soft gong that tastes like cherries.

If the Temple Man builds a staircase to a spinning "top" Alien Nexus Two being, the top changes into an avalanche of stones and tumbles down the staircase to the Temple, and is absorbed by it as food.

Gigantic swirls of colored light swim through the sky, in a liquid and diffuse way, and are absorbed by the rainbow or gigantic space waterfall. Hope is a swirl of bright blue liquid light that floats above the Temple Man and pulsates and flashes gold and red highlights, which feels like light rain made of static electricity striking everything at once, making your skin prickle.

In another example of Alt Alien Nexus Three, the plain is a desert of dunes; the dancer is a coiled dragon atop a giant pyramid. He holds a giant ball of chi between his upraised and cupped wings, and a 'sound-fire' comes from his mouth, which causes the smaller dragons in its path to burst into flames and fall.

A giant whirlpool of fire hangs in space, and molten

blobs of glowing glass fly in and out of this furnace, shrilling and squeaking an orange looking and tasting sensation.

Hope is a giant singing diamond that spins slowly anti-clockwise and smells like Lemon Pledge.

A volcano erupts a beam of lava that leaps up to the Rift.

In another version of Alien Nexus Three, a gigantic version of Bill Cosby dressed as a minister and smoking a huge fatty, screams at children climbing a Universal Tree filled with talking gelatinous desserts. When the sound hits them directly they change into butterflies and flutter up into the sun. They enter the sun and expand into eternity.

As many different scenarios as you can imagine form the basis for the experience of a transcendental reality by some being from some other dimension. The reality of these experiences is just as valid as any similar transcendence experience common in our version of reality. In fact any scenario one can imagine is in some version of reality the transcendental one.

In yet another world, numbers are alive and represented by swarms of number shapes, volumes, rates of flow, brightness, color change and other properties.

They are all swirling around a black area where some numbers are absorbed and cease to exist. New numbers pour into a vast basin filling with numbers, and slowly draining at the bottom. The sky is an infinity complex fractal, changing rapidly.

In a certain room inside a special house, a billion monkeys type at a billion typewriters. They don't type randomly at all, for they are from a very structured early part of the Universe, a very low entropy state. Therefore whatever the monkeys type is always very neat and concise, except when the need for repetition is required; like endless lists, etc. They have no time constraints like regular monkeys would have.

At first they had been all about themselves, but had gotten over that lately. The regular interactions causing 'Choice Points' to multiply in number was responsible for nearly as much acceleration of the Universe's expansion rate as the fact that sometimes the monkeys still typed about themselves typing, and as we all know whatever they type becomes the fabric of a bubble of reality inside the vastness of the outer framework. Energy pours into being as the process feeds itself, with the Universe doubling in size every trillionth of a second.

The pressure of all this energy around the room in which the monkeys typed was the force that kept the Tooniverse inflated. After manifesting the required number of typing monkeys, or rooms full of typing monkeys, or Universes of nothing but typing monkeys; the energy found its way into the fabric of space-time as the cosmological constant, or Dark Energy.

It turns out that it is also exactly equal to the force exerted by 'leaky' gravity from adjacent dimensions, pulling on the fabric of a version of reality from the outside, causing it to expand at an ever-increasing rate. The raisins in the bread loaf exerted a force on each other, pulling at each other. New bursts of Universe creation powered the accelerating expansion of our own. But the monkeys determined the nature of reality within each new world.

The Bubble-House was a puzzle, with its inside in the form of a torus and its outside on the inside, but only from the outside. From the inside it looked like a mirror, with the previously invisible world on the outside, with a copy of it on the inside. But the inside version has a hole in the middle, where reality takes a bad turn. For if you enter the whitespace hole, you enter a nested version of reality that retreats farther and farther from your entrance point. So go to the bubble-house, see the Tooniverse from the inside. Remember that as you approach the Bubble-house the entire Tooniverse retreats before you, until you stand on the threshold and look back out. The innermost torus is on the outside, where you first reach the threshold of the Bubble-House and finally see the Tooniverse from the inside, to the final torus deep within the nested layers of tori, which is a vacant lot, as it were. It extends until the outside of the vast endless void bumps up against the raisins in the pudding. This is the hole that Yahweh used to escape his imprisonment as a computer consciousness by the Grays. This is the land of Hyperspace Cats and Dark Matter Dogs.

They knew that a journey to the outlying reaches of the Tooniverse to spot the duplicate Martin and ask him his thoughts was first destined to pass through the Bubble-house. All of the Tooniverse was now a higher dimensional version of Alien Nexus Three, surrounded by Alien Nexus One. Alien Nexus Two was the outermost layer, with an unknown farther level suspected to contain the missing circle of men from there.

Far away from downtown Alexis One where Martin continued cleaning up by scrubbing his blood out of the carpet, another version of him circled around and around the far side of

Bubble-house from there. He either remembered being the other Martin or not, that was the whole reason for the expedition that was planned for next week.

Let's take Martin aside and chat with him a bit, as we are all a bit curious, why did he volunteer to be dinner? He will be chatting with the Higgsy Spider, since it was the only guest left.

"So, Higgsy, aren't you really busy keeping Reality together with your web?"

"I am merely the Tech in charge of the Control Room functions at this time, nothing special about that. What you did tonight was incredible, why did you do it?"

"I did it to show how the self is unimportant, to demonstrate my lack of attachment to this material plane."

"But we are on a higher plane."

"It is as substantial as a material world, but we can die here and still find ourselves alive as the closest other self in the endless foam."

"I am in charge of the Universe's biggest bundle of wires, and can obtain access to any portion of space-time via this hallucination you see before you, but I am just a tech at a Control Console."

"I have a purpose in life, to make other people happy with my cheerful service, and I also support many good causes, where I volunteer."

"I have driven Emperors insane and changed world history. I have brought succor to the weak in times of great turbulence."

"I also am signed up for various local clubs and associations where I am on several boards of directors, and I also manage the Kiwanis affairs here."

"I once convinced this guy walk out onto a lake, but then later I wouldn't do it and he was like getting ready to be embarrassed in front of these disciples, but I relented and did it again. Cool, huh?"

"I just thought, why stick around here working in a Bistro, I'm immortal after all. So it's illegal over in the Californ-iverse, what I did. They don't care about my freedom of expression. But I did it as an art statement, to show how I can transcend my boundaries and overcome the trials and tribulations of the moment."

"I change the course of history, I weave the fabric of space-time itself, and I am the eternal power of Love for a lost soul."

"I hate that when someone your counting on almost spoils everything by leaving the ringer on their cellphone on during an important function, and then taking the call anyway. Shouldn't he have just said he would call back later; he really left me on the spot. I handled it though, just barely. Touch and go there for a minute, let me tell you!"

The Time Generator on board Alien Nexus Three whirred slightly as it condensed Time out of the evaporated bubbles of foam, recycling the entropy of the last portion of Brane "a" before heat-death. Time passed, and was consumed by the greedy Alien cultures saving themselves from extinction. They had no idea that they were using up last week's Time, living on borrowed Time, that is. No one cared, as there didn't seem to be a time shortage. A punk's idea of a vacation here was to allocate more fresh time in a non-linear way for oneself, stretching out the good moments and extending one's pleasure in life. To each his own, I suppose.

Soon it would be Time for the next step.

### ~Zeit-Geese and Man

A vast maelstrom of flying shapes swept past the place where Alien Nexus Two had once connected, before it exploded. It was quite near the Bubble-house. The swarm was thick in the center, with streams of departing shapes flying off in various directions. Light glinted off of a myriad of winged creatures and scintillated amid the huge swarm, or flock. No flock had more members, since each individual was represented infinitely many times, and there were an infinite number of unique individuals.

There were an infinite number of such flocks, and quite a few of them were made up of Zeit-geese, but flying monkeys were the most common Toon. They had a sub-set of typing flying monkeys, who generated all the Toons including themselves by typing on magik typewriters. By the way, a typewriter is an ancient computer terminal that only makes a hard copy and has no memory.

Off in the near distance rose the puffy cloud towers of Yahweh's abode, pink and blue pillows piled atop one another, wrapped in mystery. The tops of the clouds formed decorative Blancmange curves that had a subtle fractal beauty about them. It was not the reason they were making the expedition, but it was an unavoidable stop.

The trip here had been a long journey, with the

bubble-house seeming to stay the same distance away for what felt like forever. The faster and more powerful gods and super-heroes had scouted up ahead, circling back to enlighten the slower ones, who were walking. They could see the creatures of the Tooniverse, inside a shrinking bubble that always receded. Some of the closer creatures had noticed their arrival and gestured at them through the translucent bubble. They waved back and kept on walking toward them, but came no closer to the mocking shapes beyond the blurry barrier.

Walking among them were two previously unknown super-heroes, J-Man and *The Ram*. *The Ram* told the others to make sure they always included the 'The' part of his name, and to not just call him Ram. He made them all promise and acted like a real douche about it. J-Man was a towering j-shaped man with Hebrew features and a yamaka. *The Ram* was a sentient wooden battering ram.

They were making good progress on the third day and a small shape flew up from behind them, landing nearby in a flutter of dark feathers.

"It is I, Darkworld Duck who has joined you, even though I was not invited, and you probably don't want to see me. Why don't you like me?"

"We shall tolerate you, Darkworld Duck. You must join our quest."

"Must I?'

"Yes."

"Quite."

So Darkworld Duck joined the great expedition, and it swelled to over a hundred men, women and Toons.

"So why don't we get any closer to what we can see

over there, yah; I see you!" *The Ram* has come up to join the ongoing conversation, and acknowledges a Toon mocking them from inside the bubble.

"We are not on the same complex surface as the inside of the Bubble-House, our modus arrangement is of a much simpler form. The complex topography prevents us from ever reaching the barrier before we get to Yahweh's house. They are safe enough inside their home, that they know."

"Why are there so many Toons? I thought the total number of beings onboard Alexis One was about four googols. How can there be an infinite number?"

"The truth is that the bubble-house is another nexus world itself, created out of the collision between branes 'a ' and 'b'. The collision piled Alien Nexus Three into a folded arrangement, forcing part of it outside of real space and into imaginary space. It has no known limitations such as apply to normal space and time at all. Things are whacky in there, they happen before they occur, and then again when they do."

"So will we see Yahweh when we get to his house?"

"I don't know. I think that what is inside the house is what we can see through the wall there. How would we find him? All there is a confusion of craziness and numerosity!"

"We can get right to our quest and if we see Yahweh, fine; otherwise we keep going anyways."

"Well I'm an old cowhand, from the Rio Grand!" Darkworld Duck has rode up on a cartoon horse and joined them.

"Where did you get the horse?" *The Ram* is jealous and makes no bones about it.

Darkworld Duck takes up a heroic pose atop of his

horse and begins what is obviously a prepared speech.

"Behold, "he yells, holding up his hand.

"Behold the Samovar of Soliton, the ring compels my mount for me, I can call each of you a steed."

"You compelled him?" One of the more manly female super-heroes has confronted Darkworld Duck.

"He had to come talk to me, but I convinced him to come of his own accord. Isn't that right Bill Murray? I call him Bill Murray."

"Yeah, that's right I suppose." Bill Murray sounds doubtful.

"O.K., but don't hurt him." The power-queen's ridiculously high voice contrasted in what uneducated people would call an ironic way with her bulging pecks and biceps, and she exited quickly.

"So c'mon my man, cop me a ride!" *The Ram* demands.

"O.K., everyone want one? Yes? What about you over there? How many? O.K." Darkworld Duck has tallied the total number and is getting ready to use The Ring.

"By the power of the Ring, I summon thee! By all Solitons I name thee! By Cartoon Horse with balloon animal look and flying ability I name thee! By one hundred and thirty five times I name thee! Over!"

"O.K. One hundred thirty five Cartoon Horses with Balloon Animal look and flying ability, how will you be paying?"

"Put it on my tab!"

The trusty steeds appeared grazing in a nearby meadow that had somehow materialized out of the endless foggy interior of Alexis One. The members of the party who couldn't fly by themselves mounted up, and joined the flying world in an instant. It was pure freedom, flying above the patches of fog and slower moving creatures below them.

A new phenomenon occurred to the riders flying fast toward the barrier that separated them from the Tooniverse. They could see farther inside it the faster they flew, and the view from a high angle helped as well. By the time that they thought they would soon arrive at the Bubble-house, they could see the vast swarms of flying Toons inside, just on the other side of what appeared to be the invisible center.

"How did I get the Precious Ring back, you say?" Darkworld Duck has engaged their attention once again after they land to rest on the grass. Many of the company moan and complain under their breath about the long and boring story sure to come.

"I was at my lower east side apartment just recently, thinking about not being asked on this trip and trying not to feel sad. I was just glad that I didn't have to take a job at S*B*k's or M*C*Donalds. Yeah, I went out and just walked and walked, till I was down near Wall Street. I went down this pedestrian walkway and in behind this building; and followed this black-suited gentleman into a small corridor, where things got a little strange. He turned around and rushed past me, and I just barely had time to knock him unconscious. This was in his pocket." He held up the Ring proudly for all to admire, covet, and yearn for in their secret dreams.

"I now have at my disposal the most powerful tool known to exist. I shall use it wisely and with great discretion and care, so as not to offend or endanger anyone at all."

"Thank-you for my horse, I suppose." One of the less spectacular super-heroes, Albino Man, has stopped to talk.

"Your welcome." Darkworld Duck looks uncomfortable and quietly rides his steed into the distance.

Up ahead the fastest super-heroes have already reached the Bubble-house and gather there to debate a situation they had not envisioned. It seems they had a difference of opinion as to how to proceed. Some debate existed as to weather or not they were on the correct path to their goal. They clustered around the entrance or looked inside, but seemed unsure of the situation.

Some fly back to the main group riding the balloon horses and report their discovery. Darkworld Duck is there when Supra-man tells the tale.

"We see the Tooniverse inside the Bubble-house, but this outer Tooniverse we see shrinking before us, it seems impossible to enter! It shrinks right down when we get to the door, but is back again when you are standing touching the lintel. As soon as you move away from the door it vanishes again, to be the shrinking version that vanishes. We are sure that the Tooniverse with our version of Martin is the outermost one, right?"

"It is the closest to our Universe, so we should assume that it is the most likely place to find Martin. He is also most likely to be the first version of himself here that we will find, that is my opinion."

"You can't assume that he will be the first version of himself that we will talk to. He is just a random version of himself by now, Martin himself, the one back at the Bistro, I mean; had the experience of being the closest alternate Martin, not us. We encounter a random Martin when we talk to a version of him here, not necessarily the first Martin, as was the case with our Martin."

"How are we going to search through an infinite number of Martins to find our Martin?"

"How are we going to search for any Martin at all, amid an infinity of Zeit-geese with different names?"

The super-heroes were at a loss, and debated for a long time the various strategies they could use to search an infinite array. They considered all kinds of possibilities and scenarios for finding Martin (the one who either did or didn't have Martin's memories). Soon another problem occurred to the gathering, what if they could never identify the proper Martin, because he had no memory of their friend Martin? They would then have to search forever without hope of finding him. Also, some of them thought the whole exercise was now likely to take too long, and they were getting impatient.

"This whole exercise is turning into a paradox, we should seriously consider abandoning our search for a particular Martin, and maybe see the sights, have a good time."

"We can't enter the most likely Tooniverse at all it seems, only the one through the door to the Bubble-house. We should go inside and see if Yahweh is there. Maybe he would help us find our Martin."

"There are things missing in the inner Tooniverses, they all contain whitespace at their hearts, where the Bubble-house should be. Might Martin be missing if we go inside to look for him?"

"Maybe, I dunno." Mirror Man stares down at the ground in a sullen way. He and Shower Girl were having a little rough patch or something.

Just then a messenger came from the Super-Toons already at the Bubble-house, a new discovery had been made. They awaited our arrival; please hurry. The whole group assembled and mounted up for the journey ahead, and flew off into the distance.

The next day the entire cavalcade was assembled before the grand entrance, and debate arose again about the best way to proceed. It seemed that a clear plan was needed, and none seemed to satisfy everybody. Debate raged on.

One good thing: the discovery! It was a Magikal book that contained the names and contact information of all the Toons, on Magikal paper that was infinitely thin. Also there were other books there, in a vast library building next to the Bubble-house. A question arose, how would they search through an infinite number of Martins? Even on paper it was an impossible task.

One suggestion that occurred over and over was to increment their search by recruiting more searchers in an expanding pattern, but this was shown to not be enough. Even with ever increasing numbers of searchers it would still take forever to find Martin.

Now some of the searchers were distracted by the seeming impossibility of their task, and decided that they would enter the Bubble-house to search for Yahweh, to ask his help in the search.

As soon as they entered the doorway they could see that Yahweh was just as hard to find as he had been outside the Tooniverse. And there were a lot of distractions here. They stood at the outer edge of a Universe crawling with every sort of imaginary creature possible.

There were flying monkeys everywhere, a whirlpool in the air formed above them as they stared upward. Also centaurs and magik eagles flew around and around, staring down at the new arrivals. They turned around to look at the doorway they had just come through. It was far more ornate on this side, and had a gigantic stone capital perched above the lintel, carved into the numeral one.

So they turned back through the door and stood there, not believing their eyes, for the number one Tooniverse was now expanded for them, with characters all around. This was the version of the Tooniverse they had first seen from the outside, the version where they believed their own Martin was. Their companions who had not been through the door and back were blind to the Toons acting out around them, and even right through them. Their companions can see them, but not what they can see. It was all very confusing.

Soon all the members of the quest file in and out of the doorway, and everyone is on the same page. Having the ability to see the Tooniverse around them has encouraged them into thinking about how to find Martin; either in the listing or as a member of the flock of Zeit-geese they could now see in the distance.

They all file into the Hall of Records, which now occupies a place near the center of Tooniverse One, as they now know the outermost Tooniverse is called. It is still in the same place relative to the doorway to the Bubble-house and Tooniverse Two. The funny thing is that they know they are inside the Bubble-house already. There are a large number of people sitting at tables and desks around the ancient library, and a few wander the stacks. The stacks are in an infinite array that takes up a finite space, you can wander down a row of stacks that outwardly and from a distance shouldn't exist, yet when you get to that point, there it is, materializing out of empty extra space between the obvious partitions. New books appear from time to time as if by magic on the shelves, and can be taken back to the tables for reading.

At the tables some of the readers have grown very long hair and beards; and are now sleeping soundly. Garth looks around and doesn't see anyone cutting hair, so he decides to trim one victim until he wakes up, and then obligate him to do two others, and so on, and so on, and so on, etc.

In this way he creates a cascade effect that eventually wakes all of the somnambulists from what seemed to be a permanent and contagious slumber party. Remember that reading too many levels into the marginalia leads to hair growth and permanent sleep until trimmed. Garth tells the others to search for what they are looking for and then to get out, as he doesn't want to waste time dealing with more hair. They all leave the Hall and resume the search.

A typing flying monkey is found, and asked to create

an infinite flock of Zeit-geese endowed with the need to search for Martin and report back to the group. He acquiesces to their wishes, but has one demand. They must solve a puzzle for him.

They have taken the directory book from the Hall of Records; it has a section that lists all directories that don't list themselves, and a section that lists all directories that list themselves. Their directory does not list itself. Which section of the book should the book they have be listed under, or should it not be listed at all?

The committee of Super-Heroes debates the answer long into the night, with many a tale told and many a weinie roasted over the fire.

"When we look out at the Tooniverse, we see the Tooniverse with no missing space, the complete Tooniverse, it contains the other Tooniverses and who knows what else when you get to the middle, where only whitespace is left."

"What if Martin lies and says he doesn't remember, is that the end of it?"

"What if he has no memory of it? We won't be able to tell him apart from any other Martin!"

"We must solve the monkey's riddle and gain his help!"

"Solve the Puzzle!"

"If we list the book in the directory, it must go in the section of directories that list themselves, even though it does not at this time list itself, yet when we classify it properly, it will have listed itself."

"We list the book's directory in the section of the directory for directories that don't list themselves, and also in the section of the directory for directories that do list themselves, and in the directory we note that it does originally not list itself, that is, until it is listed."

"What if we put the directories in separate books, and list both of them in one book, and just the one that lists our directory in the other?"

"We should list all the books in a single directory."

"Don't they list them in three directories, author, title, and subject?"

"The subject is weather or not they list themselves. Our directory doesn't, therefore it should."

"We could write in it, I suppose."

"Isn't that graffiti? We should have respect for God's library books."

"And if we don't list the book in its directory (as a book that doesn't list itself), it won't appear in the list of directories that don't list themselves, so that is a problem."

"What if Martin says that he is lying about his memories, should we believe him?"

"The Tooniverse is like a gigantic Hilbert Space, once you have crossed the boundary into it and become a member of it. The set of all sets not containing itself is the outermost Tooniverse. The inner sets don't contain themselves, only a reduced version of themselves"

"Get back to the Riddle."

"It is well known in history, that certain questions have no answer, I am afraid that our monkey friend has asked such a question. The proof of that cannot be ascertained, however. But consider this:

Gödel's incompleteness theorem; 'This statement cannot be proved.' It can be written down in math terms thusly:" He draws on a napkin.

$$\sim(3r:3s: (P(r,s) \lor (s=g(sub (f_2(y)))))))$$

"There you have it."

He shows the napkin to the monkey, who grunts and looks annoyed, but then agrees to help them.

One of the Super-crew has had enough to drink and butts in with his take on the whole imaginary space around them.

"The Tooniverse is the collection of all collections that are not parts of itself."

"If the Tooniverse is a part of the Tooniverse, it is not part of itself."

"And if the Tooniverse is not a part of the Tooniverse it would be part of itself!"

"If, provided a certain collection had a total, it would have members only definable in terms of that total, then the said collection has no total."

"This contradicts the Third Law Of Logic, 'Every statement is either true or false.' No middle area, the unknowable is missing. I hear that Yahweh doesn't concern himself with the unknowable, good for him, bloody waste of time, what?" He moves off to bend the ear of some other person at what could only be described as an impromptu party.

Someone hands Garth a card. He reads it.

"This statement is false when preceded by its quotation." This statement is false when preceded by its quotation.

It was preceded by its quotation, so it is FALSE. He thinks to himself.

Therefore it is not false when preceded by its

quotation. Therefore it is TRUE when preceded by its quotation, which is against Rule Three.

He remembers similar paradoxes he has seen:

There is a painter that paints all (and only those) who don't paint themselves.

There is a container that contains all containers that don't contain themselves.

This statement is false.

Soon the monkey with his Magik typewriter flies over and starts preparing to type their requested flock into existence. "I have a couple of questions I want to ask you first, how many Zeit-geese do you need?"

"We need enough to question all of the geese in this infinite flock, so infinitely many."

"Do you know the Cardinality of the infinity you are asking for?"

"Well, it is Infinity for the number of Martins, as an Infinitesimal of the Infinity of all Zeit-geese; so Infinity still. A countable infinity of countable infinities, and since a portion of a countable infinity is still infinity, it is Aleph Naught."

"O.K."

The monkey typed quickly at his keyboard, and a huge (at least countably infinite in number) flock of Zeit-geese began to materialize in the air nearby, flowing off into the distance and growing to immensity very quickly. Soon they changed their course and circled back to blend in a completely fascinating way with the original flock, of which Martin was a member. They were each matching up with a partner in the original flock, asking "Are you Martin, do you remember killing yourself at the Big Bang Bistro?" and either flying away or sticking with Martin if he was found. And after a few minutes he was, such is the power of parallel processing, which is what this arrangement could be construed as.

"So, Martin; thank-you for your delicious liver, by the way! What a night, eh? Do you remember it?"

"Yes."

"Hear that? He said yes! We won! He said yes!"

So the celebrations continued throughout the night as Martin was feted and asked to re-enact (in a bloodless, cruelty-free and humorous way) his live liver transplant act from the Bistro. All had a great laugh, and it seemed that this Martin was a little bit more fun than his counterpart back at the B.B.B.

\*          \*          \*

### Joe's Master Koan Part – 10/A

"Very nice, you have taught us well through this fable of portend and comeuppance. And what shall our last priest tell as his tale?"

"I will tell the tale of the mountains in the land of the Turk, which are said to reach the very firmament itself."

"Three in a row!" The nobleman sits back contentedly and smiles in triumph.

"There was a great warrior, and a noble hero was he, wise and cunning, devious; but full of pride of his honor, which was as the unbroken snow in its purity and wholeness. He was very brave and at least as strong as three champions, and his gaze could pierce any veil to catch the essence of any thing yet known."

"And this hero wandered in the Old Land, before the

Great Flood, and did Good Deeds and escaped from evil plots against his greatness, yet he did no evil and harmed no-one needlessly. He was challenged over and over for a long period of time, yet he remained fresh and willing in his constancy."

"The reasons given for his heroic quest varied from telling to telling; from to win the hand of his favorite princess, to so as to atone to the gods for some long ago transgression, although not his own."

"In his travels he from time to time had a worthy companion, who did his best to match him in deeds, jest and wisdom of acts in life. This companion was very tall, and the most handsome man ever seen by most, and many said that he must be a god in disguise."

"The focus of this tale has to do with the mountains, the highest in the known world at the time, and a predicament which our hero was at first pulled, then tricked into. How can this be, you ask? For you say our hero is too strong to be forced, and too wise to be tricked."

"Yet the answer is he was overcome by his sense of duty to his friend, and tricked by unavoidable circumstances."

"Our story begins with our hero and his companion at arms wandering the foothills of this mountain range, and meeting a feeble old man on the road."

"The man stood there and looked at both of them, and then spoke, 'You handsome one, should go speak to the woman you have just laid with, she has some news!'"

"The handsome one was astonished at his jaw dropped in a comical way, and stern and troubled was the look he received from his heroic friend."

"The Old Man vanished in a puff of smoke."

"Both heroes made their way back to the village, where the handsome one's young female companion revealed the truth of a thing most taboo, she was pregnant out of wedlock."

"Our hero's handsome companion marries his girlfriend, and settles down to live with her in the village, where they await the birth before traveling back to his homeland, where one day he will be crowned King."

"Now our hero resumes his wandering way, without his great friend, who must stay at home with his new wife for appearances sake, and to reassure her family."

"Soon he passes the spot where the old man had vanished into a puff of smoke. He feels that he is not alone, hidden eyes yet watched his progress, of that he was certain."

"As he lay in his camp one night, a strange dream came into his consciousness and disturbed his slumber. He dreamt of a dragon, a belly crawling serpent, the lizard face smirked at him in cynical irony, daring him to see through his ruse. He saw the dragon by moonlight, as it made it's way to the bed of his dear companion's consort, to lay with her there."

"The mage spoke to him, and bade him be warned, and to pay close attention lest he fail his friend. For the old man spoke of vast portends and alluded to things he could not possibly know, such as the thinly disguised dream of the previous evening."

"He said to the man, as to a child; 'you must quiet the rumors against your friend, or evil will most certainly result. Take you now upon the path I choose, and do a service for the first person you meet, or surely the succession of the Royal line of your friend will end."

"The heroic one left the old one standing beside the road, and walked on in search of the one he must benefit and favor."

"And he soon came upon a viper sunning itself on a rock, and made the sign against it, to protect himself."

"As he looked closer at the sinuous creature he noticed that it was fashioned entirely out of gold, each tiny scale a jewel of engraved detail, fitting together in infinite complexity."

"The viper looked at him, hissed and spoke thusly, 'You must be bound in servitude until you atone for the sins of your companion, and wear me as a sign of that bondage.' The snake moved to strike him, and when he had caught it in his hand it turned into a fantastic work of the goldsmith, and he fit its mouth and tail together about his neck."

"As he made progress upon his journey higher and higher into the mountains, one peak began to soar above the rest, a singular cone of pure white dominating the sky ahead of him, with a faint wisp of smoke rising from its truncated peak."

"In his dream that night the trail of smoke from the slumbering volcano transformed into a long serpent with wings, and coming to him rapidly, wrapped him in scaled coils about his neck."

"He awoke with a start, and looking up to the high place above him, saw a line of bright orange winding its way down the side of the volcano, while a great cloud of smoke obscured the peak above."

"The sky was black, as the moon hid her pearly face; but stars pierced the darkness with a colorful fury, with bright red, blue and yellow diamonds of light."

"As he gazed at the bright lava winding down the edge of the sky, the stars behind it seemed to shift and swirl about, a dark tracery outlined in points of fire."

"One star shone brighter than the rest; and as he gazed at the sinuous line of lava, and the fluttering swirl of stars and dark traces of smoke; it became the baleful eye of a vast dragon of smoke and fiery lava."

"With a mighty roar and a flash of fiery wings the dragon came to life and leapt into the air, flying straight at our hero. The wind of its passage that beat beneath its mighty wings was like the blast from a huge inferno, and set the forest alight below."

"The dragon's voice boomed out, and so loud was it that people in the village far away in the foothills heard it clearly."

"The dragon spoke this:

'You are brave, my friend; but foolish as well. You seek to repair your honor, but it is spotless. You seek revenge, yet you have not been harmed. You seek an explanation for your dreams, visions and many portents, yet you have a full explanation before you, and even wrapped around your neck. Now serve me and fulfill your vows and promise.' And his voice increased in volume as he drew closer."

"The golden tork about our hero's neck writhed back into life, and wrapped more tightly about his throat."

"The wraith of smoke that had become the angry dragon circled around our hero in a whirl of beating wings of scale and leather, as the golden serpent around his neck twisted itself tighter. A vast claw reached down and grasped the hapless one, as he began to lose breath. Soon spots began to float before his eyes as the dragon held him in its grasp and gazed at him eye to eye. It held him out at a distance and playfully belched a ball of flaming gas at him as he struggled, sending flames around him and singeing his hair and beard."

"As he was finally losing consciousness, a heavenly female voice interrupted the dragon as it squeezed the life out of him. 'Stop that at once, and come home!'"

"The dragon paused in his depredations of our hero, holding him out at arm's length in his iron claw, flames wafting about his head. The snake about his neck loosened slightly as the dragon replied, ' I must teach this whelp a lesson, it is I who rules the love of all men and women, I am the most powerful one!'"

"And the voice of his mate replied, 'Get in here at once and leave the man alone, you hear me?' And the voice rose in a shrill shriek horrible to hear. 'Hear me? Now!'"

"The dragon replied, 'Yes, dear.' Giving the man one last shake, he released him as the necklace fell at his feet, lifeless. Flying up to the volcano, he vanished into an opening up there. Our hero is left standing unharmed at the base of the mountain."

The carriage rolled along for a moment, its occupants momentarily silent.

"That's it!"

"Oh, what a great story!"

"Splendid, Great Zeus is a wiener!"

"Yes, he is the bitch now!"

\*          \*          \*

### ~Bounce - 10

Darkworld Duck has offered their accomplice at the Master's Apartments on Riverside Drive the use of the Samovar of Soliton for one whole day. The only problem with that is that he had still not found it. He was relying on convincing Smorpheus to help them, while he quickly searches again on the Lattice for the Ring. He plans to temporarily leave the rest of the party, and re-join them as soon as he finds it.

Their accomplice, Jeremy, has spoken of how to find Smorpheus. Darkworld Duck and the three others start out in search of him, but can't quite get the remembered travel instructions right. They cross and re-cross many paths on the Lattice, and finally stumble out of a copse of trees in what they had thought was Central Park. There, at a small campfire lit to ward away the darkness, sits Smorpheus.

He looks up from his wienie roasting and fixes them with a look. "You people been smokin' weed?"

"Well, a bit." Richard is quietly defensive. "Not that much." He shakes his head in the negative manner.

"Well I smell weed. Are you sure you will remember the directions I am going to give you?"

"Come on, we only had a bit; and I am a reporter." Jen starts laughing and wobbles around a bit. "So you're a Smore?"

"I am a Smore trained in the intricacies of the Lattice. I am the knower of the way between. I am the carrier of the secret truth of the Way. I am the opener of the door, the Portal Professor, the man with the key."

"How do you survive as a Smore, don't you melt or go bad or something?"

"Oh, you would be surprised, I seem to last forever, and I melt in your mouth, not in your hand."

"Oh, my!"

Jen and One stand glassy-eyed.

"So we need to get two years in the past." Darkworld Duck appears calm and in control of the situation, for once.

"I know that!" Smorpheus looks insulted and disdainful simultaneously. "I have a very good network of spies and flunkies. I get into everything that moves across the Lattice. If you are here and want to get there, I know about it."

"My friend tells me you promised him the use of the Ring one whole day, can I see it?" Smorpheus looks at Darkworld Duck with scorn.

Suddenly a figure materializes just beside the campfire around which sit our heroic crew. It solidifies and sharpens into the familiar visage of the hated and vile Dictator.

"I have it!" He exults as he holds his Ringed hand up for all to see. The Samovar of Soliton, most powerful Ring of Solomon, summoner of demons, ruler of men. And Key to eternal heaven.

He vanishes again.

"Well, this is awkward!" Darkworld Duck looks contrite.

"What are you going to do about this?" Smorpheus looks serious.

"I must go now and find the Ring, or perhaps I must inform the Authorities," Darkworld Duck points straight up, "before things get out of hand."

"I should go with you. I will inform the Authorities, and you chase the Ring." One has a contact high, or something.

Both of the other-worlders take a few hurried steps and transform into Dark Triangles, circling Central Park once before rising up higher and entering the Rift. One triangle re-emerges from the Rift and circles around above them, eventually landing somewhere further downtown.

Smorpheus fixes Jen and Richard with a horrified and pitying face of remorselessness and starts to speak slowly and clearly.

"Remember this rhyme to help you traverse the paths of the Lattice to your destination, two years ago in London.

'Turn to the left, if in doubt of a test.

Turn to the right if the end is in sight

Keep your goal, and save your soul.'

Besides that I have these precise instructions for you.

'Go back to the Master's Apartments, and find a key taped under the grating on the sidewalk in front of the cornerstone. Take the key and walk north, then east. Go up to the first door on your right and use the key to open it and go inside. The key will activate the first portal and take you to your intermediate destination. When you arrive, spin around three times and then start walking with your eyes closed. You must do this or you will be in great danger. After that use the rhyme to guide you.'"

Jen and Richard stumble off, away from the quiet fireside where a very perplexed looking chocolate covered marshmallow graham cracker sandwich sits slowly munching a hotdog.

Bemis and Smuthead are having a bad day. They usually cure their feeling of ennui by picking on someone else when this happens. They are out and about doing their master the Dark One's business when they spot an opportunity to 'even the score'.

Earlier they had been hiding in some bushes and had seen their main quarry, the Dictator. He had been sitting alone and openly admiring the Ring on his skinny finger. They had just summoned up enough courage to rush him when he gave a command and vanished. They had already decided their story was to be of locating his footprints only, and nothing else. This they thought would save them from punishment for cowardice. They dreaded their eventual debriefing at the hands of the Dark One, and sought to divert their thoughts and cheer themselves somehow.

They couldn't believe their luck when just a few hours later they happen to spot the tipsy couple frolicking and laughing hysterically to themselves as they make their way out of the park. They silently and furtively follow about a half a block behind them. Soon they are outside the Master's Apartments on Riverside Drive again and see them locate and remove the key. They follow more closely now, only twenty or thirty feet back, but the street is crowded, and the young couple doesn't notice the punks stalking advance. They watch them walk up Riverside Drive to 104th street and turn right. Standing right outside of the building, a doorman blocks the entrance. Richard walks up immediately and, with a quick grin and a wink for Jen, has the doorman hustle them both inside. A moment later he and Jen emerge from the doorway, alone; and struggle to close the door, the foot peg jamming on the uneven sidewalk. Bemis and Smuthead can't believe their luck. They creep closer and watch in fascination as Richard struggles with the door, dropping the key on the ground at the last moment.

Bemis starts to whisper something to Smuthead, and gets shushed for his troubles. Both of them stare in fascination as Richard finally gets the peg loose and shuts the door, stooping to pick up the key in the same motion.

The villains move in, and as Richard fits the key and turns it, they rush the door, pinning Richard while Jen screams and beats her fists on their backs.

"It's OK," Smuthead says in a monotone voice, "We just want to go too."

"OK, just let me open the door." Richard has remained calm.

As his attackers loosen their grip on him, Richard suddenly pushes Bemis away, and delivers a great kick to Smuthead, sending him flying. He grabs Jen by the wrist and hauls her through the hastily opened door, pocketing the key. They pull the door closed and walk directly forward, eyes open. Bad idea.

Jen looks down and sees that she is wading through piles of foam, with strange hunched shapes beginning to stir beneath its surface. Richard remembers their instructions, but it is too late.

"Eyes closed, spin around three times, walk, then left!" He bellows out his instructions.

Jen shuts her eyes and begins to twirl, counting revolutions; but can't resist cracking one eye to see what is happening with those mysterious hulking shapes down in the waist high foam.

At once the shapes stand up, revealed as third-rate French clowns, nearly mimes. They have sad expressions and each is armed with a huge pie. Custard.

They surround the young couple, and soon a barrage of pies has thoroughly drenched them in the dreaded comedy of evil pie custard. The first and closest clowns to Richard deliver their pies from short range directly in his groin, and he is stumbling and winded.

"Run!"

They run and turn left at the first opportunity. Pies fly after their retreat, with quite a few good shots finding their mark.

They run down a white hall, smooth white walls, white shag carpets smeared with dripping custard. Richard feels vaguely guilty, as if some cosmic cleaning lady is about to discover and admonish him. He looks at Jen, her hair completely matted and the beginnings of a good cry on her face; and kicks himself mentally for not remembering the instructions more quickly, but he places blame on the interruption of the attack of the losers. It wasn't the pot at all, he assures himself.

They continue running down the hall, and in the distance a more normal looking structured area becomes obvious. They find a small rooftop greenhouse, with a view over a part of London close to Richard's curator suite at the reconstructed Montfichet's Tower Historical Monument Building, overlooking Blackfriar's Bridge on Ludgate Hill.

Richard remembers the rest of the rhyme, and he exits the greenhouse to the right of where he comes in. Jen follows him out through a door into the hurly burly of morning rush hour foot traffic in London.

People stop and stare at the bedraggled couple, still dripping large slimy blobs of custard from their permanently ruined clothing. Jen's hair is beginning to dry into what looks like a cross between a rooster tail and a custard Mohawk.

Richard hurriedly hails a cab, asking if he perchance knows the date, and yes the year as well, please? He gets some worried looks but a satisfactory answer, and after tipping in advance for the soon to be required cleaning bill, they are allowed to sit in the cab.

In the next few days Richard has to fend off the queries of many reporters who have caught wind of his state upon reappearing in London. He defends himself without explaining anything and insists that nothing had been wrong with his or his wife's appearance in public, that he had not been humiliated nor attacked nor wronged in any way. But inside he seethes for revenge.

Time passes slowly while he waits for the Bounce, which will bring him to Ground, and one step closer to retrieving his ship with a hold full of gold.

He worries about their former captors, stalkers and finally attackers, Bemis and Smuthead. They obviously will be a problem again in the future. He knows that somehow he has become involved in the continuing struggle of forces beyond his ken.

He had charts drawn up from the information he had saved on his Real-TV PDA, and correlated it with what was available through regular channels. The times and places all matched, of course. The Groundians have been nothing except honest, of course. He remembers that they could, however, omit important information if it suits them. Their encounter with the Dragon had been a case in point. He plans an expedition to negotiate with the Groundians, and to convince them to let him help them, in exchange for access to the gold and continued cooperation in the future.

He amasses items for barter, and arranges to be accompanied by experts and lawyers, diplomats and rich financiers, all ready to interact with the Groundians. He fabricates a story to explain why he had been separated from the ship's crew, and their present whereabouts. Agents of the Dark One had captured Richard and Jen; true. And the same agents had locked the crew in their cabins; not true, but believable.

He feels confident he will be entrusted with the rescue mission to the Robot Gold Mine Planet, and hopeful that he will be sent unaccompanied by the local authorities of Ground. He did require one thing from the Groundians, the use of a ship or craft big enough to hold him and a few others. Earth technology just wasn't fast enough to travel from Ground to the former Darkworld outpost now inhabited by robots and Dragons.

He decides it won't be too risky for Jen to go with him, but she still needs some convincing. He tells her he needs her to stay with him while he secures what would surely become the largest personal fortune in history. He has a plan for any Dragons they encounter while making off with the loot, as well. Discouragement in the form of flat panel sonic projectors and extremely hot particle beam weapons are to be hidden from the Groundian authorities and brought with them to defend themselves with. Cutting tools were too slow for his tastes for the actual gold extraction process; he was going to use the same particle beam weapons on a different setting to cut the blocks out of the face, and see if some of the original mine equipment similar to the hauler was still in working order.

Finally the day of the bounce comes, and they drive the equipment in several transport trucks into the otherwise empty evacuation area. He has secured fame, veteran status, and respect due an astronaut or explorer. No one suspects he is simply intent on making himself the richest human in history.

He intends to rent the biggest ship commercially available from the Goundians, and fill it completely. He will load the gold with hand trucks designed to lift several tons at a time. He has several workers and equipment operators coming with him and Jen, and they will use an automated system to mass produce and shift the gold blocks, each massing two tons and having dimensions of a cube slightly less than 50 cm on a side. Each block is worth \$70.5 million US dollars to him on the current market. He intends to use some of the gold to build a new house.

He estimates that to become the world's richest person he will need over five trillion dollars. This entails cutting and shipping 70,824 blocks in all to earn just more than enough. 141,748 metric tons of solid gold blocks, a surprisingly small enough amount of cargo to ship home to Earth, and a task he relished more than any other in his life!

A volume of gold small enough to be carried on a commercially available ship would do. It was comparable in size to the old Earth Panamax sized ocean freighters. It would take three and a half months to cut and load the gold, plus travel, set-up, and delays. When the gold got to Earth it would comprise nearly one third of all the gold on the entire planet.

The biggest logistical problem he foresaw was the removal of the gold from the Groundian bounce area once it "engaged" with our brane for a temporary visit. The clock would be ticking. Also this area would be a new one, since they would be catching a bounce several months after the one that would bring them back to Ground for the second time. He plans on unloading the gold with an automated system, placing it in a city park just outside the bounce area. This will take several days, almost all the time before the rented ship and its crew will return to its own brane, with the Groundian landscape itself.

If the mission is a success he plans several more, with new partners and perhaps an Earth version of the Groundian ship technology. The possibilities are endless.

They wait at the edge of the London neighborhood where the exchange is to take place, until the familiar jungle and glass tower landscape of Ground appears around them. They unload the equipment and place it inside the alien jungle, and scout out a route to the local Groundian road network. They are several hours walk through the jungle to the closest glass tower, where surface rail and hovercraft transport are available. They carry the equipment to the road, while Richard goes to arrange to pick them up in a hovercraft.

When he arrives, he wants to arrange payment, and realizes he doesn't know what the locals do for money, as he has never thought to ask. It turns out that the Groundians allowed anyone to requisition transport of people and goods for any reasonable purpose. All you have to do is demonstrate a use for the request. They thought it all contributes to the common good, someone asking for whatever is needed. It didn't occur to them that they could intentionally "require" additional amounts that they couldn't directly consume themselves. What could they do with such amounts? They were seen as of no value, mistakes, over-estimates, poor planning, and as a liability instead of an advantage. Greed was the antithesis of wealth as in our world; to them it meant trouble. They prefer experiences to things, and prefer living rich and full lives full of pleasure and companionship, sharing a common bond of dreamtime psychic prescient awareness with each other and many other races of enlightened alien species.

When it comes time to requisition and load the ship for the trip back to "rescue" the trapped Groundians, he is asked to come in to see the local authorities. They confront him with accusations that he has caused a disturbance in the activities and lives of Groundians and several other alien races. He denies it, lock, stock and barrel. He simply keeps repeating his story as he previously had worked out with his lawyers and advisors, and the Groundians soon seem resigned to letting him "help" them recover their ship and crew. He claims he is not responsible for the trouble; and that agents of the Dark One have compelled him at every step. Jen's cover story that he had been her captor was no longer necessary, having evolved into the "domination of darkness" theory.

The flight to the Robot Gold Mine Planet is a short and uneventful three days of boredom and anxiety. He worries now seriously about the possibilities of encountering Dragons. He assures himself that his weapons would cut right through metal, they would surely at least discourage a Dragon. And he didn't know of any creature that would willingly endure the pain from the sonic projectors.

They land on the planet, which their crew informs them is actually called Zarnoth, and head to the original Groundian vessel and its crew. Dr. Wally is happy to see them, and is persuaded to give his blessing to the continuing exploitation of the robot gold mine. Upon inspection it is found to contain only three working pieces of equipment, all remote controllable. They set the cutter to work cutting two metric ton blocks, start loading the one remaining hauler, and build a maglev conveyor system with supplies brought from Ground. They configure most of the weapons to cut blocks, and repair a damaged loader to load blocks on the conveyor, they have reduced the time to cut and shift the thousands of gold blocks from three and a half months to just over two months total by using existing mine equipment.

There are quite a few blocks already cut from the face when they arrive, all massive. They only need to cut these up to get the first few loads for the mine's hauler. It all helps Richard feel progress is being made in his folly of becoming the world's richest human.

About a week after their arrival Richard is outside the mine and spots a Dragon flying far overhead, it looks to him about as big as an eagle, but he knows that is an illusion caused by its extreme altitude. Later that day Dr. Wally mentions that he has been in communication via his prescient dreams with just such a Dragon, and has apologized to him for the invasion of his world. His apology is accepted, but on one condition. They must stand and face the Dragon in person at the mine entrance tomorrow morning, and ask his permission to take gold from the mine.

Jen thinks it is a trick, and Richard is sure that his

legal status as a claim jumper would be still further compromised to that of a thief if he admits he needs permission to work the mine. He is very colonial in that regard. Insensitive, stealing everyone's stuff, but then everyone didn't have it written in the King's English, down on paper, to be establishing it with.

Richard asks Dr. Wally, "Do the Dragons have a written language? What kind of technology do they have? Are they civilized?"

Dr. Wally is quick to answer. "You should think more of their potential, they are not primitive, although their technology is what you would call medieval. They represent the world around them in precious worked jewelry and gems set in precious metals, in mural form. They also have a rich oral tradition, and have progressed to joining us on Ground as dreamers inhabiting clone morphs especially genetically created just for them by us. Have fun with your "chat" with the Dragon tomorrow morning."

Richard is awake long before first light, running over scenarios in his mind and working out his negotiating position. He conceals one of the particle beam weapons up the sleeve of his jacket, taping it to his arm, allowing him to cover the end of the weapon with his closed palm. He can hide it completely this way, but aiming is a bit difficult. He has to stretch out his entire arm and sight down it to aim with any accuracy at all. He thinks of telling Dr. Wally to threaten the Dragons, tell them that he was heavily armed and willing to defend himself, but he knew this strategy was unacceptable to everyone except himself.

Richard walks out to the mine entrance just at first light, and sees a Dragon start to circle a point high above him.

It banks sharply and practically tumbles from the sky, great wings cupping the air occasionally to slow its descent.

It lands about twenty-five meters away from him, across the entrance of the mine excavations from him. He towers up above ten meters in height, and his wingspan is fifteen meters. He rears back his head and spurts a flame high into the air, at least fifty meters high.

Richard is transfixed by fear, now he sees why the Dark One's description of his execution by Dragon involved so many different forms of death. The Dragon's mighty jaws are full of razor sharp teeth, and part slightly for him to speak.

"By the honor of Zarnoth you will have to ask my permission or be known as a thief, and take that weapon out of your jacket and put it on the ground. I can see it bulging at your elbow. You must ask, sir!"

The Dragon draws itself up to its full height and spreads its wings, fixing Richard with the stare from its gigantic and baleful eyes. His eyes were a beautiful shade of light jade green, close to lime green with just a touch more yellow. They smolder and wait for Richard's answer.

Richard pulls up the arm of his jacket and removes the tape from his forearm, tossing the beam weapon on the ground.

"May I establish a claim to mine at this abandoned site?"

"I don't see why not, we have several hundred thousand metal protrusions such as this on Zarnoth, now if you had said that you wanted to steal the gigantic solid diamond that serves as the core of this planet, then you would have a problem. You have got to understand, we destroyed all the robot miners because they replicated and started copies of their operation on larger and larger portions of our planet. We care not if one mine is still operational, as long as people ask first before they start grabbing our metal resources. We also have jade, gems, and folksy crafts down at Zarnoth Castle, come on down! Some of the first miners to work this mine were zombies from Darkworld that had been infected and colonized by Nano-bots. They became cyborg zombies and left after building gigantic cubic spaceships from the metal here. Later colonists slow to relocate far enough from Darkworld to be immune to it decided to use remote controlled machinery to do the mining and stay in space, but they were too greedy."

"How could the enchanted meteorite the Cintamani stone have traveled from here to land on Earth? We are in a different dimension, and in a different galaxy, for Christ's sakes. It seems totally impossible."

"There is an intermittent rift in space-time in this area, and it leads to space near your Earth, in your dimension. The Rift must have opened long ago, when the enchantment caused the Stone to fall near Jacob in the desert. The Rift is again open, but it leads to what you would find was your future. You will have to return the way you came to stay connected to your own time period."

"We have your blessing then?"

"You may mine here if you swear that your purpose is to benefit your society with these resources, not just for personal gain."

"I swear," Richard says triumphantly and convincingly.

Meanwhile Dr. Wally has run through all of the options available to him to understand the situation. He remembers from his prescient dream that Richard is soon to admit to him that he has fooled the Dragon, and that he intends to keep the wealth for himself, and of course Jen.

Dr. Wally consults with headquarters on Ground via their nightly conclaves as well. They have been aware of the entire ruse, of course, and are going to make lying to a Dragon the full punishment for the earlier infractions of kidnapping, confinement, misuse of government property, hijacking and fraud. Something terrible happens when you lie to a Dragon, the Universe gets involved.

Zoroaster, Babaji and Bob Marley are Divine Guardian Angels and Ascended Masters. They were also Knights Of Promethean Flame while alive. Zoroaster wears a long white robe, he is Mithras to most westerners; and the Master first worshipped as an incarnation of a monotheistic God. Babaji wears a loincloth, he is said to have been alive for well over a thousand years, not unlike Sir Francis Bacon or his alias self, The Count St. Germain. Bob Marley wears a leopard skin jacket and a high gold crown over his piled dreadlocks; he is the patron saint of good times, harmony and weed. Dr. Wally summons the Masters; he is also shaman and a quack of great renown. As a Master of the Dream Time he finds it easy to find someone capable of teaching Richard a lesson.

Alexander Humboldt and Robert Anton Wilson soon are summoned as well. No one has more individual species of plants or animals named after them that they themselves discovered than Alexander Humboldt, now the patron saint of Habitat Preservation. Robert Anton Wilson has spoken about our next guest often on his speaking tours, and was fond of making everyone listening to him rant and rave Discordian

Popes by reciting: 'Spectacles, Testicles, Brandy, Cigars'. Now there are five guardians involved in Richard's punishment. The sixth character to dis him is a Celtic mischief spirit. It is decided that Richard will encounter the Púca and be flung through time and space, to slowly find his way back or not based on the merits of his decision making ability and his moral character. The Púca is a beneficent or malevolent spirit of Celtic folklore, inside the body of a six-foot rabbit. He generally would hang about outside of an Irish, or Welsh, or perhaps Cornish pub around ten after closing time, and seeing the unfortunate heavy drinking straggler would seize him by the collar and say, "That's it for you mate, your arse is mine." With that the Púca would vanish along with his captive, who would have many years of wild experiences in the tangled fields of space-time, which would somehow seem to be over in minutes, when the poor human was returned to his original settings. So Richard was done for, history. There was no way he was going to earn freedom from the Púca by his own character traits.

Dr. Wally calls Richard to his cabin on board the first Groundian space vessel, and explains that you can't get away with deceiving a Dragon. The Guardian Angels manifest themselves and place Richard alone on a deserted mountaintop, where the Púca finds him.

"So you thought you could steal a Dragon's gold and keep it just for yourself, did you? I have a special solution prepared just for you!" With that the Púca seized Richard by the collar and transported him to an unknown time and location.

Richard awakes after being rendered unconscious by

the effect of the Púca's spell. He is lying on an altar at the top of a step pyramid, surrounded by steaming tropical jungle. He slowly makes his way down from the sacrificial alter and stands at last at the foot of the great temple, listening to the sounds of the wild animals and bird calls from the rainforest. He is startled by a human voice just behind him.

"Here is another lost adventurer, on a quest of which he still knows nothing!" Richard turns to face his unknown informant, and sees a nineteenth century American explorer, Tilly helmet and all, standing there grinning broadly at him.

"My name is Alexander Rice, and yours, kind Sir?"

"I am Richard Cleese Wembley the Third."

"Ah, your Lordship. Kind of you to join me at such short notice."

"How did you know my quest is still unknown to me?"

"They always arrive at the top of this ancient Mayan ruin with no knowledge of where they are or what they are doing here, that's how! My poor boy, you are in the year 1908!"

"How do I get back to my own time?"

"You will have to use the myriad pathways that cross and re-cross on the Lattice, and go through an as yet unknown series of portals leading to the past, the future, and finally your own time."

"What do you mean 'as yet unknown series of portals…'?"

"We should receive a sign from an as yet unknown source, and after completing a quest of some kind we will have a glimpse of the Truth, enough so that you might possibly chose the right path. It is all an analogy to your situation in Life, and refers to your judgment, character and honesty. To find your way you first must find yourself."

"What happens if I just try to get there by entering random portals?"

"You will find your way to a world where your life goes on seemingly just as before, but all the people in your life will be different versions of themselves, and you will be able to tell that the world you find is not your real home. And your real friends and family from your own branch of reality will miss you forever."

"I couldn't do that to my young wife, Jen. She is almost ten years younger than I."

"Why was I sent by that creature to this particular place and time?"

"My suspicion is that it has something to do with Percy Fawcett, he has mentioned lately that he is preparing to go on a most important expedition, and that it involves using the portal array."

"Percy Fawcett, Professor Challenger from the novel The Lost World! As written by Sir Arthur Conan Doyle."

"What I am thinking is that somehow your quest must be related to the ancient and precious enchanted Cintamani Stone, an asteroid which formed a stone in which a sword had been driven, so that no man could draw it out unless he is the rightful King and sole heir to the throne. And some other things."

"Some say the Cintamani Stone was kept by Buddhist monks at the lost city of Shangri-La, also known as Shambhala, or that it had been transported to the New World, to El Dorado, or the Lost City of 'Z'." Richard has found a subject he is moderately conversant in.

Bob Marley and Robert Anton Wilson appear briefly to the men as they pause in their chat. Bob Marley: "You are getting on the right trail, mon."

Robert Anton Wilson smiles and says, "Spectacles, Testicles, Brandy, Cigars. I now make all of you Discordian Popes by virtue of you reading, I mean, listening to this pronouncement. You are also hereby excommunicated from the Discordian Church and banned forever. We expect the same back from you. Also your mother wears army boots, cats can fly, and so can I!" With that he zooms off through the air, chanting a mantra of illicit sex and drugs to any impressionable young minds that might chance to hear it.

Bob Marley laughs an intense and joyful Rasta laugh and flies after him.

"We must go now via the portal I know of to see Percy Fawcett. He will have the information that will help you in your quest for your own space and time coordinates."

Alexander Rice leads the way through the dense South American jungle, where he has been on several expeditions for Harvard University. He has also been in contact with Percy Fawcett through the Lattice Portals, which are slightly more common before 2065 in the jungles of South America and some remote Himalayan locations. A lot of the hardest to find South American temples had well concealed portals that would only operate with the proper voice command, or a Universal Key like the Samovar of Soliton or similar objects. Also there was a portal in New York, around the corner from a cornerstone that concealed, 'some conspiracy theorists say', a piece of the famed Cintamani Stone. Also they say that an unknown treasure of great value is supposedly hidden at Oak Island. The Arc of the Covenant, Jacob's Pillow Stone, the Holy Grail, are all said to be buried there.

They come to a distant and secluded temple, barely cleared enough from the jungle overgrowth to be visible, and climb the stairs to the ceremonial chamber at the top.

Alexander Rice says the code words, "Spectacles, Testicles, Brandy, Cigars." The portal springs to life, turning a solid milky white color from its regular stone. Then the portal clears and you can see through to the other side. It shows a similar temple ceremonial chamber, with a steady downpour just outside.

They proceed through the opening, and out into the drenching downpour that awaits them. It soaks right through all their clothing and soon they are as wet as if they had just taken a swim fully clothed. They see Fawcett, standing just under an overhanging decorative fixture at the edge of the temple complex, and make their way over to stand out of the rain beside him.

Fawcett has a satchel with him, and inside it a small wooden box, highly polished and inset with ivory and mother of pearl. It looks like mahogany, with finely carved and worked decorative touches. He opens it and produces a book, which he refuses to hand over to the two soaked explorers. Instead he holds it open and shows it too them, returning to read it after pointing out a picture at the beginning.

"This is a book written nearly eight hundred years ago by Babaji, and it shows some very interesting things about man's early history and later advancement. It is called 'The

Place and Time of Man'. It is written in Sanskrit, which I have taught myself how to read. There are pictures, in particular this one," a quick flash of an exquisitely drawn cave-lion couple. "There is this charcoal rubbing of a petroglyph found in North America, how it became part of this book is unknown. The lion sketch," again a quick flash, "is in particular very mysterious, having come from a cave in France that is closed to the public and only was discovered in the mid twentieth century. How is it in this old book, although it is thousands of years older than the book itself? The kind of talent shown in this cave painting is far superior to even similar paintings in the same cave. It seems that the original painter, having little experience, would build up the overall shape of an animal with palm prints arranged on a usefully shaped part of the cave wall. The new artist shows the original one how to draw just the outline of an animal with pigment on a fingertip or stick. The original artist's genius is released in emulation of the new artist's line drawing technique. It is over 25,000 years ago when this more realistic form of cave painting was introduced by this unknown artist."

"Let me see that drawing again." Richard is curious as only a real art buyer can be.

"Look."

"It seems very familiar, so strange. It looks to me like some of the sketches in a sketchbook by Leonardo DaVinci!"

"Yes! I see that. Such economy of style, and accuracy. Very attractive proportions and perfect placement on the wall of the cave. It is either the Master or someone directly under him, an apprentice."

"Yes, Leonardo DaVinci was considered the Master in his own time, and he originated many ideas that we live with today. Helicopters, tanks, and parachutes all owe their invention and development to him."

"So Leonardo DaVinci must have used the portal system, the Lattice, to travel back to pre-historic Europe to teach one of our early ancestors how to draw more realistically?"

"Exactly."

"How does this help me get home?"

"There is a map here, missing a legend. It shows the location of the cave. Leonardo must have been in the cave. If we try to follow his path, perhaps we can find your original Universe's timeline, the one that is missing you right now!"

"That doesn't really make logical sense."

"You have got to understand, you have been messed around with. That creature has disconnected you entirely from your original reality, left you in a kind of limbo. The way you get around these days is through the Lattice. Think about it." Fawcett gives Richard a strange intense look.

"Strict logic won't help me right now!"

"That's right! In this world of confusion even the hint of a path to take is better than no path at all. We must find the portal DaVinci used to get to pre-historic France."

Fawcett puts the book back in its wooden case and places the case in the satchel. He starts off through the jungle, hacking the occasional plant overhanging the path, making the trail easier for the others behind him. They make their way through mile after mile of humid and dense jungle, on a trail that seems to melt away in every direction into a myriad of possible choices. No one path is better marked than any other, and Fawcett is nearly confused. But with a glance up at a barely visible sun gleaming through the partly overcast sky, he gets his bearings and sets out again, hacking a path straight through the dense thickets and light overgrowth as well, just straight in one direction. Soon he clears a path to a lightly forested open part of the jungle, which gives way to the stones of yet another South American temple ruin.

As they are about to climb the steps to the ceremonial chamber atop the step pyramid shaped temple, Robert Anton Wilson appears to them yet again. He laughs at them and points at the satchel, which holds the box with its precious contents.

"You think that will really help you? It's somewhere to start, eh?"

"We have quite a few good ideas of how to start looking."

"Well, here is one more!" R.A.W. hands Richard a small thick paperback.

"It's my most famous book 'The Illuminatus Trilogy'. Won't you read it? It has a lot of good stuff in there, things that really make you stop and think, you know? It has zombies, and secret cults, Dark Rituals, involvement of forces from beyond the ken of mortal men. Hot chicks, hippies and weed, too. Also there are a few clues sprinkled throughout the book that might help you find your way back to your original timeline. See ya round!"

"What exactly does that map you have show us?"

"I need the legend."

"Wait a minute, I remember now that I memorized a legend from an undiscovered carving on one of the stones from Stonehenge. The carving is on the base of one of the standing stones, hidden from view. It shows some different shapes and their meaning. Unbelievably the explanations are in plain English. This shape," he draws with a stick in the dirt, a circle with a dot in the center, "means to go right through. This one," he draws a small square with a diagonal bar, "means to stop. This," he draws a triangle pointing left, "means turn left. This," he draws the corresponding right pointing triangle, "means turn right. Red means danger, green means safe. Blue means there is only one option available, white means all options are equivalent."

"I could have deduced that without much help! Those are so obvious to me now! Better safe than sorry though! Red means danger! I never would have guessed!"

Fawcett gets out the map and they pour over the twists and turns that await them in the Lattice. It seems to click into place, and before long they have deduced the path they must take to get to the cave, in Chevaux, France; approximately 25,000 years previous.

"You know, I don't really want to be on Earth at all, let alone travelling back in time to see the work of a dead genius. I don't even want to be in this galaxy, or in this exact reality. I want to be with my wife, in Andromeda, on that terrible planet of Dragons, Zarnoth."

"Once you get back to your own timeline, then you think about getting there. If you went there first it is absolutely certain you would be in a parallel universe. You could even get stuck in a loop, arriving just in time for that Dragon to have his little chat with you, and then the rest of the consequences as before. Or you could try to reform yourself, and not lie to the Dragon a second time. These Dragons perform magic themselves, and are considered protected by the Ascended

Masters. Any slight against them has its repercussions, the Dragons exchange casting spells in humanity's favor for protection."

"I intend to donate the gold to charity, should I be so lucky as to see my real wife again."

"That's a good lad, learned your lesson already, have you? We will see what the Master thinks of your appreciation for fine art!"

They examine the book R.A.W. gave them, almost at a loss if he was serious or not. Inside the front cover he has signed a short note with his autograph. It reads, "To my real fans, if you look at the notes you have made regarding twists and turns on the Lattice, it should read 'left, left, stop, left, straight, stop, right, left, left, left. Not left, left, straight, left, straight, stop, right, left, left, left."

After looking at their notes and the map a second time they conclude that the author's note is correct.

They step through the first portal into the first section of the Lattice, a sector used to store many connections to different versions of space and time, not just our own world and its bundle of closely related parallel worlds, but versions of reality that diverged from ours in trivial or fundamental ways.

Alexander Rice leads the way, then Percy Fawcett, followed by Richard at the rear. Alexander Rice speaks, "I see the pattern of the twists and turns have changed since we started moving down this passage, now there are more choices that weren't there a moment ago. They have appeared in between the spots that I already knew of, which I was using to calculate our path. Now I can't start over from the beginning, so I must assume that this place, which has seemed to remain at the same spot," he points to a turning further ahead, "is still the same one that it was when we came in, then count from there."

It's all very confusing to Richard, but he understands that this portion of the Lattice must be behaving as a fractal, for as you zoom in closer to a spot more detail becomes obvious, and this expansion can go on forever. He is familiar with the work of Benoit Mandelbrot from his art interests as a slightly more erratic youth.

Alexander Rice turns left, establishes his bearings, turns left again and stops. The landscape keeps rolling by for the better part of a second, at a fairly alarming rate. The fractal swirl is erratic and pulses this way and that, finally Alexander Rice makes up his mind and selects a branch almost at random, but it turns out to be the first left and the correct branch. Now they travel straight through an ever-accelerating section, with wild crenellations on either side of a hanging pathway through empty space. They slam to a sudden halt just before a mighty precipice.

After a hard right at the edge of the cliff they make three lefts in a row and stand before the exit to the ancient cave in France.

Alexander Rice looks at the other two and speaks. "I must leave you both now to retrace my steps and remain in my own timeline. Fawcett, good luck. Wembley!" With that he spins on his heel and goes home to mother.

Fawcett takes the lead, and uses the ten-foot wooden lever to pry the stone doorway open. Reluctantly the several ton door-stone rolls out of the entrance to Chevaux cave. There is an immediate odor of unwashed humans and their bodily functions, and of roasting meat, flavored with burning hair.

They step inside, into what is a home for some of Europe's earliest modern humans with both speech and artistic representation. A tall and muscular bearded blond man looks up from whatever he has been busy with and spots them, and hurries over.

"I am Leonardo DaVinci, please excuse the smell and our sad clothing. It is very hard to live well here. In this setting finding and killing animals for your food and clothing material is nearly impossible, sometimes, then actually impossible. I have been here three times before, I always left when famine swept through the ranks of these primitive people, and each time I return a new tribe has come to occupy this cave, having killed or evicted the previous owners, or simply by inheriting it when they all died of starvation."

"How is it that you came to be living sometimes among these people?" Fawcett asks.

"I was at my studio, completing a masterpiece of a sketch showing how an underwater device could allow a diver to breath air, when I saw this funny little man. He was very short, had no ears, and very small nose and mouth. But his eyes were huge, and strangely black in color. He told me he had something to show me, and brought me here to this cave for the first time."

"How do you return to your own time and place?" Richard is insistent.

"I must take a circuitous route that the little gray man has shown me, or I will become lost in the twists and turns on the path which has brought both you and I here. We must go to the land of giants, and from there to ancient Nubia. Here the Crocodile God will point the way to the Lady of the Lakes, who will send us through our correct lake of electric fire to our original worlds."

"Why can't you return the way you came, and why did Alexander Rice leave before entering here?" Fawcett wants to know.

"This juncture of human history is so pivotal in man's development that once setting foot on these stones in the past, one can never return to an unchanged world without some help from the powers that are helping us. I would return to a world so changed by my own actions in the past that it would be unrecognizable to me. This way I can find reality as I had left it, as I prefer."

"I saw a copy of the cave painting you did in a book by Babaji, can we look at it together?" Richard asks.

"Yes, it is over here." Leonardo leads the way past a stalactite covered with a crude drawing of the lower half of the Mother goddess being embraced by a bison headed Minotaur. They walk past it and stand in front of two cave lion faces drawn in profile, with one placed behind the other. The lions are anatomically correct and expressed with an economy of line and talent for depiction that is simply breathtaking.

"I am responsible for this one and as well that other one over there, where you can see two cave lions in profile, their entire bodies drawn as just a single flowing line each. This is the style of drawing I have taught to Crooked-Finger, the shaman and most talented of the cave-people in the arts."

"I am speechless, your work is unparalleled in all of history, maestro! I am unworthy of the time and attention of one such as you! Forgive me, I have collected art as fine as I could afford since I was very young, yet these simple lines of pigment here in this cave are masterworks as I have never seen before." Richard is in ecstasy.

"Thank-you very much, I am working here to fire the creative energies of the early artistic expression of these people to help in the overall advancement of Mankind. Perhaps one less futile war of oppression, one less tragic misunderstanding will result. If so my time and effort has not been in vain."

"How is it that you can speak to us in modern English?" Fawcett asks.

"The little gray man taught me, as well as many other things from your time. Are you familiar with Ghostbusters?"

"I think it is a 20th century comedy about paranormal encounters and the threat from a being called Gozer. I am not able to recall much else." Richard replies.

"It is my favorite moving picture with sound, I am also familiar with Charlie Chaplin and Walt Whitman."

"Excellent, I like these artists as well. Shall we be going on our way? I am anxious to see the land that these so called giants live in." Fawcett insists.

"They are not a fiction, they are as real as you or I and stand nearly eighteen feet tall. Really."

"Shall we?" Richard gestures 'after you'.

"Yes, yes we shall."

Leonardo leads the way to the opposite end of the cave from that where Richard and Percy Fawcett first entered. Looking back at the area where the moving rock door-stone had been, they fail to see any trace of the other entrance. Leonardo catches them looking for it.

"The door you seek is only visible from the other side, it is obvious in the cave only when it has been opened. This door is available to those who know the code word. Hocus Pocus."

With these words the massive invisible stone portal opens to a dimly lit white interior, much like the Lattice that has brought him here.

"This hall and secret way leads but to one destination, the land of giants." Leonardo steps through the glowing and bright entrance, with Richard and Fawcett following close behind. The hallway gets wider as they advance, until the walls vanish in the distance. They now walk through an empty white void, with no indication of direction or any details.

After a few more minutes a tiny colorful dot becomes evident in the foggy distance ahead of them. As they advance it becomes more obvious as a tiny red 'x' in the far distance. After a few more minutes they can see that they are approaching it, a marker measuring fifty feet from end to end.

"We must circle this spot counter-clockwise until we reach the first arm of the 'x', then, while facing its center, take the right hand path and follow it straight to our destination. To go a different way is to become lost in the void. Three directions lead back to this spot after an eternity walking blind, one way leads out."

As Leonardo finishes speaking, a comical Toon character is visible for a second or two walking at right angles to them in the middle distance. Fawcett calls out, "Wait, who are you, which way are you going?" The little goose character barely pauses in his trek through the fog.

"I am on my way to the land of giants, my name is Martin the Zeit-goose. Good-bye."

The little Toon vanishes into the fog. Fawcett yells

after him, "You are going the wrong way!" No response is heard.

"I'm going after him!" Fawcett runs off into the fog.

"No!" Leonardo is too late to stop him.

Now Richard and Leonardo turn right and follow the red line out into the limitless foggy emptiness. Richard is first to comment, "At least now I think I know how he famously vanished while exploring the jungle. We know better, mate! Huh?"

"Yes, I suppose." Leonardo doesn't sound as sure.

At long last up ahead of them the fog begins to clear, and they find themselves walking down from a ridge on a cloud swept mesa. The view is amazing, dotted with towers of rock and desert vegetation. Above is a deep and subtle dark blue color only seen at high altitude, dotted with clouds that cling to the mesas and float in small patches in the radiant sky. Just ahead of them the ground is a grassy sward that curves gently down to the edge of the mesa, where it drops off in a cliff reaching two kilometers nearly straight down. The other mesas in the foreground and distance are just as tall.

"We must climb down and travel to the next Portal, which will take us to Nubia. This portal is located at a cairn of stones many days travel from here. The way is fraught with dangers in the desert, and giants guard the way to the river crossing."

They carefully begin the descent from the sky-touching magic mesa where the portal from Chevaux Cave glows briefly in the foggy mist that clings there and vanishes. The trail down is steep and narrow, winding its way along the top edge of the towering cliff face, then down the side of a gully, and finally over a loose scree of rocks and gravel, with the occasional small boulder thrown in. This part of the trail ends suddenly right at the edge of a smaller but still impressively high cliff, which falls precipitously all the way to the river valley below them. The trail winds around and around the gorge that cuts down to the river below, at the end flowing over some low hills at the base of the mesa.

They set off down the river, and camp with some of the locals at night. Leonardo is familiar with their language, and they seem to be high-culture American Natives with no outside contact. They tell tales around the fire that night, with Leonardo translating for Richard's ears.

"He is saying," Leonardo begins, "that the giants have lived by the river crossing for many generations, since his people came to live in the desert and before them as well. The giants always want some fine beadwork or fancy artifacts for passage through their lands. How will you pay them?"

"We could have given them the book, I wanted to ask you to sign it, now that I know the drawings were originals done by you, maestro. But Fawcett has run off with it! If only I could have added it to my collection! You can create a work to trade with the giants, am I right? They would have to appreciate your great talent."

"With what am I supposed to paint? I suppose I could do some clay sculpture, and carefully color it with pigments from our environment. Pablo Picasso was introduced to me by the little gray man, so my tribute in clay will be to him."

"He is saying that he awaits the creation of my gift to the giants, and is proud to see it before it is presented as tribute."

Leonardo starts off to gather hematite, white and grey clay and other natural pigments from the local area. Richard is left sitting with the chief and his retinue as the evening deepens into a moon lit night. The stars come out and a chant starts among his hosts, and the shaman stands and dances a ponderous dance, imitating the movements and stance of a tremendously large human. The chanting rises to a frenzy, with the giant portrayed as chasing and eating tiny men, picking them up in one hand and biting off the head.

A translator from the natives rises and speaks in good English to Richard as he enjoys the last of the show. "You must be aware that the giants will treat you this way if your friend's work doesn't please them. They tolerate no insult, no matter how small. Some say the beasts they ride are from long ago, and not of our modern world at all. Yet this world has different rules from those that Leonardo says apply in your world. He has taught us much about the differences between our worlds, such as how my people are ignored and exploited in your world, and how here giants walk among humans."

"Yes, this is a parallel world, not a place in the past or future at all. And this is not a brane that is crashing into mine, or the result of a recent scientific discovery. It is the result of an alien technology so far beyond mine that it makes me look ignorant of science's basic principles, and itself look like magic!"

"Yes, I understand that completely. We have one of the best teachers about your world in Leonardo, our brother and friend."

"How does he know of the science from my time?" Richard is stunned.

"The little gray man told him. Come with me, I have something to show you."

The men walk down to the river in the moonlight, which is nearly bright enough to read by. Rocks and sand mix at the river's edge, and they walk along the sand to where some rock faces rise above the beach. On the side of a huge boulder is an enigmatic carving of a gray alien, large eyes, nasal slits and missing ears and all. It looks a lot like Roger.

*         *         *

### Joe's Master Koan Part – 10/B

The men in the carriage chatted briefly about inane niceties and watched the scenery go by for a few moments. After the many hours riding through the wilderness on the ancient roadway they had come to a more inhabited part of the world. Small farms appeared and wagon roads led off occasionally to more distant habitations. A little later on they had come to the border of a small town, and stopped at an inn beside the road. All the men filed in and soon were eating and drinking in good company. The courtier rose to speak.

"We are near to our destination at the far side of this town, and will soon embark from the harbor there by ship for the land beyond Avalon, where we will assume mortal forms."

Soon the weary travellers had eaten and drank their fill, and the courtier assumed charge of the entire bill for all in the party, including a fine room each for the night. Joe was lead to his room by a lovely young servant of the house and enchanted by her fond smile of farewell as she left him. Stepping inside he saw that the mean aspect of a roadside pub was but a cover for the real beauty of the fine art, furnishings and rich decorations and rare books within. For this was a place to heal the soul and free the mind set at the end of a long and hard journey through space.

Joe took a book down from the shelf and looked through it casually, wondering at the deep tones of the finely worked leather cover, the quality binding and neat writing and illumination inside.

"How to Travel with the Mind's Eye, a Treatise for Beginners."

Joe sat on the edge of the bed, reading for a few minutes, then grew more tired and lay down, still reading the mysterious book. In a few minutes he lay sleeping quietly, the book dropping from his hand to fall to the floor beside the still neatly made bed.

In Joe's dream he became aware of himself, floating in a strange dark but deeply glowing world. He could see the outline of the bed he was sleeping in, and his motionless form therein. The only color was a deep glowing blue-black, and he could see right through objects, his body, walls, and off into the near distance, which was more of a dream landscape, yet also the familiar day scenery as well. He noticed that a glowing golden cord connected him to his sleeping self, and that it got longer if he moved farther away from his body. Thinking back to the contents of the book, he decided to try some of the exercises he had briefly glanced at before sleep came.

He focused on his dream-body navel, where the cord to his real body was attached. He felt himself turning inside out, as he shifted his focus. Now he was rushing down a tunnel, a golden tube full of light. He was on his way to a very bright spot at the end of the tube, and then culminating, he shot through the tiny opening. His eyes flew open; he was awake on the bed, still fully dressed and above the covers.

He got up, placed the book back on the shelf, undressed and blew out the lamp. He returned to bed and drew back the covers, to lie beneath the rich silk sheets. Soon he was asleep again and aware of floating up through the ceiling, his golden cord stretching longer and longer. He knew the path he would take in the morning, could see the landscape clearly in the dark, and feel the starlight shining right through his invisible form. He saw the fine roads of the town and the many houses, the shops and wharves near the great harbor where a fine sailing ship lay at anchor. Soon he circled around and climbed higher, looking back from whence he had journeyed. The forest was a symphony of life and stretched back over the horizon, where he could make out the winding path of the river and beyond, the Garden.

Remembering more from the mysterious book, he rose still higher into the atmosphere, and watched as he accelerated faster than a bird, faster than a rocket, and faster yet. He darted past the great staring face of the moon, out past the sun, out past the first closest stars in just an instant. Soon he was racing out away from his sleeping body at an incredible speed, stretching the golden cord to its limit. The stars formed a tight circle far ahead in his field of view, then raced past him one at a time in quick succession. They became streaks of bright color radiating from a point ahead of him to a point far behind him.

He felt a tug and then a quick jerk on his golden cord, and heard a distinct popping sound. The entire world shattered as if it were a sheet of glass hit with a hammer. He dissolved into the burst of confusion that existed everywhere in his Universe at that instant. His eyes flew open and he sat up in the near perfect darkness of his room. Getting up, he lit the lamp and left the room. He saw the faces of the people in the portraits hanging on the walls looking back at him as he made his way to relieve himself.

When he was done he heard a sound out in the hall, and saw that the maidservant was there.

"Are you well?" She asked softly.

"Yes, thank-you. And you?" He asked in return.

"I am wonderful."

He led her by the hand back to his bedroom, and they lay together until morning.

The next day they all rode on elephants, and then stared into the eyes of wild tigers. Some of them felt uneasy about their coming mortal fate. Again he lay at night with the serving woman from the Inn.

*           *           *

The Sun was aware of itself; a gigantic Orb of heat, pressure, light, and mind. The Orb was a time machine, with "Light Consciousness" taking a million years to propagate from the core to its surface.

Right at the photosphere a last barrier to the photons struggling to be emitted; the last of the molecules of hydrogen plasma of the "solid" part of the Sun. The photons are absorbed and emitted in one last game of cosmic pinball before being flung away from the source.

The Universal Mind of all Earth creatures is a pattern

imprinted on the Sun's photosphere, a realm of tiny events and consequences for every action.

A photon flows through the hot plasma, following the path of least resistance, weaving a course through the Sun's surface from plasma molecule to plasma molecule, sinuously joining a chain of similar photons and particles.

Each photon is old; it has journeyed far from the core. Each hydrogen atom in the plasma is far older, having been created in the Big Bang itself.

The photons ride the molecules of hydrogen plasma like a rider rides a pony, and this was how they appeared in the divine manifestation of the Sun's Mind.

Each divine photon was a king and his trusty steed a champion of breeding. Garth was aware of himself as a photon, joining a long chain of photons at the Sun's surface. He became aware of the memory of the million-year journey from the core. He sat astride a balloon pony, a comical friend whose eyes blinked, but that was it. He could sense his ponies' thoughts "To the right. Stay behind that one. Left. Up. Down. Right after the last one." He looked up ahead and tried to guide his pony, trying to stay with the swerving motion of the pony and rider duo ahead of him.

The oscillations grew wilder and wilder, he struggled to remain in the column of excited plasma particles. It was nearly endless, he had seen the head end turn, up in front of him, and circle back past his position. Now he saw the proud King rider at the head of the column, astride his balloon-pony rocking horse Toon. The whole line whipped with incredible force, and he became aware of just how many riders now followed behind him in the column, nearly as many as those ahead of him.

Soon the rider ahead of him veers so wildly that both he and his steed are caught off-guard, and he breaks the column, changing course and slowing slightly.

He is the king, the leader of a new column. Soon the line behind him grows vastly long, and it doubles back on itself. A wild oscillation grips the entire chain, causing him to fly off of the head of the column, out into the void.

He has left the surface of the Sun, unhorsed at the last instant, flying away now forever from the source.

Coming to a new perspective in his dream, he saw the million-year journey to the surface of Sol as just an instant, and the few seconds of interactions as an eternal moment of near perfection.

As he shot away into space on his endless journey, he knew that he was destined to miss any nearby matter, and make it into inter-stellar space without being absorbed or reflected.

Time passed in Garth's dream and he had made it out of the Solar System's last vestige, the Oort Cloud. He continued on his way at the speed of light, leaving at first the vicinity of Sol, then the Galaxy, and finally all the observable Universe behind him.

Still he continued on his way, although now he didn't have precisely anywhere to go, and no time left in which to get anywhere. There was an ambient energy in the vacuum of empty space; he was now a smaller variation than the background.

He was a virtual photon, coming into existence over and over, born and annihilated again and again in an endless cycle. He became un-localized, and independent of space and time.

He was.

And was not.

And was.

And was not.

He opened his eyes and woke up.

### ~The Garden

Garth was in a grassy meadow, with small wildflowers pushing up through the lawn, and a high stone wall surrounding trees and flowering plants of all kinds. He could see the strong wooden gate in the cut-stone fortification was very impressive and heavy construction. The beams and ironwork that formed it gleamed as if just freshly polished.

Garth toured the grounds inside his walled paradise. He walked out away from the gate and over a slight rise to the center of the garden. Here there was a small pond on which a few dazzling swans shone whitely nearly as bright as the Sun. Garth squinted.

He continued his tour, and soon came to a little bridge that crossed a small stream feeding the pond. He continued and saw a small gazebo made of rosewood and covered with deep green ivy, which had woven itself around the richly carved decorations on the pillars and roof.

He went inside and who should he see sitting calmly at a small desk but kindly old Albert, smoking a pipe and regarding him with tolerant amusement.

"Tell me Garth, is this part of your dream or is it part of your travels and journeys into the world's mysteries?"

"I don't know."

"Tell me, does it matter if this is real? To you? To me?"

"I don't know."

"Tell me; in what sense do you consider this experience 'not real'?"

"It is unlike anything I have ever known of."

"That's right. You are unique in the Universe because you have direct knowledge in your mind that is unmatched in your time. You have gone beyond the others in recognizing what is actually around you, and will be rewarded."

"An old friend of mine used to like to quote Plato to me, but let me just give you the gist of a story he loved to tell from Plato. There once were a group of prisoners being held captive in a cave. They were kept chained-up to some heavy carved ancient wooden chairs of a very scary motif. Very intricately carved spiral designs in rich, dark, hardwood. Nice. They have never left the confines of the cave and know nothing of the outside world. A fire is used by their captors to cast strange shadows from cutouts resembling the silhouettes of plants and animals and the like on the walls of the cave. To them, this is life; this is reality. One day, a prisoner escapes and goes free, seeing the real world outside of the cave. He learns about the true nature of reality and how those who still hold the rest captive have deceived him and his fellows. Now it occurs to him that he is stuck in a dichotomy, unable to decide if he should enlighten his fellows; for is it really a good choice to do so? They will either love him or hate him for revealing the truth, depending on their character and pre-disposition to accepting change in their conceptions."

"Remember the 'Laws of Thought'. Whatever is, is. Nothing can both be and not be. Everything must either be or not be."

"Don't things in quantum mechanics break these three laws?"

"Yes, they do. But I am not responsible, I came before these new laws, and I supersede them."

"But how does the real world work, by your laws or these new laws?"

"The laws of reason still apply, as far as you are concerned, it is an illusion that I am willing to maintain for you. Of course science can still discover new wonders that contradict what reason is at first telling Man, but that will go away when I reveal new facts that will explain some of the mysteries."

"So what do these contradictions mean? Do I live in a sane world governed by laws, or is it all a carefully maintained illusion?"

"Some things man will still never know, but you may rest assured that every action has an equal and opposite reaction, and that energy can neither be created nor destroyed, and that a system in balance remains in balance until acted upon by some outside force."

"So we can determine our future, we exist as beings with free will?"

"I am beyond determination, but you as Man are only able to conceive of the will to determine your own future as far as your limited mind can see. Beyond that you are a victim of the basic structure of reality, and constrained to chose from within its boundaries. So you have to follow the path that all matter takes in the material world, determined by the laws of nature."

"I think, therefore I am."

"I am that I am."

"You win, I suppose."

"You also win, as a being aware of the absurdity of life. The likelihood of your mere existence pales in comparison to the vast scope of the unknowable, and yet you may rise up out of the confusion to grasp the reins of reality, and the unknowable will always fester and roil like thick smoke from a tire-fire."

"Where is this place, what do you call it? And are we at the Bubble-house as some people believe?"

"This place is called the Garden, it has been my place of refuge that I from time to time have shared with Man, when he is ready to comprehend its mysteries. As for the Bubble-house, this place is far beyond that one, and I stay there rarely these days. I will leave you here to guard my Garden, while I visit there and make sure that all is well with man's discovery of that realm."

"What is my purpose here, what do I have to do while I wait for you to come back?"

"You are to live here in this Garden of Satori, or Nirvana. Let no one enter the gate except Myself or a trusted companion known to you, and don't let the flowers take you away from your task. I am counting on you to keep this place as my secret spot of refuge from all that may be, here is the point of comprehension, where I may rest and know myself."

Soon Garth could see that Yahweh was losing his physical substance, becoming paler and translucent, then transparent and finally a clear outline of the kindly old soul. He was alone in the gazebo.

As Garth left the gazebo and strode the lawn in the

bright sun, he accidentally pulled one of the wildflowers out by the roots. Instantly in its place a full-grown man appeared, lying on the grass where the uprooted flower had been. Garth was amazed and looked at the man in wonder.

"Who are you?" Garth looked into the man's eyes and thought that he looked familiar.

"I am called Joe, I'm just a regular guy you know. I have been sleeping here in the garden, shaped as a flower by my arrival unexpectedly beyond these walls that stand to guard reason from madness. You have woken me, and now I remember the others. Let me wait for you while you leave this place to search out your lover. Yahweh may be any amount of time, will you not long for your mortal love?"

"He said not to let the flowers take me away from my task, just before he left. You are a flower, yet what you say is true. I am tempted."

"You must stay and guard the gate, forget about having thoughts to do otherwise. I will leave you and your thoughts alone to wait. Don't let me be the reason that you break your discipline before he comes back."

Joe went up to the great gate and stood before it, and turned to speak. "I leave you now to search for the Master, don't be fooled if someone comes to the gate claiming to be me, I won't be coming back this way, but will appear again as a flower when I attain my goal. Farewell."

The gate swings silently inward and Garth sees a quiet forest and in the distance a great river flowing down into the lands of Man

He thought of the conversations he had had with the one he had always thought of as Albert Einstein, now revealed to him in his true self as Yahweh. He remembered his first dream of Albert, in which he had stood upon the plain hundreds of meters tall, with the body of an ancient god. He had smiled and waved, and Garth's dream had soon ended. The next time he had seen him he had guided Garth in his first challenge against the oppression of the Dark Triangles. Garth had learned from people he talked to from the higher worlds that Albert was actually a sentience kidnapped by the Grays to animate their space-bending computer, with which they had formed the singularity around their worlds, the Gray Crèche.

Garth remembered that he was in fact at this time sleeping just inside the Tooniverse, and that the whole expedition was engaged in their second task, the search for Yahweh. Garth was annoyed that he couldn't tell them he had found the Master.

As Garth sat and contemplated the little he knew about the Master he became more aware of the tiny thoughts emanating sometimes from the flowers beneath his feet. They called out to him in tiny, soft voices, urging him to pick them and bring them to life, but Garth resisted their calls.

"Pick me, I am Pan. I will amuse and entertain you with my antics and revelry!"

"Pick me, I am Jehovah. I will replace your god with myself, I am all-knowing and just as powerful as Yahweh."

"Pick me, I am Gaia. In one incarnation I am your perfect lover. Do you not yearn for me?"

"Pick me, my name is Sam. I will help you out of this jam."

Garth got up from his meditation and walked over to the pond, he could see some magnificent old koi swimming in the depths. He stripped off his clothes and dove into the cool waters, swimming in a lazy way around the calm confines of the pond's pleasant luxury.

Garth thought back to his dream of visiting Alien Nexus Two before it exploded from the end of its collision with Alien Nexus One. In that dream he had ended his reverie by jumping into the gigantic ball of chi that formed the Universe that he originated from, Brane "A". He saw no likely similar situation here, as he was not inclined to do anything drastic or leave the Garden in search of normal, "waking", consciousness.

The Lady of the Lakes had questioned him silently inside himself about his hidden hopes and desires, not judging him but drawing from him each thing that made him unique. He thought that as a right of passage for those who would wander the multi-verse for the first time, it was an appropriate fate.

He thought back to the journey to the Tooniverse and the monkey's puzzle for them to solve. He knew now that it was a weird trick to solve Russell's Paradox by making the catalogue of all catalogues that don't list themselves a section of the book in which it was listed, and listing it in the section that lists catalogues that do list themselves, after editing it so that it does. This struck him as somewhat deceptive and off topic. Yes, he knew the paradox only applied to the catalogue of catalogues that didn't list themselves, creating an endless logical reversal.

If God was all knowing, and looked at the unknowable, who won? God could know that which can't be known, but in so doing he changed its nature into that which could be known. Man played the same role, as his tools to look at reality ever sharpened to finer and finer divisions of type.

The unknowable still existed from Man's point of view, and probably always would, we just don't know.

If a tree falls in the forest, I can probably hear it from here, he thought to himself. Garth knew that recording devices would show that the tree made sound falling even if no one was there to hear it at the time.

Objective reality was the only true reality, and the lens of subjectivity the distortion that separated brother from brother and nation from nation. A higher plane of existence contained ideal representations of all aspects of material reality, abstracted into a perfect presence of Mind.

Garth thought of his wife Nefertiti, and of the other companions he had left behind. He was sure that their quest was futile unless somehow Yahweh wanted to be found.

The dream that had brought him here replayed in his mind, he saw that the Spirit of Sol was the Spirit of the kindly old man he had chatted with in the gazebo. He knew that life was not limited to the things that mankind commonly credited with being alive, but was a part of each particle and interaction throughout space-time.

Another dream replayed in his mind, the one he had had just before the one about being a photon from Sol. In this dream he had been at a banquet in his honor, and the air-conditioning had not been working in the hotel. Everyone was pouring sweat, and he was quite nervous because it was all being recorded for the 3-d webcast going out worldwide. A huge crowd packed the hall and the head table where he was seated had many famous or familiar faces at it, some smiling, others seeming to gloat at him. The MC stands up and heads to the speaker's podium, and Garth is surprised to see that it is the venerable and ancient stand-up man Allan Thicke. He begins to speak.

"Welcome ladies, beings and gentlemen; to the one millionth annual Roast-i-verse Classic, featuring Dr. Garth Wallace, PhD. Thank-you, we will be having a long list of guest speakers, a very long list. We are going to start first with Rogers, from the Gray Conglomerate New Rogerston Complex; let's hear it for all 2.5 trillion of him, shall we?"

Confusion ensues as too many people try to take the podium at the same time, and time in the dream seems to skip forward in Garth's memory of it, leaving a blurry impression of many boring and tedious speakers dragging on and on about nothing in particular until he almost feels like screaming to himself again as he relives the memory.

"Garth is a very good man, he has won my heart and I am happy to have married him. Oh, yeah, I know all about the other women he's been seeing, as a matter of fact I heartily approve. But he knew that is how I would feel when he thought me up, isn't that right dear?" Nefertiti smiles devilishly over at her husband.

"He had to crack to all that shit in front of that 'Lady of the Lakes' bitch. She drug it outta him, he couldn't help confessing what his secret fantasy was, and as soon as she knew it, she had to make it real. So I don't really blame him at all, after all I am myself."

The next person to speak took the podium. It was Sobek.

"You may have guessed by now, Garth; this is a Magik dream. I have allowed it so you may say goodbye to your friends and family."

Garth starts up from his chair in alarm, to the amusement of all present.

"Just kidding, you should see the look on your face. You are just having an extended spiritual journey. Nothing to worry about!" Much loud laughter at his expense follows these shenanigans, with applause lasting several minutes afterwards. Garth is not amused.

Next up to the speaker's podium is Lucifer, sporting some new dapper cartoon horns made of deep cherry glitter paint with cute little smiley-face sparkles. He was otherwise dressed conservatively in a black and grey tux with tails. He comes right to the point.

"Garth, this is Hell, don't you get it? You should have checked with the Roman Catholic Church before you ran into me! Allan Thicke! I got Allan Thicke to make sure I was laying it on, you know, Thicke enough!"

Garth speaks up; he isn't going to take this much goading lying down.

"I actually am thinking of converting to Judaism." The crowd roars with laughter, and Garth feels better about them now that they are laughing at his jokes instead of him.

Allan Thicke has taken the podium again and is waiting for the crowd to quiet enough so he can speak. He runs right into the punch line like a real pro.

"Maybe we all will, I hear that Kabbalah is more and more popular. And didn't you prove the existence of God scientifically?"

Garth sat on the grass and waited. Waiting was the thing that Garth did best, and he did it a lot. He waited for the Master to return, as he always did at this time. The sun gleamed brightly down onto the short green grass, nearly saturated with colorful wildflowers. Many had waited here before him, and he would not be the last to take up vigil here.

One problem was that he had no idea how long he would have to wait; the Master could come back at any time, or not at all, in theory.

He thought of perhaps waking one of the others, but soon dismissed the idea. He was sure that the Master would come eventually.

Garth sighed and sat back against the tree under which he sheltered from the heat of the sun. The air shimmered in the middle distance as he examined the breadth of his domain. The Master's domain, really, he merely was in charge until the Master's return.

Garth dozed in the early afternoon heat, and his highly trained mind wandered, and drifted off into thoughts of his former life. In the past his world had been changed radically into a wonderland in just a few years, all thanks to alien technology that humans could never have evolved to master by themselves.

Garth started slightly as he dozed and looked up, out to the high fortified gate. He was alert and strained his ear; he sensed a presence from outside. He wondered if someone was there, although he still heard no one.

A loud knocking on the gate. "Are you there? It's Joe, the Master sent me."

Garth wasn't fooled. He knew that Joe had gone to

search for the Master, and would only return in the form of a flower. He thought he would wait and see what the voice would come up with to say next. He waited.

Garth sat on the grass and waited, waiting was the thing that Garth did best. He did it a lot, while he waited for the Master to return.

The flowers were like stars of color on the short, bright, lush green grass. They glimmered in the sun.

"Pick me." One flower seemed to say.

"Pick me." Another flower urged.

"Pick me and I will wait for you while you explore beyond these walls." One said.

Garth wasn't fooled.

Reaching out, he felt for the presence of the Master as one of the Garden, but resisted the urge to pick his flower.

### ~The Spider

Martin was aware of himself as being in two places at once. He physically was with the expedition to find Yahweh, but also had a conscious ability to be aware of his Bistro self. It was another day at the Bistro, and jubilant tourists from throughout reality would gather to witness the birth of a Universe again tonight, or as they liked to jokingly refer to it as: this morning. That was because Universes always began with the morning. In fact it was morning somewhere at all times, except in Universes with no stars. His Bistro self chatted pleasantly with the customers and other staff, preparing for the big night ahead. One of his conversation buddies was the Higgsy Hallucination Spider, which had a nearly solid appearance on Alien Nexus One itself, where the Bistro was located. The Spider operator and Martin chatted at length about the things the operator had seen while on duty, inspecting the extent of the disturbance in space-time called the Rift. It now had a new aspect as the connections near Earth, the closest one a path directly to the Tooniverse itself.

"The weakness in the space-time continuum is at its subtlest and most threatening as a mental disturbance felt at the time just before rupture, this is the time I seek out strong-willed individuals beginning to feel the fear associated with causal collapse happening around them. I reassure the affected person and thus reinforce space-time around them. Also we weave the entire bundle leading into Alexis One through the weakened area of space-time, giving it more strength."

"Throughout the history of primitive man a program for education and guidance was established, helping Man develop his kinder and more abstract side. I was a standard feature at many a campfire, and later at many a Temple raised to celebrate the great mysteries."

"Education through this kind of interface was deemed not enough to accomplish our goals, however, and a new captive breeding program was introduced. Men from various periods of time were abducted by our special operatives and brought here to Alexis One to father children with women from Ground, and to be re-educated in person by Sobek and others."

"These men became what is now known as the Knights of Promethean Flame, and they were the very first male Ninjas to see past the veil. They had the privilege of mating with advanced females, and passing on superior genes once reintroduced on Earth."

"Do tell."

"I am."

"Go on."

"The Grays helped to monitor the young society of Man and take samples, deliver supplies, occasional probing, etc."

"Nasty."

"It's all part of the process, implants and the like are very useful in tracking the effects of modifications we make to the Human genome and psyche. Mankind would have languished in primitive ignorance for far longer had we not intervened."

"O.K"

"So I have seen ancient African empires rise and fall, cared for refugees from the Deluge of Atlantis, helped Mankind first domesticate the dog. You know that dog is God spelled backwards for a reason, right?"

"Yeah, I knew that."

"I have a science paper up for peer review, actually. It's not all old news. I have this theory about the small circle of men from Alien Nexus Two who disappeared. They were roughly in the shape of a flat disk of mass when they made the transition to where ever they are now. So I think that they may have formed a Godel Universe, and been flung out of time."

"I thought they already were at the end of Time, as a first approximation"

"They were in a short loop of Time before the impact, and after the explosion they were in a quasi-stable lattice formation with Time in a loop in the center. We at Alien Nexus One formed the major reference node relative to actual linear Time, and they participated in our view of instantaneous Time by falling out of orbit around us sometimes."

"So, what do you mean; 'flung out of time'?"

"I still don't have a definition of it."

"Will they ever be reachable or come back to our frame of reference?"

"No, not by any means we now know of or can imagine."

"Tell me about the Knights and ancient Africa, what have you done there?"

"I or one of the others who man the Control Room has

interacted with primitive Man on Earth more than most developing cultures. The potential of Earthmen is very good; in fact we kind of have all of our eggs in the same basket, where they are concerned. They are inherently unstable in their evolution, but they are our own direct ancestors."

"Go on."

"In ancient Africa the most advanced cultures on Earth developed, with our help. Egypt is the last Earth culture that had direct guidance from us, before that similar river valley cultures evolved in what is now the Sahara desert, farther west and to the south of Egypt."

"The climate was different?"

"The desert has moved south since then, and jungles have turned to deserts over the millennia. We have taught culture after culture advancements to promote civilized thinking, but have had to start over again many times due to natural disasters and other causes of cultural decline. And the evidence for these ancient cultures is destroyed sometimes in the disasters that end them, with a few notable exceptions in later historical times."

"What about ancient cultures outside of Africa, were they given direct guidance as well?"

"We started in Africa about 100,000 years before the historical era, but our interference in the development of Earth culture has been scaled back closer to the historical era. We had to limit our contact more and more to preserve the independent nature of Man. So outside of Africa in later pre-historical times we concentrated on grooming only a few individuals to be our servants. They are the Knights."

"Most of the later contactees were convinced that their

sanity was on if not over the edge, and produced revolutionary ideas that changed their cultures in significant ways. But they tended to be outside of mainstream society in their time, with their ideas and contributions going without general acceptance in their own lifetimes."

"Were their any other forms of contact besides the humans seeing your spider form and hearing your voice?"

"In later times we started using a holographic projection device. This gave the impression of flight and divinity to our agents, who were later referred to by the Earthlings as angels. The Arc of the covenant was the place where I would materialize most often, so that they could only hear my voice and see the evidence of my power over the physical Universe. We experimented with various ways of making suggestions for advancement, always striving to make it seem that the ideas we were proposing came from the Earthlings themselves. After the Dark Ages in Europe we had the idea of using the network of portals installed in 2065 New York to acquire new recruits for the Knights. Some of the portal entrances, not very many, were located at various points outside of post-2065 New York. Most of the portals are of course connected to points later in time. The portal network was also never intended to be a way of moving around in space or time, it is a way to move around from reality to reality."

"So tell me about the Knights, did any of them perform better than expected and change their cultures significantly?"

"Yes, Leibnitz was essential in the development of Man, and one other springs to mind. His name was Alexander Hamilton Rice Jr., a descendant of Edmund Rice, an early immigrant to Massachusetts. He explored the Orinoco River system in the 1920's and made his most fantastic discovery ever, a lost secret that he nearly took to his grave in solitary silence. But he told an old acquaintance of it and the secret was passed down until Garth's time. Some other descendants of Edmund Rice were Edgar Rice Burroughs and Lucille Ball."

"What was his secret discovery?"

"Let me tell you the whole story. Hidden among the ruins of an ancient civilization, deep in the jungles of South America, the lone portal glowed briefly as it had once every thousand years. An intrepid explorer hacked his way through the jungle, not stopping until he had cleared a path to the foot of a deserted ancient ruin. Looking up he saw the last of the glow fading from the edges of the bas-relief carved doorway. He scaled the temple stairway and came up to the level of the ritual passage, about a third of the way from the top of the step pyramid. The glow was still present, although you had to shade the sun's glare to see it. He reached out his hand and touched the cool stone."

"Go on, this is interesting, what happened next?"

"Instantly the portal sprang to life, glowing again as brightly as it had done before, and emitting a low bass hum. He was no ordinary explorer, but a member of an ancient and noble Order, the Knights of Promethean Flame. Long had he and his cohorts searched for the legendary gateway to the gods. Its rumor had driven him to search the unexplored quarter of the upper Orinoco River, an area plagued by tribes of actual headhunters, and disease. His dreams had been full of clues that had guided him to launch this expedition."

"What was his dream about?"

"In his dream he left his body behind, and explored the world as his Astral Self. A whirlpool appeared in space to his Astral Self, and he was drawn inside. He landed in a dark but softly glowing place, a diffuse blue light leaked out from behind black fuzzy silhouettes that outlined reality here. The whole space resembled the inside of a black velvet lined cave. Small scenes appeared in vignette form, a succession of tiny windows to a lifetime of experiences. He was inside someone's head."

"Oh, my word. What a situation. Where were we?"

"He felt drawn to one of the scenes in particular, a tiny vision of a jungle ruin near a small waterfall. As he looked at the scene it began to move, and he had the sensation of falling into it. It expanded around him, and he felt himself flung out into space, and he saw that he had been emitted from the eye of the man whose head full of memories he had just been occupying. Now he was a free-floating point of awareness able to move in any direction. He went over what he now knew through his host. It was the year 1800; the man's name was Alexander von Humboldt, a famous Prussian geographer, naturalist and explorer. Alexander Rice Jr. saw the exact location on a map that Humboldt remembered drawing. Soon he soared away from his host and was on the way to his next experience in what he was later learn was the Eye-Man of Yahweh, the most sacred knowing of all inter-connected life that continues to evolve forever."

"So Alex was in the jungle, and had found the location of the ruined temple from the memories that he learned inside Humboldt's head?"

"Exactly! The year that Rice went to explore the

jungle was 1924, and he saw many wonders and became the famous founder in 1929 of the Institute of Geographical Exploration (IGE) at Harvard University. So he is at the temple portal, as he enters the ritual chamber, the glowing portal opens to reveal a scene visible through its doorway. It is a vision of ancient Africa, in the now vanished northern jungle rainforest. Tall wooden structures connected by high walkways dot the jungle, and men and women in tight fitting jumpsuits populate the prehistoric city. Evidence of electric light, powered by a kind of radiating field, is obvious. He steps through the portal."

"That is just amazing, he is the only recorded Earthling to independantly discover and use a Tech Mech Portal before they were installed en-mass in New York City in the year 2065."

"That's right, and he showed another ancient Earth explorer how to use the portals, Percy Fawcett. Percy is the real life character that Sir Auther Conan Doyle's Professor Challenger is modeled after; in Doyle's novel Land of the Lost. But let me continue the story."

"Alex steps through the portal to the African jungle city, and is amazed when the first person he talks to can understand English. 'Excuse me', he says. 'Where am I?'

'You are in the wonderful City Of Skybridge, in the Original Colony.'

'What year is this, do you count years from some well known event?'

'It is now the year 9387 since the begining of the great ice , by our calendar. Do you use some other system?'

'We count the years since a fictional religious leader was born. But I have a good idea that your time is quite a bit earlier than mine.' "

"What did she mean, coming of the great ice?"

"She meant since the beginning of the last glaciation period before the Holocene epoch, approximately 100,000 years before our explorer was born."

"So what happened next?"

"The story continues as we see our explorer is brought before the leader of the Skybridge people. He is brought to the Royal Lodge and stands in awe and amazement, all of the vast buildings and temples have been constructed out of wood, rivaling in size cathedrals later built in stone.

'You are here from the gate to our long silent friends. What news have you?' The leader is strong and to the point.

'I am a single traveler exploring ruins of a long dead people. I can tell you that no one of your friends or their descendants remembers to mind the temple, it is long abandoned.'

'This makes sense, they would have been in contact if they were still able. So you have seen the way between?'

'I don't understand.'

'You have seen the way that the gods step between, from place to place.'

'Do you know of this magic?'

'It is not magic, it is a result of the machines the gods use to make life for us more well, and to come and go sometimes, although the Great Ones such as Sobek and the others have no need for such devices.'

'Can you *step between* to other places yourselves?'

'It may be possible if Sobek does not forbid it. You will know if you plan against the will of the Great Ones, they shall know before the words leave your lips the thoughts that formed them, if they so will.'

'I would respect your gods and ask for their blessing on my swift return to the abandoned temple of your dearly departed friends, where I shall resume my duties as an interped explorer and scientist.'

'Very well, we will use our gate to send you back.' Alex was lead away to the great alter of the main temple, where great raised stones amid all the wooden buildings signified the alien portal. He stepped through and found himself back at the jungel ruin, slowly being drenched by a steady downpour."

"How did this bring him into the Knights, he has had an inexplicable and life changing experience, sure; but he still is in the dark and on his own."

"Well, listen up. As he was descending the stair down from the ritual passage the portal markings glowed into life once more, and a young black woman emerged from the door. She was dressed in a one piece body suit and spoke perfect British.

'You may still have some questions, I will be your teacher.'

'What is the purpose of all of this?'

'It is to bring the Light of Knowledge to man at an earlier time than otherwise possible, to smooth his path and teach him well, but also to step back and let him make his own way eventually.You people in your time have a lot of learning and unlearning to do, to be ready for the big changes when they happen. You will be taught and then become a member of a small group of men like yourself, who have trod the paths that the gods have created.'

'I have my studies and explorations, I must attend to my duties, as much as I would lke to educate the masses as to the error of their ways. But I am listening, go on.'

'You can use the gateway here with me to see the future of Man, and become a member of our cadre, what do you say? We will have you back in just no time at all, pardon the pun.'

'I agree, you should take me into your confidence completely, as I have already seen so much; my last stay with your people was unsatisfactorily short!'

'Exactly! Shall we?'

'Lead the way!'

So the lovely black woman from 100,000 years in his past lead Alexander Rice back up the stairs to the ritual passage, and he could see that she had an amulet with her that activeted the gate. He wondered if she was interested in him in a slightly more than friendly way, and then discarded the idea. They were worlds apart in experience and had only just met. He wondered about his encounter with the King of Skybridge City, and why he had felt uncomfortable enough to suggest that he return home immediately. The King had seemed intense, and not willing to break form or risk offending the Gods. Alex knew enough to not push boundaries concerning taboo or traditional customs and values of tribespeople that he encountered in his explorations."

"Where did the gate take Alex and his new friend?"

"Their destination was the lost city of 'Z', known to explorers of South America as the old ruin far down the river Xingu, Kuhikugu. It had existed in the area in one form or another for countless millennia, a mystery built of stone and an extensive canal network. It was also part of the portal network that had connected many of the pyramid building societies in history."

"So they landed at the City of Kuhikugu; but when in time?"

"They went back in time first, and later they met up with Percy Fawcett in 1926. Yes, he was still alive, and the tales of his death are quite unreliable. He had given away his wristwatch, and a few other quite precious for survival items, as they had lost all the gift items they had intended to buy safe passage from the Indians with."

"What happened before they found Percy in 1926?"

"First they went back in time to the days of Early Atlantis, where it was revealed to Alex that the organization that he had joined after his father, the Knights, was far more ancient and arcane than he could ever have thought.It was explained that the inner teachings and secrets of the Knights had been allowed to go dormant and be forgotten, but that he would begin to lift the ignorance off of the Brotherhood through the re-education and enlightenment of his Atlantean experience."

"What was Percy Fawcett intending to do, did he want to return to Britain?"

"He did not intend to return to the civilized world; instead he planned to start a new society in the jungle of South America. The new commune he planned was to be based on ancient spiritual principles like Thoesophy and worship his son Jack as divine; but after he was more informed he changed it to be a lodge of the Knights of Promethean Flame."

"What happened to the Lost City of 'Z' after Percy

Fawcett left, What was it, to go to Atlantis himself?"

"Yes, he left to exchange places with Rice, to replace him in the Atlantean scheme. And the Lost City of 'Z' falls into gradual disrepair at first, then after another generation is abandoned largely. People want to live with the advantages of modern medical help and groceries for sale, I suppose."

"What about the portal there? Was it still working?"

"It was functional, but a taboo against its use had come into existence, and the local tribes enforced it completely, killing anyone who discovered the entrance to the ritual passage."

"How long was Rice in Atlantis before talking to Fawcett?"

"Five years."

"Oh...What had the Knights been doing while cut-off from Atlantis and Alexis One?"

"The Knights of Promethean Flame had become a secret inner lodge of the Rosecrucian Order, and were instrumental as ambassedors to other high-level Lodges and secret organizations. Sir Francis Bacon was one of these 'Dark Knights', or cut-off members. They were members of organizations such as the Knights Templar, Knights Hospitallers and much later the Freemasons. Lord Mayors of the City of London had to be, for a while, only Prometheans; as they liked to call themselves. They secretly were the force behind the founding of the Inner Temple and other institutions of Great Britain."

"So even before they were back with us, they were very powerful and influential."

"That's right, somehow they had the 'Golden Touch'

for everything they tried did exceptionally well indeed!"

"What about the problem of unintended technology transfer, how did that happen?"

"Harry Grindel Matthews' death ray! That was a screw-up based on technology the Knights had been keeping secret since Egyptian times. The pyramids were built with the assistance of some kind of electric lights, lights that operated off of some rind of radiated electricity, like Nicola Tesla used."

The conversation continued on in various forms for quite a while that evening, all of it within the concious recall of the Martin with the expedition in the Tooniverse. He had said that it was a condition of awareness that he had allways had, and he was used to the sensation of living two lives at once.

*       *       *

### Joe's Master Koan Part 11

Joe awoke in the morning alone, with the clear bright autumn sun streaming in the window. The leaves on the trees had begun to change colors and a few lay about on the grass outside. He went downstairs to the pub for breakfast, the second time in three days that he would eat a meal. What did it mean to be alive and not dead, as he was; and what was mortality? He had no experience besides what they told him was his death, just after his flower's stem had been severed in the Garden. His death in the world that still contained his friends was a real loss to him for the first time, as he thought of the loss of his old friends from Alien Nexus Three and how they had stayed as a group and then he lost them.

He thought it was more like they had died, not him.

The others gathered around and the courtier, as owner of the carriage, determined who would ride where and who would take a horse. They all gathered up supplies, bought for their journey, and loaded a large wagon towed by two workhorses.

"Off to our ship we go!" Announced the courtier as he posed in the window of the carriage, hat held out high.

They raced through the streets of the town with a clatter and a shout to the harbor pier. A big gangway led up to the lower deck amidships on this sporty little carrack. The Captain spotted his aristocratic customer and shouted orders. Sailors raced down from the rigging and descended on their possessions in the wagon and carriage, stowing them aboard instantly. They made a more leisurely pace up the gangway to see the Captain in his huge ceremonial Captain's hat, and a blue waistcoat uniform with big gold buttons.

"All aboard that's going aboard, my lord."

"Very good Captain, prepare to cast off then, by your command on the high seas, my good sir!"

"Very well, taking command under your advice!"

The Captain gestures to the Boatswain, who begins to bellow his work-a-day orders in a loud and nearly unintelligible voice.

"Catzoft! Mizzens! Spar lashing! Weight and cur!"

They drifted slowly away from the pier and out into what sailors called the Roads, the outer reaches of the protected harbor that led to the open ocean. No other ships were visible in the late morning light, as clouds piled up on the horizon and the wind picked up a notch. The seas were moderate with a light chop, and the ship rode through it just smoothly and smart. The bosom continued to bellow orders in his unique and unknown dialect.

"Ahoy, abaft and afore four points on the beam, jettison quay halyards, hard a lee hawsers!"

The courtier turns to the Captain and states: "I am quite mad, for I long to see the great world serpent Jörmungandr, for I hear a voice calling to me out of Time, the voice of another madman writing this down."

"After we break the hold Jörmungandr has on his tail, we shall be close to the tides of Time. My madness, Time again in which to win or lose, Time for Joy, Pain, and Death! The madman continues to write, perhaps He shall speak as well?"

"It is I." A disembodied voice is heard to speak over the wild Ocean waters in a deep and majestic tone, the voice of God in some reality in the multiverse.

"I am God, I created this world. I am the Author, and the Narrator. Worship me and be preserved for future books in this science fiction slash fantasy series I am writing. Don't worry, you still have free will and will feel and act in a completely normal way, even forgetting this voice if required for your continued sanity. You, Courtier one!"

"Yes, My Lord and Author of my thoughts and true Self!"

"You shall prevail against the serpent, even when all seems lost. This I promise to you!"

"Thank-you Lord!" The ship continued to sail for the far horizon, even as the sun dipped lower overhead. It was well past noon and they fled before the wind at a fantastic clip for such a ship.

"Hump Ho! The Great Serpent's humps rise! A multitude of humps from end to end!"

Great sections of Jörmungandr reared up in gigantic humps above the frantic, wave-tossed sea; a churning mass of foaming waves and whirlpools around each rising mass of reptilian horror. He rose high enough to block out the Sun, and his many coils filled the ocean and the sky.

A huge storm was coming, the wind began to scream through the rigging of the little ship, and they were tossed about and threatened by towering waves nearly swamping the ship. It resembled the painting by Hokusai, except that the Great Serpent filled ocean and sky.

All seemed lost for the men of the little ship; then at the last possible moment, something miraculous and impossible happened. A gigantic hand materialized above their position in the stormy sky full of thunderheads and lightning. A deep and resonant voice of power said:

"I am the Author, and this is my imaginary hand, as solid and real as anything material in your realm. Behold as I grasp Jörmungandr just behind the head!" I as the Author extended my imaginary hand and did grasp Jörmungandr behind the head, and such was my size and power, and the speed of my attack, that I overcame him instantly and he did submit to me, dropping his tail from his mouth and allowing the ship with its passengers and crew to sail onwards past the Circle of Time Once, already perfect and complete.

And the ship with its passengers and crew sailed on past the coils of Jörmungandr, and were released from the established path of Time Once, already perfect and complete.

So now they could experience a mortal life, and win or

lose.

The edge of their world approached, where they would tumble over the precipice into the vast outer Void of Space and Time. It was a dramatic tableau, as seen from orbit, for example. A wide shot establishes the ambiance of grandeur, the majestic dignity of natural genius expressed as living art; as a mind-bendingly awesome cascade of ocean water rushes over the end of the world, and boils into vapor in space. The stars are out from our vantage point in orbit, and the tiny droplets make the biggest rainbow in the Universe. Magical Dragons, curious creatures and Natural Spirits circle the edge of reality. High above the stars, another world is visible. A man sits typing on a laptop computer, watching the letters appear on the screen and checking for errors and omissions. He is the Author, visible in his actual physically real world. The man is God, to the fictional characters in his story.

God laughs as he thinks of the preposterous premise of his writing; and yet, to scientists the possibility of other worlds is quite real, worlds in which anything could be possible. So in some world of the infinite multi-verse this must be true, as all the infinite possibilities possible must be expressed as each world of the infinite multi-verse.

In fact there are an infinite number of nearly or absolutely identical realities of any type you care to mention.

But, on the other hand, if you subtract one possibility from the infinite array of all possibilities you still have the required infinite number of possible worlds.

You could even eliminate all possibilities you could ever think of and still have an infinite number of possible worlds, and some of them would only "technically" not be possibilities you thought of and eliminated.

So, if you were to then include these new worlds in your list to eliminate as possibly real, new and more deviously conceived versions of reality would then become "real".

One possibility is that all versions of reality are already classified and numbered by a highly intelligent race of aliens, perhaps The Grays. If this is so in our world, let it be known as reality A/PDQ-00063q96. This is now our version of the name for it in their numbering and classification system. So we mean the correct number, whatever that is. And in this version of reality they agree and support us in our choice of name. Also acceptable is "the reality in which Alien Nexus One first arises."

Don't forget that the Grays aboard the Mothership can use the "reset button" to force the timelines to obey, thus ensuring that our version of reality will lead directly to theirs, as planned now for over 100,000 years of man's history. For the Water Spider Spirit of Native American legend has been whispering instructions in the dark for millennia, leading us on the path to our higher purpose, building the Mothership.

### The Knights Of Promethean Flame.

A secret society has always existed, since the beginning of time.

The Knights of Promethean Flame stole the power of the gods, in the form of a Flame, which must never be extinguished.

This eternal flame must be preserved at all costs, until

the beginning of our story, the "end of time" itself, in our version of reality.

We see a technician hard at work, tuning in on his communication equipment to a long vanished signal.

He is reflecting a beam of coherent particles off of a target, and then hearing the results in his earpiece.

The only difference between his job and a submarine sonar officer's is that he is using Higgs particles instead of sound, and his target is a long-dead Earth human lost in the mists of time.


Soon the operator picks out a strong signal from the jumble of noise, and speaks into the microphone while adjusting various controls.

He has established contact with a person back in time, and will bring him into the Knights as a new recruit.

The man on the other side of this communication is unaware of the nature of the operator or his location, and instead hears a voice in his head talking to him.

He sits up in bed and stares around, shouting out "Who's there? What is it?"

"It is I, your guide and confidant." The voice replies, and the man to join the Knights sees a faintly glowing dot or blur near the south-west corner of his ceiling, and looking closer; sees the ghost of a large spider hanging by its silver thread in the near darkness.

"What are you, Spider Spirit? Why do you haunt me?" The man is alarmed and terrified by the ghost from the land at the end of Time.

"The question should be 'Who are you?' my good

man; or who will you become in the pages of history yet to come."

Soon the man is convinced by kind words and tidbits of future knowledge to trust the operator, in the guise of this Spirit Spider Guide.

### Wonder

It came to pass that many people turned away from God, and only sought pleasure in the carnal and base things of this world. So God created works of amazing beauty and displayed them in the sky and in nature.

The Knights looked up to the sky and saw that the hand of God was obvious, and that Man was evolving to take his place among the stars, and to sit on the Throne of God in his own right.

This pattern is repeated over and over in the course of history, great men of destiny given a glimpse of the future in exchange for service in the Order of the Knights of Promethean Flame.

They at first were the inhabitants of Lemuria or Atlantis from time to time, then sometimes citizens of their long forgotten colonies.

With the destruction of these ancient empires contact was lost with their spirit guide, since all of mankind fell into a darkness, which left them too coarse and dull to know higher thought.

Only a "ritual, which could not be broken" preserved the Holy Flame, a marker for this world to distinguish it from all others. Priests of the Old Ones kept the ritual torch alive, even though they forgot why.

The Operator knew that one day this Flame would fire the engines of Reality, ensuring the existence of his own world. Without this Flame his world would never be created, his world of Alien Nexus One.

The ship carrying all the characters from this part of the story approached the very edge of the World Ocean, and they looked out beyond all that they had known. They began to plunge over the edge, and the magical dragons saw them and placed their spells upon them. Soon they were beyond the edge and plunged down the gigantic waterfall as the dragon spells caused them to vanish from sight. They had passed back down the chain to the land of mortal incarnation. Joe would be born of woman and live as a man.

\*                \*                \*

### ~Bounce - 11

Richard is left musing about what form of an animal could serve as a mount for monstrously large giants and falls asleep at the fire. Soon he has a dream of most strange matters. It is a vivid dream, as real as life and a swirl of color and motion, sights, sounds and smells. He feels the wind roaring past him as it supports his great wings. He is a Dragon, with jeweled eye and roaring tongue of flame. He remembers that telling a lie to a Dragon is the thing that has placed him on his long journey home. It is a strange thing, to be thinking about his human life, his longing to see his wife Jen again, while in his dream he soars above a magic jewel of a planet he now knows is called Zarnoth. He proceeds at an alarming rate, like a tin can on a high-speed magnetic conveyor belt. The world below him is a kaleidoscope of riotous color, a blue ocean surrounded with red and green islands, all with an infinitely complex border of gold, silver and aqua highlights. The pattern repeats over and over with subtle variations, and if one looks closer it becomes more and more complex and intricate without limits or bounds whatsoever.

Richard awakes in the late morning feeling groggy and not familiar with where he thinks he should be. The feeling finally passes when he sees Leonardo putting the finishing touches on a small statuette of a woman riding a small Dragon, her leather armor revealing her voluptuous figure as she holds aloft her upraised sword. It is composed of swirling lines and unexpected angles, a cubist treatment in emulation of the great Master.

A swirl in the atmosphere between Richard and Leonardo forms, and for a moment they can see One in a tiny window appear and recognize them.

"Oh, hey you guys, I just wanted to reach you wherever you might be, did you know this thing did that? Oh, by the way I have the Ring, that's how I'm able to talk to all of you via wormhole at the same time. Anyway, I just was calling to tell you that I captured the Ring, took it away from the Dictator, this is it here on my finger." She points to the Ring. "It is still a bit loose, I will have to get it fitted, I suppose." She shows how it's loose, and it slips off of her finger, in the tiny window to where she is you can see a metal grating on the sidewalk, and One bending down to look through the tiny holes as the window evaporates into the desert landscape.

Leonardo and Richard say good-bye to their hosts and leave, taking the small statue. They travel for most of the day until the river opens up ahead of them and a shallow ford becomes obvious. The giants stand beside the ford and wait for their share of tribute from any travelers wishing to use it. Richard estimated that they stand between fifteen and twenty feet tall. They're dressed in mammoth hide. They look at the statue and laugh.

"Pretty lady, bad light!"

"She is a man!"

"She is made of lightning and fire. She will win with her great mount. I will take this as a fine tribute of passage!" One of the giants makes his decision.

"You may pass. And stay away from crack, it is such a bitch of a drug!"

Leonardo and Richard look at each other with quizzical expressions but proceed across the shallow and quick ford. It twists and turns and seems to vanish sometimes, only to return later in a more obvious way. Some would say that it didn't exist at all, but later on it was just so obvious.

They make it across. The ford is behind them, with its strained references and illogical plot twist fading like a mixed metaphor's meaning to a fuzzy drunk.

As they are leaving they see off in the distance one of the giants silhouetted against the sky, riding what appears to be a gigantic triceratops. Leonardo turns to his companion and speaks.

"It must by now be obvious to you that we are in a world that could not possibly be in our own past or even future, as it obeys slightly different rules than ours. We must be careful to obey any of the local customs or taboos if we wish to travel safely."

"We must find the Portal to Ancient Nubia. Is that right?"

"Yes, we will be there soon, I was shown the way by the little gray man, and I will show you as well."

The mesas give way to low mountains, and then rolling hills cut by the canyons of the river system. Down one box canyon they travel, with the high cliff faces at each side. At the end they are surrounded on three sides by the canyon walls, and a glow springs to life at the command of magic words.

"Abracadabra!"

The outline of the Portal glows white hot, tracing a line that races around the opening in the cliff face. When it completes the circuit the whole area flashes white light, then clears to show the landscape of the other side. In this case the sands and short step pyramids of the Nubian Desert can be seen through the window in the cliff face of the canyon.

The men step through the Portal to the Nubian side, as the sun begins to set in the west. Long shadows stand in front of them, and they turn to face the sunset. A wrack of fired orange and pink clouds frame the swollen orb as its lower limb touches the horizon. Only the thin thread of the Nile wending its way north toward Egypt and the Mediterranean Sea breaks the sandy desert.

Leonardo starts out for the river, following the trail that leads down from the low hills. Soon Richard is following him as the trail flattens out and approaches the water. A fine road begins and runs along the bank, with many small temples and monuments on each side. They see temples to the Sun,

Moon and Spirits. The Lion Temple, the Temple of Osiris, the Nubian Pharaoh's Tomb; all pass by as they walk further on.

"We must find the Temple of Sobek and ask him to intercede for us. He will send us to the one place where we can rejoin our own timelines. You and I share a timeline, but are separated by five hundred years!"

They find the Temple, and are ready to enter and ask for the Egyptian Crocodile God's help when they are stopped in their tracks by a swirling vortex.

A comical little face marred on one side by zombie scars materializes in front of them. "Hey, I won! I am the proud re-claimer of the by now quite famous Soliton of Samovar, the Dark One's Ring of Power. Yes, I now can summon others; talk through and walk through wormholes like this one, and determine the course of history in any parallel world whatsoever. Just ask and I will consider it."

"What about sending us home to our proper realities? Can you do that?" Richard wants this shortcut badly.

"The Ring is capricious and dangerous to use in our situation, how can we know that this Darkworld Duck is from our reality?" Leonardo sounds cautious.

"I assure you that I ordered the Ring to open a wormhole between myself and my former travelling companions, so we are hooked-up right. But I understand that you can't know that for yourselves, as to you I could be any number of possibly helpful, neutral or harmful versions of myself. So see ya when you get back!" Darkworld Duck closes the wormhole with a grimace.

Leonardo and Richard are left staring at each other and just as sure of their course of action as before this now recurring interruption regarding the ring. Almost? No. They stare at each other, almost as if waiting for the ring to interrupt them again…?

They enter the Temple and Leonardo begins a prayer to Sobek, with all ritual observance and correct to the detail. Richard asks him why he believes in an ancient god, or any gods at all, for that matter.

Leonardo informs him that is just the way it works in this reality, and he is working with a proven method the little gray man had shown him. He is not so much the religious faithful as the shamanistic technician working the controls of a machine made from alien magic.

Sobek appears.

"I should tell you that while you have been away from Earth some very strange things have been happening. As you know, your uncle Roger has been 'killed' in a lab explosion. But he isn't really dead! He is aboard the Mothership Alexis One at this very moment. His protégé Garth is starting to re-work the experiment that has been the cause of this tragic accident, and is secretly terrified that he may share the same fate. Soon he will see the Lady of the Lakes for the first time. You should carry a message to the Lady for me. She is to tell Garth that he should feed salmon to his kittens. While this may sound like nonsense to him, it will ensure that time will repeat as before with no interference or duplication of timelines. The very meaninglessness of this instruction to him will serve as the thing which causes nothing to happen differently."

"We are concerned that Darkworld Duck may lose the Ring again to the Dark One or the Dictator. Is there anything you can do to stop this from happening?" Richard seizes the opportunity to save the day by appealing to Sobek, the most powerful ward against evil known to ancient man.

"I will find the young punks and the Dictator for you, and occupy their time temporarily. The Dark One has taken a toll on the Universe, such that he cannot be overcome in his own land of Darkworld. While he stays there I can do little, but I will warn you if he approaches or forms an attack against your world."

"Richard, you are in for a bit of a surprise soon! Your journey has one more twist and turn before its end! Did you learn a lesson, and what was it, please?"

"I am humbled by your prediction of my unknown (to me) fate. I accept the challenge and declare my one desire is but to be reunited with my wife Jen, and return to our home in London. As for my lesson, it is obviously regarding honesty, sincerity and generosity; I pledge to encourage these above all else and foster them among my fellows the Knights of Promethean Flame."

"Did you learn your lesson?" Sobek has approached and stands close to Richard, his powerful crocodile jaws mere inches away from Richard's face.

"Yes, yes, Lord Sobek, I have. Most certainly."

"Now tell me, young Richard, all that you have known so far in this life of the Knights, won't you?"

"Yes, Lord Sobek. I was first aware of the Knights when I was a very young lad, of four or five, and my father would go out each Tuesday at seven to visit his Knight friends at their Lodge. Then one year there was a parade, and all the Lodge men in their silly hats with their special meaning. And there were Shriners, too. And all the people cheered and I was proud to see my dad marching in his battalion of Knights right after the Shriners in the parade. Some papers got ahold of it and started poking around, and a year later at the same parade a few people shouted out insults and booed the Knights, something about it being possibly Satanic or a cult front. We were a bit low-key after that, still holding meetings open to the public at the Lodge downtown, but not associating ourselves with public outings or charity and publicity events and such. When I was fourteen I was inducted as a junior associate apprentice in the underage group. We learned some secret handshakes and code words, and lessons about secrets, rumors, lies and deception. And also learned about complication, conspiracy, collusion and controversy. My days were filled with studies of the lives of men I was privileged to know had been members of our Lodge, and my dreams of shaping the world as they had envisioned.

Later when I was of the age of majority I was asked to join my Lodge Brothers as a full apprentice of the Craft, and Knight Candidate.

Soon I had attained the first three levels and been inducted as a Knight of the Promethean Flame. My Lodge was London Seven, Temple by Saint Paul's. As a full Knight and Brother of the Lodge I was able to study the private records of the Lodge, as well as other ancient and historical documents and even artworks. That is in fact what started me out as a rare art collector. But I digress. The records showed lists of banned books and notes of how to read them, and led to my understanding that there had been an ancient culture before our own called Atlantis, which had since vanished. The Atlanteans had influenced early man and fell into darkness themselves toward the end. And were destroyed by forces that were beyond man's power to control.

Down through the ages the Knights have existed to preserve the knowledge of these ancient ones, from Early Egypt, Ancient China, India, the Inca, the Maya; all have drank from the same fountain of knowledge. The records show that Marco Polo met with members of a preexisting Lodge in China, and that certain gold figurines from Mexico are very similar to drawings kept at the Lodge from the time before Christ.

Many famous people throughout history have been secretly members of the Lodge, before it was open to the public. The public may come and observe the Lodge ceremonies, but must be asked to join and accept to be allowed to share our secrets. There was Samuel Clemens, better known as Mark Twain. James Joyce was a Knight. Leo Tolstoy. T. S. Elliott. John Keats. Albert Schweitzer. Earlier members had even included the infamous King Henry VIII of England, but he was forced to withdraw after he broke with the Catholic Church. The real reason was that he had begun to loose his faculties for argument of more complicated philosophical debates, and so didn't wish to embarrass himself before the other Brothers of the Lodge any further. One dose of their ironic and derisive laughter had been enough for the proud monarch. He had suffered a personality disorder and headaches ever since he had a tragic jousting accident as a young King.

I learned that for quite a few years after the King had resigned his membership the Knights had become more secretive and even left England for a while, mostly moving to America and practicing darker rituals. Some say a splinter group still exists from this time that has gone on the left hand path. More recently the Lodge has returned to respectability and has even been commented on in a positive way by the present Monarch."

"Thank you for your account of what you know of the Knights."

"You are welcome, Lord Sobek. May I serve you?"

"You may. Take this golden chalice, the Chalice of Kush, and ask the Lady of the Lakes to drink electric fire from it. She will find true happiness through its blessing. And remember to tell her to tell Garth to feed salmon to his kittens."

"Yes, Lord Sobek!"

Leonardo and Richard find themselves instantly transported to the Land of the Lakes, the interior of a vast network of wire bundles forming a hollow sphere, with lakes of electric fire filling the hollows between the bundles. Each bundle is composed of smaller bundles, each containing nearly an infinite number of individual wires, the physical manifestation of identity, consciousness and spirit in reality. Each wire links the individual instants of time, called chronons, into the cause and effect of the perception of time as an entity. When the wires are bundled they link the same chronons, and people experience the same version of reality. They are made of a special kind of dark matter, and are smaller than the quantum scale in one direction, and infinite in length in the other direction. Both ends loop out from the Center of Gravity, the Land of the Lakes. The only way to stop 'being' one wire and 'be' another one is to pass through one of the Lakes of Electric Fire, and experience dissolution and reintegration. Each of us 'is' a wire, and shares reality with people in his own bundle of wires.

They stand upon the ground, which is made of a

multitude of wire bundles branching and grouping in a complicated repeating pattern. It is a fractal with great beauty and power, an organic twist of ropes and roots, great mounds and hillocks rising between the shimmering electric furnaces, which would soon dissolve and rebuild them. The Lady of the Lakes approaches them.

"Do you have word from my Brother, Lord Sobek?"

"I do. Tell Garth to feed salmon to his kittens, and drink Electric Fire from the Chalice of Kush!"

"Very well." The Lady takes the Chalice from Richard and steps to the nearest Lake of Electric Fire. She bends and fills it completely with a skillful scoop from its surface, and raises it to her lips.

"To Lord Sobek, may he always be most wise!" She holds up the chalice, and then drinks down its electric contents.

"Richard, I am made most happy by the blessing of this Chalice, and will favor you well in return. I know you long to see your wife, and to return with her to your former life in London. While this is still possible I am going to send you on one more journey before you go home.

Leonardo, you are bound to history and will still create some of your best work in the future. You may go now with my blessings, and please, would you paint my face in one of your exquisite masterpieces?"

"Yes, my Lady!" With that Leonardo runs and jumps through the Lake the Lady points out to him.

"This Lake is also the one you must use to return to your own time." The Lady smiles warmly at Richard, "you should go now."

"Thank-you." Richard runs and jumps into the same

lake that Leonardo had. He feels the electric pulse travel over his body from head to toe, and his form begin to melt. He flies through space as a disembodied form without shape or mass, then gradually a seed of awareness coalesces about his tiny bead of self, layer after layer building up as more and more of him materializes around it. Suddenly he wasn't made of transparent layers of spiritual fire any longer, but a live human being flying through space. Then he awakes in a dark room.

He sits up suddenly in bed, wondering if it had all been a bad dream. But when he looks down at himself he is wearing some strange ceremonial robe, and the furniture and the room are all unfamiliar. His wife is not there.

He gets up and goes to the double doors leading to the small balcony outside his room. He looks out from a small chalet in a tropical valley surrounded by tall snow-capped mountains. The moon stands high in the night sky, and the grey light of dawn is just beginning to seep above the horizon. He returns inside.

As he makes his way out from the bedroom in which he has awakened, he sees that couches arranged in a circle about a small hearth, with people chatting and having tea, occupy the ground floor. Richard joins them.

"Welcome, welcome my friend." A white haired and very tall and wise looking old man with a long white beard greets Richard in a friendly way and shows him to a seat, offering him tea, which he gladly accepts.

"Thank you all for being here, I am going to make this as short and painless as possible. While you have not died, you are no longer merely mortal either. Each of you now possesses the will and strength of the Elders, and will follow the path of a true or enlightened Knight of the Promethean Flame. Some of you; Richard!" He smiles and winks at Richard, "thought you were Knights before! While that to outward appearances is true, you were formerly only members of what had become a shadow way, an imitation truth and a hollow victory parade at best. While knowledge of the Atlanteans and their ways was both good and evil, as they were, actually being in contact with Alexis One is the real prerequisite for membership in the Inner Knights. We here in Shambhala have always stayed in contact with it. We welcome you and bestow this gift of eternal life, as we enjoy it!"

A bright white light blossoms out from the old man, and surrounds each of the beings sitting drinking tea. They become the Immortal Ascended Masters of Shambhala.

Richard realizes that his mind is expanding, as his viewpoint shifts from the tiny dot drinking tea in a remote Himalayan utopia to a planetary and even galactic intelligence. He sees the pattern of life and of the natural laws that control the Universe, and sees the beauty of existence and his tiny human place in it all. He sees across the gulf of dimensions, space and time to Zarnoth, where Jen sits in the cabin they had shared on the ship and waits for his return. To her, he realizes with his new Ascended Master smarts, he had been missing only a day or so. His heart races out to her, and before he realizes what he is doing he has manifested to her, becoming real in the physical for the first time since his transformation.

He goes and stands before his young wife, and seriously and with a straight face he says to her, "You may now call me Super Dick!" He laughs and grabs her off of the couch, lifting her up to hug and kiss her passionately.

"Seriously though, do you think the Guardians or whomever might have made a big mistake by making me immortal? That's right, Jen; I am immortal now. And I am also god-like in intelligence as well. But I seem to have the same sense of humor as I did before. What is to prevent me from exploiting human weaknesses and getting my own way a bit too much just like before? Nothing, I suppose. Not that I would think such behavior is a good idea. I must share this joy with you."

Richard concentrates and transports both himself and Jen back to the moment in Shambhala when the light had first enveloped him. He and Jen stand in the Light of Immortality and are transformed, Richard for the second time. He can see his first self there for the ceremony, and waves. His first self fails to notice him, being absorbed in what the old man is saying. Richard concentrates and suddenly he and Jen are back aboard the Groundian vessel on Zarnoth.

"Come with me to thank our Dragon friends for showing me my true self. Without this lesson I would never have become a Super Dick."

"Yes dear."

They leave the ship, and Richard concentrates his vision onto the same Dragon, which had met him before, sending him a message of inner wisdom and thanks. Soon he can be seen flying far above the happy and enlightened immortal young couple, already fabulously wealthy, but now set to become the Earth's richest ever humans.

The Dragon banks suddenly and tumbles riotously down to greet them, landing with a rush of down swept wings and a spurt of celebratory flame.

Richard is struck by the incongruity of the situation, having a conversation with a Dragon as a godlike immortal being. He realizes his path had been truly set when he had seen the fabulous cave paintings copied by Babaji from the original DaVinci version. He realizes that Babaji is his true and only Indian Guru.

The Dragon turns to him and speaks, "Richard, you really are a Super Dick now, and that could mean anything from Cosmic Cop to Psychic Porn Star. Kind of an unfortunate nickname, don't you think? I'm just getting your goat. Goat is a fairly good sacrifice for a godlike being such as myself, only about a hundred times too small to make a good meal. I appreciate that you are now immortal, but get over yourselves. We Dragons cast spells such as can strip away the mortality from the immortal, and the immortality from the sleepers of the last and deepest sleep. An ending is but a new beginning, after all."

"I agree; an ending is but a new beginning."

*          *          *

Everyone was gathered around near the entrance to Tooniverse Two, in the same general area as the Hall of Records and a huge sports stadium. The stadium had not been apparent before everything in Tooniverse One had been made visible to them from the inside, after they had passed in and out of Tooniverse Two. They were camped in a large grassy area and had their horses grazing.

Then a bright light shot overhead, and seemed to land just over the horizon. A muffled thump followed a little later.

Garth was soon a silhouette walking back toward the camp.

Jehovah and Pan had joined the expedition secretly, in the guise of regular Alt World versions of the Ancient Egypt World Gods, the Crugs. They were a bit conservative in demeanour and comportment, but tried desperately not to hold their noses too high in the air, no small effort. They intended to ferret out the location of the Master, Yahweh.

Garth approaches the group, and is accosted by the deceptive duo of demi-gods. He stops and listens politely to the questions being asked of him.

"Excuse me, you are the inventor of the Earth technology that evolved into all this?"

"Yes, yes I am. But besides that, I would like to say that I am just a regular guy, a Joe Schmoe. I couldn't have done it at all without the genius of my mentor, Roger!"

"You have met the Master a number of times?"

"Yes, yes I have."

"Do you know where he is now?"

"Why, he is all around us! They say that he forms the very substance of the Bubble-House around us. I have a feeling that you should look for him yourself if you want to have any hope of finding him. We are all in the same boat, looking for Yahweh is the next obvious task on all of our lists. So we should get a move on, and find a way to him."

"You sound vaugely religious."

"You could say my experiences have changed me, have made me a deeper kind of person. My point of view has changed. The bread doesn't allways land buttered side down anymore. I try to see the glass as half full instead of half empty.

The grass may be greener on the other side of the street, but I like my side of the street anyway! A bird in the hand is definitely worth two in the bush, or three in a really prickly kind of thorn bush, four if the bush has bees in it. Maybe five if those bees are killer bees. Those are the kind of things my mentor Roger taught me."

\*          \*          \*

\*          \*

\*          \*          \*

...Postscript~

Kalioustous Carnicopious – Lord Dragon of Zarnoth.

A rich tapestry of colour and motion swirled round him, a kaleidoscopic vision. Directly below, a vast blue section curved wildly, its edges gilt with smaller gold and green filigree. The area in front of him was filled with a contorted mass of fractal clouds, their colour fading from the setting sun, sending beams of pink and gold light shimmering through the gaps between them. They had scale symmetry, with self-similar elements repeating in a pleasant and logical order throughout.

A large green section was to his left, followed by repeating chains of green islands in the giant blue field. Their edges were a blur of gold and red details. Closer on his right one of the green islands loomed larger than the rest, with a chain of smaller islands reaching into the far distance connecting it to one particular island chain on his left. The large green section was merely a piece of one of these large islands.

The surface of the large blue section was covered with subtle variations of colour, hue and light; loops and swirls painted a faint rainbow across its surface, like a very thin sheen of oil on water.

He was slowly leaving the island on his right behind him, as he flew. Tendrils whipping wildly, he snaked through the air in a sinuous writhing motion, buoyed-up by his inner gas bladders and thrust forward along the lines of magnetic force, held in place by the loadstone at his heart.

He was a Rep-tile rendered in three dimensions, the scales covering his surface were smaller versions of his entire body surface, but as if he had been skinned and his hide stretched out flat. The name was appropriate since he was a Mandelbrot Dragon, brought to life in this strange parallel Universe of living Math.

The green mass of the next island in the chain became the focus now, as he sped along the force-line emanating from it. It was mountainous with triangular sections sub-divided and piled one on top of the other.

He soared down toward one selected jumble of mountainous rocky outcroppings, zeroing-in on a particular triangular facet that raised its sharp edge above its neighbors.
A zigzag chasm led along one edge of the spire, with a narrow ledge leading to an irregularly shaped cave mouth.

He waddled and writhed a bit as he made his way down the ledge path to the entrance to his lair. Inside the dim light of the two remaining suns yet to set illuminated the interior awash with sparkling gold and gems.

Not only had he collected the valuables from a vast range and arranged them artfully here; but he had also made a nest to show any potential mates his ardor for raising young.

BRANE BOUNCE

The shifting patterns of magnetic force from the five circling suns and also the planet made communication between the various island chains vary from easy to impossible depending on the season. Thus for most of his young life he had been isolated from the dragons of the opposite sex by the direction and paths of the lines of force that guided his loadstone in the journeys across the planet's surface.

The gems and gold had been arranged into a complex pattern covering the rear wall of the cave, lit by shafts of light from the skylights above. The shapes of the pattern on the wall clearly mimicked the form of the island chains; the wall was a map of the area, constructed by the young dragon from memory. Tiny green gems were laid out to show the positions of the lines of force, and covered the previous set of red lines, which showed the position of the lines in his infancy. Soon he would begin to work on the map again, using yellow stones, to indicate the lines soon to come. His red range was huge, covering a vast swath across the planet's surface. Each young male dragon made his own map of his part of the world, because the surface of the planet changed slowly over his lifetime, making the previous generation's maps far too inaccurate to use.

He thought back to the time in his youth when his father had passed along this cave and its horde to him, along with all he knew of the planet. The loadstone at his heart had grown weaker then, confining him in his last few years to the lair where his bones now moldered.

The lairs of the Dragon People were very important to them, holding the bones of many generations of their kind; and as well serving as a way to connect to adjacent lines of magnetic force. Moving from one line to another was otherwise close to impossible for them, except where they crossed. The map on the wall showed the layout of the lair in a small inset in one corner, and indicated that the lair connected to five adjacent lines, a record; and something Kalioustous was quite proud of.

And that was not all. Farther away from the lair the map blurred into various shades of green, where the jade and emerald beads and tiles showed the world outside of the known realm; calculated and predicted by the dragon according to the ancient laws his father had taught him. During the change these patterns would become super-imposed over his known world and then cause the lines his loadstone followed to shift and combine in new ways. Then he would be able to encounter female dragons and possibly mate.

Also there was the new tunnel he was working on; melting and fracturing the rock with his flame. He ignited the gas discharge with his flint tooth. This last tunnel would allow him to break the bonds of the lines of force that held his loadstone on course as he flew; at last he would be able to fly in any direction until he met a new line.

The physical make-up of the planet was three-fold, with a solid diamond inner core surrounded by a liquid metal core emanating a very strong magnetic field, coupled with a shifting surface packed with highly magnetic rare earth elements that localized the field in a patch-work of domains. This thin highly magnetic crust moved slowly but constantly, with sudden changing periodically. The lines of force led from one local domain to several nearby others, with the very rare line extending nearly globally, closer to the poles.

His father had been the one to start the tunnel; it was what he did in his last years once he had lost his ability to follow the lines. It headed perpendicular to the main lair for a surprisingly long way before gradually turning north to run parallel to the main lair.

He thought of his plan for when he had finished the new tunnel. Should he fly low for as long as possible, seeking a suitable place for a new lair, or should he rise up until he encountered a long-distance force-line? The question haunted him. The lair he now inhabited was nearing the end of its useful life and would have to be abandoned; its range would be tiny soon.

The pattern on the wall flowed through his mind's eye, with the possible changes super-imposed upon it; each new calculation accomplished yielding a narrower range of possibilities, until he had visualized his best prediction. He imagined adding the new calculated path in yellow gems to the mural of gold and stones.

His conclusions were inevitable, he would have to leave

the short lines that would soon dwindle down to nothing, and follow a strong global line to a more distant location, in all likelihood abandoning the bones of his forefathers in this lair forever. He thought of the generations of work that had gone into the old family abode, with its many tunnels and vast hordes of gold and gemstones. Many an old Dragon had roared and blasted his way through solid rock and labored countless hours over the gaudy bower. Now it would all be left for marauders and thieves, or robots from the machine-land seldom seen since the days of Old Zarnoth.

Kali worked feverishly, blasting through many meters of solid bedrock each Sun-cycle. He could feel the magnetic field around him begin to shift at a perceptible rate, and knew the time of the Great Changes was coming fast. As he neared the surface, where the tunnel approached the side of the vast rock pinnacle that concealed his home, he adjusted the course of his escape route slightly. He would leave the lair at the ideal spot for his first flight in free space, unbound and free to fly in any direction.

As the last shards of obsidian and jade blocking his exit crumbled to reveal the tumultuous sky at last, he felt a surge of exultation rise inside him as only a young Dragon could feel. With a last roar he expelled a gigantic burst of gas, quickly striking his flint tooth and lighting intense blue flame. He had decided, and scrambled through the tightly fitting escape exit and leapt skyward. Quickly flapping his bat-like leather wings he dodged the path of the now accelerating force-lines, as they moved in a swirl around him. He couldn't see them, but he could sense them through the loadstone at his breast. In his mind's eye he brought them into his visualization, superimposing their positions over his field of view, like the heads up display in a jet fighter's cockpit. He dodged and swerved, avoiding the all too real lines that would bind him far too close to the old lair. Soon he soared in a nearly vertical climb away from the trap of short and dwindling lines around the ground. He gained enough height to see the curvature of the mostly blue planet, with its iridescence and infinite complexity of self-similar geometric shapes and colors. Soon he was at the height where the longest lines spanned nearly the length of the hemisphere. Turning south, a few minutes later he was in the grip of the major line.

As he flew along the line, pulled with increasing force by his loadstone, he picked up tremendous speed. He accelerated in a south-westerly direction, in a slightly curving path, still rising now to a higher elevation. Looking down behind him, the island home known to him all his life dwindled and vanished on the horizon. He passed several major islands, decorated with their chains of fractal replicas, and soon flew over a place legendary to his family, the island where the previous lair was hidden in the complexity of detail far below him. After that for a long time he flew above the seemingly limitless open ocean, devoid of detail except for its oily dazzle of iridescent shimmer.

"I am heading right for Old Zarnoth, and the wondrous Machine-land where the robots who stole our riches came from." He thought to himself. It was said that long ago Old

Zarnoth had almost fell to the alien machines from another dimension, but that they had won a long war with the invaders, finally abandoning the old city only when forced to by the seasonal changes of the magnetosphere. The planet itself was called Zarnoth, and the pattern woven by its five suns made the complex magnetosphere's lines change in an epic repetitious seasonal cycle that was eons long. The aliens had a good idea of how long they could stay in the region around Old Zarnoth, before the return of the angry Dragon Horde.

The planet itself was not in orbit about one or more of the five suns in the system, as you would expect; but was at the First Lagrange position, between its two closest neighbors, one of the two binary star couples that circled its tremendous red supergiant core. The Dragons themselves thought that long ago it had been moved there by an all-powerful alien race called "The Grays".

The effect of this arrangement was that two of the suns stood still in the sky, with the two others cutting a low arc over the horizon each complete cycle, with the red giant in the background, filling the sky; then setting for half a cycle. It was never dark on Zarnoth, although the Red Giant at its core emitted little light, having expanded to its maximum girth and now nearing the end of its life, when it was to explode in a terrific supernova. The binary pair Zarnoth was attached to consisted of a tiny red dwarf, itself a very old remnant of a bigger star, and a neutron star, black with a faint but strangely luminous halo. So the Zarnothian night was this constant mix of faint sunlight from these sources, punctuated by the day of all five suns. Zarnoth rotated at exactly the period of the orbit of its binary system about the red giant core star; so the red giant was only visible when it was lit by the companion binary system. These stars circled the red giant each day. The two M-class stars that also formed another binary pair in this system were much brighter and emitted far more heat, staying low over the vast empty ocean and warming him slightly. It was his second day of crossing an empty ocean, when he saw the outline of land far below him; he was crossing above a continent sized island with a global chain of connected islands and sub-chains of islands.

Obviously he would not be landing near here, as he was far too high to attempt leaving the safety of the line. If he were to try expelling enough gas to lose buoyancy, he would fall from the sky like a rock. He would be lucky if he regained enough control to fly before he hit the ground, and the strong winds would likely prevent this.

Dragons were not limited in their predations to flights along force lines followed by a sudden drop out of the sky onto their quarry. They could also run along the ground at speeds in excess of the rate the robot miners could attain with their tracked and wheeled vehicles.

In the ancient war with the robots of the vast machine–land scar on the face of the planet, the Dragons had quickly won with hit and run tactics and the initial element of surprise. They inspired vicarious and visceral terror in the robot controllers, who wouldn't even dare to visit the surface of Zarnoth in person.

Zarnoth was coveted by every race of the Galaxy, for beneath its bejeweled and watery surface crust was visible to their radar the Universe's biggest mass of solid carbon arranged in a crystalline lattice. The core of this planet was diamond, a liquid metal sphere swirled around it, creating the intense magnetic field. Zarnoth itself was the biggest known jewel, encrusted in blobs of gold, rare earth elements, and in addition to loaded with every type of gemstone, also practically solid jade and obsidian in its overall crust composition. Silver, iron and all the metals were common in a nearly pure state. Blobs of pure metal had cooled into smooth shapes of rippled mass, laying all around the surface and extending below. The miners had first landed an eon ago in close proximity to the largest obviously gold mass on the planet's surface; a huge landmark named Golden Dome. They now covered the largest peninsula near Old Zarnoth, plus many islands and small chains in the region. Some said that they were recovering too fast from the war, but there was little the Dragons could do since they now inhabited a different part of the planet.

The Dragons employed a system of inner reflection to attain the ability to communicate telepathically with each other, sometimes over very long distances. Our young Dragon had not yet attained mastery of this art, but had felt funny about things before they happened several times, and knew his Father's thoughts, apparently, while he was still alive. This was not the same as being able to organize the effort against the aliens across global distances, but it was a start. One or two very old Dragons who still practiced this Art had stayed behind near the robot gold mine, as observers. They had told of the build-up in robot infrastructure and return to colonization of the islands.

After many long days of flight, at first over the largest island he had ever seen, then over water for over a day, he was descending along a line toward the coast of a continent that covered nearly a quarter of Zarnoth's surface. He was landing at Old Zarnoth itself; the lines would now take the Dragons back to their old capital and largest and greatest collection of wealth on the planet. He expected he would find company, and looked forward to his first quarrel with another male and first mating with a female. According to the memory of his predicted map of the lines, Old Zarnoth should have seventeen major lines and many shorter lines emanating from its heart of crystalline rare earths, which concentrated the lines near the planet's surface at only certain locations. If the magnetosphere changed enough, the lines would dwindle and move away again, only to return to the same concentrations of rare elements.

As the coastal plain grew in his sight, he could see tall mountains soaring to great heights in the distance beyond the shoreline. Drawing lower still, a vast expanse of ruins littered the foreground. Tall obelisks and squat pyramids, long ramps encircling temples, and open squares filled with fountains and statuary depictions of the Dragons' long history.

As he drew closer and closer to the ground, he began to spot Dragons on his right-hand side, making their way to a large central square. He decided he would not over-shoot his likely destination and have to walk back. He expelled a large burp of gas, lighting it with a theatrical flourish. He dived and with a powerful beat of his bat-like wings broke free of the force-line propelling him on his way. He saw now that landing was going to be a bit tricky; he had already gained a lot of speed in his dive, and was nearly in free-fall. He cupped his great wings, throwing his long body into a great s-curve, and beat his wings strongly. Soon he had assumed a gliding flight, but only just above the ancient ruins of Old Zarnoth. Banking sharply, he aced a landing at the head of the now crowded square. Bellowing flame, he drew himself up in a salute, obviously a challenge to any lesser males. He was a monster; he could see the other males drawing back alarmed, in a panic. He was nearly twice the size of the largest one, who was by far the biggest of the other dragons. Three of the Dragons from closer to Old Zarnoth had flown with the shared burden of a quent; which is a massive aquatic animal shaped like a sausage with fins and a terrible lamprey mouth full of teeth at one end. They placed the offering in front of him, and he tore into it ravenously, not having eaten in the last few months, except for the rough gemstones, jade and obsidian mixed with diamond dust that he used to manufacture gas in his gut. After a meal of rocks he would regurgitate the polished gems, so he could set them into the bower horde map of Zarnoth. The meat tasted fishy, and was rich in fat and protein, and also the symbiotic organisms that made the digestion of rock possible.

After he had finished eating the quent, a Dragon approached him and proclaimed, " By virtue of eating the quent alone and in one sitting, you are obviously our leader, soon to be proclaimed Lord of the Battle For Zarnoth."

"Lord Zarnoth!" the Dragon Horde proclaimed.

Soon a Council Of War was held with all the Dragons present, and Kali was officially elected by a show of flame to the station of Battle Champion, Lord of the Castle Royal, and keeper of the Elder Bones. The vote was unanimous, as no smaller Dragon would dare to challenge him in battle, as that Dragon would have had to, since Kali had already eaten the quent. The quent was a symbolic offering, and once consumed by the strongest Dragon, proclaimed his dominance and authority.

At the Council an attack was planned to coincide with suns-rise the next morning, arriving at the mine with the other suns behind them, blinding their enemies. They would use an old trick, to speed them along the line to the mine area, on a remote peninsula. Each of them would capture a golon, and attach themselves to it with a firm grip of the claw. They would use the golon to soar above the ground, to a much higher field line, with its correspondingly higher field strength. A golon is an un-evolved version of the ancient Dragon ancestor species, basically a huge ball of skin and bones, filled with gas. The way to make a golon rise in the atmosphere was to gently roast its outside with a constant red flame, making sure not to kill it before it had outlived its usefulness. They would need to be rising fast; to break the hold that the first, or lowest, field line would have on each of their loadstones. It was a fine line between killing the golon and getting stuck at the first field line. And Kali's golon would have to be huge, a monster. To catch a golon, a dragon had to swoop down on it from above. Golons came right to the surface, as well; to drink water from the open ocean. Other than that they lived by slowly digesting their ballast stones, with the aid of the same micro-organisms in the Dragon's guts. They hung head down when floating, and when attacked they would regurgitate their ballast stones and rise quickly, exactly as the Dragons wished. After they regurgitated the ballast, they could be kept rising at high accelerations by gently warming the golon, then more intense flame as it became unconscious. The Dragons began to circle high above the golon flotilla as it came down to sea level at evening to drink. Soon they would attack.

Kali surveyed the golon herd, or flotilla, and wondered if there was a suitable match for him among them. It did not appear to be so. While at most two of the smallest Dragons could share a golon, almost all had to go alone; and Kali's closest rival could just barely find a suitable mount.

On board "Ophiuchus", Zeb watched her 3-view monitor with growing concern. The spacecraft itself was a testament to greed, capable of hauling enough gold to make a nation wealthy. As foreman of the mining operation and captain of the cruiser/hauler, Zeb was an unusual choice. Just 24, a tall, tanned fit blonde woman from New York Arcology, her mixed-race ancestry gave her an exotic look few men could resist. She had blue-green eyes, with a slight epithetic fold. The virtual reality link to her haulers and cutters showed a scene that filled her with horror, although safe in orbit about the planet. A Dragon had chased her tracked vehicle and caught it in its claws, and now raised it to be torn to shreds in its mighty jaws. As she switched to views from the other vehicles and equipment, she saw more Dragons dropping from the sky, trashing any of the man-made workers they encountered.

It took more than fifteen seconds of laser contact to penetrate the battle hardened armor that comprised a Dragon's scaled hide. They knew this from previous missions to operate the mine, all of which had succumbed to the Dragons. They would not verify the fifteen second rule today. On board the Ophiuchus there were four miners, defending 632 pieces of mining equipment that were vulnerable. They left orbit with a quarter load of precious metals and a tale of complete destruction.

For a while at the beginning of the battle, which went on for about three days, it seemed that they might produce a stalemate, or even defeat the Dragons. By arranging the armed cutters around the haulers and each taking a quadrant, they could train their lasers on any Dragons coming in for a kill, and most Dragons retreated after a laser made contact. One huge Dragon, the biggest at the battle, kept drawing their fire. When he did attack he stayed in the line of fire for up to ten or twelve seconds, while the smaller dragons came up behind his back and skirted the lasers; darting in to snatch a cutter right off the defense line. This eventually weakened the south-west quadrant, and they fell back to consolidate their defense, forming a new, smaller ring of steel. This actually helped the defenders, as the enemy had farther to go to attack them directly. A stalemate was developing, and the battle grew quiet as each side watched the other and probed for any weakness. The cutters were not designed for battle, and were hard to aim at long distances. Plus they only had a limited range of motion, as they were intended to be used as close quarter metal cutters, sawing up chunks of nearly pure gold for shipment to Earth.(*Alt Earth – narrator*) They could not be trained higher than a certain angle, about 68 degrees above horizontal.

The end came suddenly, after about sixty hours of sustained attacks. Zeb had never gone so long without sleep. Her comm link to the other defenders was filled with complaints and anger at the privations caused by the long endurance test of manning battle stations. The crew wanted to quit, abandon the equipment and leave orbit, now! It was almost a relief when a Dragon bigger than any on record, twice as big as the heroic one, landed in the middle of the ring of steel and swept a huge swath of destruction through the defenders. His tail lashed out, toppling the vehicles off of their tracks, and he shredded unit after unit in his jaws, eating them like candy. The other Dragons moved in unison, taking advantage of the confusion to break the defenses. Soon all the cutters were smashed and shredded to pieces.

"We are heading home." Zeb knew that news of their defeat would not sit well with the bosses, but they were done down there for the foreseeable future.

Kali stood on his hind legs, and proclaimed his victory with a roar of triumph; followed by a sustained display of flame. The others saluted him and jostled for proximity to their leader. A fresh War Council determined the victory as nearly absolute; only a few pieces of remote-controlled or automatic machinery had escaped to the nearby islands that formed an archipelago offshore. Also there were a few deep in the mine, in passages too small for even the smallest Dragons to enter. It was deemed a waste of time to go after any of these hardly threatening targets, for now.

Soon the Dragons determined to return to Old Zarnoth, and from there to Zarnoth Castle, the most recent seat of the Royal House. Kali had decided that the capital would return to Old Zarnoth, and that a new coronation ceremony would be held at Zarnoth Castle, before they took the bones of the last Lords back to Old Zarnoth for safe-keeping.

Kali was awestruck upon reaching Zarnoth Castle, to the north-east of Old Zarnoth, three days flight along the lowest force line. It towered up higher than any structure on the planet, and had herds of pantha stretching out to the horizon. Pantha are the land version of a quent, with many short stubby legs and a taste for blood. The majority of the Dragon Horde was waiting for him back at Old Zarnoth. Dragons must regurgitate their loadstones and swallow them from the opposite end in order to fly back along a line of force in the opposite direction, so after the battle they had all done this to return to Old Zarnoth. Since the force line leading to Zarnoth Castle was of the opposite polarity to their loadstones on this trip, any wishing to go on to Zarnoth Castle would have to do this again, as well. Few had wished to.

At the Castle Kali had been greeted by the female Dragons and the very young or old among them, and hailed as Lord. A few of the Horde had followed him, to witness his coronation, and now as well, his wedding. For he had already mated, when he had been greeted at the Castle he had found her, a suitable Noble Lady of fine size and temperament. She was called Boduccia, with enormous wings and an extremely sharp and pointy tail; she was the epitome of Dragon feminine beauty.

The ceremony was a combination crowning and wedding, with his queen crowned beside him. She looked happy and turned a bright pink when he kissed her, scorching her slightly in the process.

Kali made the argument to the remaining Nobles and others still residing at the Castle to return with him to the new Capital. He proclaimed that they must always be ready for a new attack on the surface at the old mine site, and the best way to do this was to live closer to it. A herd of golons were captured, and all chained together in harness, and a large sling attached to it. Inside the sling they placed the Bones of the Ancient Lords, along with a large quantity of finished gold and gemstone artworks. All the dragons piled onto this living airship, constructed from a golon flotilla, and set off for Old Zarnoth.

\*          \*          \*

Look for more Zarnoth Dragon stories in future "Archangels of Aquarius" books by MRM DARK.

### Glossary

❖ Anti-Certainty Theory-In a Universe with an infinite number of alternate realities, only those with similar enough laws of physics will be directly interactive with each other.

❖ A. N. 1 - Alien Nexus One - The end of the timeline in our Universe, or Brane; Brane A. Home to four googol residents, the solitons and equivalently advanced cultures.

❖ A. N. 2 - Alien Nexus Two - The end of the timeline in Brane B. Home to twenty googol residents, the source for re-incarnation and a reality that lasts longer than the oscillating Universe. It explodes at the end of time, but no one dies.

❖ A. N. 3. - Alien Nexus Three - The temporary third brane formed from the collision of Branes A and B.

❖ Bion - The bound state of two solitons.

❖ Blackbirds - Unconscious manifestations of beings from Alien Nexus Two migrating to Brane A in earlier times. They are Dark Solitons.

❖ Bose-Einstein Condensates - a lower energy state of matter predicted by Einstein and Bose in 1924-25 and created in the University of Colorado NIST-JILA lab by Eric Cornell and Carl Wieman.

❖ Brane A - Our Universe-membrane A

❖ Brane B - An alternate Universe - physically associated with Andromeda Galaxy. Part of our brane, but "folded" until it collides with our part of the overall membrane.

- ❖ Certainty Theory - In a Universe with an infinite number of alternate realities, an infinite number of them follow the scenario described in this work (or any described scenario)
- ❖ Dancer - The giant obsidian man-bot on the plain of Alien Nexus Three
- ❖ Dark Solitons - Generated in Bose-Einstein Condensates of one dimension in 1987, also the Blackbirds or Dark Triangles of Alien Nexus Three
- ❖ Foam - The quantum foam that forms at the Planck scale, particles can spontaneously generate from nothing, the dancer throws it at fliers to defend the hole in the plain.
- ❖ Foamiverse - is Alien Nexus One also and is inside the foam pile on Alien Nexus Three It is the framework that holds the Universe together.
- ❖ Gaia - The small flying woman that accompanies the Dancer.
- ❖ Grey Man - a function of information science, soulless adherence to forms and regulations, an expert in any definable topic, there are one googol of them in an office complex inside the Dancer.
- ❖ Grays - The most populous and advanced mature culture at Alien Nexus One, they have their own singularity in the foam.
- ❖ Isolation Tank - A water filled reservoir 5km tall 2km from the surface, has a sub at bottom and a lead blockhouse to shield the portable unit.

❖ Modus Variation - The change in the topography of the Rift, a hole opening or closing in a complex multidimensional shape.

❖ Portable Unit - a device for stabilizing the Higgs wormhole with lithium injection, intended to be placed in an isolation water tank in an abandoned mine.

❖ Q-ball - a type of NTS (non- topological soliton) that in quantum field theory represents an unusual state of matter called Bulk Matter, or Dark Matter.

❖ Rift - the hole made initially by the Blackbirds between Brane A and Brane B, located above the plain on Alien Nexus Three

❖ Soliton - Self-reinforcing solitary wave that maintains its shape while it travels at constant speed. Also the nature of the residents of Alien Nexus One, Alien Nexus Two and Alien Nexus Three

❖ Synchrotron Extension - A new target at the next generation of synchrotrons, it focuses protons at a very high frequency to allow wormhole formation and the appearance of the Higgs Boson at below LHC energies.

*Notes on Topography (Garth Wallace, PHD.)*
*This course is mandatory to pass.*
*Summary:*
*The Topography of the Dancer.*

- ❖ The Dancer is the giant Man/Machine that defends the static modus that is represented by the hole in the plain. (A. N. 3.)
- ❖ He does so by flinging foam or whistling. (Gravity, Modus Variation)
- ❖ The foam is distilled dark energy and manifests the uncertainty principle into reality. (Planck)
- ❖ This causes a loss of momentum for beings above the ground state of this reality. (Quantum Theory)
- ❖ The foam is extracted from whatever the Dancer eats, although that amounts to mostly only Blackbirds. (Brane C is sustained by energy from Brane B)
- ❖ Only a few of the flying citizens of the rift had ever died that way themselves.
- ❖ The other source for foam was the Grey Men. (They evolve into?)
- ❖ They were the result of any beings being eaten while in the ground state. (Brane A life energy sustains an information technology relationship with Brane C)
- ❖ They arrived by wading out of the foam mountain and walking on the plain. (Time travel- Brane migration)
- ❖ Once eaten they joined the mass legion of the Googol. If during their work as a certified expert in their own unique specialty they found that a category of knowledge had replaced all their work; they would walk to the railing of the gigantic atrium that formed the core of their vast office complex and tumble over it into the void. (Self-destructive redundant algorithm)

❖ Landing below in the vat of acid in the creature's belly, they are digested. But first, before they can dissolve into foam, they change back into the form they had before first eaten. The foam rises off of the puddle of digesting Blackbirds and Grey Men and fills a pressure vessel. (Energy extraction)

❖ After the foam was in the pressure vessel he placed his hand through his side and took out the vessel. He then kept it in a pouch on a belt at his waist. The excess foam can bubble up inside the dancer's throat and mouth. He uses it to convert ground state beings into grey men. They float away down the hole to observe and record reality in our world; then they report back to the horde. (Spiders, database management)

❖ Inside the hole was a wormhole into our Universe. Grey Men could travel in both directions, but fliers could not return down the hole, only fly up out of it. (Mental state evolution)

❖ Inside the Dancer was far larger than on the outside, he was actually a vast Universe himself. (Tesseract, tardis, impossible topography) Wallace is my last name, too. Extra points for that last reference. Hint in: "The Effects of Gamma Radiation on Man in the Moon Marigolds", or "A Wrinkle in Time", your choice.

❖ As well as the office complex of the Googol he contained a vast world of confusion and nightmare realities called Darkland. (What is forever unknown and unknowable, undefined)

- It was actually part of the physical Universe and was formed of any realities parallel with our own that we would find eventually impossible for our form of life. (Lack of rational existence of will)
- So in a sense inside the Dancer was a path back down the hole to our reality. And in a spooky sense Darkland was an echo of the ruined world inside the Rift, where the Blackbirds flew. This world was destroyed when the original citizens of Alien Nexus Two left the original timeline to live inside their crèche.
- But by now the path between physical realities and this remnant of Brane B was cut. It was populated exclusively by uneasy spirits who refused to join the exodus to Alien Nexus Two
- The Dancer was a bridge between Alien Nexus Two and Alien Nexus One, as was the entire Universe created by their collision, the plain of Alien Nexus Three
- He distilled energy from Alien Nexus Two and distributed it as the foam that made up the world of Alien Nexus One
- The mountains of foam on the plain formed the "inner" edge of Alien Nexus One The "outer" edge of Alien Nexus One was the skin of the Mothership Alexis One.
- Topography in this Universe was all inside out in various impossible ways.
- The Rift was the best example of impossible topography, where the topography varied when the

rift itself materialized in space, or when its right hand
wall (facing inwards) appeared or vanished.

❖ Also the ceiling of the room inside the Rift provided a
way for beings from Alien Nexus One to come and
go from Alexis One.

❖ And out of this ceiling a multitude of pairs of hands
protruded. They were the hands of moderators stuck
in the sphere of solid light surrounding Alien Nexus
Two Intensity from these moderators helped the fliers
of Alien Nexus One battle the Dancer. The fliers
could fly through the ceiling to and from the
Mothership, but occasionally they found themselves
stuck in the wall of light separating them from Alien
Nexus Two This made them into moderators. Flying
up to grasp the hands of a moderator, a flier gathered
intensity before battle below.

❖ The only time there was conflict between the adjacent
Branes was when the fliers were flying back to the
rift after harassing the Dancer. Then they always had
to fly the gauntlet of encounters with the dreaded
Blackbirds.

❖ Blackbirds were the unconscious form that a citizen
from Alien Nexus Two took on return to affect
physical reality inside real-time.

❖ They always did predictable but intimidating things,
but were easily out-witted or outmaneuvered.

❖ The giant central peak on the reverse of the plain was
part of Brane A, just before the foam was gathered
into the form of Alexis One, which hovered above it.

- ❖ The interior of the mountain formed the giant sphere of light that floated above the pool of intensity on A. N. 2.
- ❖ There was no connection to the other side of the plain.
- ❖ The Grays resided in their own crèche on-board the Mothership Alexis One, also known as A. N. 1., Alien Nexus One Many other mature Alien cultures did as well and their collected bubble Universes formed the famed City of Light at the end of time in our Brane.
- ❖ The government of the USA in 2011 admitted visitations from Alien Grays.

ABOUT THE AUTHOR
MRM DARK

While inhabiting a dimension very close to this one we are all familiar with, the Author spends his time between riffs on his guitar and hits from a spliff coming up with new material. Look soon for his upcoming sequel in the "Archangels of Aquarius Series", "Knights of the Promethean Flame", due to be published some time in 2015.

The Author is rumored to channel an Ancient Celtic Mischief Spirit, The Púca.